28
1̶4̶ X **DAY BOOK**

FIC Cosic
Cosic, Dobrica, 1921-
South to destiny.

1

19 95

FIC Cosic
Cosic, Dobrica, 1921-
South to destiny.

FEB 8 1982

South
to
Destiny

Also by Dobrica Ćosić

A Time of Death
Reach to Eternity

Dobrica Ćosić

South
to
Destiny

translated by
Muriel Heppell

Harcourt Brace Jovanovich, Publishers
New York and London

Library of Congress Cataloging in Publication Data

Ćosić, Dobrica, 1921–
South to destiny.

Translation of: Vreme smrti, vol. 4 / D. Ćosić.
1. World War, 1914–1918—Fiction.
I. Title.
PG1418.C63V7213   891.8′235   80–8764
ISBN 0–15–184486–0   AACR2

Printed in the United States of America

First edition

B C D E

South
to
Destiny

1

Letters from Serbian prisoners of war in Austro-Hungarian camps, 1915.

From Gretig to Prokuplje:
Dear Mother,

Now you can sleep in peace. I'm protected from the world here, guarded by walls three meters high, topped with two rows of barbed wire and a strong garrison. We can look at the sky, thank God.

From Boldogašonj to Cetinje:
Dear Father!

There's been a great deal of sickness here—a lot of Montenegrins have died and God only knows how many Serbs. In our camp of twelve thousand, more than five thousand have already perished, and in each of the other two camps with sixteen thousand there have been nine thousand deaths. For two and a half months I was ill with typhus—it would have been better if I hadn't survived. . . .

From Mauthausen to Zaječar:
Dear Lala,

Your letters are as rare as snow in summer. God has forgotten us here, and so have you. What about that international agreement? And the resolution of the Hague Convention? And where is almighty and inviolable God?

There's no hope for the future, but our children are growing up. . . . Will there be anybody to help them? No! Will anybody offer us a crust of bread? No! Will anybody in this world sacrifice himself for another? No. No such person has ever been born, nor ever will be!

I'm alive yet I'm not, because here you don't know who is alive and who isn't. I equally despise life and death, just as I despise the world, the universe, and God—especially merciful God!

From Nežider to Velika Drenova:
My dear mother, children, wife, family, and neighbors,

I'm living here like a mouse in a pumpkin. I hope you are well.

Letters from Serbian prisoners of war conscripted into the Austro-Hungarian army who were taken prisoner by the Russians and Italians, or had surrendered to them.

From Russia to Bačka:
Last time I wrote to you, we had entered the Carpathians, and on February 28 just after daybreak we set out to attack the Russians. Not even the officers knew what it would be like with the Russians. The snow was deep, they shouted "Hurrah" and the officers pushed us forward, and when I saw how things were going I leaped into a ditch because I thought the Russians would attack us from all sides and that's exactly what happened. We started yelling and the Russians turned around and fired. All those on the hillside were dead and wounded, and those of us in the ditches didn't know where to go. Then all of a sudden the Russians surrounded us and seized us, and we were taken to Russia. . . .

From Russia to Srem:
Greetings to Mother, Smilja, Žarko—my dear, dear children! And to Seja and anyone who asks after me. And to my poor dear wife—do you dream about me? Do you hope to see me and are you behaving yourself?
God bless you all, my wife and children and home.

From Italy to America:
My dear Cousin Mića,

I hope you and all your Serbian brothers are alive and well. At Soča, I fled to the Italians. And you, Mića, can be thankful to God that you're not in this damned Austria and that you can't see what this country is doing to us Serbs. Here in Bosnia and Hercegovina they've hanged thousands of our Serbian brothers—all the best people, priests, doctors, teachers, and all the learned folk. . . . We Serbs have suffered terribly. There's more than twenty thousand people in prison—men, women, children. And just think, they force us Serbian soldiers to go to the front to defend Austria, to kill our Serbian brothers and the

Russians and Italians and French who are fighting for justice. What a bitch this Austria is! She's hanged her Serbian subjects, men, women and children, burned our houses, and on top of that wants us to defend her! But the Serbs run away as soon as they get to the front—I fled with two others. Here in Porto Mauricio there're plenty of us Serbian deserters and we've all volunteered to fight for Serbia in the war against Austria.

From Kiev to Tashkent:
Dear Ilija!

There're plenty of us from Srem here, but mostly they're from Bosnia, Banat, and Bačka. Over eight hundred of us who have volunteered to fight for Serbia. In fact all the Serbs are going as volunteers to defend Serbia, they've all put in applications—from your regiment, too. Soon there'll be a supply unit of four hundred leaving, and I hear that up till now sixty-eight thousand people have applied, some of other nationalities. Don't you put it off, Ilija!

(These letters and cards were seized by the Censorship Division of the Gemeinsames Zentral Nachweisbureau in Vienna.)

Milena Katić was startled from her reflections. A sudden commotion interrupted the quiet of the sultry August afternoon in Niš; she heard women's cries, joyous and sorrowful, the banging of doors, people calling to each other, clogs clattering on the cobblestones.

"The mailman!" said Milena. She looked at her mother, who sat reading in a wicker chair in the shade of a pear tree.

Olga dropped the book onto her lap; they had not heard from Ivan or Vukašin for a long time.

"Mother! A letter from Bogdan and a card from Ivan!" Milena cried.

"Anything from Father?" asked Olga, laying down her book on the burnt grass.

Milena just handed her the card from Ivan and started to read Bogdan's letter from Rama on the Danube front. Olga's hands shook:

Nežider, July 20, 1915

My dear mother and sister,

I have received a parcel, money, and two cards. You must believe that I'm not unhappy. That's very important to me. Unhappiness is a prewar feeling [three words deleted by the censor]. I've had letters from Bogdan and from Sava, who came to my rescue on Suvobor. The stars are indeed high above; one cannot hear them breathe. Please ask

Uncle Najdan to send me the French translation of Don Quixote, *both volumes, through the Red Cross in Geneva. I wish you [rest of the sentence deleted by the censor]*

Ivan

"He still hasn't answered my question about his glasses. And not a word about his health, Milena."

"That means everything is all right, Mother."

"But his handwriting is larger, and more shaky."

"His handwriting is normal. And what he says about unhappiness simply isn't true. It's only now that I know what happiness is." Milena turned back to Bogdan's letter:

. . . I'm better, my dearest, I'm really well at last! Once more I can smell plants, fruits, and the August nights as I could before I got typhus. A few days ago when I set out at dawn to check on the sentries guarding the bank of the Danube, the smell of the river, the willow trees, and the mud hit me—I sneezed and sneezed. I just couldn't believe it. My eyes filled with tears. By God, I'm better! I shouted out loud and breathed in the dawn, the mist over the Danube, the enormous river, the whole valley. I bent down and smelled the earth, pressed corn tassels to my lips, and thrust my head into the pumpkin stalks. Sounds crazy, doesn't it?

Do you remember how sad I was because I couldn't smell the quince in full bloom outside our window in Valjevo? The quince tree that you used to look at for hours from your bed, grieving for your hair that had fallen out. And I never told you how I suffered because I couldn't smell my father's candles and my mother's lilac. I felt like a cripple, although my wounds had healed and my hair and moustache had grown again. Then I understood my commanding officer, Gavrilo Stanković: he killed himself because he loved life!

The smell of the Danube valley and the departing summer intoxicates me, the way the smell of my father's boiling wax intoxicated me. I take off my uniform and swim in the Danube. Let the Germans spray me with machine-gun fire, I say to myself. I'm in love, and all I'm doing is watching the river! What happiness that is! What happiness to smell the ripeness of late summer, to be as healthy as I was before the war, and to love Milena, my Milena.

Olga gazed at Ivan's card: so unhappiness was a prewar feeling. *What about the feeling that has come with the war, my dearest boy?*

What have you written me that is forbidden? Why is the Austro-Hungarian Empire afraid of what you have to say?

Milena wanted to embrace her mother, but was cut short by the look in her eyes—the look she had first seen one morning after her mother had spent the night on duty at the hospital. So she simply placed her hands on Olga's shoulders and said:

"I'm better now, Mother. I'm happy. You needn't feel sorry for me any more. I want to live!" She embraced her mother. "I want to live. It's like thirst. Remember when I had high fever and snatched that mug of water from you?"

Olga eased out of Milena's embrace. "Are you sure Ivan's handwriting isn't bigger than it used to be?"

Milena's face clouded. "I can't comfort you, can I?"

Olga leaned back into the chair. "No, not even you."

Suddenly they heard someone shouting: "Has the mail come?" It was Dušanka, Milena's friend, running toward them and waving her parasol. Two days ago she had come to see Milena and tomorrow she would go back to her duties in the hospital at Valjevo.

"You'll never believe it—never—but it's true!" Dušanka threw down her parasol. "Guess who I just saw in the park. I was standing by the Nišava in that awful heat, feeling miserable. And out of nowhere someone called my name. I recognized his voice right away. There he was, rising from the bench and smiling—Doctor Radić! Doctor Radić, I swear it! He was so pale, you could see through him. His eyes were enormous, and there were tears in them! I stood petrified as he took my hands in his. It was incredible! I told him I was staying with you, and he said he would visit us after six o'clock. Aren't the flies unbearable today? No one can remember such heat."

"I'll be delighted to see Doctor Radić," said Milena.

Olga went into her room without a word.

Mihajlo Radić walked along the main street in Niš to the Ministry of War. His morning appointment with the chief had been postponed until half past one, and for fear of meeting Olga Katić he had hidden in the park. But even there he wasn't safe. Whom should he run into but his nurse Dušanka! Valjevo once again whirled inside of him; his whole body ached from the memory. He had been afraid to go to Niš and hadn't made his mind up until he was at the station. How could he now have promised to visit Olga?

People in the street were shouting: "Has the ice arrived? Two freight-car loads are coming this evening. Warsaw's fallen—it won't be long before we're off the map. The Germans are advancing on all fronts. That's a sight for you—a defeatist Serb! The ice . . ."

This current of words was drowned out by a resounding noise: ragged, crippled soldiers, torn caps before them, were sitting on the pavement, banging their bayonets against the cobblestones. Radić was ashamed to see tomatoes, green peppers, pears, a piece of bread, but rarely a coin in their caps; he tossed a ten-dinar piece to a soldier who had lost both arms.

At the War Ministry, the man on duty pointed to the office of the chief of the medical service. Radić paused in front of the door: in his request for a transfer from the Valjevo hospital, why had he cited health reasons? They meant nothing under the circumstances. If health was a factor in the performance of one's duty, then half the Serbian army should be pronounced unfit for military service. But how else could he justify his wish not to return to Valjevo when his sick leave was up? Memories, traumas, a personal defeat—who cared about those things today? He decided to return to the front, to the troops.

"Come in, Doctor Radić, I was expecting you."

In the doorway stood Paun Aleksić, the unscrupulous hospital super-intendent whom he had replaced during the typhus epidemic. Aleksić was stunned: in front of him was, not the unpleasant humanitarian and ambitious reformer he remembered, but a worn and exhausted typhus patient seeking a transfer from Valjevo to any kind of medical duty, no matter where.

"I wish to see the chief."

"The colonel is in France, on official business."

"I don't understand."

"Take another look at the signature on the letter summoning you to the ministry."

Radić took the letter out of his pocket and read aloud: "Major Paun Aleksić, on behalf of the chief." "Impossible!" he whispered to himself. He had not noticed the signature.

"It is possible. Much is possible in this world, my dear Doctor."

"But you're a district physician in Požarevac!"

"I was. However, winter was approaching, so I moved south."

"You moved south?" Radić entered the office. "Now I understand. There's no hope for us, then."

"Who is 'us'?"

"The people in the trenches. The people in Valjevo."

"You mean all those who believe that Serbia is leaping onto bayonets, charging under shellfire, flying into the kingdom of heaven? For you, Doctor Radić, Serbia is people who are dying for freedom and can scarcely wait to sacrifice themselves. Isn't that so?"

Radić looked at him in amazement, as if he had never seen him before.

"What's wrong, Captain?"

"I'm still convalescent. There must be some misunderstanding."

"No, everything is in order."

"I don't believe that."

"Listen to me. The Serbia that boasts about its heroism and sacrifice—that Serbia is no more. It doesn't exist, Doctor Radić. Finished. It has made the supreme sacrifice. But there is a living Serbia: the Serbia that flees from anyone stronger than herself, that has the sense to get out of the way of evil and unhappiness, that cheats emperors and lice and thieves, that can manage quite nicely under anyone's heel. Yes, indeed, the Serbia which has become impervious to evil, that is my fatherland, Doctor Radić. And some day it'll be yours too."

Aleksić shut the door and sat down at his desk. Torn between a desire to berate Radić and a twinge of compassion, he rang for the man on duty and ordered coffee and cognac. He asked Radić to sit down and offered him a Greek cigarette.

"I haven't smoked since my illness."

"Amazing! You were constantly chewing tobacco."

Radić took a cigarette; Aleksić lit it for him, pleased at Radić's reversal. He had always derived particular satisfaction from breaking "strong men," from witnessing the violation of "oaths" and "vows."

"In this stupid, filthy war," Aleksić went on, "life is impossible without strong tobacco, easy women, and huge lies—magnificent, monstrous lies. Only for such lies will the rabble shed blood. Of course, it all depends on who tells the lies." He stopped and looked at Radić: should he treat him like a gentleman? "The higher the title and the greater the authority, the bigger the lie must be. And the bigger the lie, the more subtle it must be. This morning one of our diplomats gave me a German newspaper with the Kaiser's speech for the anniversary of the outbreak of the war."

"I'm not interested in German newspapers."

"Just listen now to what Kaiser Wilhelm has to say: 'Times of unprecedented bloodshed have come to pass in Europe, but my conscience is clear before God and history. I did not want war, and it was not desire for conquest that drew Germany into the war. We are fighting a defensive war, a war to secure our national survival.' "

Radić's cigarette tasted bitter, but he didn't want to extinguish it. He would go back to the hospital in Valjevo, where he was needed.

"And now, Radić, comes a truly imperial *volte-face:* 'Go to church and pray to God! For the glory of Great Germany.' Only an emperor could get away with such rubbish! By God, how power justifies all words, all lies, all stupidity. I have always found that phenomenon exciting." Radić's face was ashen. "How's your heart?"

"I'd like you to know that as far as I'm concerned . . ." He came up to the desk and brusquely extinguished his half-smoked cigarette.

"I understand. Things look bad. A decisive attack is expected soon. Bulgaria is mobilizing. We cannot fight on three fronts even for a week. . . ."

Radić broke in: "Major Aleksić, would you please ignore my application for a transfer?"

"Why? I don't understand."

"I've decided to go back to my post in Valjevo."

Confused by this unexpected turn, Aleksić offered Radić another cigarette, which he firmly refused. So Radić was up to his old tricks. In a scathing voice he said, "I'm sorry, Radić, but I'm in no position to comply with your request. I've just signed a letter appointing a new superintendent for the Second Valjevo Hospital. You're now at our disposal. At the end of this month you'll be assigned new duties. Do you have any preference?"

"No," said Radić loudly.

"It would give me great pleasure if you would lunch with me today in the Hotel Europe."

"Thank you, but I already have an invitation for lunch."

"With Mrs. Katić? I saw her yesterday. She looks marvelous. Her husband is in France."

"Don't be crude, Major!"

Aleksić laughed. "Crude? I assure you that women are at their best toward the end of August and at the beginning of March. Come on! War is the slow death of the male between the hills of Venus, on the one hand, and the Drina and the Sava on the other. But from the woman's point of view . . . Well, here's my card. I'll be expecting you tonight for a game of poker."

Red in the face, Radić left without saying good-by and walked down the scorching street, which reverberated with the sound of a drum. He hurried past the assembled crowd, to whom the drummer was announcing that ice for the townspeople would arrive at seven o'clock the next morning.

Olga curled up on her suitcase in the corner of her room. Next door, the clock struck a quarter to six.

Was he coming? The blood ran cold in her veins. What would she say to him? Her hand would be in his. In his pale, bony hand. She would feel the warmth of his joints and fingertips. Perhaps he remembered her silence as he lay unconscious and she held his hand. She had left him ill, dying. Did he still greedily smoke one cigarette after another?

Ever since he had come into her life, Mihajlo Radić had been the spark of a cigarette in the darkness of the train to Valjevo. What about those thin, restless fingers that sought out the pain in the sick: were they now still? Had his sadness disappeared with his recovery and deliverance from death?

It was good that he was coming. She would be able to tell him that what they felt for each other had grown out of the painful experience of the hospital. Each had understood the other's fear of death, the other's loneliness. It had been friendship, not love—a friendship which had given her hope that her son was alive. It was compassion, his compassion and hers. A compassion of the soul, a holy thing, something higher than all her wishes and desires. And it was now no longer possible. But why? Why was it no longer possible?

Helplessly she wrapped her arms around her knees.

How could she have left before he had regained consciousness? Why had she sent only a few meaningless words with that parcel? They had been ordinary words, the only ones she could find after tearing up ten drafts. She knew well how he took them, and that was the hardest part of all: he thought she had run away from suffering. But she no longer feared pain. How would she convince him of that? She fled from the shame that, amid so much suffering, and in spite of her children, she could still feel something that was hers alone.

Did he have any idea how she had fought against coming back to him—how many times she had left the room with her bags packed? She had gone to Belgrade to see her ruined house, but she had really intended to go to Valjevo to see him.

Her shame hurt her. *You want to take all I have. But I don't believe in sacrificial love. Go back to Valjevo.*

His cigarette would glimmer in the dusk, as it had on the train, under the eaves of the Warehouse of the Dead. *You are sensible. Yes, you are. I don't believe you could forgive still another desertion. In Valjevo I believed in you completely. That was why I could go away. Pity me, so that I may believe forever that you did come to me.*

She began to cry.

Milena burst into the room.

"Mother, why don't you believe that Ivan's handwriting is the same as before?"

Olga curled up even more and pressed her face against her knees.

"Why don't you compare this card with the letters from Skoplje?"

Olga did not respond.

"It's nearly seven o'clock, Mother. Obviously Doctor Radić isn't coming."

Olga let go of her knees and stared at the floor.

Milena hugged her: "Remember Valjevo? The Warehouse of the Dead? Nadežda's death and my illness? We've survived an epidemic. Why are you so fearful?"

"We must forget Valjevo!"

"But I don't want to forget it. It was there that Nadežda and Vladimir died. I don't want to forget those nights with Sergeev during the occupation. And I'll never forget Gavrilo Stanković. Or a single wound or a single night on duty. I don't want to forget even a single curse uttered by a wounded man. I want so much to live, Mother!" Milena felt her mother start. She couldn't tell her how much she wanted to dance, how this desire had flared up suddenly in her feet and her whole body. "Is that bad, Mother?" she asked softly.

"No, it isn't. It's a sign that you've recovered, that you're forgetting Valjevo. But why does Ivan want to read *Don Quixote?*"

"Because it's a fable. Right now I too love everything fanciful. I read nothing but poetry. I'd like to go out, Mother. What dress should I wear?" She walked toward the wardrobe.

"Your white dress with the navy blue dots."

"I wore that one when I went for a walk with Vladimir. I'll never wear it again."

"Then your silk dress with the embroidered décolletage."

"You're right. That has always looked well on me. If only my hair was two inches longer." She put on her dress and stood in front of her mother. "You don't think I'm being disloyal to Bogdan?"

"Don't deny yourself anything that gives you pleasure, Milena. Why isn't Dušanka going with you?"

"She'll wait for Doctor Radić till all hours. She's fallen in love with him." Milena kissed her mother and hurried off to the dance, her first dance since the beginning of the war.

Olga lay down on the bed. So Dušanka had fallen in love with him! What about him? A good thing it was getting dark. He wouldn't come now.

Dušanka entered the room. "I can't understand why he hasn't come. He was so pleased when I told him I was staying with you." She sat down on the bed and placed her hand near Olga's; she wanted to touch her.

Olga was aware of this desire for intimacy, but she withdrew her hand. Suddenly she spoke, loudly and in a firm, hard voice: "Are you really in love with him, Dušanka?"

"I adore him, Mrs. Katić! I could die for him!"

"Die for him?"

"If he wished it, even if the thought just crossed his mind. You know, he got sick at the end of the epidemic, and by then we all feared for our lives. His getting ill frightened us more than all the eight thousand sick people in Valjevo. The nurses ran away and the orderlies pretended to be sick, but Doctor Sergeev, Miss Inglis, and I remained faithful to Doctor Radić. We worked in the hospital from dawn till dusk, and at night we sat up with him. Sometimes I'd be overcome with exhaustion and simply fall down by his bed. But I'll never forget the morning when his spots came out."

Where was I that morning? thought Olga, envious of this naive girl who believed that one could die for love.

Dušanka suddenly fell silent. Olga sensed that Dušanka wanted words of comfort from her, but she had no strength for such an enormous lie. The dusk enveloped the walls and bed, the boxes and cases. It spread its shadow over Dušanka, transforming her into someone unknown. Something like hope was burning up in the air. Something was turning dark inside Olga, perhaps forever. The clock struck loudly, but she felt that time had stopped again as it had before she went to Valjevo.

"Why did he promise?" cried Dušanka.

Olga rose from the bed to get away from her, but when she saw Dušanka trembling, she sank back on her pillow, helpless and ashamed.

The curtain billowed before the windows, and the old walnut tree in the courtyard creaked in the wind. Olga took hold of Dušanka's hand and squeezed it tightly: "It's wartime. Even love means suffering now, Dušanka. It brings fear, too. It humiliates us."

"Oh, come now!" cried Dušanka, and snatched her hand away. Then she whispered: "I'd have fled from Valjevo after the first night in the hospital, if I hadn't been in love with someone. When a handsome young man is wounded, there's no more wonderful feeling than pity for him. The expression in his eyes then. How moving it is, when the shadow of death passes across his face and you can do him some good—no one else but you."

Olga was embarrassed by this strange woman with a sturdy frame. Her presence seemed to suck the air from the room.

"Mrs. Katić, there's a storm brewing. Take your things in," cried her neighbor from the entrance hall.

Olga grew rigid.

Dušanka went over to the window and looked at the sky. "Well, he won't be able to come now!"

Nikola Pašić didn't like storms: they destroyed the order and harmony of nature, bringing the highest things crashing down and disfiguring the most beautiful. But this time he was glad to see the storm: maybe now, on his way to the government headquarters, he wouldn't be accosted by crowds demanding news of the latest telegrams from St. Petersburg, Paris, and London, or his reply to the latest Allied note. His wife Djurdjina touched his hand:

"Wait for the storm to blow over, Nikola."

"Misfortunes never come singly, Djurdjina," he said, and set off.

Silently she accompanied him into the street, where the coachman and a policeman were raising the fiacre's top to protect Pašić from the wind and rain. A crowd of men and women crouching under the eaves of neighboring houses rushed toward him as if carried by the storm. He greeted them politely, raising his hat, then he slowly climbed into the fiacre, now surrounded by the crowd. They seized hold of the horses, the mudguards, the wheels.

"Prime Minister, my husband was killed at Gučevo and left me with two children. I've received no help from the local authorities. You know better than anyone that we're in for hard times."

"Ask them again at the town hall, my good woman."

"I've done it a hundred times."

"Go again and say you've been to see me."

"Mr. Pašić, tell me like a brother: in view of what's going on, should I send my family to Bitolj or Salonika?"

"Send them to any safe place you can."

One of his card-playing friends sidled over. "Nikola, a word with you in confidence. What bank should I transfer my money to?"

"An English bank."

"Prime Minister, please take my petition. My husband is an innocent man in prison."

"Don't worry, my good woman. People may be better off in prison."

"Is there any hope, Prime Minister?" cried a voice from the crowd.

The rain drummed on the taut leather top of the fiacre, the wind blew away the petitions and requests, the horses moved off. Pašić raised his hat and inclined his head. It didn't matter that no one could see him: one must learn from the relationship between God and the people; God is all-powerful and the people respond to the invisible. He moved to the middle of the seat so his knees wouldn't get wet, relieved that at least today his drive to the government headquarters would be free of pavements filled with people. The people didn't make him particularly happy with their praise or unhappy with their hatred and curses; what troubled him deeply was their indifference, which he regarded as a sign of how little his authority meant to those he ruled. The coachman whipped the horses, and the wind beat against the top of the fiacre as it clattered over the cobblestones. The policeman, curled up next to the coachman, started at every flash of lightning and every clap of thunder. Pašić tapped the coachman with his stick and asked him to slow down.

In front of the government headquarters the horses stopped suddenly; the policeman bent over to help him out of the fiacre. Pašić would have liked to sit there alone, protected against the rain. A damp face poked itself under the top of the fiacre and asked angrily: "When will you hold a secret session of the National Assembly, Prime Minister?"

Pašić reflected, then replied deliberately: "When the President of the Assembly orders it."

He bowed slightly to the journalist, then entered the government headquarters, moving slowly through the downpour. He walked through the anteroom past two secretaries and Jovan Jovanović Pižon, who was waiting for him with telegrams and reports. Immediately he closed the door and the windows, although it was stifling. Still wearing his hat, he went to his desk. He was glad to be alone: if only God would keep up this bad weather for at least two days! If only it would hail and thunder, so that the Allied ambassadors could not pay the visits he had delayed until this evening. The Allies were demanding a reply from the Serbian government to their note of August 4. Pašić had postponed the reply for fifteen days, wishing he could postpone it for fifteen years. The Serbian army had replied to that note at Kumanovo and Bregalnica, but no small nation ever wins a war forever, nor does the man who serves a small nation. Anyway, a fall from the heights on which he now stood would be fatal. But a man cannot be advised about his own fate, he reflected; he is alone, and in the dark. The advice of people who thought as he did was of no use now—they would lead him to an easy decision. Right now only an opponent could give useful advice; a wise fool who believed that the truth could do him no harm. Someone like Vukašin Katić. Why hadn't Vukašin replied to his last letter?

The lightning flashed and the lights went out.

"Prime Minister, here's a telegram from Paris—very urgent," said his secretary.

"It can wait till tomorrow."

"I must remind you that Mr. Vesnić has twice pressed us for your reply. Yesterday you postponed it until today."

"Just because it's so urgent, let it wait until tomorrow," said Pašić, without turning his face toward him, both his hands resting on the table. This man was far too conscientious and ambitious. He must get him promoted and out of the way. There was nothing more dangerous than an intelligent employee.

"Prime Minister, the daughter of that important person has offered you her father's memoirs. You know who I mean."

"How much does she want?"

"Three thousand dinars."

"That's a lot. But tell her I'll have a look at them."

"I'm sure she'll settle for two thousand. She's in a hurry to get to Salonika."

"You talk to her. See what you can find out about Stojan's memoirs in the next few days." He waved his secretary away. That Stojan Novaković knew both the people and the government. These days one could stay in power only if one knew what people were trying to hide. Democracy had brought with it newspapers and the right to lie.

A servant brought in the lamps.

"Prime Minister, the news of an imminent attack on Serbia has been confirmed today from both Bucharest and Athens," warned Jovan Jovanović, his foreign-affairs assistant. This man was his right hand in diplomatic matters, but he was a great scribbler and believed whatever was on paper. Pašić looked at him hard and said:

"If I were in the shoes of those people in Vienna and Berlin, I too would be hurrying to finish Serbia off." He turned his back on Jovanović and folded his arms.

Nikola Pašić's father had been a peasant, but he himself had sat at imperial dining tables and had talked with the Czar of Russia. He had been an anarchist, a friend of Bakunin; under his leadership the Serbian state had been at its strongest since the time of the Nemanjići. In Switzerland he had learned what democracy was, and from Bakunin personally what revolution was. His countrymen hadn't wanted him as an educator, but had been forced to choose him as the leader of the biggest political party. He had attained power the hard way: he had worked like a slave and made his way up the ladder despite slander, disgrace, and betrayal. He had bent and twisted; he had bowed to the throne of the Obrenovići. He had alternately been spat on as a traitor and hailed as a prophet. He had fled the country like a man who had cheated petty shopkeepers, and had returned as the savior of Serbia. He had eaten the bread of exile and the salt of the Bulgarians. Nothing had come to him easily. He hadn't even met his wife Djurdjina in Belgrade: he had found her in Trieste and faced the difficult task of bringing her to Belgrade. Day after day he had suppressed the suffering of political defeat, and had triumphed over popular vengeance that had almost cost him his life; he had offered the heads of his friends and renounced his principles. He couldn't have acted otherwise. He was guiltless before God, and much more so before men. In a land where a human head is no dearer than that of a sheep, one can't always behave honorably. There is neither treachery nor dishonor where human life has no real value, and where punishment is part of the order of things.

After an unpleasant lunch in a tavern where the stifling heat stank of onions and brandy, Mihajlo Radić set out along the Nišava. Having walked out into the fields, he suddenly turned back in order to make it to Olga's by six o'clock, but at the corner of her street he changed his mind and breathlessly climbed a hill above the town. It was by now a quarter past six and he was so far from Olga's house that it would have taken him at least half an hour to get there. Once more he hurried toward her and once more changed his mind—as if again in the delirium which had marked the beginning of his typhus. He was in a state of shock, a feeling mixing equally his great desire to see Olga and his resistance to doing so. He could not forgive her for leaving Valjevo while he lay unconscious. It was not the usual disppointment one feels in a woman, he had to admit, no matter how painful that admission. He had no right to feel such disappointment. He continued walking.

Olga's departure from Valjevo had demolished his shaky self-esteem, which had sustained him during the epidemic as he fought for the lives of his patients. He had been betrayed by a woman whose suffering he had believed in. He wanted never to forget the morning he recovered consciousness from the delirium of typhus, when the objects in his room were suddenly illuminated by a brilliant light, and he gazed at the door expecting her to appear. Instead, Dušanka cheerfully announced that Olga and Milena had left for Niš three days before. For days he didn't speak or open his eyes. He couldn't even look at Sergeev or Dušanka, who were treating him. Their kindness and consideration irritated him: he found Sergeev intolerable, and Dušanka's tenderness aroused only disgust. But recovery had brought with it the strength to suffer. His pulse had quickened with the whistle of the morning train—perhaps Olga was coming?

Someone was clattering along behind him, breathing heavily. He turned around and saw a one-legged soldier on crutches staring dumbly at him. Radić hurried to get away from him, but without success. In the distance he could hear the man's moans and the noise of his crutches.

When he received a parcel from Olga he had ordered the contents distributed among the patients without even looking at it. That day his temperature had gone up again. As soon as he could stand on his feet, he had asked Sergeev to take him to the station and help him into a train—the same train in which he had traveled with Olga to Valjevo.

The man with one leg was now breathing down his neck. Radić wheeled around and stared at the soldier, then continued walking in the direction of the fortress walls.

The west wind, which blew down from the mountain on Niš, extinguishing the street lights, caught Radić within the walls of the fortress: how could he visit Olga in such a storm? He sought shelter under a tree. A few paces away the soldier on crutches also stopped under a tree.

Flashes of lightning rent the dusk, illuminating the walls of the fortress, and claps of thunder broke over Niš like the shells around the regimental dressing station at Mačkov Kamen, where Radić had amputated the limbs of wounded men. Everything had been so uncertain there, yet he had been so calm. Why was he in such a state now?

He pressed himself against the tree trunk. The rain had soaked through to his skin.

The wind whipped the trees.

Tomorrow he would visit Paun Aleksić and Olga Katić. These two, although completely different, were one—they both belonged to a world in which pangs of conscience were pointless.

"Are you Doctor Radić?" a nasal voice asked. A flash of lightning lit up the soldier on crutches. "Ah, I'm glad it's you, Doctor Radić."

"What can I do for you, soldier?"

"I was a soldier until you cut off my leg at Mačkov Kamen. Lopped it off right up to the balls!"

"It was necessary."

"So you think you did me a good turn?" He shook his stick and took a step toward Radić.

"Probably not."

"When I saw you in town, something made me follow you. I want to shake your hand. Do you think there's any more of me you could cut off?"

"Who are you?" asked Radić, withdrawing from the soldier's touch.

"I'm Rightleg."

"Rightleg?"

"I was the sixteenth to be operated on, but the first to lose his right leg. Don't you remember, Doctor? They carried me into the operating room and I shut my eyes because I didn't want to see you. Then you lifted up the tent flap and said: 'This is the sixteenth today, but the first right one.' I can hear you plainly. I hear your voice all the time."

The nasal voice made Radić shudder. He remembered the incident: one day in the divisional hospital he had amputated ten arms and fifteen legs, but all left legs. Rightleg had lost one of his ears, his nose and half his face had been blown off, and he was full of shrapnel. His gangrenous right leg had to be cut off, but the morphia had been used up for the arms and the left legs amputated earlier, and there was only a quarter of an injection left. Radić had explained the situation to the man and asked him to make the decision. Rightleg immediately replied: "If it's my decision, then let me die." Radić had then attended to an arm with a crushed elbow and amputated it near the shoulder, but without using the quarter injection. In the evening he had given the quarter injection to Rightleg and amputated without asking Rightleg's permission. The man hadn't even groaned. His silence had made Radić's hand tremble and he screamed at the nurse and the orderly for no reason. He had wiped the soldier's dry, cracked lips with a piece of damp gauze, taken hold of his sound arm, and asked, "What's your name, soldier?" "It used to be Stevan, Doctor. But for you I'm Rightleg." In the hospital and throughout the retreat before the Austrian attack, Stevan Rightleg had never once groaned. He had talked only when he had to.

The lightning illuminated Stevan's disfigured face.

"Did you go home after you left the hospital?" Radić asked.

"It was a mistake. When my wife saw me she began to wail as if I were dead. She ran away. What could she do—sleep with a cripple?"

Radić thought of Olga: she had fled from him, too. The rain slithered down his back.

"When I saw you on that street corner, I'd have chased you all the way to the Drina, just to touch you and ask you—"

"What are you doing in Niš, Stevan? Have you been up before a board?" stammered Radić.

"No, I haven't. I ran away from my mother's wailing. So people who knew me as I used to be can't see me. Here in Niš nobody knows me; there are lots of cripples and I go around with them. I putter around the hospital, they give me some food."

"Perhaps I could help."

"All I need is justice, Doctor. That's all we cripples need. Do you think there'll be justice when the war's over?"

"There will be freedom, Stevan."

"It's those behind the lines that need freedom, Doctor. Those thieves and shirkers. Those fine folks—merchants and scoundrels! Those who aren't fit for the army, or so they say, but they're fit enough to pester our wives and sisters while we're having our heads smashed up and our legs sawn off out there. They're all right for our wives—they open their legs for them, for those fucking bastards. Will there be justice after the war, so we can get even with those shirkers and scoundrels, pay them back in their own coin?"

"I don't think so, Rightleg. No, I don't really think so."

"Why have I lost my ear, then? Why did you cut off my leg?"

His stick banged in the darkness. The thunder rumbled and the rain fell in torrents.

Although they were alone in the office, Jovan Jovanović whispered to Nikola Pašić that the English ambassador had arrived.

Pašić looked doubtful. How could that gentleman have come, in such terrible weather? Jovan Jovanović added that De Graz had in fact arrived one minute before the time fixed for his audience. When Jovanović then asked whether he should act as interpreter, since the Englishman didn't speak French very well, Pašić shook his head. He was determined to conduct his conversation with the Englishman in French.

Pašić greeted the severe, rain-spattered diplomat with a nod of his head, gestured toward the sofa, then dropped back into his armchair.

"You seem very anxious, Your Excellency," he said.

Sir Charles de Graz sighed. "We cannot feel at ease, Prime Minister. I have information that the number of German and Austrian troops on the Sava and the Danube is increasing. During the next few days Serbia can expect the worst."

"I know that. The Germans are in a hurry to get to the Bosphorus."

"That's so—there can be no other aim. Our Foreign Secretary has ordered me to convey to you his disappointment at your reception of the proposition of His Majesty's government, and at the Serbian government's delay in replying."

Pašić sat motionless with folded arms and looked right through him.

Sir Charles went on uninterrupted. "In spite of all my efforts to put myself in your position, I can't understand your hesitation. It's a perfectly simple calculation. In compensation for Macedonian territory ceded to Bulgaria, Serbia will be given Bosnia, Hercegovina, Srem, Bačka, Slavonia, and part of Dalmatia with the harbors of Split and Dubrovnik. What more can your government expect of the Allies today, when you're on the brink of disaster?"

"Since you've mentioned the word calculation, I'm obliged to say that what the Allies are offering Serbia is Serbian land. For us there's no question of bargaining with regard to these territories. In fact, Your Excellency, Austria-Hungary attacked us to prevent just such a unification of the Serbs."

"However, Prime Minister, we're talking of territory which is now included in Austria-Hungary, not in the kingdom of Serbia. Your historic right is quite another matter." Sir Charles started at a peal of thunder; he was silent a few moments, then continued. "We must return to incontrovertible facts. The Serbian reply to our note will determine whether the situation in the Balkans can be settled without conflict. If the Balkans are united in accordance with our proposals, then the German and Austrian penetration to the east can't succeed. If Serbia doesn't give way and the Balkans remain in a state of discord, our common enemy will easily reach the Dardanelles. Bulgaria will then get Macedonia from Berlin and Vienna. In view of the situation, how can you hesitate?"

"Well, I can assure you that Bulgaria, along with Austria-Hungary and Germany, will attack Serbia unless the Allies intervene with military force."

"That can't happen, Prime Minister. We know Bulgaria's intentions very well. And because we know them, we insist that Serbia behave constructively and help bring Bulgaria over to the Allies as soon as possible."

"I find it hard to believe that the British government bases its Balkan policy on such a mistaken notion. How can you be so naive, Sir Charles?"

"Prime Minister, Britain is just one small island, but we have the most powerful empire in the world. People believe that we rule through our navy. That's nonsense."

Pašić looked at him gravely, intercepting his ironical smile: "How does England regard our union with the Croats and Slovenes?"

"In principle His Majesty's government is not against your unification. But in this connection we mustn't forget Italian demands on the eastern Adriatic."

"We won't agree to split up Croatia."

"I really can't understand your great anxiety over the Croatian problem under the circumstances, Prime Minister."

"It is Serbia's duty to be concerned on behalf of her enslaved brothers. We are a single people, Your Excellency."

"War compels us to be realistic in everything. Romantic attitudes are wonderful, but—"

"I don't think much of romantic attitudes, Your Excellency. Would you really say that you English, Scots, Irish, and Welsh live in a single state for romantic reasons?"

"Of course not, but today we must think only of victory. It's obvious that great sacrifices must be made if we're to win this terrible war."

"If we're to win the war, the sacrifices must be fairly divided among the Allies. The Serbian nation is ready to fight courageously only if it knows it's fighting for freedom and justice. That's the kind of nation we are."

Sir Charles de Graz asked permission to light a cigarette, then continued: "As regards Banat, the Rumanians are very insistent, unfortunately."

"You must talk to some other prime minister of Serbia about surrendering Banat to Rumania."

"I ask you, Prime Minister, to consider what the position of Serbia would be if Rumania and Bulgaria were fighting on her side."

"Serbia never has the good fortune of having her neighbors fighting on her side."

"But Serbia can now change her fate. She can choose between a brilliant future and total ruin. I sincerely envy the role which history has entrusted to you, Prime Minister. But a decision must be made. We have very little time left to prevent the worst."

"Don't be anxious. We have plenty of time for wise and honorable decisions."

Sir Charles de Graz got up, looked out the window, then spoke slowly in Serbian: "I'm an optimist, Mr. Pašić."

Still seated, Pašić muttered in English. "I no longer am, Your Excellency."

"I'm sorry, extremely sorry to hear that. When can we expect your reply?"

"It's important for us to know as soon as possible when Serbia will get the loan which has been approved. We no longer have the means to wage war."

"There are great difficulties in connection with the loan, but I'll do all I can. What dreadful weather!"

They shook hands.

Pašić paused in the middle of the room and reflected on what he had said to his visitor. Had he perhaps pulled the reins too tightly on the British lion? Now, having pressed him on the paw like a hare, he must behave like a fox. But a fox caught in a trap bites off its own paw. If he did this, could he still save himself?"

Jovan Jovanović announced Prince Trubetskoy.

Pašić would have a much harder job with the Russian than with the Englishman. In front of England he had to bend occasionally, but he could straighten up again; in front of Russia he could only bend. Russia treated Serbia like a child, yet she was Serbia's only kin in this dog-eat-dog world.

The Russian ambassador greeted him in a mild, melancholy voice and stood before him, blinking in bewilderment.

Pašić addressed him in Russian: "Prince Trubetskoy, I'd like to know your government's position on the mobilization of Bulgaria and the concentration of troops in the direction of Serbia."

"I'm afraid you've received false information, Mr. Pašić. Russia has given a guarantee to Serbia that Bulgaria will not attack. I must tell you that Russia's attitude is very close to England's."

Pašić didn't ask Trubetskoy to sit down: "When the Serbian people learn of your position, they'll despair. In a day or two I'll have to tell them about our critical situation."

"You're doing all you can to make Bulgaria decide against the Allies and therefore against Serbia, Mr. Pašić. The Slav cause in the Balkans is becoming hopeless."

"By her compassionate policy toward the Bulgarians, Russia is simply encouraging them to stab Serbia in the back!"

Trubetskoy raised his voice. "Russia, Mr. Pašić, is the true protector of all the Slavs. But you Serbs, with your boundless ambition, have always obstructed our good intentions. Every one of them!"

"I'm sorry. I cannot agree to your demand that the Bulgarians take eastern Macedonia."

"So you reject the advice we give you as a friend and an ally?"

"We Serbs can distinguish quite clearly between advice and an ultimatum, Your Excellency."

"If you make no distinction between Vienna and St. Petersburg, then . . . then, Mr. Pašić, Russian absolves herself of all responsibility for the fate of Serbia."

Pašić stared at the floor. A secretary brought in tea. "If there must be some compensation," Pašić asked, "can the Czar's government guarantee our union with the Croats and Slovenes? And that you won't touch Banat?"

"Regarding your unification with the Croats, I'll tell you in confidence, as a brother, that we can't promise it. The English have a very reserved attitude toward the Slav cause. Italy is definitely opposed to it. You must never forget, Mr. Pašić, that Italy entered the war on the Allied side only because we promised her the greater part of the Adriatic coast and a chunk of Albania. The situation on our fronts necessitated this concession to Rome."

Pašić seemed to be listening to the storm outside, then said in a low voice: "Yes, yes, I understand. You make arrangements for the Balkans and the Adriatic coast, as if Serbia weren't your ally. This time, you've really done us in!"

"Are you implying that Russia is indifferent to the Slav cause in the Balkans?"

Pašić said nothing.

"I'll convey your opinion faithfully to Mr. Sazonov. I hardly need tell you that they'll be deeply disappointed in St. Petersburg. I'm extremely anxious about the fate of Serbia. Very soon you're going to face an attack of tremendous force. How will you resist it alone?"

Pašić looked at him calmly and replied, speaking now in French: "In the way we must."

Trubetskoy looked him straight in the eye. "You know very well that Russia has the means to force you to give up Macedonia to Bulgaria! It's for your own good. And to prevent disunity among the Balkan Slavs!"

"Thank you, Your Excellency. You've spared me the decision of how to respond to the blackmailing demands of the Allies. My task is easier now. Serbia must fight to the limits of her strength, naked and barefoot, not only against Austria and Germany, but also against her allies, who are dividing her up like an African colony."

"I strongly protest this reproach of Russia!"

Pašić paused, then said, again in French: "I believe that Russia has done all she could to defend Serbia's interests. Nevertheless, Russia should not expect the impossible from us."

Trubetskoy sat down, finished his tea, then responded excitedly in Russian: "Listen, Mr. Pašić. Serbia is on the verge of suicide. If you ask for everything, you'll lose what you have. I understand how difficult it is for you . . . the pressure of public opinion, the army, national ideals . . . but do understand that you must choose between Macedonia and the interests of the South Slavs."

"If that's our choice, we'll choose Macedonia."   .

Trubetskoy stood up: "I'm sorry to hear that. And I'll be even sorrier if it happens, which God forbid. I place my trust in God. God will save Serbia, if her best sons cannot do so. Good night, Prime Minister."

Pašić didn't close the door behind Trubetskoy.

A dejected Jovanović came in, shut the door, and whispered: "The German with a Greek passport who arrived yesterday from Istanbul insists on your receiving him tomorrow morning."

"Have him come at once. Send the secretaries and cipher experts away. I don't want even a policeman in front of my door when you bring him in. And tomorrow morning will you please visit Trubetskoy and be soft as butter, but don't give way on the important point. In the afternoon go see De Graz. Tell him casually that I'm thinking of resigning if the Allies continue to blackmail Serbia. And press him for a loan by all possible means."

Left alone in his office, Pašić extinguished one lamp and dimmed the other, putting it on the floor in a corner of the room. It was still raining. Niš was in darkness, but he couldn't be sure someone wasn't watching his windows from the river bank or from the bridge. What would happen if the Allies stuck to their position and things turned out as they predicted? Then he would be blamed for the downfall of Serbia. Perhaps he didn't see things clearly or know everything. . . . Should he yield to their demands?

After standing for three hours on the open track, blocked by the flood, the train from Salonika slowly started up, and Vukašin Katić leaned out of the window to look at Niš in the darkness pierced by infrequent, blinking lights. He was seeking that spark of light which housed his wife and child. Those poor, wretched lights lost in the darkness—could that be the wartime capital of Serbia? No previous feeling of sadness on encountering his homeland had resembled the uneasiness he felt this night—fear of Niš and of what tomorrow would bring, welling up from the damp darkness.

He wasn't sure if they had entered the station. The train had stopped, a light was flickering from a window somewhere, and a railwayman was swinging a lantern beside the engine. Vukašin was confused by the mad rush, the pushing and shoving of the incoming passengers. Confronted with this panic-stricken surge, he retreated to his compartment. "Where are you people going?" he shouted.

"Skoplje's the first stop."

"For me it's Bitolj."

"Well I'm not getting off till Salonika."

They were refugees from Niš, but Vukašin didn't ask them whether the final attack on Serbia had begun that evening. He took his suitcase, pushed his way through the crowded corridor, and jumped off the train into a muddy puddle, barely managing to regain his balance. He called for a porter, then for a fiacre, and heard a voice saying, "This man's from Mars." He set off with his suitcase, stepping over puddles. Again he called for a fiacre, but, finding none, he continued on foot through the mud and darkness, toward the center of Niš and his own house. As he walked, he remembered riding to the Gare de Lyon in the Serbian ambassador's car.

Lanterns were swinging, and he could hear people shouting: "Take the woolen cloth first, you fool—leave the chintz! Woolen cloth costs five times as much. Take the sugar and leave the flour. Forget the rice! Why does lightning always strike the power station? Where are the municipal authorities? Where is our army to protect the old folks and our property? This is the capital. Pašić should be here in person. Thieves are looting my workshop! Where are those damned policemen?"

Vukašin thought of the young Parisians in the Tuileries, then stopped in his tracks to listen to the voices in the darkness. He wondered how he could bear the injustice that those people on the Thames and the Seine directed against his own people. Disappointed as he was with Europe, how would he keep a cool head in front of Pašić and his party? Nothing was more odious to him than a disappointed politician. It was starting to rain.

His hands began to ache from carrying his suitcase, so he put it on his back like a porter. As soon as he had rested from his journey and reported to Pašić on his mission to Paris and London, he would go straight to his father in Prerovo! He was just barely able to find the gate and stumbled on the path to his house. He would hug his wife and his daughter both at once. He would not knock until he had composed himself, he decided. But while still on the steps he found himself in Milena's arms. "No matter how long the war lasts, we won't be separated again!" Milena exclaimed.

"No, my pet, we won't," he said. He had hardly stepped into the dark room and put his suitcase down when he collided with Olga, who dropped her head onto his shoulder. "What's going to happen to us?" she asked. He hugged her tightly, kissing her hair and cheeks, and didn't release her until Milena lit the candles. A card had come from Ivan that day, Milena told her father. Vukašin asked to see it; he read it twice by the candlelight.

Milena looked at her father bending over Ivan's card in his crumpled, mud-spattered clothes, and concluded that it was not only mud and rain which had disfigured his dress and behavior, ordinarily so refined. The only time he had looked like this had been in Valjevo on his return from Maljen, where he'd been searching for Ivan. How had she been able to live without her father for almost a year? She told her mother to bring him clean clothes, then took off his boots and poured water for him to wash with. She would tell him that she had fallen in love with Bogdan; he would surely be pleased.

Vukašin yielded to her attentions, saying how much he had missed her and her mother and reproaching them for not writing more often. After he had washed and changed his clothes he gave them some chocolate, the only present he had brought. Milena sat on his lap and hugged him. He was a bit embarrassed, but mostly pleased that this evening she was behaving as she used to before she went to work as a volunteer nurse. He caressed her as she told how she had missed him and feared he wouldn't return before the new attack on Serbia.

Olga was silent, interpreting Milena's excessive tenderness toward

Vukašin as a reproach for her own silence and tension. Her conversation with Dušanka and her long wait for Mihajlo Radić had upset her. She noticed that Vukašin had grown thinner, that his sideburns were gray. He had aged. He had never behaved with much tenderness toward her in front of the children, but now he held and stroked her hand in front of Milena. She began to tremble. What change had come over him? What change had come over her? What was going to happen to the two of them? She must tell him the whole truth. What if he didn't understand, if his masculine pride was stronger than his understanding?

Vukašin interrupted her thoughts: "What happened to you after I left, Olga?"

She met his anxious glance and broke her silence: "We suffered a great deal, Vukašin. Not a single trouble passed us by in Valjevo—not one." She should have been more direct, but Milena was there. "Do you know anything more about Ivan?"

"I've had only two cards from him. I've sent him money and a few parcels through the Swiss Red Cross. His first card described a certain bench in the Luxembourg Gardens and his wish to sit on it again some day. The second card asked me to go for a walk around the Ile Saint-Louis and toward the Bastille. Nothing about himself."

"Did you carry out his wish?" asked Milena.

"I sat on his bench whenever I was free. I wandered around the Sorbonne for hours. I found his lodgings in the Rue des Quatre Vents. Two Spaniards were staying in the room. I asked them if I could have a look around. My son's lodging was poorer than mine, Aćim's son, yes, indeed. A bed, a bare table, a washstand with a mirror, and a picture of the Eiffel Tower on the wall. But objects are silent."

"No they aren't. They too can remember," said Olga, getting up to prepare his supper. She went into the other room, which served as a kitchen, lit the lamp, and busied herself at the stove.

Ah, my self-confident man, you were indifferent to those objects, so they were silent. You've always been reserved with me. You approved of everything. You have no idea how painful it was for me that you never opposed anything I did. You never thought that you could lose anything. Why should my confession humiliate you? I'm not reproaching you. At one time I even saw your certainty of my love as a reason for my happiness. That's why I did what I could to preserve your dignity in a world that stains everything that is clean and undermines everyone who is strong. You never gave any sign that you needed my devotion. What mattered to you was what was done in public, what everyone could see. Ah, Vukašin! The only thing I valued in our life was what was ours alone. You and the children were everything to me, but to you I was just someone you came back to when you were tired. A person you left to go to someone more important. That's how it was, and had to be. It wasn't an injustice on your part or a sacrifice on mine. You aren't obligated to me in any way. It was in Valjevo that I chose to sacrifice for the first time in my life.

Vukašin called to her.

The German with the Greek passport stepped hesitantly into the Prime Minister's half-darkened office, looking around to see if there were anyone there besides this old man with a full beard, his long shadow broken up by the wall.

"You're here on the recommendation of King Constantine?" asked Pašić, addressing him from a distance.

"Yes. The Greek ambassador has full instructions. What language should we speak?" he asked in German, speaking more loudly than the occasion demanded.

"Of necessity I also speak the language of the country with which we are at war," Pašić replied in French. He wondered whether this "Greek" with his drenched cloak, holding a cap in his hand, could have arrived at his office unnoticed. He waved to the couch as he himself sat down in the armchair, bending forward to gain a good view of his visitor's face.

"Prime Minister, I'm sure you've checked my identity through your ambassador in Athens. I'm authorized by highly placed persons."

"Civil or military?"

"Military. I've been authorized to convey to you the German proposal for peace with Serbia. Are you aware of what lies in store for you, Prime Minister?"

"Yes, I am. And I'm waiting."

"Preparations are complete for the imminent destruction of Serbia. The last obstacle to Germany's passage to Istanbul must be removed."

"We've been aware of your intentions for a long time."

"During the next few days they'll be carried out by extremely efficacious means," he said, then fell silent.

Pašić was also silent as he recollected earlier offers for a separate peace. The Austrians had been more insolent than this man, who now said forthrightly: "Serbia can be saved only if she accepts our generous offer of peace."

"There are other ways in which Serbia can be saved."

"Let me tell you this also. Our ally Austria-Hungary is not at all enthusiastic about Germany's wish to come to a peaceful understanding with Serbia. She's convinced that Serbia will never be a trustworthy neighbor. Vienna is determined to settle all disputes with you on the battlefield."

"That's not the most useful course of action for Vienna. Germany should advise her ally not to persist in this method."

"Vienna believes it the quickest way. All circumstances indicate that the decisive moment is now. The Russian bear is mortally wounded and rolling eastward. On the western front all preparations have been made for dealing France her death blow. Our submarines are harrying the English on the seas with great success. As regards Serbia, Berlin has other hopes, serious hopes. You have shown that you're a brave and gifted nation."

"We too cherish certain hopes."

"What's your opinion on this matter, Prime Minister?"

"I think our opinions are well known to Germany."

"Could you give me your latest word?"

"We're determined to survive."

"How? With whom?"

"With our friends, as best we can. With our enemies, as necessity dictates."

"Germany cannot permit a Serbia of this kind to exist."

"That won't be easy for you. Not easy at all. We do exist, you see. And we have waged war successfully with the Austro-Hungarian Empire for one year."

"Germany sincerely desires peace with Serbia."

"Serbia desires it even more. The only question is the kind of peace Germany is offering."

"Germany has only two conditions: the capitulation of the Serbian army and the unhindered passage of the Central Powers armies through Serbia to the Dardanelles and Turkey. Otherwise your army will be destroyed without mercy. Belgrade will be leveled. And every village from which a gun is fired will be burned."

They looked at each other in silence. Then Pašić whispered: "Apart from the demand for capitulation, has Germany any other proposal?"

"Immediately upon the capitulation of your army, Serbia will be united with Montenegro and Albania. Under the Montenegrin Petrović dynasty, of course. In a new constellation of the Balkans and Europe, and with an outlet to the sea, Serbia can develop her many resources."

"Is that all that Germany is offering Serbia?"

"Do you honestly believe that so little?" asked the German, lowering his voice to a whisper and leaning toward Pašić.

Pašić looked at him thoughtfully: for the third time that night, he had heard the same question. Both her allies and her enemies were surprised at Serbia's failure to agree to their plans to save her. "Germany, a great country, is not offering us much. Very little, in fact. Would you please, sir, convey to the right quarters my disappointment that a power such as Germany offers Serbia so little in return for peace." He spoke loudly and with conviction.

"Germany knows very well that the Allies offer Serbia only false promises in return for a war of total extinction. Isn't this so, Prime Minister?"

"I regret that Germany is not more anxious to secure peace with Serbia."

"I can wait until noon tomorrow for your final reply, Prime Minister. Or even perhaps until the evening train for Salonika."

"I'll have nothing more to say."

"That's your last word?"

"It's my firm conviction."

Pašić stood up and held out his hand. The German with the Greek passport tried to salute him, but in confusion shook hands and made a deep bow. Pašić didn't accompany him out of the room. Had he said too much to this German? There was no need to close all doors; in fact, he mustn't close any door. He summoned Jovanović: "See if you can get that German to stay in Niš two more days. And make sure the Allied ambassadors hear that we've received serious peace proposals from Germany. I'll give the Bulgarian Chaprasnikov as much information as I have to. Now find Dragiša Lapčević, the socialist. I'll summon the liberals in the morning. It would also be a good idea to see one of the freemasons tonight—a grand master. Who else can I see tonight?"

"Apis is in Niš."

"Let Apis come after the freemason."

"Najdan Tošić is here. He says it's important."

"Tell him to come in right away. The others should follow in the order I've indicated."

"Some manuscript was delivered for you this evening, Prime Minister."

"I'll look at it later, after everyone has gone."

He sat down at his desk to receive formally this contractor who had caused him so much trouble over the pharmacist affair. He was presumably the only Serb for whom defeat would mean salvation: a man with more money than sense, but one who knew more about the current situation than the Serbian press bureau. What would Najdan Tošić have done in his position? he wondered. He would definitely have obeyed the Allies.

Najdan Tošić sat in the dark waiting room, lighting one cigarette after another. On his way to the government headquarters, who should he have run into but Vukašin Katić with a suitcase on his back! He could hardly believe his eyes. Vukašin had returned unexpectedly, in terrible weather—like a vampire!

Everyone had been relieved when Pašić sent Vukašin off to Paris that spring with a group of professors. The atmosphere in the Assembly was peaceful and easygoing. Had it not been for those two socialist fools and three or four shrewd peasants, the Serbian Assembly would have resembled the British Parliament. Even Vukašin's most fiery supporters (fortunately few in number) had enjoyed the respite from his crazy arguments in the name of "law and honor." The press coverage of the "supplies affair" had been polite that summer, vague and indirect. Najdan had arranged it so that the Assembly commission to investigate army supplies had postponed the interrogation of the Ministry of War supply officers until December. He had also arranged to have an "important witness"—one of his own men—included in a delegation to France, where he would supervise deliveries of military material. Meanwhile the great events in the offing had reduced to nonsense that wartime harangue about his selling to the army boots made of cardboard, flour mixed with sand, bicarbonate of soda as quinine, and aspirin as a cure for typhus. Everything had settled down nicely, and the people and the newspapers turned their attention to real problems: cannon on the Serbian frontiers, Bulgarian bayonets. And now his brother-in-law, Vukašin, would turn everything around. The day after tomorrow his editorial about the contractors, thieves, and bloodsuckers of the nation would appear in the *Echo*. At the first Assembly meeting he would ask when the Assembly's commission would submit its report on the contractors. Then all the headaches of last spring would start in again. All his old enterprises were going splendidly, and the new ones had got off to a good start, too—the buying of gold which was then sent to Switzerland, a traffic connected with the flight of the intelligent and wealthy to Salonika and France. If Serbia still wasn't occupied by November, 1915 would be for him a year of exceptional business success. Yet all this could be ruined by his own brother-in-law, the man whose children stood to inherit these "blood-stained and shameful millions." Really, there was nothing like it even in fiction! His efforts to send Olga and Milena to Athens and save the top hospital personnel would be frustrated by that "exemplary patriot." That meddling "domestic moralist" would sacrifice everything for power and glory!

Only Pašić could hush things up in the Assembly. Skilled as he was at putting off the most urgent and pressing matters, if it suited him, he could certainly put off answering any special investigation "until the next meeting." Without that levelheaded man as Prime Minister, the state would have been splintered by the "honor" and "love" of the Serbian opposition. That wily Italian, Baron Squitti, was right when he said of Pašić: "Your Prime Minister possesses one quality of a great leader: he understands criminals and fools. And they constitute the majority in this world." Indeed, if there was any hope for Serbia— if it was at all possible to save her—it rested in this man who didn't fear evil, who was more cunning than all his enemies and allies put together.

What should he say to Pašić this evening? Perhaps he shouldn't divulge Mišan's conversation with Filoliti about Italy's games with the English and the Russians, and Trubetskoy's statement about the future boundary between Serbia and Greece. He would talk to Pašić only about the Bulgarians that evening, and offer him the rest if Pašić offered a higher price for it. Which he very well might, if complications developed when the report of the Assembly's commission was released.

Jovan Jovanović, whose excessive seriousness was always distasteful to him, came up with a candle and guided him to Pašić's office. At the sight of that long, full beard glimmering in the darkness, he stopped, humbled, as if in church. In front of that beard he was always filled with awe: whatever secret he was about to communicate, it seemed that Pašić already knew it. He had never been able to surprise him with anything. And Pašić's deep silence always compelled him to say more than he wanted to. At such moments he no longer felt sure of himself, he couldn't stop talking, his voice trembled, he stammered, and his hands shook. Then anger would well up inside him against this dignified old man whom he feared, even though he wasn't dependent on him or indebted to him in any way. Now, forgetting to greet him, he was suddenly overwhelmed by the question: was there behind that saintly beard some saving grace in which everyone believed, even those who hated him? Or was this belief just Serbian folly and desperation? Pašić invited him to take a chair and come closer.

He pulled the chair right up to the desk and looked at Pašić: was Pašić frightened by coming events? The old actor didn't show his feelings.

"This bad weather has done a lot of damage in Niš and the surrounding area," said Pašić coldly.

Najdan decided to say nothing until asked why he had sought this interview in such bad weather and so late at night.

"How are your cousin and her daughter? What do they hear from Vukašin?"

"I saw Vukašin a while ago with a suitcase on his back. He's come back just in time."

"When you see him tomorrow, tell him I want to talk to him."

"Prime Minister, I wanted to inform you about certain important matters. A few days ago Baron Squitti delivered to Chaprasnikov a confidential note that the Allies had sent to our government. The Bulgarians know all about the latest pressure on us by the Allies to give them Macedonia."

"That could be expected."

Najdan paused before making his most important pronouncement: "In ten days Bulgaria will conclude an alliance with Germany. The Bulgarians claim that all their important differences have been resolved. A secret delegation from the Bulgarian General Staff will leave for Germany within the next few days."

"They've been in Germany for some time, Najdan. There never were any important differences between them."

The indifference in Pašić's voice offended Najdan's self-importance as a purveyor of information. He had expected astonishment, anxiety, and despair. Was it true that such a service to his government and fatherland had no significance for Pašić? Pašić was silent, so Najdan started again: "Two days ago Baron Squitti said to Chaprasnikov: 'You Bulgarians must be reasonable. If you join us, the Entente powers, Germany will destroy you. You have nothing to expect from Serbia. Now is the time to attack Serbia and take Macedonia and the lands which Europe considers yours.' That's exactly what he said."

"From the Italian point of view, that is undoubtedly good advice."

Najdan felt increasingly irritated by Pašić's reception of such important information. Had he received it from someone else, or was the old actor just feigning indifference? He leaned over and said in a threatening voice: "We are all alone, Prime Minister."

Pašić simply crossed one palm over the other.

Najdan waited for Pašić to say something, but the Prime Minister's lips were shut tight, his face expressionless. Najdan said bitterly: "At lunch today Chaprasnikov said: 'The bird that you Allies are offering us Bulgarians is much smaller than the one the Germans offer.'"

"Tell Chaprasnikov that I advise the Bulgarians to keep their eyes open, or they may end up with a pigeon instead of an eagle."

Najdan waited for a more lucid message, but Pašić stood up and asked softly: "Do you know what the Allies are asking of us?"

"Yes, I do."

"Should we give in to them?"

"We'll gain nothing by giving in to them. The Bulgarians will attack us regardless of what we give them now."

Pašić held out his hand: "Tell Vukašin to come early tomorrow."

Najdan put on his cloak and plunged out into the darkness, offended by Pašić's lack of confidence and his failure to attach significance to his information. All Najdan ended up with was a request to perform an extremely unpleasant task, a job for a village policeman. He had hoped that the information would put the government under an obligation, and that he would have one more laugh at those who questioned his patriotism. The thought of Vukašin made him even more upset. Suddenly the dull, heavy roar of the swollen Nišava filled him with the sense of some supernatural menace. All his business plans and ideas, his calculations, all his pleasure in work and women, lost their meaning, vanished. He felt weak before this unknown force. He stopped on the bridge, his whole body tense. That force was stronger than anything in him or in this world. *What am I, where am I?* he thought. If a man saves himself, is he saved? Shame welled up in him, and for the first time a sense of futility overwhelmed him. And a feeling of disgust, like dampness.

Suddenly, in the distance, he heard the sweet laughter of the girl he had left in his bed that evening, who had charmed him with her fear of thunder and lightning. He hurried home.

"Were you lonely while you were away, Father?" asked Milena cautiously, trying to guess why her father had come back from Paris in such a state. She looked at his face: there was a network of wrinkles around his stern eyes, eyes which judged everything they looked at, and which would not tolerate jokes or disorder even when they were bright and gentle.

"I found people harder to bear than loneliness, Milena. And I was with people all the time. I had to walk through the crowded boulevards of Paris and the streets of London and look at the people. They were buying and selling, making love; they were cheerful—as if the war was on another planet. Meanwhile I was forcing my way through the doors of French and English politicians, professors, and journalists, trying to justify the unification of the Croats and Slovenes with the Serbs."

He had aged. Yes, that summer he had grown old. She felt a spasm of pain at the thought and was afraid: he may die! She took his hand tenderly in both of hers. "What did they say?" she asked.

"They were kind. They were nearly always kind, my child. But nobody in Europe is concerned about freedom and the rights of small nations. Or about justice."

His embittered tone and "my child" alarmed Milena. Her father had never used endearments with her, except when he was reproaching her, or wanted to show special affection. Only then was she "my child."

"You are still a child, but war is making you grow up fast. I must tell you something that weighs on me heavily. I'm disappointed in Europe. Either my generation was blind, or this war has turned everything upside down."

Milena couldn't understand her father's disappointment. How much had he loved France and Europe, to feel such pain? How could one love a country anyway, how could one love something that could not give love in return?

"I found our people even harder to take. If our nation knew the truth about the situation . . ."

"Who are these people, Father?"

"There's a whole colony of them in Paris. Diplomatic officials, members of the Yugoslav committee and various other missions, army contractors—all of them with fat expense accounts from the Serbian government, and all slandering Serbia."

"Why? I don't understand."

"What is ours, what is Serbian, is no good for them, Milena. For our Yugoslavs, Belgrade is a smelly Turkish provincial town, and we Serbs a dangerous and corrupt people—Byzantines. I'm sure that in Vienna and Budapest they haven't nearly so bad an opinion of Serbia as do many of those fighting for unification."

"Don't they know what happened at Mačkov Kamen, Suvobor, and Valjevo? Don't they know about those reprisals at Podrinije and Mačva?"

"My dear girl, I had to defend to those Serbian patriots and ardent

Yugoslavs what I've been attacking for thirty years. I had to eat my own words."

Olga listened to them as she prepared supper. Talk about politics was distasteful to her. As she was setting the table, she said, "But surely they're not all like that, Vukašin. Some of them are your friends and people who think as you do."

"You're right. But war and emigration reveal people as they are—strip them bare. Reveal the evil in them." He paused for a moment, then added, "Anyway, politics and power are dark, turbid passions. Dirty work!"

"Then why do you do it?" Olga looked him in the eye. Since her return from Valjevo she had thought a great deal about their quarrel just before Ivan's departure for the front, when she had asked Vukašin to arrange through their friends that Ivan should not go to the battlefield. She had despised him then because he was sacrificing their son for his political and moral principles. Later she had resolved to ask his forgiveness for her lack of understanding. Now she listened intently.

"I know that politics is war by all possible means, Olga, even politics with the most honorable motives. I never accepted it before. But now I see that in struggles for even the highest aims and the most honorable principles, the need for truth is lost. I realize now that I haven't always been fair to my opponents. I haven't always spoken the truth. I'm glad Ivan isn't interested in politics."

Olga said nothing, but Milena could not remain silent. "If politics is so disgusting and degrading, Father, why have you devoted your life to it?"

"It's a long story. History has forced my generation to be concerned with politics. The best of my generation have lived for the fulfillment of national goals and the creation of a modern state. We entered life convinced that all great evils, all misfortunes have come to our nation from bad government. I myself believed that government was the power through which the common good could be accomplished."

"Have people with your convictions ever been in the government?"

"A few. For a short time." He fell silent, anticipating Milena's next question, but Olga asked it first:

"You won't be involved in politics any more, Vukašin, will you?"

He paused a moment, then replied, "I must destroy some national misconceptions. My own, too."

"It may be too late for that."

"It's my duty."

For the first time that evening Olga and Vukašin looked at each other with a full, steady gaze. Her soft, oval face, sensitive to every change of feeling, was strained by anxiety and resolution; her eyes darkened with reproach; her slender frame seemed filled with strength. She was more beautiful than ever. What happiness to have her at his side, what comfort to have her at a time like this! He wanted to embrace her.

When had she last seen tears in his eyes? Perhaps it was not just his political disappointments that had made him downcast. He had always been secretive. There was darkness inside him, but he made great efforts to be strong and sensible. Had that brought him happiness? She turned her head away to hide her own tears. *What will I do,* she thought, *now that there stands between us a man who has offered me what I don't have? What I have never had? What I never even wished for, because I didn't know it existed? This is a misfortune, I know, but one I don't want to escape.*

Embarrassed by the sudden and prolonged silence between her father and mother, Milena said, "I never thought that people could deceive you."

What could he say to her? She had lived through the military hospitals and Valjevo, she was no longer a child. But she wasn't even nineteen. He stroked her short, curly hair and said, "Milena, ever since my last year of high school, when I read certain Russian authors, I've had nothing but contempt for disappointed idealists and defeated politicians."

Olga stood behind her husband and daughter: as the space between them diminished, so did the distance between kindness and sincerity—now a distance of just a few steps. She stepped forward, then paused. Both the man she'd been waiting for and the one who had arrived sought from her all she had. How could she then not lose herself? Can people love their own sacrifice? *I don't believe so,* she thought. Perhaps pride was her excuse. Even weak people defend themselves with pride. Perhaps sincerity was her revenge. The weak also defend themselves with sincerity. *I'm weak, Vukašin,* she thought. She stroked his neck; then suddenly, deep down, she realized that silence and kindness extended to this exhausted, disappointed man were more humane than her sincerity. She felt better.

"You must be hungry, Vukašin. Let's have supper."

Vukašin found his first morning back in Niš strange and exciting. He was quite unlike himself. Ever since he could remember, he had got out of bed as soon as he woke up. He despised lying unwashed in a rumpled bed, wasting the finest moments of the day—the freshness and light of the morning. But that morning he found lying in bed and looking at the light filtering in through the curtains strangely pleasant. To him that light represented a deep wish now fulfilled. He delighted in Olga's gentle movements as she busied herself in the room cluttered with boxes and suitcases. He also found pleasure in the sound of their neighbors' voices, and in the clanking around the well and the chirping of sparrows in the yard. Had he not received a message that Pašić was expecting him, he wouldn't have left the room all day. It was so good to be with Milena and Olga—he had never looked at them with such excitement, never listened to them with such enjoyment. Suddenly a shudder ran through him at the memory of Paris and London: that long, tormented summer now so remote from the reality of Serbia.

Dušanka had left early; at noon she would catch a train to Valjevo. As the three of them were eating breakfast, Milena timidly confessed to her father that she'd fallen in love with Bogdan Dragović and wanted to hear what he knew about Ivan's best friend. But Vukašin felt only a melancholy gladness that she had fallen in love—it didn't matter with whom. Olga frequently put her hand on his shoulder, but lightly, as if by chance, and enveloped him in a glance sometimes surprised, sometimes questioning. He noticed that every word he spoke, every movement he made had meaning for her. That pleased him enormously. For a long time she had been oblivious to his presence. He had taken this as something inevitable, something that liberated him from those vain efforts of married couples to persuade each other that they were resisting the passage of time. Now he felt that his long absence enhanced the time they spent together, healed some wounds, erased the banalities of everyday existence. A shiver of fear and uncertainty went through him as he reviewed the value of what bound them together. His affair with Radmila no longer weighed on his conscience. His world was in flux.

Milena was telling him how Bogdan Dragović had been wounded, but he could concentrate only on his own thoughts. Was it in defeat that he had discovered his true values, his real power? Perhaps his lack of success in life lay in his inability to be happy, to find satisfaction in what he had achieved, what was possible. He had concealed this flaw by despising happiness in the name of commitment to higher goals. Had he not come to recognize these things rather late? Or had he demanded too much of life, spurred on by his father's ambition? He had undervalued all that was ordinary, everything he had, everything the majority of his contemporaries could do. His joy at home with Olga and the children had seemed trivial, but now the fruits of a civic career, based on his schooling and political loyalty, seemed insignificant. He hated the parvenus of the Balkans and was ashamed of all the privileges enjoyed by an intellectual in an unenlightened and poverty-stricken land. He yearned for great deeds, public successes, and political victories; he wished to drive the royal dynasty out of Serbia, make her a republic, change her laws and institutions. He was excited by the possibility of doing good on a grand scale; he lived for such a victory. He had always placed that victory above personal happiness. It would appear on the horizon, near at hand and brightly shining, then move away again and dissolve into uncertainty. With the onset of the war the meaning of all things changed. He resisted many internal changes; even now there were some he couldn't accept without being untrue to himself. Yet something was nudging him to admit that the great ideas he had believed in were destroyed. What was left for him? What would it be like to live in defeat? He would be like a gambler full of regrets for losing a fortune. Even if the scorn of men passed him by, their understanding would be no comfort.

Olga reminded Vukašin that Pašić was waiting. He embraced her and Milena and set off reluctantly for government headquarters, fearful of meeting friends and acquaintances. The houses in Niš, the crowds, the fallen trees seemed unreal in the brilliant sunshine. He walked through the town as if in a dream, his footsteps uncertain. Only when he found himself in front of Nikola Pašić did reality reassert itself. He greeted Pasić, and sat down in the nearest armchair without being asked.

"Why did you come back without my consent? I wanted you in London now," said Pašić sternly.

"I couldn't be away from my country during the coming crisis. Or away from my family," he added in a somewhat lower tone. "What is the situation, Prime Minister?"

"It's never been more serious. The attack hasn't begun yet, but the Allies are pressuring us to accept their demands. The government can't decide what to do. We're holding a secret session of the National Assembly the day after tomorrow. How are our affairs out there in the world?"

"To put it briefly, many people oppose the unification of the South

Slavs. The Great Powers don't want a strong, ambitious state in the Balkans which would change the balance among themselves."

"We must convince them it's in their interest."

"That's not so easy. The entire Balkan policy of the Allies turns on the Dardanelles and Istanbul. They're helping us only to the extent that we bar the Germans from the Dardanelles."

"Is there anyone who's less strongly opposed to the unification? Who would allow it?"

"Well, the English don't favor the breakup of Austria-Hungary because they fear Russian domination of the Balkans and southeastern Europe, the more so as the Russians have been promised Istanbul. And we Serbs have a bad reputation with the English, because they think us Russophiles and Slavophiles."

"Whatever made you tell the English you're a Russophile? When in England you have to be an Anglophile; when in France, a Francophile. What you are in your soul is entirely your own affair."

"As for the French, they follow Russia in their policy toward Serbia, and Russia, as you know, doesn't want a Yugoslav state for reasons of her own connected with her position as a Great Power, and an Orthodox Great Power to boot. Italy wants to replace Austria-Hungary in the Balkans, and is doing all she can to bring about the defeat of Serbia and prevent her from becoming a Yugloslav Piedmont. In general, the Catholics and the Clericalists in France and the rest of Europe are bitter enemies of Serbia. They're working for Italy and Bulgaria. No political idea in Europe today has as many powerful opponents as our Yugoslav cause."

"Do you think we should abandon it?"

"No, I don't. But we must adapt our entire national policy to that idea."

"Do you think we should give up Macedonia?"

"Since we must decide between Macedonia and our own destruction, between Macedonia and union with the Croats and Slovenes, common sense dictates that we should renounce eastern Macedonia as Serbian territory forever." Vukašin could see that Pašić was unconvinced. This man, the greatest opportunist in Serbian politics, was at the same time a nationalist fanatic. A disaster for Serbia.

"But God will be on our side," said Pašić evenly.

"We have no evidence of that, Prime Minister. The Balkans are only small change; the petty accounts of the Great Powers will always be settled at the expense of a Balkan nation, and Serbia's first of all."

"What else did our Allies try to convince you of in London?"

"They assured me that Serbia doesn't have a friend in the world. Every other small nation has somehow managed to find itself a protector. Only we Serbs don't have one."

"That's not true. Serbia has friends. What about Russia and France? If they weren't our friends, we would have been done for long ago."

"Those friends have shown little interest in Serbia. In any case, not enough to save us."

"I'm convinced that it's enough, Vukašin. If we don't act with that conviction, we are lost."

"We must deceive both ourselves and the people?"

"If there's no other way, yes, let's pretend we believe them."

"Our pretense is convincing to the Allies only as long as we give our lives. As long as we die like fools for the Dardanelles."

"That's what we must do. There's no other way."

"If I recall my historical facts correctly, Prime Minister, that's the one lie for which a government will sacrifice a whole nation. To try and prove that lie to be true. Sacrifice without mercy."

Pašić walked over to his desk as if looking for something, but came back with his hands empty. "It's no use being disgusted with the world, with the Allies and their injustice toward Serbia," he said slowly, almost crossly. "They are our friends as long as it suits them. Our despair over such a situation can only benefit our enemies. The solution to all this, Vukašin, is that we who wear lamb's clothing must have a little of the fox's intelligence."

"That's our Serbian, our Balkan, delusion. A fairy tale, that disastrous naiveté that the wolf and the lion don't have the fox's intelligence. As long as we go on living under that misconception, the wolves will devour us even when they aren't hungry."

"I believe the great must sometimes do the small a good turn. They must. Even wolves make a virtue of necessity."

"I'm afraid of such a belief, Prime Minister. I wonder if Serbia can be victorious with such a belief."

The telephone rang. Pašić walked over, answered, and came back.

"Did you ever go to church in Paris, my boy, to forget about the truth and pray to God for a bit of hope? You should go to church sometimes. Whenever I was in Paris and had the time, I used to go to mass in Sainte Geneviève."

Vukašin left, aware of the futility of his mission to Paris and London, of his powerlessness to influence Pašić's policies and the course of events. There was no way out of the present situation. Some irrational force had taken hold of even the most rational Serbian minds. One could no longer save even one's conscience.

On the bridge over the Nišava, crowded with people, he ran into some of his party supporters: "You've come back at the right time! Pašić is wavering before the Allies, but we're not giving up Macedonia or Banat!"

He listened and quickly left. He would be a traitor, and to no purpose. At the other end of the bridge he ran into the French ambassador, Auguste Boppe, who tried to convince him that it was in the vital interest of Serbia to abandon Macedonia and Banat. "I'm delighted you have returned, Monsieur Katić. Try to put some sense into the Opposition, who are pushing Monsieur Pašić further than he wants to go. Use your influence in the Assembly the day after tomorrow. Save your nation."

Katić said nothing. But the French ambassador's fervor demanded a reply: "So you believe Serbia can be saved only if we listen to our Allies?"

"Yes, I do. I believe that as I believe in France."

"I have my doubts about France. And even more so about the other Allies."

"You have doubts about France, about Europe and her spirit? You, Monsieur Katić?"

"The things that we thought constituted the greatness of Europe before the war no longer exist, Monsieur Boppe. Perhaps they never did. Europe is a battleground and a marketplace of thieves. It's gone mad with nationalism and lies. One can no longer believe in any European political ideal. The socialists have betrayed us, too. Everything has been betrayed!"

"What has so discouraged you, Monsieur Katić?"

"Your cruel indifference. The persistent determination of the Allies to save us in their own way. Your international agreements. Your anger that we don't feel you are saving us. Don't you see that we can't be saved within the limits of your calculations?"

Boppe looked at him in astonishment.

Ambassador Boppe anounced to Nikola Pašić very briefly that he would, in accordance with the instructions from his government, associate himself with the positions of England and Russia. He appeared more worried than Pašić, the head of the Serbian government. He was holding his pocket watch and nervously rubbing his thumb across the glass. It was as if he wanted to break the hands, erase the figures, and destroy the human measurement of time in a single circular motion.

"In history everything begins in the dark," said Pašić softly, as if to himself. "The greater the events, the deeper the darkness."

"That's a law of the East, Prime Minister."

"Maybe. But I learned in the West not to be surprised at anything men do. Except when they work against themselves."

"I believe, Prime Minister, that in historical storms such as this one, one survives by choosing the lesser evil. Salvation lies in understanding the inevitable and retreating in the face of the greater evil. Do you seriously believe that you will save Macedonia, Prime Minister, if you don't follow our advice?"

"Do *you* believe, Your Excellency, that by handing over Macedonia to Bulgaria you'll buy her entry into the war against Turkey and the Central Powers?"

"If we didn't believe in that possibility, we wouldn't have occupied ourselves with it for a whole year."

"I assure you that you won't buy Bulgaria with Macedonia. The Bulgarians want a Greater Bulgaria."

"I don't deny that the Bulgarians have such aims. However, if you don't immediately give Macedonia to Bulgaria in return for her joining the Allies, Bulgaria will attack you in conjunction with Germany and Austria-Hungary. That will be catastrophic for you. There's no third possibility, Prime Minister."

"Undoubtedly that's how matters stand, from your point of view. Because you think you'll buy Rumania with our territory in Banat and Bulgaria with our territory in Macedonia. Just as you bought Italy's entry into the war with our territory in Dalmatia. I give you my word of honor, Monsieur Boppe: Bulgaria wants more, and she wants to be on the winning side. Right now our enemies are winning—they are stronger. Bulgaria has decided for them."

Boppe rubbed his thumb over the glass of his gold watch for a few moments, then added with unconcealed emotion: "If the Serbian government doesn't accept the Allied proposals, Serbia is finished. In which case, for me personally, this war would be lost, because it would be morally lost for Europe. It is Serbia and Belgium which have given a moral basis to this slaughter in Europe."

"In rejecting the Austrian ultimatum," Pašić said firmly, "Serbia entered the war not only to defend herself. By not accepting the ultimatum from Vienna, Serbia sacrificed herself for the European democracies and Russia. Just as she sacrificed herself for Christianity and

Europe in the fourteenth century, in the face of the impending Turkish invasion."

"I have the greatest admiration for your action, Prime Minister, an action in the spirit of Kossovo.* An action demonstrating greatness of soul. On the field of Kossovo you decided once and for all for European civilization and became a European nation. Now you stand again before a new and brilliant confirmation of your spirit and your greatness. In this tragic European cataclysm, you have been called upon to make a contribution which will place you forever among the great nations."

Pašić interrupted his eloquence: "By her entry into the war and her dearly bought victories over the Austrian army, Serbia made it impossible for the Central Powers to conquer the Balkans and the Dardanelles and penetrate to the east. For more than a year Serbia postponed that calamity for the Entente states, a calamity that might have proved catastrophic. Imagine where your Eastern front would be today if Serbia hadn't stopped the Germans and Austrians. Yet even so you present Serbia with an ultimatum to surrender her lands to a country that tomorrow will be our enemy and yours. That's all I have to say to you."

"Please believe me that I understand your difficulties and will make every effort to interpret them faithfully to my government. But please accept our proposal without delay! That's the only way you can save your country. Whatever happens, I'll remain your friend as long as I live." Making no attempt to hide his disappointment, Boppe left the office.

Pašić wondered whether it would have been more useful to have made this last statement to the English and Russian ambassadors. But he had no time for reflection: the Italian ambassador was announced.

Baron Squitti, the Italian ambassador, made a deep bow while still in the doorway, and said fervently in French, "I beg you to believe me, Excellency, that I have a profound understanding of Serbia's drama, and your personal drama as well."

Pašić greeted Squitti coldly but politely, and before the baron could sit down tentatively on the edge of the couch, as was his custom, Pašić asked: "Why doesn't Italy agree to the unification of the South Slavs according to the same principle by which she was united and became what she is today?"

* In the battle of Kossovo in 1389, the Serbs were disastrously defeated by the Ottoman Turks. [Translator's note.]

45

Squitti straightened up, and his mild, smiling face was abruptly transformed into handsome severity. "You wished to ask me, Excellency, why Italy desires to have the eastern Adriatic coast? Because she has a rightful historic claim to it, a claim known to the entire civilized world."

"There is a Slav population living on the eastern Adriatic coast, Your Excellency, which is equally known to the civilized world."

"We will not dispute that conditional fact. But we affirm that, not counting the rocks and plants that belong to the Creator, everything else that men have created on the eastern Adriatic is Italian. The towns, the churches, the culture are all ours. It is our civilization. Of course the villagers are of Slavic origin. But they have no history. Anyway, a Roman emperor planted cabbages in Split—or rather Spalato." His smile lingered. "You, Excellency, as a statesman must ask yourself why Italy entered the war when she was not threatened, unless she expected that the future peace would bring the final solution of the Adriatic problem."

"I understand all too well why you entered the war. You were given fine promises."

Squitti shifted, smiled again, and straightened his pince-nez. "Today we must be realistic, Excellency. Notwithstanding the honorable military achievements of the kingdom of Serbia, she doesn't and cannot have the rank of a Great Power. That's your good fortune. You don't have to fulfill the obligations of a Great Power. You seem to think otherwise."

"I think realistically. Right now the kingdom of Serbia is defending singlehandedly the route to Istanbul and the East. That's the role of a Great Power."

"Italy values that. Therefore she agrees that you should be given the territory from the Cape of Planco to ten kilometers below Cavtat, including the harbors of Split and Dubrovnik."

"But the rest of our territory will be yours?"

"Isn't yours the lion's share? True, the English have promised you a lot. But of course it's hard to believe such generosity is feasible. Rome understands your doubts, Excellency."

"Has Rome reflected on what will happen to your claim to the Adriatic coast if the Germans and Austrians take the Dardanelles this fall and turn everything upside down? Where will your front against Austria be then?"

Squitti's face clouded. "Rome has no doubts as to the outcome of the war."

"That's nice for you, but we're afraid."

"That's understandable. For that reason we're waiting with the greatest anxiety for your reply concerning compensation for Bulgaria. My government wishes to know when Serbia will give her final answer."

"We're thinking about it, Your Excellency."

"It isn't easy for you. But time rushes on furiously, and will soon overtake us."

Pašić suddenly interrupted him: "Were you born in Florence, Mr. Squitti?"

Baron Squitti gave a sour smile, then frowned slightly: "I'm a Venetian, but I like Florence very much. I know it well."

"Have you ever been in the church of Santa Maria Novella?"

"Yes, I have. An extremely well-proportioned church. Yet by comparison to the other churches in Florence, its architecture is modest, not to say stereotyped. Why this curious question, Excellency?"

"In that beautiful church I've prayed to God for my wife's happiness."

"You, an Orthodox, prayed in a Catholic church?"

"Whenever I'm in Europe and have the time, I go to mass. The organ music suits my soul, fills me with courage. A man can pray for whatever he likes to the accompaniment of organ music. When the choir sings during our liturgy, when the people sing in a cathedral, I'm seized by an immeasurable sadness. Thank you, Your Excellency, for this pleasant reminder of the past." Pašić rose slowly and held out his hand.

"Allow me to remind you once more of the future. How soon can we expect the Serbian reply to the Allied note, Excellency?"

"You know, Your Excellency, in politics prediction is a dangerous thing."

"I marvel at your persistence."

"That's my duty."

As he closed the door behind Squitti, Pašić thought to himself: I must be more persistent than the most persistent of the Allies. Perhaps Serbia can be saved that way. It can also be destroyed that way. One must be flexible. One must be persistent and flexible, but persistent in both.

"The heavens are infinitely greater than the earth. Because of this absurdly disproportionate relationship, it is improbable that the infinitely great heavens would revolve around the infinitely small earth."

Vojvoda Putnik was reading Copernicus in the office of the High Command of the Serbian army in Kragujevac. He was so absorbed that he didn't hear a knock on the door.

When Colonel Živko Pavlović entered, the chief of the High Command was sitting in a large, iron bed, propped up against a pile of pillows, in his uniform and woolen socks. He was deep in his book, and a cat lay at his feet. Pavlović stopped in the middle of the enormous room sparsely furnished with a table and three wicker chairs. He looked anxiously at the vojvoda, who was again laid low with asthma. How can we oppose three powerful General Staffs, he thought, with a seriously ill commanding officer, a worn-out old man?

"May I have a word with you, Vojvoda?" he asked timidly.

"The heavens are boundless when we compare them to the earth. Very little is known about how far this boundless space extends."

"I'm sorry, Vojvoda, but I must disturb you." Vojvoda Putnik raised his eyes and noticed that the third button from the bottom of his assistant's jacket was unfastened. It was the first time this exemplary officer had exhibited such slovenliness. A button. A circle, a perfect form, the form of the earth and the planets. What was one button in comparison to the earth and the planets? What was one button in comparison to the earth, and to the sun? Yet this unfastened button revealed disorder in the man and the army. Disorder was a sign of absence of will. And absence of faith.

"Please do disturb me, Colonel."

Colonel Pavlović faced a glance that could halt a division.

"I'm listening, Colonel."

"Our military attachés in Paris, Bucharest, and Athens confirm the telegram received yesterday from St. Petersburg about the movement of enemy armies toward the Sava and the Danube. We are also informed from Sofia that Bulgaria is rapidly preparing to mobilize." He handed him the telegrams.

Putnik looked at the telegrams. He didn't see the words, only marks on white paper. He saw an infinitely small Serbia on an infinitely small earth in the infinite universe. He reached for a bell on his bedside table and rang it.

Pavlović grew more despondent. Vojvoda Putnik didn't have the strength to call an orderly, but he had to lead an army against three others vastly larger and stronger.

After entering swiftly and noiselessly, full of self-importance, Sergeant Milorad, Putnik's orderly, stood at attention. "Shall I take Gavra out, Vojvoda?" he asked, looking at the large, gray cat on the bed, which he was ordered to remove whenever the vojvoda received official visitors or issued orders to the army.

"Shut the windows, Milorad. It's getting dark."

Milorad walked over to the windows, disappointed by the vojvoda's petty command. It was the end of summer, and the air was full of pungent harvest odors, and dampness at night, which was harmful to the vojvoda's breathing. How will he feel when the rains come and the fog settles in? Pavlović wondered.

"Order the source of this information to be confirmed, Colonel. Especially about the new German cannons. I want precise information on their caliber and range."

"The sources are reliable, Vojvoda. The only information we lack is the date of the Bulgarian mobilization."

"Well, check again. I can only make responsible decisions on the basis of facts."

Putnik was left alone. The air was growing thick. There wasn't enough of it in this small room in Kragujevac, or in Serbia, pinned between an infuriated Austria-Hungary and Germany to the west and north, a vengeful Bulgaria to the east, and a powerless Montenegro to the south, along with Greece, a small and unreliable ally, and the Albanian rebels lying in ambush.

What is Serbia on this infinitely small earth, itself whirling, and turning around the sun? A lump of earth between rivers. Between the Danube, the Sava, and the Drina, and the lakes of Macedonia: dark red mountains rising like waves; garlands of coniferous forest and bare slopes bending and curving; valleys yellow with corn and slopes with stubble, and flocks scattered over them. The three green Morava rivers and the Ibar going their meandering ways; the Kolubara, Pek, Timok, and Nišava gleaming brightly from their willow groves and meadows; the Vardar glinting in the Macedonian sun through its burning valley. Over the hills and vales a white scattering of villages with swollen graveyards, small towns nesting in the valleys, crowded with frightened inhabitants ready to flee when they hear cannons. Along the Drina, Sava, and Danube, the trenches of the Serbian army stretch like an unwinding skein. Behind them rises the smoke of regimental and battalion field kitchens with the staff tents half-hidden in enclosed fields and copses. Dust rising over white roads constructed with devilish difficulty, rising behind the baggage trains as they crawl toward the front lines, and between them and the quartermaster stores. On the hillsides and riverbanks, the soft deciduous trees are already turning golden. Women and children are scattered through the fields, gardens, and plum orchards: the gathering of plums has already started, but without the shouts and curses of the men. They are with the army in trenches and command posts, or they lie rotting beneath a shallow layer of soil. The dead are more than two whole armies, and the prisoners of war, almost two divisions.

How to resist? With what means and whose help?

The Drina, Sava, and Danube do not effectively bar the passage of the Austro-Hungarian and German armies; Serbia is neatly cut in two by the Morava valley, just right for flank attacks and for encircling the main body of the defending army. Serbia lies open to Bulgarian attack along the Nišava valley and the Strumitsa plain, while from the Stratsina direction the Bulgarians could quickly plunge into the Kumanovo ravine. From there they would meet no obstacle as far as Skoplje and Kossovo. The shortest approach to Salonika and Greece for the Serbian army is barred by the Grdelica ravine, where it would be impossible to withstand a Bulgarian flank attack. The one railroad to Salonika and Allied help would soon be cut. And then what? Crowd the army toward Kossovo, Albania, and Montenegro, with no way out? But the enemy would surround us on three sides and annihilate us on the undulating slopes toward Skoplje, Šara, and Kossovo—wipe out every last pocket of resistance. The Vardar valley would be open to the conquerors on their way to the Dardanelles and the Mediterranean. Would it be better to lose the battle, lose all the battles, but save the army? Where would we go then?

His glance roamed overhead. Clouds were approaching from all directions, wrapping themselves around Serbia and her battlefields. The rains silenced the rivers, the dust rose no more behind the baggage trains, and the unharvested meadows, fields, and plum orchards darkened.

Serbia has an earthy face, with its dirt roads and villages, and an earthy people, milling between the shallow trenches and graveyards, fleeing along the roads to the south, frightened, naked, impoverished, and emaciated, not yet recovered from the great typhus epidemic. How can we defend this people? What could a man do in the face of events which were changing the natural course of history? Human time, human deeds were but a moment, a crumb. Everything great happened in accordance with the laws of the universe and the Creator. But something great must be done today, to save Serbia. And great deeds demand great faith.

The cat climbed up his arm and began to lick his moustache. Here at the High Command, only this cat dared to behave contrary to the rules of military service, and only to the cat did he dare show feelings of tenderness. He stroked this creature, which had learned tenderness from women, playfulness from children, and disobedience from men.

He picked up the bell and rang it.

"Turn the light on, Milorad. And bring two lamps." He felt uncomfortable, dirty in the feeble light of the bulb. He got out of bed and slowly walked to the window with his head thrown back, accompanied by the cat. The telephone rang and he walked back to the table.

Nikola Pašić's voice. "Good evening. How's your health, Vojvoda?"

"No worse than yesterday, Prime Minister."

"What are the latest reports about the enemy?"

"According to the reports I received yesterday and today, the Austro-Hungarians and the Germans are speeding up the concentration of their armies for an attack on Serbia. The information about the Bulgarian mobilization was confirmed today."

"Our allies are demanding—it's practically an ultimatum—that we immediately give Macedonia to Bulgaria and Banat to Rumania."

"Who will keep the Germans from the Dardanelles if Serbia is dismembered?"

"Until we fulfill their requests, the Allies won't let us use the loan already approved for the purchase of military equipment and munitions."

"What should we do, then?"

"Go on as we have been."

"That's no longer sufficient, Prime Minister."

"What can be done is sufficient. You do what can be done for defense. That's all I can tell you now. A secret session of the National Assembly has been called for tomorrow. I'll let you know the outcome."

Putnik leaned against the back of the wicker chair to ease his breathing.

"You must tell the Allies firmly that the Serbian army cannot take responsibility before the court of History . . ."

He didn't finish, as Pašić had already hung up. Anyway, what did "responsibility before History" mean? Responsibility in ceasing to exist? Human responsibility in the universe? Before *what* history? One was lost on a small piece of earth between three little streams—what did that represent for the existence of a cluster of stars?

Later he drank a bowl of milk and told his orderly to prepare his bed.

How could he wage war when attacked simultaneously by three armies, each one stronger than his own? Should he retreat? But where to, in a small country? Should he lose the battles, but not the war? Did the Serbian army have the strength to wage war for defeats, and the will and faith to go from defeat to victory? Had this ever happened, O Creator, on this ancient earth?

He went over to the window, opened it just a crack, and gazed at the starry depths of the sky, into infinity. Suddenly he felt calm.

2

Letters to Serbian prisoners of war from their women.

From Belgrade to Boldogašonj:
My dear brother!

If you only knew how much I suffer because I can't do anything for you and all my Serbian brothers in prison! I can't even help the people I love most. My dearest brother, I feel more unhappy than you fellows there. Your sister begs you to be patient. Be patient and stick it out. Our enemies can't hold out, for all their power.

From Prijedor to Nafmeder:
My dearest son Nikola,

Everything is misery. Since the war started, the Fritzies have put all the Serbs in Bosnia behind bars. Children have been born but not christened. The priests, if they're not hanged, are in jail. My dear boy, if Big Russia and Little Serbia don't free us, there's no more life for us in Bosnia.

From Loznica to Mauthausen:
My dearest Čeda,

My companion whom I can never forget, how hard it is for me to live without you! I pray to God that you may keep well, and that God will bring you back home, because there's nothing worse than having your heart torn in two. Oh my heart, why don't you split my body in two, so I don't yearn for my handsome Čeda! My darling Čeda, my Dark Eyes, how I long for you! Čeda, my dear companion, will the merciful God bring you home, will we see each other once more, my darling?

I get up and go to bed crying, "O God, I'm unhappy!" It's so hard for me, living alone inside these four walls.

Čeda, my dearest Čeda, can you hear what I'm saying to you? I'm waiting for you, Čeda, waiting for you, my dear heart!

From Serbia to Boldogašonj, postmark not clear:
Dear Veljko!

Your father won't answer your letter because you're a coward. He doesn't want to hear anything about you either. He curses you and says you're a misfortune come down on his head. He even curses our children and wants them to die. He says: I don't need the offspring of a coward, a man who has brought me the greatest pain and shame!

I don't think any better of you, Veljko. All the women are proud of their husbands and praise their heroism, but you have brought shame on me and on our house. I've sent you some money to buy poison, so your village need never see you again.

This is Stanojka's greeting to you.

(These letters and cards were seized by the Censorship Division of the Gemeinsames Zentral Nachweisbureau in Vienna on July 20, 1915.)

The train from Skoplje, due in Niš the previous night, arrived at daybreak. But Kosara, with her baby wrapped in a yellow shawl, was sorry when the train reached its destination. She would have liked to travel to the end of the world. If it weren't necessary to buy a ticket, she would have traveled anywhere, simply to be moving. During the day she would look out the window into the unfamiliar, changing countryside, and at night she didn't sleep, but simply gazed into the darkness at the garland of live coals which was hurrying the train along, the train that whistled from sadness at leaving and from joy at arriving. But a war was on and she had only five dinars to her name, so she could go no further.

We must get out, Života my son. You're fast asleep—you don't care, do you, that your mother has brought you to a big town to live among real gentlefolk. I can't imagine anything better. Why should we wander about Skoplje, or flee to Salonika? Fall is coming, and rain and cold. If the Germans and Bulgarians arrive, what'll I do? Do they really throw babies onto bayonets, then set them on fire with the house? Where do such people come from? Did they suck their mothers' breasts or did they lick knives, God forbid. I can see from your forehead that you're going to be handsome, and from your legs that you're going to grow tall. You've got a gentle nature, you don't cry like other children. There's nothing finer in a man than a gentle nature. I don't know how I'm going to pull through such troubles with this helpless creature in my arms. For a month now I haven't slept, or looked at a man in uniform. I heard someone inside my soul cry out, "Bear him, Kosara!" So I did. Sleep, sleep, my son.

Let them all get off the train—we two won't yet. I thought to myself: What if it's a boy? So many men are dying, after the war every man and boy will live like a king. Why shouldn't my son, too? I knew you were a boy, Života my pet, I knew it. When the war's over, your mother will take you away from these fine folk, and you'll learn to be a locomotive engineer. You'll drive a train, drive your mother from Skoplje to Niš and Belgrade and back. And you'll whistle—ah, how you'll whistle! All of Serbia along the railway track will know that you're at the engine. But today we have to find Father and Mother. I hope they're not cruel and nasty. I'll find them if I have to go to the end of the world. I'll say: Madam, this is your grandson Života. Sir, this is your son's son. If the name Života isn't good enough for you, you can change it to Miloš. I won't agree to any other name. Dear God, don't let everything I've planned fall through.

Nowadays people just save their own skins. They ditch their children to travel faster and farther. When you grow up, your mother will tell you what people are like, men and women. And she'll tell you how to grab at happiness in this cruel world, how to steal it!

Where are you rushing off to, gentlemen? You'll get to Salonika, don't worry. Who cares whether it's first class! There's no first class when you're fleeing from Serbia. I'm not getting off the train until it's broad daylight. I have no money for a room, and I'm not about to drag my child through the streets of Niš. I'm going to a really fine house, to some gentlefolk from Belgrade, and you know what time they get up. Sorry, you can stand and wait till my baby wakes up.

"I can see you're decent, Soldier. The war's bitten off your leg. Old man, pump me some water, bless you, to wash my baby. As soon as he's been fed he makes a mess. I'm going to a fine house, it's the first time Grandma and Grandpa will see their grandchild, and he should be clean. No, it isn't too cold. He hasn't been washed in warm water three times since he was born. It's still summer, he's a boy, thank God, and I want him to get used to cold water. Not so fast, the jet will hurt him. See, cold water doesn't make him cry, my little hero. Just hold him, won't you, while I wash his diapers? Thank you, my friend."

Now, my son, you're going to see Niš for the first time. When you grow up I'll tell you how the two of us traveled in an empty train from Skoplje to Niš, and first class, too.

"Excuse me, madam, do you happen to know a Mrs. Katić from Belgrade, the mother of Ivan Katić? He's a student, and they say he's a prisoner of war now."

Vukašin Katić stayed awake all night: if he announced his convictions in the Assembly that day and didn't vote with all the others, he'd be proclaimed a traitor; but if he didn't stand up for his convictions, he'd betray himself. Either course, if carried to its logical conclusion, would disrupt his life. He couldn't accept such an outcome. He had examined numerous other possibilities, but rejected them all. Why couldn't he act like the majority in such circumstances?

All night Olga was restless. She knew Vukašin wasn't asleep. Several times she wanted to caress him, but refrained. That night he didn't want her tenderness. The thought made her sad, and she could hardly wait for daybreak so she could get up, go into town, and buy him the newspapers. On her way she met the mailman, who handed her several letters. None from Ivan.

Vukašin didn't even look at the newspapers; he knew that they all had the same feeling about the Allied demands, that conceding to the demands was more important than saving Serbia. Among the letters he recognized his father's handwriting and felt afraid: why was he writing to him, today of all days? His father had never replied to the letter informing him that Ivan was missing. Trembling slightly, Vukašin opened the letter:

My dear son,

I sense that we're approaching the end. The millers say that last night, before the midnight cockcrow, the millstone stopped. The Morava stood still, Vukašin! This always happens before some great misfortune hits Serbia. Yes, our river stood still. I see that just about everybody is after Serbia. I hear that southern Serbia is being given to the Bulgarians. Why did we fight two wars? Why did so many of our young men perish? Why have things gone badly for us after great victories and glory that Russia and the whole world acknowledge? Here in Prerovo we're waiting for the Day of Judgment.

I can't go on like this any longer. I'm asking you to come home, my boy. I want to see you. From what Tola says, you're already an old man, and I've had one foot in the grave for a long time.

I suppose I'm not the worst father and you're not the worst son in Serbia. Why is it that for twenty-two years the two of us have behaved as if we had no heart or soul? I don't know. I'm rotting away, nothing but bones and misery. I no longer recognize myself. Nor can I tell what would have become of me if I hadn't forsaken my own son.

I'm waiting for a letter from my grandson Ivan. I'm waiting, but I know it won't come. I wait for you too every evening at suppertime. That was the hour you came home when you were a student. I know you won't come. You haven't yet gotten to where you mean to go.

Then I think again and I know you're not bad. If you can manage it, come to Prerovo. Bring my granddaughter Milena, if you can. And if it isn't asking too much, I'd like to see my daughter-in-law Olga. If hell exists, it's at night in my room. I've served out my sentence for all the sins my stupid heart has committed, and paid off all the debts of my obstinate head.

If you don't think I have, Vukašin, then go wherever you must to the end of your life.

May God grant you and your children and your wife health and freedom. Your loving father,

Aćim

Vukašin decided to go to Prerovo the next day, as soon as the secret session was over. He remembered his last visit to the village, on Christmas Eve, and the dinner with his father and brother. No, he hadn't betrayed his father, nor had his father repudiated him. No one was to blame for that misfortune. The rift between them had been unavoidable, something which fate brings about whenever men attempt to reach beyond it. His father too had realized that time and the war made their conflict pointless. Their differences had lost their significance, and all that remained were the eternal truths: love, pain, remorse. Did twenty-two years have to pass for him, Vukašin, to grasp that? Is war the time for reassessing values? He had tried to explain his feelings to Olga in one of his letters, but apparently he made no impression; she was silent on the subject. Why had such a letter come from Aćim today? Was it a warning before his entry into the Assembly? Perhaps the nation could not escape its fate. Perhaps its downfall was inevitable. Perhaps the nation would not settle its accounts with History, it would not be ruled by reason, it could not. Why didn't he believe in God?

Olga prepared his breakfast and sat down at the table to wait for him. She could hear paper rustling, but she felt it would be awkward to ask, Whose letter makes you tremble so?

"You'll be late, Vukašin," she said.

He washed, dressed, and ate in silence. As he was setting out she put both her hands on his shoulders, looked anxiously into his eyes, and said firmly: "You must do today what you would have done before the war."

"I'm no longer sure whether that would be a good thing, Olga."

"Follow your conscience and we'll take what comes."

Vukašin gave her a long, questioning look: Is she sorry for me, or is that what she really believes? She had talked differently when Ivan left for the front. He said thoughtfully: "The awful thing is that today even my conscience cannot be my guide."

"It must be, Vukašin. No matter where it takes you."

"I have a feeling that nobody will follow me. I'll lose my reputation and the respect of the people. That's what I've always cared about most."

"If a man has no respect for himself, he has no right to expect it from anyone else."

"Sometimes it's difficult to respect oneself."

"I found that out in Valjevo."

"Only then?"

"Yes."

They looked at each other despondently. Suddenly he set off, then came back to kiss Milena, who was asleep. She smiled without opening her eyes. That smile cheered him up, and he set out once again. But at the gate he stopped: after the speech he would deliver in the Assembly, he couldn't go to Prerovo to his father. Not even his father would approve. He shouldn't leave Niš for the next few days anyway. He'd send Milena to Prerovo. Let her span the time the two of them had put between them. He returned to the house and timidly told Olga about his father's letter and his wish that Milena go to Prerovo. Olga didn't oppose the idea, which pleased him a great deal. He woke Milena up and told her. She embraced him, happy that she would at last meet her grandfather.

Nikola Pašić refused to read the morning telegrams from the Serbian ambassadors to the Allied capitals. He weighed his decision carefully. He told his secretary that he would receive no one before he left for the Assembly. He then sat down at his desk and placed a finely sharpened pencil across a sheet of paper. Few things helped him to collect his thoughts like the whiteness of blank paper, which had the potential for lines and numbers and all kinds of constructions.

Ever since he'd lost faith in Bakunin, he'd behaved in accordance with the laws of the world, not the imperatives of an ideal. He was convinced that this was wiser for both men and nations. Fireflies had never been his guide in the dark. He'd never proposed to either himself, his party, or the State any goal which only the future could prove. Politics wasn't like engineering, for its material was human beings, the most unreliable construction material. Politics was perhaps more like agriculture: each task had its own time and tools; one sowed in order to reap, one planted in order to gather. If sowing weren't balanced by harvest, it was useless; if one worked without profit, the work was pointless. Every policy but a practical one was evil and senseless. And when a policy demanded sacrifices, the calculations must be as exact as the calculations for the construction of a bridge. Nothing in human history aroused such revulsion in him as sacrifice for an ideal. National leaders whose policies required great sacrifices were narcissists—tyrants who deserved only contempt and curses. He had never admired Caesar or Napoleon.

Today all circumstances conspired to force Serbia to sacrifice. Even her village policemen knew that. Many wise people thought that not much could be accomplished through politics, that their only choice was a dignified collapse. A collapse for honor, legends, and a new Kossovo. On the other hand, those without ambition weren't concerned about dignity. They believed that Serbia was no longer in a position to choose honorable capitulation. Today in the Assembly none of the more intelligent members would take his side, because for them the boundary between the grave and salvation was too thin for comfort. Certainly the majority had no hope in their hearts, and people without hope cannot make wise decisions about their own fates, let alone the fate of a nation.

He must tell them the worst. The tide of the war was turning against Serbia. *History is pulling us under,* he thought; *if we succumb, we'll suffer for it; if we oppose her, we may die.* He would shatter idealists with facts. The Serbs couldn't wage war against Franz Josef, Wilhelm II, the Vatican, Count Tisa, and Radoslavov with ideals. Only fools could be idealists in Serbia when her allies were Lord Kitchener, Delcassé, Sazonov, and Sonino. The right course was to accept the inevitable and act accordingly, to use all means to secure survival and victory. To persevere as long as it was profitable.

To Vukašin Katić and the like he would say: I know, gentlemen, that the Allies have been heartless and unjust to Serbia, and this isn't the first time. They're sacrificing us now, and it doesn't bother them much. If we rebel or declare, "We don't believe you, we don't want to go along," we'll only make it easier for them to get rid of us. So we must believe in them, or at least in their rules. By persevering in our belief we'll exert pressure on them, put them under an obligation to us before Europe and the entire world. After the war not even the meanest of Allied statesmen will be able to renege on their obligations to Serbia. Auguste Boppe was right: he who betrays Serbia in this war cannot be the victor.

After all, war hadn't changed politics, it had merely made it naked and unashamed. Yet not even his own supporters in the Assembly had grasped this, let alone his opponents. Why was it so hard for people to understand the simplest truth? He hadn't suffered unduly because of the fate of his people, nor had he made much of an effort to understand them. He respected their stupidity, their mistakes. He had always behaved toward his supporters as if he believed in them, and had agreed to be what they wanted him to be. He had lived up to what his opponents expected of him. He had never tried to reform people or change their opinions about himself. Because he had never been consistent, and in any case was more than the sum total of his actions, nobody except Djurdjina had seen the soul behind the beard. He had stayed in power at the head of his party at a time when this was considered impossible, when he was thought gullible, cowardly, and incompetent. He hadn't wasted time refuting such charges. He had just continued steadily in his own fashion, acting in the way that seemed most useful. Long ago he had grasped that anyone in politics who wanted to be a democrat and rule without violence had first to learn to bear injustice and patiently disarm his opponents. A politician must be discreet, he mustn't use freedom for his own defense. Freedom was the right to oppose the government. Nothing was more useful for the government than such freedom. Things weren't so bad as long as the people were making à noise; when they were silent, it was dangerous. This held good now, too. Today he'd have to endure attacks. And not only from his opponents. Perhaps Vukašin Katić and Jaša Prodanović would give him a little support—presumably their principles would not be all-important to them today. Once he had believed that any good government would be strenuously defended at critical times by those not in power. Could he still believe that?

Well, let his allies and enemies think what they liked. He'd hold out on his own. After all, this time of imperatives, of no choice and no way out, was *his* time.

Vukašin Katić paused in confusion: in front of the Officers' Club, where the National Assembly had held its meetings since the beginning of the war, was a huge crowd of people, overflowing the street and the park. Alongside this subdued, multicolored, swelling throng walked Austro-Hungarian prisoners of war, maintaining a strict hierarchy; they had no sabers, but their uniforms were carefully pressed. Between them and the anxious populace, servant girls pushed babies in carriages. The cries of news vendors fused with the rhythmic brushes of the shoeshine boys. Aware of being watched closely, Vukašin felt awkward as he hurried into the Assembly building. His political supporters moved in on him, and the crowd grew agitated. "Don't give the Bulgarians any Serbian territory!" they shouted. "Why is Pašić beating about the bush? Down with Pašić! Defend Macedonia! Join the army—Serbia is placing her trust in you! Tell the Allies Serbia isn't a scared rabbit. Get a word in now, Vukašin, tell them we'll die fighting! Defend our cause, Katić!"

Dazed, he stopped, then slowly continued on his way, lowering his head as he passed among a group of war invalids who were banging with their crutches and bayonets, begging for coins. "Don't give anything of Serbia's to our murderers!" they called out to him. "Were we crippled for nothing? We'll kill you, if you give up Macedonia!"

He looked at the man who shouted this threat: his face had been disfigured by shrapnel, his chin blown away, and his lips twisted into a blob of flesh.

Vukašin entered the Assembly Hall with his self-confidence shattered. He shook hands with his party associates and sat down in his seat. Around him he heard the deputies talking:

"We hoped the Russians would be in Vienna or close to Berlin by now. Instead, the Germans are pushing toward St. Petersburg. Russia always suffers defeat, but never loses a war. Remember Napoleon's Moscow campaign? That's no comfort. History doesn't repeat itself, gentlemen. Kaiser Wilhelm's Germany isn't Napoleon's France. The fortress of Kovno will fall, I bet you. Nonsense, Kovno is impregnable. If we can stick it out until winter and not surrender Macedonia . . ."

Some of these people, perhaps a third of the Assembly, held a point of view similar to his own, thought Vukašin. Yet they'd go along with the majority, he was sure. And they wouldn't consider such action dishonorable either. On the contrary, they'd consider such flexibility a sign of political wisdom. Perhaps that was indeed so. In science and scholarship one could be alone, but not in politics. To be in the right and alone, to act according to one's conscience, was senseless. Crazy. Between his own convictions and the opinions of the crowd outside who believed in him and called on him to speak in their name, he could not emerge honorably. He would have to make a decision and betray himself. Still, it was easier to betray oneself than other people, the majority. Integrity was not always a sign of strength, nor was honorable behavior always a virtue. Everything he'd experienced since the first secret session of the Assembly last fall and that infernal meeting with the government and the High Command in Valjevo—everything since his disappointments in Paris and London, everything that had troubled him since his return to Niš—all that was his own personal affair, something he didn't admit even to himself. That terrible vice of power—something inherited from his father, but concealed under high principles and adorned with moral sanctions. Olga had actually said as much the night she'd begged him to intervene on Ivan's behalf, to save him from going to the front.

To divert his thoughts, he began to read that day's *Echo* and his own unsigned leading article: "Not since 1804 have our national representatives been called on to make such a difficult decision. We have experienced more difficult days, but never a more difficult decision. Today we are making a decision about our fate. We need to be wise, tolerant, calm."

Was that good advice, or just the echo of his own moral weakness? Abruptly he turned the paper over and read the last column on the back page: "There are more dogs in Niš than in any town in Asia Minor. The authorities have decided on measures to exterminate them, but have not fully implemented them. The dogs go around in packs and frequently attack the townspeople. How can we protect ourselves from this nuisance?"

Andra Nikolić, the president of the Assembly, rang his bell, and called on the secretary to read the minutes of the last meeting.

Nikola Pašić felt a spasm of fear at the silence that met him as he walked toward the rostrum: though he'd spent decades in the Assembly, both as a member of the Opposition and as a government minister, and had never known such silence. Moved by it, he stood for a few moments with his head bowed toward the deputies, grateful for their acknowledgment of the seriousness of the moment.

"Gentlemen. History is turning in a direction contrary to our wishes and hopes." His voice was so broken that he had to stop speaking. The emotion on the faces of the Opposition deputies gave him strength. He continued in a quieter tone: "The Great Powers are not prepared to take our rights into consideration. They demand from us exceptional sacrifices. Serbia must again dig up her own foundations. The government will inform you about its present and future foreign policy, and you will have a chance to comment. This is how matters stand. . . ."

Vukašin was confused by Pašić's position on the Allies, which so closely resembled his own. Was it the tactical plan of an old parliamentary master, or had Pašić substantially changed his opinion since their talk yesterday morning? Later the previous day Vukašin had met him in the street while taking a ride with Olga and Milena. Pašić had stopped his fiacre, bowed deeply to the two ladies, and called Vukašin aside:

"Keep quiet tomorrow, Vukašin," he had said.

"How can anyone keep quiet tomorrow, Prime Minister?"

"If you can't keep quiet, at least don't lose sight of certain facts. The State, the socialists, and I, we all stand together. The army, Vojvoda Putnik, the men with the Karageorge Star, and all those shirkers in front of the cafés stand together. The townspeople—that's you, your brother-in-law Najdan Tošić, the actors, the businessmen—they're all together. That's Serbia now—all of us, honorable and dishonorable, happy and unhappy, heroes and cowards. We must all stand together."

"I know that. But we must fulfill our obligations today."

"Don't divide the nation. Don't separate the wise and honorable. What can we do with them?"

Vukašin was only half listening.

Back in the Assembly Hall, documents were being read aloud about Serbia's foreign policy, including telegrams and notes exchanged between the Serbian and Allied governments about the Balkan question and territorial compensation.

Nikola Pašić sat in his place, his arms folded submissively, and looked at all the deputies in turn, weighing their moods and their possible criticisms of the government. His replies to his opponents mustn't sound as if he were a member of the Opposition, nor should the minutes of the session indicate that anyone had disagreed with him. Tomorrow nobody would be able to say that he had opposed Pašić, clung to his own opinion, or refrained from voting. No one must be allowed to climb to power and fame by way of this meeting. Only fools must be allowed to fall. He carefully observed Vukašin, who sat dejectedly. The deputies were growing more and more bitter about the escalating Allied pressure on the Serbian government; the final messages from the Allies were drowned in a swelling murmur of protest. Pašić decided to take the rostrum and intensify the discontent. Before midday the ambassadors of Russia, England, France, and Italy would know just how bitterly the Serbian National Assembly felt about their policy toward Serbia. That would be his strongest support in resisting their demands. The noise gradually subsided and the president's bell became silent. Pašić spoke:

"You have heard, gentlemen and brothers, that Italy is to have Dalmatia and Istria, Rumania Banat, and Bulgaria Macedonia."

"Disgrace!" shouted one of the deputies.

"Of course we are guaranteed Bosnia and Hercegovina, Srem, Bačka, Slavonia, and the Adriatic coast, including Split and Dubrovnik."

"What about Slovenia, Prime Minister?"

"They've divided that up. Italy is to have Primorje and Ljubljana, and the northern part will go to Austria-Hungary if she still exists, otherwise to Croatia."

"Injustice! Those people are our brothers. We're being put up for sale!"

The shouting died down and Pašić continued to cite the disagreeable political facts. Speaking without emotion, using the technical language of geography, he cited the number of inhabitants, square kilometers, and material resources which Serbia would lose and gain according to the Allied intentions and initiatives.

Vukašin thought of Richelieu, Cavour, Bismarck, and Prince Miloš. Pašić was one of them. In him too the passion for unification and the creation of a great state never wavered. He shrank from no sacrifice or action. His allies were everybody who could help. The only thing he couldn't tolerate was obstinacy in matters of principle, and lack of perseverance in achieving the main objective. He refrained from no deception; insults never troubled him. He was prepared to go along with everybody, so long as they went along with him. He had all the qualities of a great and successful statesman. But even a man like that could accomplish nothing now.

"What will happen," shouted a deputy, "if we say we won't give up what's ours?"

"The Allies maintain," said Pašić, "that if Serbia doesn't fulfill their demands, they'll give her no more weapons or munitions. They'll give them to those who want to fight on their side."

"There are no such people in the Balkans!"

"Let me ask you this, gentlemen: if the Allies abandon us, what will happen? What will we do?"

"You're asking that too late! Much too late!"

"It's not too late. So long as people are working for their salvation, they can be saved. Now I think it's time for the president of the Assembly to give us a short break." Pašić wiped the sweat off his forehead with a handkerchief.

"What will we say after the break, Vukašin?"

"We'll say what we think."

"Who dares say what he thinks today?"

Vukašin did not reply.

On his way to the Café Paris for a business meeting, Najdan Tošić noticed that the town was half-empty, and that the older, predominantly male upper-class, society was missing from the sidewalk cafés. Those passing along the street were for the most part prisoners of war, peasants, wounded soldiers, and women. He felt uneasy: right now in Serbia it was twilight one moment, dawn the next. He bought a copy of *Politika*. Apart from bad news from the fronts (especially the Russian), he saw nothing in the newspaper that could have removed the usual crowd from the streets of Niš. Now one must live at a much faster pace, see through only the most important business deals. Not a moment to spare for fools and sluts; he could no longer waste his nights on despairing women whose husbands were prisoners of war, whose brothers were at the front. As for war strategists and national pessimists, he couldn't even drink a glass of beer with them!

The Bulgarian ambassador Chaprasnikov suddenly turned the corner. To avoid meeting him, Najdan quickly turned down the first side street. These days he felt more ashamed to be seen in public on friendly terms with Chaprasnikov than to be implicated in new scandals concerning drugs and boots, even though those who needed to know did in fact know why he and Chaprasnikov were friends. In Serbia the café was a courthouse which never closed: everything and everyone was judged and sentenced there; evidence, witnesses, and appeals were of no avail. The mob had its own laws and its own scorecard, and that was what counted right now.

He went into the empty café and stopped dead: he hadn't entered an empty café since the war started. The Café Paris was ordinarily full of people, but now there were only Dimitrije Lepenac and Melamed Albahari, two merchants sitting at a corner table, waiting for him. "What's up?" asked Najdan, pointing to the empty tables.

"Everyone is over at the Assembly, waiting for the decision."

"How could I have forgotten? Why aren't you there? Why are you waiting for me?"

"Listen, Najdan, how long is it since we have met in a café to talk in peace, like sensible human beings?" said Lepenac, smiling. "Today is Franz Josef's birthday. They're preparing a celebration feast in the prison camp."

"The Fritzies have emptied the shops—there isn't a bottle of champagne left in Niš," interrupted Albahari.

"I don't give a damn about that!" said Najdan. He was particularly irritated by Lepenac, who before the war had been a partner in a small tannery and was now the biggest leather merchant in Serbia, a man involved in all deals with a rapid turnover. Notwithstanding his abilities and the large profits he had made in deals with him, Najdan found him uncongenial. Lepenac's crudeness disgusted him. He sat down at Lepenac's table, and after Albahari told him about the rapid fall of the Serbian dinar and the termination of deals with his partners in Rumania and Bulgaria, Najdan leaped up again: "I refuse to discuss our affairs in this deadly place, gentlemen. It's like the beginning of the occupation. Come to my house at six o'clock." He turned and started for the door.

"Don't put on such airs, Najdan!" said Lepenac. "Millions are being lost every day. A month from now you'll be able to light gypsies' fires with paper money."

"We must get into real estate, or convert the paper into gold and silver," added Albahari, rising from his chair.

"You convert it, then!"

Najdan left them in front of the café and hurried off to see Olga. Vukašin was now in the Assembly, so he could have a serious talk with her about leaving Niš soon.

Olga was stricken by some private grief. He looked at her anxiously: every melancholy mood of hers affected him deeply, clouded his spirits and spoiled his day. He sat down on the edge of the bed, afraid to ask why she had such dark circles under her eyes. If only he could help her and Milena, save them! But what if Olga wouldn't go to Athens—if Vukašin prevented her with his "moral principles"? As she made coffee in the other room, she asked: "What's happening in town?"

"The Fritzies in the prison camp are celebrating Franz Josef's birthday."

"What's going on at the Assembly?"

"For heaven's sake, Olga, what decisions can wretched Serbia make, when it's clear to every street vendor in Niš that Serbia's fate is sealed?"

She stood in the doorway and said timidly: "Vukašin will propose the acceptance of the Allied demands."

He didn't conceal his mirth: "That will be his last speech in the Assembly! He won't be able to save his skin by putting army contractors on the spot this time." He moved closer to her. "I'll tell you something, Olga. That would be the most sensible proposal made by your husband in his political career. However, our fall can no longer be prevented by any means. Serbia is on the verge of collapse."

"Vukašin thinks that the worst might be prevented by sensible policies."

"Sensible policies? When have we ever had sensible policies in this country—or anywhere in the Balkans, for that matter? We've only one sensible politician, and that's Pašić. And today every bum is cursing him on all counts. Today, my dear Olga, all intelligent people are packing their bags and fleeing to Greece. People know that the vengeance of the Germans and Bulgarians will be terrible."

"What will happen to our people?"

"They'll keep out of the way and adapt themselves as they did under the Turks. They'll manage all right, don't worry."

"What about you, Najdan?"

"I'll keep close to Pašić. I don't want to be away from the government. I'll take you and Milena and Aunt Selena to Athens in my car. Then we'll see what happens. You can take three suitcases with you."

"What are you talking about, Najdan?"

"Even the gypsies will be fleeing to Greece, you idiot!"

"When they go, I'll go. Anyway, this is a matter for Vukašin to decide."

Milena came in with a parcel in her arms. "Mother, I ran into Doctor Radić! He's in bad shape. Hello, Uncle." She kissed Najdan on both cheeks. "Has Mother told you that I'm going to see my grandfather in Prerovo? I'm happy about that. Mother, the whole of Niš has gathered in front of the Assembly. They're silent as the grave. I'm afraid for Father."

Najdan looked at Milena in amazement. Going to Prerovo? This wasn't war, it was a self-destructive sickness. Serbia was perishing. The will to live and the capacity to survive was used up, burned out, and now collapse was inevitable. He left without drinking his coffee.

The president of the Assembly found it difficult to subdue the angry clamor; again and again he called for order.

First deputy: "If we accept the Allied demands and cede Macedonia to Bulgaria, seventy thousand South Serbs and Macedonians will desert from the Serbian trenches, and the rest of the Serbian army will follow. Mr. Pašić should resign at once. Only a new government can resist the Allies."

Pašić: "I would like to state that neither I nor any of my ministers wish to be in the government at this time. We are not resigning lest we appear to desert Serbia in her most difficult days. However, if you gentlemen are of the opinion that the government should resign, register your decision at once."

Second deputy: "Mr. Pašić should know that even the most difficult acts of those in power should not be determined by personal convictions. In a democratic country no ruler has the right to judge how long he should remain in power."

Third deputy: "In discussing the question of the government's resignation, gentlemen, we deputies must ask ourselves whether the Serbian government or Assembly dares surrender territory for which our people have fought three wars in the last five years. No assembly has the right to surrender its people to another state. The government and the army must examine the wishes and demands of our allies within the framework of their legal competence. To bring our national frontiers into question in the name of 'higher interests' is to forget that the highest interest and the sole valid law is our country."

Pašić: "The government has made no decision concerning our territory. I've told you what has been asked of us and predicted what will happen if we don't fulfill the requests of the Allies. I repeat that I will carry out any decision you make."

Fourth deputy: "Brothers, the Great Powers of the Entente didn't enter the war to protect Serbia and Belgium, but to defend themselves and their empires. *We* are fighting for our own liberation and unity; *they* are fighting for conquests, colonies, and the Dardanelles. No good will come to Serbia from this war. If God doesn't save us, we are lost. I suggest that we not insult one another, that we talk gently and quietly, and discuss only those things within our competence. Let the Great Powers act according to their intentions, as they have done since the beginning of time."

Fifth deputy: "We will not give up Macedonia! We will not give up what is ours! Let them take it from us if we're defeated. Brothers, let us fall with our heads high! Our defeats are our most enduring victories!"

Pašić: "In bad weather the wolf finds a new den. When the storms blow, old oaks bend before the blast and the eagles descend into the undergrowth. Such a time has come for us. If we must fall, let's not die, but crouch and shield our faces with our hands. Let's cling to our land. No one will lament us. No one will even remember us. That's how people are."

Vukašin Katić: "I propose that we postpone our decision for twenty-four hours."

The deputies: "Why should we? We know our decision!"

Katić: "Let's reflect, gentlemen. Let's consult one another and seek the advice of the people around us. Let the president of the Assembly consult with the High Command and the generals. And with the policemen who are holding the people back from our doors and windows, so they won't hear what we're saying. Ask the priests and teachers what they think, gentlemen. Let's go out to the market early tomorrow and ask the peasants what they would do in our place."

Najdan Tošić ran into Chaprasnikov on the bank of the Nišava. The Bulgarian joyfully stretched out both hands toward him: "Why are you running away from me, Mr. Tošić?" he said, mixing Serbian and Bulgarian. "You see what's happening? The whole of Niš has gathered to watch poor Mr. Pašić twisting and turning in the Allied mousetrap."

"People also watch the mating of dogs in the street, Mr. Chaprasnikov."

"This is different, Mr. Tošić. Dostoyevsky has observed that people delight in spectacles of great misfortune."

"I don't care for Dostoyevsky."

"I know. You like French writers. But Russian literature is embedded in my heart. Let's walk along the river bank in front of this silent crowd. A distressing sight. I don't like witnessing this event," said Chaprasnikov softly.

"Nevertheless, before noon you'll be sending a telegram about it to Sofia."

"I'll have to send something, unfortunately. But let's talk like brothers. The fate of politicians and statesmen is indeed tragic. The greater and more successful the statesman, the greater his tragedy."

With a slight inclination of his head Chaprasnikov dropped a few coins into the caps of begging soldiers. He did so every time he walked through the streets of Niš. The beggars knew the time and the route of his walks and arranged themselves to receive his charity. It was said that, in addition to the dinars, Chaprasnikov invariably gave one beggar a napoleon, whispering: "This is from the Czar of Bulgaria." Najdan had never brought up these gifts of napoleons in his conversations with Chaprasnikov. Although this small-scale charity didn't give him any satisfaction, until this moment Najdan hadn't found Chaprasnikov's generosity distasteful. But on this occasion he felt humiliated by it.

They ran into Baron Squitti. They greeted one another cordially and proceeded together.

"I have decided, Monsieur Chaprasnikov, that you Bulgarians are the children of the Goddess Thalia," said the baron. "By her first marriage, too. Everything works to your advantage—everything!"

"My dear Baron, there dwells in us Slavs what you might call a primeval feeling of solidarity. Grief and fire in my neighbor's house are in mine, too."

"This romantic patriarchal spirit and Slav superstition, which is really a particular kind of animism according to our Western, Cartesian mentality, once represented true virtue. Look at this scene in front of us, gentlemen. It's like the agora in Athens! This is how the assembly of the *polis* deliberated in Athens before the Persian invasions. It's true they did so openly under a clear sky, so the *demos* could hear. But Xerxes didn't have our espionage system, and there were no diplomats or newspapers. If there had been, those wise Greeks would surely have deliberated in secret, like the Serbs today. It makes no difference. The setting here in Niš is an almost exact replica of the Athenian model. There too the assembly was surrounded by spearmen —that is, by policemen—and beggars and courtesans stood in front where those actresses and beggars are standing. The citizens sat in a hierarchical order, just as they are doing here in this park in Niš. Beyond them were probably slaves and small boys. Here we have prisoners of war, of the same historical category. The scene is magnificent, gentlemen!"

"I'm not so delighted by this scene, my dear Baron. Speaking as a Bulgarian, I'd say that my unfortunate Serbian brothers have reached the end."

Najdan didn't hear this last remark. Seeing the deputies coming out of the Assembly, he interrupted his companions: "The heat is intolerable. Let's have some cold beer. There's still some ice in Niš."

"An excellent idea! But do allow me, Monsieur Tošić, to watch Pašić emerge from the Assembly and climb into his fiacre. Look at that saintly dignity, the wisdom and refinement of old age. A pity he isn't wearing a coat and tails. I assure you, gentlemen, there's no politician in all Europe who looks so ordinary while maintaining his dignity as Pašić, no statesman who is such a true gentleman."

As soon as the secretary of the Assembly had completed the roll call, which showed that today fewer deputies were present than yesterday, Nikola Pašić began to speak:

"Gentlemen, European diplomats define the existence and freedom of the Balkan nations as the 'Eastern Question.' But serious misconceptions are prevalent in Europe about the so-called Eastern Question."

First deputy: "A naive remark, Prime Minister! If those erroneous notions weren't useful to them, the Great Powers would have got rid of them at the Congress of Berlin. We must protect our rights."

Pašić: "Being in the right isn't enough to win even a civil lawsuit. To be in the right in a war in which everybody is digging everyone else's grave offers little hope. History's judgment on the rights of small nations is made by sleepy judges, gentlemen."

Second deputy: "Let's not play hide-and-seek, Mr. Pašić! You've promised the Allies eastern Macedonia and they aren't satisfied. Now you want us to give you a mandate to bargain with them."

Pašić: "I haven't promised them anything, but I must indeed bargain with them. We won't give them an inch more than we have to."

Third deputy: "Before we give the government a mandate to decide how much of our land should be given to the Bulgarians and Rumanians, gentlemen, I propose the following resolution: that we dig up the graves of our fallen sons, so the Bulgarians won't desecrate them; that we take out of our libraries all works on our history, all books and poems about our kings and nobles, and burn them. Let's burn everything that reminds us of our greatness and glory, let's level our tombs, destroy our churches and monasteries. Let's bring all the priests and monks here to sing a requiem for Serbia!"

Fourth deputy: "In this great darkness and discord, I don't know what we should do. We suffer evil at the hands of friend and foe alike. Is there no way to minimize the pain?"

Fifth deputy: "Brothers, we won't give anything to anybody! Not a single town or village, not a stream or cowshed. Let's cut short this meeting and demand guns, then go straight to the trenches and finish our debate there!"

Pašić: "If we let our emotions rule us, we won't attain our objectives. You say we should tell the Allies: 'We won't give you an inch of land or a single cowshed!' Gentlemen, if we don't give them an inch, we'll lose the entire estate. If we don't give them a cowshed, they'll destroy our houses! I believe that the honorable and sensible course, and indeed the most patriotic, is a different one."

Sixth deputy: "If it was wise to enter this war, it can't be wise now to give up what we had at the start."

Seventh deputy: "Our country is not a shop beset by thieves. You don't give up something less valuable in order to keep what's worth more. Our country is a heritage for our sons which cannot be sold piecemeal! In its soul, our land is a single entity, and you must be at one with it, or it isn't yours!"

Eighth deputy: "Serbia is not a state acquired by conquest or as a royal dowry. Serbia was founded on two words: *I won't!* Impale me, but I won't become a Moslem like the Turks. Hang me, but I won't become a German! Nor a Russian or Italian! Serbia means the freedom to say 'I won't' to everyone at all times. This should be conveyed to the gentlemen in London, Paris, and St. Petersburg!"

In the sudden silence Pašić said in a low voice: "Gentlemen, we're all talking with our heads in a noose. However, even with his head in a noose, a man shouldn't give up. As long as his brain is working, he can talk with his executioners and come to an understanding."

First deputy: "Yes, you'll bargain and haggle, twist and turn, you old opportunist!"

Pašić: "That's right, you old socialist! I'll bargain and haggle, twist and turn, so that we give as little and gain as much as possible. That's the law of survival!"

Second deputy: "I agree with Mr. Pašić. Serbia must stay with the Allies. Any other way will bring greater misfortune and greater sacrifice. Make your proposal, Prime Minister."

Pašić: "All indications are that we must give up some part of Macedonia. But we certainly won't repudiate the unification of all the Serbian lands with Croatia and Slovenia."

A tremendous clamor broke out, with arguments and threats aimed at Pašić. The president rang the bell and asked for silence.

Vukašin Katić surprised his friends in his own party: why was he still silent? He must go to the rostrum and say what he had planned to say. Bathed in sweat, he raised his hand to speak, felt it tremble, and dropped it. The deputies around him informed the president that Vukašin wanted to speak. He was about to cry out that he would speak later, but he had no voice. He sat mute and motionless in an overwhelming silence, then the bell summoning him to the rostrum echoed inside him. Hearing his name, he walked over to the rostrum without an idea in his head. An unfamiliar and threatening voice called out: "What are you waiting for, Katić?" Suddenly he began to speak, softly, as if in conversation:

"In history even the wisest men have made mistakes. In the accursed business of politics, conscientious and brave men alike make wrong decisions." He paused, lacking the strength to go against them. He couldn't find a single familiar face in front of him.

"What do you propose, Vukašin?"

"I'll tell you, but not until political hatreds in all of us have yielded to a common concern for the future of our country."

Once again tempers flared. Vukašin waited for silence, but wished for an earthquake or a flood. Unconvinced about what he had intended to say, he decided not to wait for the deputies to calm down, and walked slowly back to his seat.

Several deputies requested adjournment until the next day. Pašić nodded in approval, and the president closed the session. The deputies took out their handkerchiefs and wiped the sweat off their faces.

After a prolonged telephone conversation with the stationmaster at Niš, Major Paun Aleksić hung up and swore violently.

"It's astounding how corrupt and rotten this damned country is! For God's sake, Radić, why don't you sit down?"

"I'm here officially to ask—"

"What's the rush, Radić? Hello there! Bring two large cups of strong coffee to Major Aleksić's office, and a bottle of cognac. Tell them in the canteen that Doctor Aleksić wants French cognac." He turned to Radić. "This heat is driving me crazy. I can't wait for the summer to be over, to get rid of the flies. I'll take ice and snow any day. You've started smoking again, I see."

"Yes, while waiting for you to give me my assignment. I want to tell you—"

"Sensible man! Anything that gives you pleasure, anything at all, grab it. Help yourself to my Greek cigarettes. We'll be smoking real tobacco for a few more days, then corn silk and elm leaves. The situation is catastrophic. Not even the newspapers lie any more. The Assembly is in secret session, and Serbia is finished. I'll have a stroke, I swear—they're playing dirty tricks on me!"

"I'd appreciate it if we could attend to official business first."

"It's exactly three weeks since I asked the stationmaster—an outright thief—for a freight car to Bitolj. My furniture and the household goods my wife didn't take with her are falling apart. I shoved them into a shed, but the storm smashed the roof. See what kind of people we are! The Serbian state railway is now working for government ministers, generals, ambassadors, members of national councils, and their friends and relatives, taking them to Greece to save their lives and possessions. What kind of law is that? Maybe Cromwell pumped some order into the blood of the English, but here whoever has power has the law behind him. Meanwhile the Austrian prisoners are celebrating victory in their camps. Their music and noise kept half of Niš awake last night."

"I want to be assigned a duty schedule immediately, or I'll go straight to Vojvoda Mišić."

"All in good time. What's your hurry anyway? I must have a cognac to calm my nerves. Have some yourself. To hell with formalities in this chaos!"

"Thank you, but I don't drink in the morning."

"Ah, but this cognac is heavenly, a drink for the gods! If it's true that any country with good liquor has good women, the French are lucky! They've got a reason to die for their country. I'll get to France somehow before the winter, if I have to swim."

"Major Aleksić, I want to go to the front tomorrow. To a division hospital."

"So you want to sacrifice yourself for freedom? Freedom, fancy that! An idealist or a weakling? In your case, virtue and principle! Just the right combination for deception. I've been free of that since I started to walk and realized that human shit stinks worse than cow manure. I enjoy my freedom in any state, under any government. That's because I'm not afraid to enjoy myself. Not because I'm a doctor or because our profession pays well, but because I can always be happy. Always! What do I care what national anthem is being played, or whose flag is fluttering in the courtyard? I've never been ashamed of any pleasure or any vice. What a powerful experience vice is! Don't laugh, Doctor Radić! You know as well as I that there are few virtuous people in this world. With apologies to all moralists, I maintain that there are even fewer with real vices."

"That may be so, but it's beside the point, Major Aleksić."

"Listen to me, Doctor. Enjoy your vices, cherish them. That's real happiness. Of course you must have some common sense to enjoy such happiness. Do you know any man with vices who's a fool? Such a specimen would merit scientific study. Won't you humanitarians and moralists ever learn?"

"There's probably some truth in what you say. I'm not contradicting you. But I'm a weakling and a fool, so I'm asking to be sent to the front tomorrow. I repeat that I'll see Vojvoda Mišić."

"By all means. It's pride that causes wars. Courage, the defense of one's honor, dignity. If we liberate the vice in people, the world will be free! Vice has no frontiers, languages, uniforms, sacred national objects. Please don't go. I want to confide in you. There's no one else in this stinking hole I can talk to."

"I must go, Doctor Aleksić. I'll be back at eight tomorrow morning. I ask you once again to have a letter ready arranging my transfer to a division hospital."

"There's something I must tell you. I've fallen madly in love. The woman is a relative of mine. What a woman, Radić! My God, what thighs, what breasts! And a lustful, selfish whore. But there it is, the room spins around me. She's been in Niš for a few days now. She has lunch with me, but she has supper with some lieutenant. I'm crazy about her—crazy! Incestuous, you might call it. The only blood relative I acknowledge is my mother. Well, I suppose that's carrying cynicism too far. Last night she told me she'd rather hang than sleep with me—it's a knife in my heart. Why, I asked her, why? But she just shook her mane—what glorious hair! I wanted to strangle her."

Aleksić banged his fists on the table and burst into tears of rage, then buried his head in his hands. Radić left quickly, lest Aleksić call him back.

Delighted by yet another letter from Bogdan and excited by the prospect of meeting her grandfather the next day, Milena refused to leave her father in his gloom during supper. She wanted him to tell her more about her grandfather, her uncle, and the people she would meet. In fact, she wanted to know the whole truth about the breach between her father and his family, since she suspected that her father's explanations had been neither complete nor correct.

But Vukašin answered her absentmindedly in but few words. It was hard to describe his father and his brother, who were to meet her at Palanka station. Aćim probably still had his forked beard. Djordje also had a beard, as he had noticed that night in front of the hospital in Valjevo when he had lit his cigarette for him. He couldn't tell her more than this. Twenty-two years had passed since they had seen each other. He told her to stand in front of the stationmaster's office. They'd recognize her from her likeness to her father.

"Milena, don't stay away more than a week," said Olga.

"I'll be back by Saturday, Mother. Perhaps Bogdan will get three days' leave and come to Niš on Sunday. Don't worry, Father." She kissed him and went to her room.

Olga tried to turn the conversation to the Assembly session. Vukašin couldn't tell her that he had walked away from the rostrum, or that he'd been greeted at the entrance by shouts from townsfolk and wounded soldiers to defend the Serbian land and its honor. Was it simply a political disagreement with the majority, or was this something deeper, some crisis of fate? Perhaps he, Vukašin, the grandson of Luka Došljak, who had been left in diapers under a willow tree where refugees from the Turkish janissaries were camping, was troubled by that ancestral fear for survival. An inborn fear that was in his blood stirred in the face of danger hovering over Serbia. Perhaps they were on the verge of a new migration, of flight and long bondage. This would be a different kind of bondage, under a modern Europe which ruled not only by force but by money and deception. Bondage under the masters of machines and of lies, against whom peasant risings would be exercises in futility. Was Serbia about to experience the fate of the Czechs and Croats and the other South Slavs, but with the brand and guilt of schismatic Orthodoxy?

Olga washed the dishes, prepared the bed, and wandered restlessly about the room. She didn't know how to help him. She could no longer watch him bent over his cigarette, staring at the floor, so she turned off the light. The spark of his cigarette in the darkness reminded her of Radić. She trembled and approached Vukašin, restraining a desire to stroke his neck. He didn't move. She couldn't even hear him breathing. Now she could only hear herself.

"In times like these," she said hesitantly, "perhaps the only right thing is to look to our children. They'll need their freedom and their country for a long time."

"If only I were sure what is good for them."

"Do what is most natural to you."

"What if we make a mistake which a whole century of effort can't change?"

They went to bed. Olga grew numb as she lay on her back, motionless. She pretended to sleep. She couldn't turn away from him now, curled up on her right side, the position in which she always fell asleep most quickly. It would have been an act of crude indifference, betrayal, to turn her back to him that night. He had never been closer to her, though she had once loved him more and in a different way than she did now, tormented as she was by Radić's presence in Niš, filled with anxiety that he might visit her, and at the same time wanting, yearning to see him. Vukašin had not slept for two nights, so anxious was he that he might make the wrong decision. He had lost his self-confidence for the first time. Since his return from Paris he had talked softly and moved cautiously as if fearing he might cause a disturbance. He was even a little bent as he walked. Sometimes this Vukašin seemed to be the older brother of the prewar Vukašin, who'd been so strong, resolute, confident, and stern.

The big clock struck one. Vukašin lit another cigarette with a long-drawn-out sigh. Olga raised herself above him and placed her hand on his sweating forehead.

"Vukašin, I'm afraid to give Milena advice, let alone you. But I can't bear your silence any longer. You know that I've never babbled about love, I've lived it." She felt that she was talking too loud, that she would wake Milena and the rest of the people sleeping in the house. She paused with burning confusion and anxiety inside her.

"What is it, Olga?"

His words made her tremble. She wiped the sweat off his face and neck with the sleeve of her nightgown, raised him up, and turned over his pillow. That soothed her. She took his hand, raised herself onto the pillow, and said firmly: "With all the troubles ahead, Vukašin, I'd squelch my ideas and principles. It's more honorable now to be loyal to the people than to stick to ideas of one's own."

"I've written at least twenty articles about our public honor and conscience. I've always told our children to serve truth and remember their pride. It's difficult for me. I can't act otherwise now."

"In times of suffering, people have the least need of truth, Vukašin. I became convinced of this in Valjevo. In misfortune people look for comfort and goodness."

"I can't apply your Valjevo experience in the Assembly, unfortunately. The Assembly isn't a hospital. Though from the moaning you hear at times, it seems like one."

"Niš is a hospital. Serbia is a hospital. And so is all Europe. A person who isn't sick today, whose soul is not full of pain, isn't a real person."

"I understand. But goodness can't save us from the great evil threatening us." He paused, then added: "You want me to be different, don't you, Olga? I've felt it since I came back."

"I've never wanted you to be different from what you are, Vukašin. I haven't tried to twist and break you to suit myself, even though it has never been easy for me to live with you."

"I know. Go to sleep now."

He rested his face on her breast and she embraced him gently. He yielded to her tenderness and lay close against her. Now she was powerful and protective. Only as a child had he lain in such a dejected state, next to his mother. He felt himself shrinking, no longer able to think, his fear draining out of him. He had only one wish: that the night would be long.

She listened to his heartbeats, which made her at one with herself, as with all her heart and soul she wished to be, as she had been before Valjevo. But an inexplicable anxiety prevented her from falling asleep. Her left arm ached from the weight of his body. Well, she thought, let it.

Gently and wearily, Bora Jackpot gathered up the cards from the table, wrapped them in a white handkerchief, and placed them in his inside jacket pocket. He emptied his pockets of all the money he had won, and threw it on the table with a faint feeling of disgust: "Take as much as you need, gentlemen," he said to the officers whose pockets he had emptied that evening, "or borrow it until the first of the month. You won't get your pay for another week." He looked at his mother: her head ached from fear that he had won so much at cards, and that soon he would be leaving for the front—and going to Belgrade, too, which the Germans would level to the ground, so people said.

The officers refused the money they had lost. Some were even offended by his generosity, but they arranged a poker party at another house the next evening, since the host had won three evenings in succession. Almost guiltily, Bora's mother offered them coffee, wine, and cakes. They thanked her and left.

Bora Jackpot stared at the money on the table. His feelings were similar to those he had experienced in a brothel beside a woman who had surrendered to sleep the moment he required no further service from her. At this moment of victory he thought: A filthy little pile after so much excitement! Is this victory? The end of so much passion?

"Mother, I'm going out for a while to clear my head. I'll be back, don't worry." He kissed his mother's disappointed face, and hurried into the street. He caught up with Mihajlo Radić, who was walking in the opposite direction from the other two members of the poker party.

"May I accompany you to your lodging, Captain?"

"Please do. And please don't call me Captain."

"Tell me, if I'm ever brought wounded to your hospital, will you amputate my arm? To me my arm is the most important part of my body. My arms and my eyes."

"Yes, I know. Blind men don't gamble."

They walked on in silence. The streetlamps were few and far between, but it was a starry night. The sound of barking dogs echoed all around.

"Every night there's a massacre of dogs in Niš. Or so I think. I can't get to sleep from my horror at this barking. Doctor, what can we do about that bloodsucker, grief?"

"Tell someone about it. Let it out. Fear sprouts in silence like mushrooms after rain."

"I've no one to share it with—all my close friends have been killed. Besides, if one doesn't talk about grief the right way, it turns into disgust."

"You don't need wise people to open your heart to. You need people who've suffered. There are plenty of those in Niš."

"I avoid people who've suffered. They're vain, and always offended by somebody or something. They require futile effort and they like lies, don't you find?"

"I'm listening from a different perspective. But we were talking about grief."

"Yes. I had a friend in the Cadet Battalion in Skoplje whose name was Ivan Katić. He was taken prisoner. He had a great talent for talking about grief."

Radić stopped under a streetlamp and, playing with his shadow, whispered as if to himself: "His mother knows how to suffer, too."

"Do you know her?"

"Yes." He stepped forward as if to catch up with his shadow. "We worked together in a hospital in Valjevo."

Bora Jackpot kept up with him. "I've seen that lady two or three times when she came to visit Ivan. She seemed arrogant and not very nice. But I respect Vukašin Katić, Ivan's father."

"I'm indifferent to politicians."

"Vukašin is different, Doctor. All my life I'll remember the dinner party he gave in Kragujevac just before we left for the front. That was the first night I fell asleep without feeling hatred for the people who killed my father."

The barking of the dogs from both sides of the street interrupted them. Bora Jackpot went on: "In Niš I feel as if I were in a dugout full of smoke. I feel nauseous."

"Have you been disappointed in love?"

"I haven't had the opportunity. Girls consider me gloomy and boring. I'm not often enthusiastic about them either. Actually, two days ago a girl broke a date with me. Such a lovely smile, too. I worshipped her. She's studying to be a schoolteacher, but now she's a volunteer nurse in Valjevo."

"Is her name Dušanka?"

"Yes! Do you know her?"

"She was a nurse in the hospital where I was superintendent."

"Well, we all know one another in this poverty-stricken Serbia, don't we? If I don't get killed, I think I'll go to Asia—an ocean of people. There I'll know only my friends. Tell me, Doctor, seriously now: did that girl have the same radiant expression on her face in the hospital? She's truly humble, a real madonna."

"Dušanka's just a nice, ordinary girl. A kindhearted creature with some imagination. She's easily hurt, but not for long."

"Why does she get hurt?"

"In that Valjevo hellhole her smiling face—or, as you call it, her radiance—made people think she was a loose-living woman, and it aroused resistance in the sick and wounded. Something about her offended them."

"I see. Doctor, don't think that I'm sad tonight because Dušanka didn't keep her date with me. That's a petty little grief. A successful game of poker can wipe it out."

"I don't believe you."

"Tonight you must believe everything I say. Since high school I've struggled hard to be a cynic. I realized that people have little capacity to believe. They have an exceptional variety of skills to deceive others about what they believe and understand, and where their sympathies lie."

They were slowing down and their shadows lengthened, fleeing from their footsteps. The crowing of cocks mingled with the barking.

"I'm on leave now. That makes me even more fed up with life. But I've been transferred to the Belgrade Defense Force. In four days I'll be leaving this dog pound and going to Kalamegdan—where I grew up—to wait for the Germans."

"I know how you feel. This uncertainty would drive anyone to despair."

"I don't give a damn about the troubles in Niš. My official and national worry is grief. Grief in my soul, under my skin, in my every thought and sensation. I feel as if the cobbles we're walking on have rotted from grief, that these houses and fences, and those trees under the streetlamps, are all disintegrating from grief. They're like dough. I could plunge my arms up to the elbows into grief."

Radić stretched out his hand to place it on the young man's shoulder, but Bora Jackpot pulled away: gestures of tenderness disgusted him. They continued walking, dragging their long shadows behind them.

"You know, Bora," Radić said, "time transforms all our feelings. When fear lasts a long time, we no longer feel it."

"But I haven't felt afraid for a long time. Fear has never been the most difficult feeling for me."

"Well, fear *isn't* the most difficult. It moves us to action. There's hope in fear, and time. The hardest feelings are those where there's no sensation of time. No passage of time."

"That's true. When I was rigid with fear on Suvobor, waiting for the enemy attack, I could see and hear time."

"The hardest thing to achieve these days is hope. Any kind of hope."

"I've only known petty, ordinary hopes. I place really important hope in chance, in what can't be foreseen or expected, like a stray bullet."

"We need something more certain than a stray bullet."

A cat crossed their path. Bora paused, then asked: "What should I believe in? Could you suggest some ideals for me?"

"I suggest that you think out your own view of the world. Find some kind of justification or purpose."

"And then sacrifice myself for it? Is that what you mean, Doctor?"

"If your view demands it, yes, you should sacrifice yourself. Anyway, we're all compelled to sacrifice ourselves. We already have. That's how everything that makes up our lives has been created."

"Does that give you comfort, Doctor?"

"Yes, it does. If we don't accept it, we end up corrupt or despairing."

"All right, Doctor, what does our country mean to you?"

"Our country? Suffering, that's my country. People who suffer, who are tormented by pain."

"And your patriotism is therapy—treating sick people! For you your country is an enormous hospital under a clear sky. Why, Hungary could be that, Doctor! An interesting thought." Bora Jackpot gazed at the stars above. "You've identified patriotism with doing good. With philanthropy."

"Not exactly. You've narrowed down my ideas considerably. For me my country is above all a world where there's some sense in striving for virtue. Where the struggles and torments of reason and conscience are not without meaning."

"If that's your country, then the people in this world have no countries. No such country exists!"

"You have to fight hard to have such a country, Bora."

"Don't be offended by my frankness, but it would be difficult to endure a burst of artillery fire with your type of patriotism. As for moving against bayonets—not a chance! Really, Doctor Radić, do you think so highly of others that you would rush forward to kill with bayonets and grenades, to defend them in a rain of bullets? Or lie in mud and snow for a week for them?"

"Yes, I would, and not because I believe the Serbs to be good, or because people in general have qualities that make them worthy of sacrifice. I'm not convinced of this—I'm not particularly impressed with the human species. I'm not in love with Serbia or any other nation. But among the people who are killing each other today throughout Europe and the seas around it there do exist here and there creatures desiring goodness and love, and capable of doing good and loving. And of thinking. People who think without gaining advantage from it. That's what counts. Nothing equals such a creature. Nothing at all! And there are such creatures in Serbia."

Bora Jackpot spoke caustically, too loudly for the time of night and the empty street. "So why does that sweet, rare animal—man—wish to do good? Why does he love?"

"This is where I am lodging. But if you don't feel like sleeping yet, we can continue."

"That's fine by me, Doctor."

"In talking about the motives for doing good, we'll pass up the reasons. I speak only for myself. I have no way of fighting human worthlessness, except by doing good. I've always been tormented by the idea of eternity. And it wasn't a book or a word that started me thinking, but a stone. A stone in Prince Lazar's tower, the stones in the rosette of the Lazarica church, and the marble portal of Studenica monastery. Stones set to outlive man. This striving for eternity, however pointless in the end, is the invisible foundation of our world."

"I don't see the connection between eternity and doing good."

"It's a close one. If I can't think in stone, if I don't have the gift to express myself that way, or the power to utter words which will outlive me, I have the power to exist in people beyond the span of my own existence. I can implant myself in several people, multiply myself in them."

"You have a high opinion of yourself!"

"I see great power in doing good. All other things should serve that power—freedom above all."

"Emperors and tyrants and the so-called popular teachers have the same wish, though it is fulfilled in a different way. They too yearn for great kingdoms and empires in their lifetime. They're the only people who work successfully for eternity."

"No, Bora, the two things are totally opposed."

"No, they're not! Because there is no better way of ruling people than doing good. I don't admire your passion or fall on my knees before it. You want people to depend on you, you long for gratitude!" Bora's voice made the dogs bark even more loudly. "In the hospital among the sick and wounded you probably feel like Moses, like Caesar or Napoleon! You feel like a savior, a victor!"

Mihajlo Radić said nothing and waited for the barking to die down.

Kosara spent the first night in Niš with Života in her arms, enjoying the sound of waltzes with which the captured Austro-Hungarian officers were celebrating their Emperor's birthday. She spent the next night in a rented shack which by midnight was full of drunken soldiers. At the crack of dawn she fled from their prowling hands and offers of brandy and sat under a lime tree, with Života wrapped in her yellow shawl, opposite the house which she had learned the previous evening was the home of Mr. and Mrs. Katić. Suddenly she grew numb at the thought that those fine people might send her packing: "Show us your certificate from the local authority, so we can see who and what you are. Give us proof that it's our son's child, young woman! Get out, you whore!" She decided to wait until morning and barge in on them at breakfast time. She had spent her last dinar on the night's lodging, and had no way of getting back to Skoplje. She thought of the night the students left Skoplje to go to their death. And of Ivan. He was a lanky fellow, half-blind, in a muddle, God help him, but honorable and not at all like a student. Before a week was out there was that letter: "Please forgive me. My name's not Stepanović, but Katić." How did the name Stepanović come into his head? He was dead drunk, too. The student thought that when a woman heard Stepa Stepanović's name she would keel over. . . . But how long were those folks from Belgrade going to sleep?

She hoped they would never wake up!

Women with baskets and bags came out of the courtyards and hurried off to the market and the shops.

Let's wait a little longer. It wouldn't be nice to barge in on them before breakfast. It would be good if you could whine a little when we go in. A noise like a pussycat, then I'll know whether they have hearts of stone. Ah, my beautiful boy, if you knew all that might happen to us today! But if blood is thicker than water, then we'll be all right. Let's have a little feed so you won't wet your lips like a puppy over there. Let the servants get back from the market, then we'll go in and give them a surprise. We don't have a penny. I'll treat them as they treat me. If they're stiff, I'll be stiff; if they're nice, I'll be nice. Until things are settled. Then your mother will behave like a saint. That's a stern-looking man coming out of their courtyard with that beautiful young lady. He's carrying a suitcase, must be hurrying off to Salonika. He did say something about a sister, but his sister couldn't be a beauty. That gentleman is tall, like the student. The way he carries himself, you'd think he was the only person in Niš. I wouldn't like him to be your grandfather. Well, now we must go in, Života, my son, and see what God has in store for us. The Germans are moving against Serbia, they'll trample everybody. I must save you. Yes, I'll save you, if I have to deceive God Himself!

"Could you please tell me, madam, whether Mr. and Mrs. Katić from Belgrade live here? I need to see Mrs. Katić. Good morning, madam. Are you the mother of Ivan Katić who was in the Cadet Battalion in Skoplje last year?"

Olga faltered in front of the woman with a baby in her arms, wrapped in a yellow shawl. "Yes, I am. Please come in," she stammered, and shut the door behind them so the neighbors couldn't see them and hear their conversation. "Who are you?"

"This is your grandson Života, madam. My name is Kosara."

Olga steadied herself against the table and opened her eyes wide. Could she be dreaming?

The engine was clanking against the coaches, wreathed in smoke before pulling out, and he had stood there smiling mournfully, behaving like a little boy again.

"Are you in love, Ivan? Why are you ashamed of it, my darling? So many of your friends have girls. Look at them hugging each other."

"I don't want to talk about it."

"You must. Do I know her? Is she from Belgrade? Is it a French girl? It's all the same to me who and what she is. I don't care if she's a gypsy, as long as you love her and she loves you. Why are you so pale, my darling?"

"Mother, I have a woman. Her name is Kosara. She lives in Skoplje."

"Where do you live?" asked Olga.

"Since the war, I've lived in Skoplje. The way you are living here in Niš."

"On what street?"

"Prince George Street, madam."

"Number 46?"

"There is no Number 46, I live at Number 36. I have one room on the courtyard, but it's pleasant."

"This is my first love, Mother. Don't you like her name?"

"I do like it, my darling. Kosara is an old Serbian name. Please write to her often. Don't behave as they all do to their women today."

"Has Ivan written you?"

"I don't know why he hasn't. He has sent greetings to me regularly through some of the other students. To tell you the truth, madam, it surprises me very much that Ivan hasn't written. He's so well bred."

"Don't hold it against him. He's a prisoner of war." She looked at her with disappointment: a common girl, and homely. My God, she thought, can this be true?

"Kosara is a charming girl, Mother. She's pretty, sensible, proud, and dignified. You'd like her. I really am lucky, Mother. I'm going off to the war in love with someone. Someone else loves me besides you and Milena."

"Please don't be angry with me, madam, but my baby's awake. It's time for me to feed him."

Olga stepped toward Kosara, took the child from her arms, and stared intently at its face: it blinked and made a clucking sound. Ivan's forehead had been like that. Yes, it was Ivan's forehead. But the nose? The nose was like his mother's. Oh God, Holy Mother of God, was it his child?

Her hands shook, and Kosara was afraid she'd drop Života, so she placed her own hands underneath him.

"I can tell you, madam, this child never cries. When he's hungry he makes a clucking noise, as he's doing now. After I feed him, he sleeps like a little log. Good-natured, just like Ivan. Forgive me, but I'm upset, too. Who wouldn't be—I understand your feelings as a mother. If the same thing happened to me, if a son of Života's arrived on the scene . . . Now let me feed him, and afterward we'll talk. We've traveled by train all night, so we're tired. Does Ivan write you regularly?"

Tears were running down Olga's cheeks. She didn't know what to say or do.

After he had seen Milena off, Vukašin hurried to the Assembly. In front of the Assembly, and in the park stretching down to the Nišava, there were even more people than on the previous day. Once again they greeted him with shouts and cries, but now they were angry: "How long will you keep quiet, Katić? You aren't hiding behind Pašić's petticoats too, are you?" He turned: a few straw hats were raised in greeting. He returned the greeting and hurried off to his seat in the hall, determined to be the first to speak.

The deputies were talking about the German capture of the Russian fortress of Kovno, which even the most pessimistic Serbs had not believed possible. The deputies closest to the government were discussing the Russian press's charging Serbia with lack of consideration and obstructing decisive Allied military action in the Balkans. These conversations and the mood in the Assembly seemed favorable to the point of view Vukašin was going to express. He awaited the entry of Pašić and the ministers with impatience.

The secretary of the Assembly was taking attendance. Often the response was, "He's not here—he slipped off to Salonika last night," or "He's spread his wings southward!" The anger against the departed deputies only strengthened Vukašin's resolve to be the first to speak, but Pašić was already at the rostrum. Without agitation, even with a certain indifference, he asked for a mandate for the government to initiate talks with the Allies, and the right to wage war to victory. Even before he had sat down, several deputies approached the rostrum demanding his government's resignation and the formation of a new one which would resist Allied blackmail and the sacrifice of national territory.

Vukašin was afraid, but he asked angrily for permission to speak, then stood at the rostrum in silence. The deep, penetrating quiet cut right through his self-confidence. He began to speak in a firm voice, but not as he had intended.

"Gentlemen, the greatest weakness in any policy is making decisions under dire necessity. When decisions are the result of necessity and not of our own will, they're always bad. We're now in that position: we must act on something which might in fact mean acceptance of a decision made by others."

"What acceptance? Speak for yourself, Katić!"

"It's our misfortune, gentlemen, that at this time and in this place we don't have the right to speak only for ourselves or our party. We must speak for the world of tomorrow—a responsibility without limits."

"Don't beat about the bush!"

"The German and Austrian armies have all but crossed the Sava. Bulgaria is on the point of mobilizing, the Russians are in retreat, the English have been defeated at Gallipoli. Among the Allied governments and general staffs the opinion is growing that the Balkans must be abandoned."

"They'll lose the war."

"Our army is reduced to half its strength, our people are worn thin with sickness, crop failure, and poverty. The state treasury is empty. We have nothing to continue the war with." He paused and saw Pašić's beard nodding affirmatively. "If the Allies abandon us, as they surely will unless we meet their demands, we'll be annihilated."

"They dare not abandon us, they need Serbia!"

"They *will* abandon us. I know. I returned from Paris three days ago. We mustn't be deceived by self-importance and our earlier victory. We mustn't be intoxicated by hope. The rights and freedom of small nations are empty words in the mouths of Allied statesmen. Deception!"

"Don't insult Russia, Katić! This is the Serbian Assembly!"

"Russia too, no less than England and France, bases her policies on calculation! Today the small and the weak offer themselves as sacrificial lambs to the great and powerful, as they have done since the beginning of time. We mustn't let them run away, before the world and before history, from their guilt for our fate."

He fell silent in face of a tumult of protest. The president of the Assembly rang his bell and demanded silence.

"I'll come to the point, gentlemen, and be brief. We don't have the strength to carry out all our national obligations. Therefore, with no less pain in my heart than those of you who think differently, I propose . . ." He paused. "I propose that we accept the Allied demands without delay."

"He's out of his mind! Do you hear him?"

"I propose that, in return for the surrender of eastern Macedonia to Bulgaria, we demand that the Allies guarantee the unification of all the South Slav peoples. However hard it may be for us now, we must renounce forever our southern territories and our boundaries with Czar Dušan's empire. The cities of our national epics, the lands of King Milutin, will continue to exist in our poetry. Let's not ruin our future for the sake of legend and former glory."

"Who's paying you for this treason?"

"In whose name is this monster speaking?"

"I'm speaking in the name of our children, gentlemen! Their future doesn't lie in the south and in dreams of ancient times. It doesn't lie in a victory over Bulgaria!"

"To share your own inheritance with the Bulgarians! Shame! They've greased your palm for this in London and Paris. Where are you gentlemen of the Opposition now? This man was your pride and glory—this Judas!"

Vukašin listened, tense and strained, but he wasn't offended. As soon as the shouts had abated, he continued, speaking firmly without raising his voice. "We must offer the Bulgarians the hand of reconciliation, so that we're never again divided by a Slivnica or Bregalnica. This is reasonable and necessary. If we don't do this, we'll be giving formal agreement to a national catastrophe. Serbia will be buried in the ashes of a European conflagration."

"Capitulation will destroy us!"

"I doubt that, gentlemen!"

"May God preserve Serbia from such wisdom!"

Vukašin concluded his speech to jeers, without any applause or a single glance of support. For the first time in his political career, only disagreement accompanied him back to his seat. But a burden had fallen from his soul, and he looked with serenity straight into the eyes of the very people who had attacked him most bitterly. He folded his arms and listened attentively to a fellow member of his party, a man known for his measured manner at the rostrum.

But only Pašić could calm the Assembly: "All the deputies have spoken from their hearts and according to their own views of the welfare and freedom of our country. I blame no one for any personal insult."

After Pašić had finished his short speech, the president of the Assembly announced that a vote would be taken on a mandate for the government. The secretary began calling the names to confirm the majority in the Assembly. Some deputies left. The quarreling flared up again: "Where are you off to, you coward? Come back and vote! Shut the door! We must shut the door, Mr. President! He wants to tell the people outside that he was against the proposal. He can't do it! Don't allow anyone outside! We must all share the responsibility. Serbia will ask for the heads of all of us!"

The voting proceeded.

Mihajlo Radić felt depressed at being at the disposal of the Ministry of War and having to report to its adjutant every morning at eight. He decided to go see Bora Jackpot, the one man in Niš with whom he could talk about matters other than the war.

But he must see Olga—he must! What would she think if she found out that he was still in Niš, with nothing to do but play cards all night? A peacock's vanity—that peacock's resentment at unrequited love—had taken hold of him. A vulgar feeling. He would visit her that very day, that afternoon, and have a friendly talk. How good was this purely spiritual feeling toward her, devoid of all passion! How love restricted a man, how much evil was in it! The greater the love, the less love there was. If only he could feel goodness and gentleness even for a few hours, and be free from those other feelings, from confusion and pain.

In front of the Assembly the huge mass of people suddenly stirred. He didn't approve of their intense preoccupation with politics and state affairs; it put him in a bad mood. A nation preoccupied with politics lost its moral health, its sense of proportion. During the last few days he had avoided the mob, but now, on his way to Bora Jackpot's, he could not, and so forced his way through the jostling crowd.

"Who'd have thought he'd betray us? Only Vukašin Katić voted for giving Macedonia to the Bulgarians! He was the best man at my wedding—he'll bring a curse on my children! Are you saying Vukašin Katić's a traitor, gentlemen? Macedonia's gone! No, Pašić won't give up Macedonia!"

Mihajlo Radić quickened his step. So Vukašin had come back! He was here, they were together. That was natural, inevitable. They were man and wife. What did that have to do with him? Why did he have such stupid thoughts, why did he feel so humiliated? Tomorrow he would visit them both—no, he would do it today, this afternoon. A courtesy visit by an acquaintance. Why an acquaintance? He would visit them as a friend. They'd greet each other warmly as people who had kept watch together over so many deathbeds. What a poor, weak idiot he was!

The crowd in front of him was shouting at Vukašin Katić: a menacing, repulsive crowd. Something drew him forward. He pushed his way through the angry mass of people and found himself in front of Vukašin, who stood motionless, his hat and cane in his hand.

"Traitor! You've sold your soul! They bought you in Paris! Whose Opposition do you belong to anyway?"

Wide-eyed, Radić listened. He wanted to understand what was happening, but couldn't make sense out of the way the crowd was treating this eminent member of the Opposition, even though Radić himself despised politics and the struggle for power. He hadn't been able to grasp how Olga could love a man like this with such devotion. He remembered his conversation with Vukašin over Milena's sickbed, and that painful distance which had come between them—something not caused by Vukašin's words and manner, since his suffering and anxiety for his sick daughter were indeed moving; yet it was then that he had felt remote from him, even hated him. This same man was standing in strained but dignified silence, listening to horrible insults. He must have known what awaited him, and yet he had done what he believed was his duty. His very self-control showed that he had known what the consequences of his behavior would be. This was a man with a strong conscience. How many men would stand up for their convictions at the risk of being cursed and spat upon by a rabble? *I don't give a damn about his convictions,* thought Radić. *I don't give a damn about Macedonia!*

Tomatoes, melon rind, and the sticks of wounded soldiers were hurled at Vukašin. A woman with a parasol cried out: "He's an honorable man! He loves Serbia!"

Vukašin smiled, as if about to say something, but someone spat in his face: "That's for you, you traitor! We voted for you, we believed in you!"

Vukašin closed his eyes and swayed. Radić rushed through the crowd, stood in front of him, and shouted: "Get back! Get back!"

The angry crowd retreated, still cursing; two policemen came up to protect the deputy, but Radić took Vukašin by the arm and led him away into the blazing sunshine.

"Where do you live, Mr. Katić?"

"We have rooms on Sindjelić Street. Thank you, Doctor. I can get home by myself."

Radić let go of his arm and continued walking close beside him, touching him, feeling a strange excitement—a mixture of hostility and intimacy, but also of shame. He turned around: the woman with the parasol, who had tried to defend Vukašin, was following them at a distance of some twenty paces. What was the connection between them? He must know her, he had twice turned around to look at her. But why didn't he ask her to join them?

They reached the house so familiar to Radić, who had hung around it for several nights. Vukašin opened the gate. "Please come in, Doctor," he said warmly.

"No thank you, Mr. Katić. But if it means anything to you, I'm your political supporter today."

"We can't part here, Doctor. You must come see Olga. She'll be hurt if you don't. You've done so much for her and Milena, for all my family. Do come in."

"No, thank you. I can't stay now. I must be at the Ministry of War at twelve o'clock sharp; I'm already ten minutes late. But now I know where you live, so I'll drop in one of these days. Do give Milena and Mrs. Katić my best."

Before he shook Vukašin's hand he looked back: there was no sign of the woman with the parasol.

Doctor Radić had held out his hand with such a resolute expression and spoken so firmly that Vukašin could only beg him to visit them as soon as possible. But now it was essential for him to be alone with Olga. Numb from his recent humiliation, he passed some neighbors under a walnut tree without greeting; they fell silent as he passed by. He stopped in front of the apartment. He was returning home beaten, wounded, and disappointed. He was in despair. Never before had he experienced anything like it. Olga had been spat upon, and Milena and Ivan, his honor and his whole life. Tomorrow morning he and Olga would follow Milena to Prerovo, where they would wait for the time of bondage. Hearing an unfamiliar voice in his room, he walked in uncertainly and found Olga changing a baby on their bed. She paused with her hands on the child's chest.

"Whose child is this?" he asked, raising his voice.

Olga stood up, and her eyes filled with tears. "It's our grandson, Vukašin. And this is Kosara, the girl Ivan fell in love with in Skoplje while he was in the Cadet Battalion."

"Ivan's child? Ivan's son?"

He stood over the baby, trembling: his grandfather Luka had been discovered at the foot of a willow tree, abandoned by his mother in her flight from the Turks. His grandmother Kata, after her husband had died in an uprising, had taken her servant Luka into her bed and given birth to Aćim. Živana had borne Vukašin and Djordje during the brief calm between that uprising and the wars with the Turks.

Adam, too, had come into the world in some strange way. And now a grandson had been born to him between the barracks and the battle-field, between the battle on Suvobor and the prison camp. This was his grandson.

Olga could not bear the expression in his eyes; to keep from sobbing, she disappeared into the other room.

A real gentleman crying—that was too much to take, so Kosara slipped noiselessly into the hallway and leaned against the wall. From shame she dug her nails into her thighs. The gentleman called out: "Why didn't you come here yesterday? Why didn't you come to us at once, when he was born?"

Kosara trembled and looked about for the gate.

The next day all the Niš newspapers carried the following statement from the National Assembly of the Kingdom of Serbia:

AFTER HEARING THE STATEMENTS OF THE GOVERNMENT IN SECRET SESSION, AND WHILE PAYING DUE RESPECT TO OUR FALLEN HEROES AND EXPRESSING A DETERMINATION TO CONTINUE THE STRUGGLE FOR THE LIBERATION AND UNIFICATION OF THE SERBS, CROATS, AND SLOVENES ON THE SIDE OF THE ALLIES—THOUGH AT THE PRICE OF SACRIFICES ESSENTIAL TO SECURE THE VITAL INTERESTS OF OUR NATION—THE NATIONAL ASSEMBLY APPROVED THE GOVERNMENT'S POLICY AND PASSED ON TO ROUTINE BUSINESS.

3

Vojvoda Putnik was devoting himself to the stars. Ever since he became a soldier, his days had been given to work and his nights to freedom. In wartime he had always tried to avoid night duty. Tonight he even tried to avoid Pašić's questions about the war, and to ignore his worries about the next day's meeting of the government and the High Command. He wanted nothing in his mind but Orion and Taurus, the most beautiful constellations over Serbia on August nights. Not even the loveliest seasons of the year held so much beauty for him as the masses of stars, nor did the power he held over men excite him so much as the curving arc of blue space at which he now gazed.

The earth was turning soundlessly on its axis; Serbia was sinking ever more deeply into shadow; Kragujevac, his room with its bed, the cat Gavra, and he himself were now flying through space at a speed of 334 meters per second; the High Command and his officers and soldiers neither knew nor felt this. Serbia was not aware of her flight toward Orion and the Pleiades that night, and did not hear herself whirling around the earth's axis, nor the earth whirling around the sun and the constellations. Man notes all the trivia of his little world, but the great things either escape him entirely or are lost in illusion. The illusion of history is even greater than the illusion that the sun rises and sets. History? It is the crucifixion of man between illusions, between deceptive possibilities and immoderate goals. The proof of this is that we kill easily, and these acts of human stupidity endure. Also our faith that happiness lies just beyond the horizon. He had no such thoughts as a captain or major; he had no such thoughts even as a general. No, he never had such thoughts. For surely at every stage of life, in every station, human fate is different. History. It was always the same movement in ascending and descending arcs, with only one outcome. But the average person acknowledges this only when his own cycle is completed, when he goes down for the last time. Copernicus demonstrated centuries ago the true order of our infinite universe, but within ourselves we still believe that we're at its center. All our progress and all our knowledge haven't budged us from this illusion.

His breathing was painful. But he couldn't resist the clear, stony expanse of the night sky. He got up, wrapped his cloak around him, and moved with difficulty to the window.

Thick masses of stars. There in Orion were Aldeboran, Rigel, and Betelgeuse; the Pleiades shone in Taurus. That was Canis Major, and there were Sirius and Dositheus, just rising. What were those military leaders—Alexander the Great, Caesar, Napoleon—compared with Copernicus, the priest who had understood, communicated with the stars? Simply men who sowed the seeds of death for their own insatiable love of glory. Light does not bring great knowledge. Copernicus didn't discover that the earth revolved around the sun by looking at the sun; it was in the darkness that he saw the sun at the center of our planetary system. The greatest human knowledge has come into existence by night. A great nation, like the Great Bear, is most visible in the darkest night. A great man is like the morning, gleaming on the horizon above a dark rim.

Today one more cycle of Serbian history would be completed, when the meeting at Valjevo was resumed. When Serbia moved noiselessly from west to east, when it turned to the sun, a circle would be formed: some would be cursed for conscience' sake; some would win glory by their cowardice; others would retain power through cunning. Some of the victors of Valjevo might well be defeated today. Virtues would fall by the wayside and be slowly trodden down by the heavy boots of generals and the light shoes of ministers.

Whenever he reflected on the mistakes he had made in this war, he would recall the meeting in Valjevo of the High Command, the government, and the Opposition, when he had proposed making peace with the enemy because he was convinced that the Serbian army was exhausted. That was a defeat from which he could not recover. He had been accused of lack of faith. An army commander may make a mistake in estimating the situation on the battlefield, but he dare not lose faith in the war being fought to defend his country. Without faith he has no right to command, for then he is a murderer, not a warrior. After the meeting in Valjevo, Putnik's subordinates and some malicious people called him a defeatist. Although he knew that most people persist in denouncing those in the right, and that in Serbia a man in the right must endure denunciation with dignity, the memory of the Valjevo meeting stung him. He saw it as a moment when he had lost his perspective in the face of adversity. Would he have to confess again in front of his subordinates and the ministers, caught in a vise between Mišić's soldierly optimism and Stepa's pigheaded caution? No, he would not. No war had been won by assemblies, votes, and majorities. Napoleon hated deliberating with his staff more than anything. An army commander is alone in the middle of the battlefield. He makes dispositions, weighs things, considers facts, and believes in himself. He listens not to the chattering of men, but to the wind and the silence. He looks not into the eyes of his subordinates, but at the stars. He turns to God, to the universe, for advice. Not to his subordinates.

The dawn chill and the crowing of the roosters made him shiver. He went back to bed and closed his eyes.

He was awakened by the pain in his chest. The cat was still dozing at his feet. The creaking of the wooden staircase announced the relief of the night sentry and the beginning of the High Command's morning routine. Every day he felt his illness more keenly; it detracted from that perfect severity and control which had made him confident even when his front was collapsing under the blows of the Austro-Hungarians and he was ordering his staff to shoot deserters. He knew that the illness of a commander bothered an army like their first lost battle. His soldiers, though coarse and hard, were compassionate and extraordinarily sensitive. They felt the eye of everyone from God to the corporal, and heard everything from the High Command to the buzzing of bees. His illness was even more disastrous for staff morale: it aggravated the faintheartedness of tired men and fed the rancor of subordinates. The faith of the entire Serbian army was being poisoned.

He didn't feel well that morning, but he couldn't delay getting up. At half past seven the commanders of the armies would arrive. He dared not receive in bed even the people closest to him for it would arouse their pity and scorn. Yes, their scorn! The human animal never misses an opportunity for that blow to the heart. If his wife were still alive, it would be the same; the only person to whom he dared complain was his eldest daughter. He wouldn't give his sons the opportunity to pity him. He rang vigorously for his orderly.

Corporal Zarubac deftly assisted him in washing, put on his boots, and buttoned his jacket. The fatigue caused by buttoning his jacket humiliated and angered Putnik. The orderly brought him tea and removed the cat. Another orderly placed on the table the previous night's telegrams from the front and from the military representatives in the Allied commands. Putnik didn't look at the telegrams. He went to the window to breathe in the morning freshness. He looked wearily at the roofs of Kragujevac and the trees spotted with sunlight. The countryside and the sky had the fragrance of the departing summer, perhaps his last. Ah, if only I could say nothing today, he thought. If only he could say nothing until the artillery started to thunder on the Sava and the Danube.

The creaking stairs announced the arrival of the army commanders. He returned to the table feeling so tired that he could hardly smooth down his short beard. He returned their salutes with an inclination of his head and indicated the chairs with his eyes. Agitated by a loud, uncontrolled sigh from Vojvoda Mišić, he said immediately in a stern tone: "Gentlemen, the Prime Minister has submitted some very difficult questions to the High Command, to which he asks a joint response in writing. Colonel Pavlović will keep minutes of our conversations. The first question is: What are our chances of success if we are attacked by Austria-Hungary and Germany during the next few days?"

Their faces darkened.

"Let me help you. This is what I think: if the Austro-German forces don't exceed thirty thousand men, we have a chance of success."

"I'm not so sure about that, Vojvoda," said Vojvoda Stepa Stepanović, the commander of the Second Army, with conviction. "Our cadre of officers is reduced to half strength. The same is true of the army. They're weakened by sickness and malnutrition. With superhuman efforts we could perhaps hope for partial success."

Putnik looked at each general in turn, and then at Mišić: did they think his modest optimism unjustified? He thought so himself, but today it was his duty to have faith.

"How should we reply to this question, gentlemen?"

"Any way you think," said General Pavle Jurišić-Šturm, the commander of the Third Army, in a quiet voice.

Putnik knew that this man—a German by birth and a former Prussian officer who had come to Serbia as a lieutenant, joined Putnik's army, become Orthodox, and risen to an army command because of his abilities—always spoke sincerely. "Do you agree with Šturm, Mišić?"

"Yes, I do, Vojvoda."

"I should like to have my dissenting opinion recorded in the minutes," announced Stepanović.

"Very well. Next, what are our prospects in a war with Bulgaria without the assistance or agreement of the Allies? Let me again offer my view first. I think we can count on success, especially if the Greeks fulfill their obligations as our ally."

"I'm convinced that the Greeks won't enter the war," said Stepanović confidently. "Fighting the Bulgarians alone, and under pressure from the Austrians and the Germans, we'd have little chance of success."

"If the Austrians and Germans didn't attack us with strong forces," said General Ilija Gojković, commander of the Timok army, "I believe we could hold out for a while."

"It would be difficult, gentlemen," said Šturm. "Isolated, and without help from the Allies, we can't fight a long war. We could do it last year, before the offensive and the typhus epidemic. That's what every soldier thinks today."

The deep, clear voice of General Mihajlo Živković, commander of the Belgrade Defense Force, broke in: "I'm convinced, gentlemen, that the Serbian army will once again astonish the world." He stared hard at Putnik as he spoke.

Putnik wasn't pleased by this support from the "Iron General."

Mišić kept his eyes on the floor: what lay behind this chessboard questionnaire of Pašić's? Did he want to make the High Command responsible for defeat in the eyes of the people? To have a written record to condemn the guilty? It was bad for a nation to have such a wily leader. He felt so strong a desire to smoke that he wanted to gnaw his fingers.

"Do you wish to record a dissenting opinion, Mišić?"

"No, I don't, Vojvoda. I think the same as all of you and our soldiers."

"Perhaps there are some small differences among us. In times of great uncertainty, small differences carry weight. In all probability Mr. Pašić knows that."

"Unlike Mr. Pašić, I don't believe that Serbia is confronted with four possible courses of action," said Mišić. "There is only one, and that one inevitable. We all know it."

The generals looked at each other anxiously, and Stepanović nodded in confirmation. Mišić's position was unacceptable to Putnik, who continued:

"The easiest question submitted by the Prime Minister is the following: What are our prospects of success if Austria-Hungary, Germany, and Bulgaria attack us at the same time? In this case our prospects would be doubtful, I believe, but not hopeless." He saw the uncertainty on their faces and added: "No, not hopeless. The fate of Serbia would hang in the balance, and once the soldiers know that, they can do even more than they must do. It wouldn't be so easy to defeat a man aware of this fact."

All the commanders except Mišić stated briefly and firmly that in a war on three fronts against superior forces Serbia had little chance of success. And by all accounts such a war was in store for Serbia, and soon.

Putnik was worried by the ease with which he had secured the agreement of the army commanders to a course of action different from his own. If they were so easily swayed, how could they guarantee the loyalty of the officers beneath them? But Mišić, famous for his optimism at the Valjevo meeting, sat in gloomy silence, twiddling his thumbs.

"Do you have anything to say in answer to the question just put, Mišić?"

"I'll never give an order which I don't believe my soldiers can carry out, Vojvoda."

"That's as it should be, Mišić. On condition that you not proclaim the limits of your faith to be the limits of the fighting power of your troops." Putnik was still not saying what he really thought.

"Živojin, do you believe we can defend ourselves against the attack in store for us?" asked Stepanović softly.

"Yes, under certain conditions."

"Under what conditions?" asked Putnik with a start.

"If we immediately eliminate Bulgaria as an enemy."

Putnik turned to Mišić: "You mean if we attack before their mobilization is completed? Take Sofia by surprise?"

"Yes, absolutely."

Putnik repeated to himself: "Yes, absolutely."

"And if the Lord God put some sense into the heads of our allies," said Mišić," they'd realize that the Serbian, or rather the Balkan, battlefield is the one where Austria-Hungary can and should be smashed, and for that purpose they'd immediately move at least fifteen divisions to our front. Less than they lost in their senseless Gallipoli campaign!"

"What if the events don't work out in our favor?" asked Putnik quietly.

"Then our collapse would be inevitable. And very quick, too, Vojvoda."

Živković moved his chair a little and frowned. Gojković's face was like wax and expressed no emotion. Šturm looked anxiously at Putnik with his small blue eyes. Stepanović raised his head and stared into space.

Putnik knew that Mišić had said nothing outside the general opinion in the army, and this impressed him. On the other hand, he objected to Mišić's confident tone, and felt it was a suitable occasion to give a warning to the other commanders:

"Gentlemen, this is a difficult time in Serbia for people who think logically and see only the obvious. They can see only defeat—nothing else. The logical conclusion is: we must capitulate. But we can save ourselves only by victory. To win a victory, gentlemen, we must have faith in defiance of logic and reality. Therein lies the problem." He paused to summon his strength, then raised his voice: "If we are to survive, it is essential that we have great faith, the greatest faith, true faith, which is faith in a miracle. The faith with which we won on Suvobor and on the Kolubara. That faith is proof that victory is possible."

"Faith in oneself is not enough now," someone whispered.

In the strained silence Mišić announced, "We can still place our trust in God, as we have always done."

Again someone whispered, "That's not enough now, either."

Putnik grasped the arms of his wicker chair, his voice hoarse and trembling. "We must believe in something that our enemies would never believe in, if they were in our position. Our miltiary superiority depends on that spirit alone."

"That's crazy!" someone whispered.

Putnik fell silent and then looked at each commander in turn; he looked at them like the president of the examination board for their promotion, like their commanding officer, like the chief of the General Staff and the first Serbian vojvoda of his century. They met his gaze in their customary military manner. He drank up the rest of his medicine, breathed more deeply, and continued:

"It's our duty to have faith, and when people have faith anything is possible. Belief in the impossible is now the sole proof that victory is possible." He stopped speaking; he had difficulty regaining his breath. Stepanović and Mišić were frowning; they didn't have faith. He breathed in as much as he could and went on in a threatening voice: "Even when we retreat and lose battles, we can still have faith that we're working for victory. Yes, gentlemen, victory!" He wheezed and coughed and became deathly pale.

Someone said in a clear, ringing voice: "Nonsense!"

As he coughed, Putnik shook his head in disagreement. The commanders exchanged inquiring glances, wondering who had said this. Stepanović spoke in a challenging tone: "How can we, few in number, naked and barefoot, have such a spirit?"

"Even faith is hard for a small nation," said Gojković cautiously.

"We've believed in freedom longer than anyone—that fatal freedom," said Stepanović bitterly. But Putnik, supporting himself on the table, replied: "Freedom is necessary to a man who believes in himself, Stepa."

"But it's the man who doubts himself who deserves freedom," said Mišić thoughtfully.

"Doubt yourself, Mišić, but only until you sign the orders for your army."

"I do doubt myself, Vojvoda. And I often doubt the orders given to me. But I must carry them out."

"Yes, you must," whispered Putnik, wiping his brow with great effort. "Subordination is part of the order of the universe."

Colonel Pavlović cut short his suffering: "Please sign these minutes, Vojvoda. Your car is waiting for you. The doctor thinks you should go to your vineyard immediately. For rest and fresh air."

Putnik nodded to the commanders, scornfully signed the minutes, and slowly descended the wooden staircase with the help of two orderlies. As he was leaving the High Command he ran into Nikola Pašić, who was disturbed to learn that Putnik would not attend the meeting.

"Can't you stay just for the beginning? The Serbian army hangs on your every word, Vojvoda."

"I'm not responsible for words. I'm a soldier and I take responsibility for the nation's frontiers, Prime Minister."

"What about me, Vojvoda?"

"You are responsible for words."

"What should I do?"

"Nothing that will destroy the faith of the people and the army.

Their faith in the purpose of the war." He slowly raised his hand to his cap, and with the help of his adjutant got into the car.

The sound of thunder awakened King Peter—or was it artillery? Raising himself on his elbows, he listened intently to the silence of early dawn. Perhaps he had been dreaming about artillery fire; he had dreamed about all sorts of things last night, and when not asleep he'd thought about the battle on the Loire in 1871 when he was wounded by the Germans while fighting as a second lieutenant in the French army. The dawn light in the window. The time for an artillery bombardment before a big attack. If Serbia were attacked now or in the next few days, he wouldn't be able to cover the church with a copper roof, or finish the crypt, or bury his grandfather Karageorge. And an unfinished church was more shameful than the evil deeds of men, more despicable than the destruction of sacred objects.

"Zdravko! Zdravko!" he called to his servant, and banged the chair with his stick. Zdravko was a peasant, yet he slept late. He had grown fat at the King's table and become lazy and insolent. Last night he had again come into the room without knocking, despite instructions that he was never to do so. Still, King Peter had to put up with him because he had one virtue: he could keep his mouth shut. "Zdravko!" As soon as he got out of bed he knew he'd have trouble that day with his contractors. Those liars from the Venčac quarry wouldn't polish the marble slabs for the tomb. The builders, those lazy bums, had spent the whole summer paneling the altar and laying down the floor of the church. And he hadn't thought of buying stained glass before the attack on Serbia. Now he had no money, and these days there was no one to borrow from. On the contrary, everyone stole from him as if he were the Turkish Sultan and not the King of Serbia. It was a bad sign when stealing from the State and cheating the King was a greater achievement and a source of greater joy for a Serb than any heroic deed. "Get up, Zdravko!" He banged with his stick. Zdravko slept the sleep of the dead. Much he cared that the German cannon were pounding the Serbian trenches. King Peter went out into the hall and opened the door to the little room where Corporal Zdravko slept. He called again, but the man didn't stir. He hit him on the legs with his stick.

Zdravko jumped up and stood at attention before the King, who was still wearing his nightshirt. "What can I do for you, Your Majesty?"

"What do you hear?"

"The roosters, Your Majesty."

"Only the roosters?"

"I hear barking in the distance, and the cows mooing in Topola. And a little bell on a yoke nearby."

"What else?"

"I hear the ravens cawing and the blackbirds whistling in your forest, Your Majesty."

"You don't hear any cannon?"

"No, I don't."

"I've told you a hundred times to think carefully before you answer my questions."

"I hear some crickets, Your Majesty."

"Now do your duty and be quick about it," said the King despondently.

He did so love the crickets, those invisible musicians, and that year he didn't hear any. Last night he had thrust his head into the underbrush and put his ear to a lump of earth, but hadn't heard any. He went back to his room to get dressed, feeling calmer, but depressed because he had been mistaken in thinking he could hear artillery from the north. Zdravko brought him fresh water from the well and poured it on his hands. The King gave a start: he had forgotten to write down in yesterday's expenses, eleven dinars for medication and five groschen to the peasant woman for a melon. Damn it! The contractor and the chief engineer would fleece him! Zdravko deftly helped him to dress. No reason to scold him. Who knew how many dinars and groschen slipped through for no known reason. He wouldn't even be able to complete the altar in his church. If Putnik's information about the enemy's intentions was correct, the main door and the road leading to the church would remain unfinished. The equipment for the hospital wouldn't be ready either. He'd have to hand the hospital over to the people and the army before the German attack.

He went out and stared at his church, surrounded by scaffolding and lit now by the rosy, spectral light of dawn. It was as if the lower scaffolding had already burned up, and the upper scaffolding and the dome were on fire. He shuddered; grasping his stick with both hands, he stabbed it into the ground. He stood there, leaning toward his church in the menacing silence, while the thickness of night filtered down from the dome and the upper scaffolding, until the great building stood sharply etched against the clearing sky—the building which was a symbol of man's eternal quest and the king's authority. And of freedom. And of the victory of Serbian faith.

In the heart of Šumadija, on this poplar-covered hill where his grandfather Karageorge, his father Alexander, and he himself had pastured their flocks, in the midst of plum orchards, vineyards, and enclosed fields, the five-domed church would tower over everything, a sister to the Church of the Holy Apostles in Constantinople. The enemy was on the threshold, had all but rushed in to kill and burn and destroy, but he was building a church which would survive all human misdeeds and outlast all the bondage and misery of this century. Šumadija would await the dealer of death and slavery with a magnificent new cathedral. After the churches of Vienna and Budapest, it would be the biggest on the way to the East. The first great Orthodox cathedral.

His cathedral and mausoleum. A high, marble cathedral that would gleam in the sun and moon, and shine in the dawn and dusk of Šumadija. Her enemies would respect the nation that had such a great structure rising up in the midst of its huts. There was no great nation without a great cathedral. It would outlast all contemporary buildings, it would outlive ancient roads and cemeteries. Tales would be told about the king who lived in a house less than half the size of the houses in the village of Topola, but who had built this marble cathedral next to his house, a cathedral no smaller than the one in Constantinople built by two emperors, Constantine and Justinian. That was how he had lived his life: everything that served him should be small, so that he might build something great for eternity.

He stood in front of the altar, knelt down facing eastward, and crossed himself:

"O Lord God Almighty, put off the autumn rains and the attack on Serbia so that I may finish this church built to Thy glory. Grant to Serbia a fine and peaceful autumn, so that all may be quiet in the trenches of my army. O Most High, may the roads be dry so that I can bring the marble from the quarry. May the weather last, so the sculptors can finish carving the tombs. And preserve, O God, the health of the workmen and contractors and the architect."

He said the Lord's Prayer, then hurried toward the eaves to waken the workmen and builders: "Get up, children, the sun is rising. Get up, the days are getting shorter and the nights longer. You've had a good sleep and you're well rested. We must hurry, the enemy will attack soon!"

When, slowly and sluggishly, the workmen had begun to wash, he returned to his room. He was depressed by their lack of energy. It was as if they were determined not to finish the church while the war lasted, as if they'd conspired with the contractors and the architect to squander his money until they had taken his last groschen, until the Germans arrived at Topola to find the mess and rubble of a building site. He sat down at the table to check the previous day's accounts, counted his ready money, added up his debts, set aside cash for that day's expenses, then recorded it in his notebook. He checked his calendar, as he did every morning, to see whether something important had happened on that date in the past. Was it possible that nothing of significance had happened that day? He returned to his desk and his accounts.

Zdravko brought him some preserves and a glass of water. Just to be on the safe side, the King reminded him once again to set a place for the Prime Minister, Mr. Pašić, who should arrive that morning and would certainly bring worrisome news. There was sure to be an ultimatum from the Allies. Even when he had lived abroad as an émigré, and particularly as king, he had had little patience with politics, and after withdrawing from his royal duties he disliked discussing politics with Pašić, who didn't talk about politics like a politician. Should he ask Pašić to tell the minister of finance to give him something on account? Dare he? In a country where the right to break the law increased in proportion to the power of one's position, he was the only one who didn't take advantage. He continued adding up the previous day's accounts; his calculations showed a deficit of one dinar and thirteen groschen. Why, this was the daily wage of a common workman!

"May I have a word with you, Your Majesty?" said his adjutant.

"Did you give me exact accounts yesterday, Colonel?"

"Yes, I did, Your Majesty."

"And what if I show you that somewhere you calculated one dinar and thirteen groschen too much?"

"In that case the deficit will be made good."

"That's not the point, Colonel. Every embezzler in Serbia says he'll make up the deficit. I want at least one account book in this country to be correct. I'm warning you for the last time to present me with exact accounts!"

"Mr. Pašić has arrived, Your Majesty."

"A Serbian peasant had to toil and sweat until midday for that dinar, and now his son is in the trenches wearing torn boots." More dejected than angry, he went into the dining room to meet the Prime Minister.

They greeted each other in silence with stiff, formal gestures, then sat down opposite each other at the small table laid for breakfast. Pašić asked the King whether his rheumatism was troubling him. This question made the King uneasy, so he replied with his own question: "Do you still believe, Mr. Pašić, that a monarchy serves the cause of freedom in a war better than a republican government?"

"Yes, I do, Your Majesty."

"I haven't been sleeping well the last few nights. I've been worrying about this unhappy nation and my unfinished church. I've been reviewing my principles and enumerating the advantages of a republican government."

"A good government depends on its people, Your Majesty."

"However you look at it, Prime Minister, there's more chance of freedom in a republic. But to our misfortune, we still haven't taught the Serbs how to use freedom."

"We'll discuss this after the war, Your Majesty. Now I must get down to business. Our situation is grave. Soon we'll be attacked on three sides."

"I know. Vojvoda Putnik has informed me."

"I've brought you personal telegrams from Czar Nicholas, King George, King Emmanuel, and President Poincaré."

"What do they want?"

"They appeal to you to make Serbia cooperate with them, to make new sacrifices for the Allied cause."

"Sacrifices? They're always asking us to make sacrifices. But let's have breakfast, Prime Minister." He drank his tea and thought: Dare I oppose him?

Over breakfast Pašić related the decisions of the National Assembly, the High Command, and the government. The King nodded but didn't respond. Instead, he complained to Pašić about his foreman, contractors, and workmen. When the King paused for a moment, Pašić handed him the telegrams. The King read them and said angrily:

"So Their Majesties ask me to give up Macedonia and Banat as if they were my own private property! They ask me to force the government of Serbia to fulfill the demands of the Allies as if this country had no constitution, as if it didn't have its own freely elected Assembly to decide state policy in the name of the people. What extraordinary insolence! Typical of kings and emperors! I'm sorry Poincaré is associated with them. France is my second homeland."

"Things are going badly for the Allies, Your Majesty. That's why they're appealing to you to use your authority at this critical time."

"The royal authority in a democratic, parliamentary state? I'm offended that the Allies refuse to recognize that the sole authority in Serbia is the constitution and the law. You know best what your duty is at this critical time."

"Yes, we do. And we have made the decision that had to be made. But I'd advise you, Your Majesty, to respond to these telegrams immediately, indicating that you fully understand their appeals and will do all you can to see that Serbia carries out her obligations as an ally."

"You write and I'll sign."

Pašić made suggestions about the reply to Czar Nicholas, whose support meant most. The King listened carefully and agreed, then said hesitatingly: "Prime Minister, I'm afraid I must violate one of my principles. I too think this is a critical time for Serbia and I won't see my church finished. I've used up nearly all my savings. Each day the contractors present me with another bill. I'm compelled to ask you, Mr. Pašić, with full confidence that you'll understand my position, whether—if it wouldn't interfere too much with the budget—Mr. Pacu could order the court treasury to give me two months' pay in advance, so I can make all my payments."

"I'll see what I can do, Your Majesty. As you know, Pacu doesn't like to go against government regulations."

"He's quite right. That's how a finance minister should be."

Pašić paused for a moment, then said: "No, he's not right. Not even the law is always right, Your Majesty. The law was made by man. For men. Don't worry, I'll take care of it. And I'll send the telegrams—subject to your approval—for your signature in two days."

Pašić stood up and they took leave of each other, once more with strict formality and great seriousness. The King accompanied Pašić to the door, regretting that he had mentioned his request. He returned to his room, sat in an armchair with his eyes closed, and thought: The Allies are sacrificing us, it's all over. So many wars and uprisings, so much death and suffering for a bit of damned freedom, then bondage once more. He wouldn't flee Serbia. He had gone into exile as a prince, and he didn't wish to do so as a king. An émigré king was not a king; a king could be a king only in a state of freedom.

Once again he devoted himself to his accounts, tracking down the deficit and searching for ways of cutting the kitchen expenses. He remained thus occupied until just before lunch, when his adjutant reported that Vojvoda Mišić had requested an interview. He could hardly restrain himself from crying out: "What does he want from me?" But he couldn't refuse to receive a man like Mišić.

"Ask the Vojvoda to lunch."

When he saw Mišić an hour later, he stopped at the sight of his gloomy face: "Have we been attacked, Vojvoda?"

"Not yet, Your Majesty."

"Thank God. If only they'd leave us in peace for two months."

"You won't see your church finished, unfortunately."

"You think they'll attack before? Sit down, Vojvoda."

"They'll attack in two weeks. They must get to the Dardanelles before winter."

The King stared sadly through the open window at his unfinished church. The workmen were loafing. For him there was nothing more distasteful than bad and lazy workmanship.

"Vojvoda, look at those idlers on the scaffolding. I've begged them, bribed them, but to no effect. The other day I threatened to send them to the front. Still no effect."

"Recent events and our own policies promise no hope. We're set on a course toward darkness and uncertainty, Your Majesty. This unhappy future for the Serbian nation can be avoided only by your will, Your Majesty."

"By my will? What are you saying, Vojvoda? Surely you haven't forgotten, as the Allies have, that Serbia is a democratic state, and that the rights of the monarch are clearly defined? And—fortunately for the Serbian nation—defined in such a way that the king doesn't have the right to make his people happy or unhappy. His duty is simply to serve the country, and to watch over its freedom. Our nation is responsible for its own happiness."

The King looked at the scaffolding and strained his ears in vain to hear the stonecutters. Mišić, disappointed by the King's answer, listened to the threatening squeak of chisel on stone. He leaned toward the King, raising his voice to make himself heard above the hammers: "Do you believe, Your Majesty, that Serbia should be sacrificed for a mythological unified state which professors and hotheaded politicians have conjured up from books? For unification with those who have given little indication that they care about it?"

"Mr. Pašić has informed me about the decision of the Assembly and the government. I've taken note of it. My role ends there, Vojvoda."

"Your role can't end there, Your Majesty."

"It must. As a Serb and a European I believe that this terrible war can bring nothing more just and progressive to Europe from the dissolution of Austria-Hungary than the unification of the South Slav peoples, and the unification of the unfortunate Poles into a single state."

"Forgive me, Your Majesty, but I must remind you that it's your duty and right to prevent Serbia from suffering a historical misfortune into which it's being recklessly pushed by our ambitious politicians, by people who believe that a whole nation should be sacrificed for an ideal expounded in their political pamphlets."

The King raised his voice: "I would ask you, Vojvoda, not to define my duty in such an arbitrary way, nor to assign me the right to oppose a decision of the National Assembly and the government. As King I can't allow even you to oppose a decision which has been made. You forget that . . ." He sounded as if he were about to raise his voice even higher, when suddenly he fell silent.

Mišić was upset. During lunch he said nothing, while the King praised the Czech prisoners of war who were working on his church. They were exceptionally conscientious and capable, which was proof to him that there was no greater injustice in Europe than the Czech nation's not being free. Then the King moved closer to Mišić and whispered: "We're both soldiers, Vojvoda. It's our right to stay out of any dirty work in wartime. To have nothing to do with national politics at a time when kings and emperors are lying more shamelessly than their valets and grooms. Please help yourself to coffee."

REPLY OF THE SERBIAN GOVERNMENT TO THE NOTE FROM THE FOUR ALLIED STATES:
THE SERBIAN GOVERNMENT, AWARE OF THE GRAVE SITUATION IN VARIOUS THEATERS OF THE WAR, HAS DECIDED, NOT WITHOUT A PROLONGED AND DIFFICULT MORAL STRUGGLE, AND GUIDED ALMOST EXCLUSIVELY BY CONSIDERATIONS OF GRATITUDE TOWARD RUSSIA AND HER ALLIES, TO SATISFY THE WISH OF THE ALLIED STATES, TO MAKE ONE MORE SACRIFICE, THE GREATEST OF ALL, AND TO ACCEPT IN PRINCIPLE THE LINE PROPOSED BY THE OLD SERBO-BULGARIAN AGREEMENT OF 1912, WITH THE FOLLOWING LIMITATIONS WHICH ARE ESSENTIAL AND FROM WHICH THERE CAN BE NO DEVIATION. . . .

SEPTEMBER 5, 1915
PROPOSAL FROM SIR EDWARD GREY, FOREIGN SECRETARY OF GREAT BRITAIN, TO SAZONOV, THE RUSSIAN MINISTER FOR FOREIGN AFFAIRS:
THE ALLIED STATES CANNOT CONCEAL THEIR DISAPPOINTMENT THAT THE

SERBIAN GOVERNMENT HAS REFUSED TO AGREE TO THE CESSION OF THE WHOLE UNDISPUTED ZONE TO BULGARIA. THE ALLIED STATES CANNOT ACCEPT ANY ALTERATION OF THE PROPOSAL SUBMITTED TO THE SERBIAN GOVERNMENT, AND THEY INSIST THAT SERBIA MUST ACCEPT THESE PROPOSALS IN THEIR ENTIRETY AND WITHOUT DELAY.

SEPTEMBER 14, 1915

MEMORANDUM FROM THE RUSSIAN MINISTRY OF FOREIGN AFFAIRS TO ENGLAND, FRANCE, AND ITALY:

MINISTER SAZONOV BELIEVES IT IS ESSENTIAL FOR THE ALLIES TO USE THOSE MEANS OF EXERTING FINANCIAL PRESSURE ON THE SERBIAN GOVERNMENT WHICH THEY HAVE AT THEIR DISPOSAL. PRESSURE SHOULD BE APPLIED BY DELAYING RESPONSE TO THE NEW APPLICATION FOR CREDIT SUBMITTED BY SERBIA.

SEPTEMBER 22, 1915

LETTER TO ALL AMBASSADORS OF THE KINGDOM OF SERBIA ABROAD:

A FEW DAYS AGO WE RECEIVED A REPORT FROM SOFIA THAT BULGARIA WAS PREPARING TO ATTACK SERBIA.

THE SUCCESS OF AUSTRIA-HUNGARY AND GERMANY IN THE BALKANS WITH THE HELP OF BULGARIA WOULD BE THE DECISIVE ELEMENT IN THE OUTCOME OF THE WAR! SERBIA WOULD SUCCUMB.

THIS DANGER CAN BE AVERTED ONLY BY RAPID AND VIGOROUS MEASURES ON THE PART OF THE QUADRUPLE ENTENTE. THE QUADRUPLE ENTENTE MUST PREVENT THE MOBILIZATION OF THE BULGARIAN ARMY AGAINST SERBIA BY AN ULTIMATUM THREATENING MILITARY ACTION AGAINST BULGARIA IN THE BLACK SEA AND THE AEGEAN. IF BULGARIA DOES NOT DESIST FROM MOBILIZATION, THE ENTENTE MUST OCCUPY VARNA, BURGAS, AND DEDEAGAČ, AND SEND MILITARY HELP TO SERBIA FORTHWITH TO STOP THE BULGARIAN ATTACK.

PLEASE LAY OUR REQUEST AND VIEW BEFORE THE ALLIES AND BEG THEM TO TAKE THE NECESSARY STEPS AT ONCE.

PAŠIĆ

Vojvoda Putnik studied the report of the miltary attaché in Sofia regarding the concentration of Bulgarian troops in the direction of Serbia. He calculated time and distance. Both favored the enemy. He pushed the report aside, took a fresh sheet of paper, and began to doodle roses.

Perhaps salvation lay in a crucial risk—a decision which was not just a matter of the commander's rational estimate of the situation. An occasion for such a crucial decision was a military commander's good fortune. He could enter the textbook of the Military Academy and win himself a large statue in the nation's capital. However, the decison that he, Vojvoda Putnik, faced, although it could bring victory in war, could bring defeat in time of peace—a defeat which would wipe out the vojvoda's victory and glory. It would outlast them and bring shame upon them. Even his wisest commanders did not see this. Threatened, they thought only of immediate salvation. The peace after the war did not trouble them today. Two days ago, in trying to convince Pašić, he had almost succeeded in convincing himself: "We can be saved," he had said, "only if we attack Bulgaria before she completes her mobilization, only if we forestall an attack from the east and avoid an annihilating encirclement in the Morava valley. Only by eliminating Bulgaria can the Serbian army receive the blows from the north and west and then, with its rear wide open, retreat toward Greece and Salonika until an Allied army arrives." In that case he would wage his sixth war for liberation as an aggressor in a foreign land. Long ago, while still at the Academy, he had grasped the fact that an army is a liberator only of its own people. A foreign army of liberation brings envy, humiliation, a debt which cannot be paid off. If a people must sometimes receive its freedom from a great nation it will never do so from one equal to itself. That's how human beings are made. It's possible to feel gratitude for freedom toward a great nation, but only hatred and resentment toward a small one like one's own. Even if the majority of the Bulgarian people felt themselves liberated from German influences and the pro-German court and government by a Serbian attack on Sofia, that would simply stir fresh resentment among the Bulgarians toward their Serbian liberators— new hatreds on top of the deep-rooted old ones, new wounds. Would that not also be the case with our captive brothers in the unified state of tomorrow? One more arc of history would bend into a circle.

Živko Pavlović brought in for his signature an order to move troops toward Bulgaria. He waited for the vojvoda to stop drawing roses, something Putnik always did before making big decisions.

"Put that order on my desk, Mr. Pavlović. I'll call you when I need you."

"Lieutenant Colonel Apis would like to see you with some new reports from Bulgaria."

"Tell him to come at once."

Apis greeted him correctly, but with a hint of contempt.

"Sit down, Lieutenant Colonel. What's up?"

"I made connection with some people close to Stambolisky, Vojvoda, and with some politicians opposed to the court and the pro-German element. They affirm that the Bulgarian people are frightened by the intention of the King and government to push the country into a war against Serbia and the Allies. The people don't want a war with Russia."

"The people never decide about the beginning of a war; they decide how long it will last and how it ends. Go on."

"The people I'm in contact with are enthusiastic at the thought of our attacking Bulgaria in order to prevent mobilization and an attack on Serbia. They believe that our attack would provoke an uprising which would overthrow Radoslavov, remove the Coburgs from the throne, and turn Bulgaria toward Russia and the Entente."

"Do you seriously believe that if we crossed the frontier, the Bulgarians would respond with an anti-German uprising?"

"I'm convinced, Vojvoda, that the Bulgarian people don't like their king and hate the pro-German government. And I know some people there, Macedonians, who could do away with King Ferdinand."

"That idea doesn't interest me."

"I understand."

Putnik wanted to go to the window but suddenly felt weak. He sank back despondently in his armchair, took a deep breath, and said: "Come to think of it, Lieutenant Colonel, neither individuals nor nations love their saviors."

"That's true, Vojvoda. But sometimes things turn out differently."

"What are you trying to say?'

"Perhaps spilling the blood of those Coburgs on the throne in Sofia would make the Serbs and Bulgarians brothers."

Putnik asked sternly, "What else do you have to tell me about the Bulgarians?"

"There's a rapid turnover in their army and General Staff, and anti-German officers are being retired."

"Give me all the important facts. Don't hold anything back."

Apis hesitated a moment, then got up to say good-by with a cold politeness. Putnik stopped him at the door: "Do you believe in luck?"

Turning toward him, Apis answered automatically, "Yes, I do."

Putnik thought a moment, then said abruptly, "Take care of your health, Lieutenant Colonel."

He pulled the telephone toward him and felt fatigued from just dialing. He was so weak. How could he be an aggressor? "Get me the commander of the First Army. Mišić, are you still of the same opinion concerning Bulgaria?"

"I'm more convinced than ever, Vojvoda. If we don't frustrate their attack on our rear and flanks, our collapse is just a matter of time."

"You're less afraid if we attack?"

"I'm more afraid of defense that comes too late."

"What if the Bulgarians don't understand? What nation can accept an army which crosses its frontier to remove a foreign king and a pro-German government?"

"I'd take that into consideration if I felt sure that this same Bulgarian nation wasn't about to attack us. But since I'm convinced that the opposite is true, and that ten days from now . . . Forgive me, Vojvoda, but I don't understand your questions."

"I'm putting them to you, Mišić, because I believe you *do* understand them."

"We're not attacking Bulgaria to take her territory. We simply want to prevent her from attacking us from the rear, while we're defending ourselves against Austria and Germany."

"Is that your real reason, Mišić?"

"I'm sure that any intelligent commander in our position would make such a decision. I don't know what purpose is served by further justification."

"You should reflect, Mišić, on the fact that a war is remembered more by its results than by its intentions. Aren't you concerned about what future generations will think of our attack?"

"No, I'm not. We're only doing what we can and must do for our survival."

"Wise soldiers don't wage war only by military means."

"Surely you know that resolute action is wisest at this time."

"Perhaps. But caution isn't always the same as vacillation. All my instructions remain in force. Good-by, Mišić!"

He slowly put down the receiver and carried his cat over to the window: roofs, treetops already turning golden, an overcast sky. He could see little and during the day felt too cramped in this room to think. He needed space, but that was a blessing he wouldn't experience again: to be alone on some beautiful upland, on a hill, on a plain. To step out alone on a plateau. To walk with nothing to hinder his steps, to let his eyes range over open spaces. For him this would overcome even despair.

"What is it, Mr. Pavlović?" he said, without turning.

"Today's air reconnaissance has established that strong enemy forces are moving toward the Sava and the Danube."

"So it'll begin soon. Very well. Have the troops designated for the attack on Bulgaria move to their positions immediately."

"There's a new factor in the situation. I've just seen off a group of Allied military envoys led by Colonel Artamonov. They've found out about our troops' moving toward Bulgaria and protested vigorously."

"What disturbs these gentlemen?"

"They insist that our action will be a fatal mistake for Serbia. All four of them tried unanimously to convince me that the Allied talks with Bulgaria will come to a successful conclusion, and that in a few days Bulgaria will move against Turkey. Naturally I pointed out that Bulgaria was hand in glove with Germany and would attack us very shortly."

Putnik turned slowly toward him. "What did they say to that?"

"Not even an enemy would have threatened us so crudely. They said that not only would all military help be cut off, but that something would happen to us that nobody wanted. Artamonov threatened to use military force if we touched Bulgaria. I couldn't believe I was talking with our wartime allies and diplomats."

Putnik trembled: should he withdraw the order to move troops toward Bulgaria? That would be the beginning of capitulation. No, by no means. The Serbian High Command couldn't act according to the whims of generals in St. Petersburg, London, and Rome.

"Please put this question to the Prime Minister again," he said firmly. "If we attack Bulgaria, will Greece and Rumania remain neutral, or will they join us?"

"A telegram just arrived from the Prime Minister saying that Greece and Rumania are hesitant, waiting to see what measures the Quadruple Entente will take."

Putnik interrupted him: "That means we're alone."

"That's certain—we're alone."

"So we have to settle all the Balkan accounts. Have our troops continue their movement toward Bulgaria. And Stepa Stepanović—"

He didn't finish his sentence, for his agitation had brought on a severe attack of asthma. His assistant hurried from the room to call the doctor.

THE MILITARY ATTACHÉ OF THE KINGDOM OF SERBIA IN SOFIA TO THE HIGH
COMMAND IN KRAGUJEVAC:
BULGARIA ANNOUNCED MOBILIZATION AT 12:00 LAST NIGHT. ALL MEN UP TO
THE AGE OF 50 INCLUSIVE ARE TO REPORT NO LATER THAN 1:00 A.M. SEP-
TEMBER 25.

Nikola Pašić knew that every request for an interview on the part
of the Allied ambassadors was to renew pressure on Serbia, so he didn't
leave the government meeting until his secretary whispered to him for
the second time that Prince Trubetskoy had been waiting in his office
for a quarter of an hour. This was their first meeting since the mobilization of Bulgaria. Neither Trubetskoy nor any other Allied diplomat believed that events would turn out as he had predicted—namely,
that Bulgaria would align herself with Germany at her convenience.
He decided not to apologize for being late. He asked the Prince to sit
down and said in Russian: "You're not well, Prince?"

"I'm worried about your fate."

"Serbia expects such anxiety from her mighty protector, Russia."

"Events are moving against us with dizzying speed."

"I'm grateful that you see this, Prince."

"That's not enough for our relations, Prime Minister."

Pašić looked at Trubetskoy calmly, waiting for him to comment on
the Bulgarian mobilization. But Trubetskoy said imperiously: "Russia
and the other members of the Quadruple Entente demand that Serbia
cede Macedonia to Bulgaria immediately. Our patience is at an end,
Prime Minister!"

Pašić showed no anxiety. He looked at Trubetskoy as if he hadn't
heard, determined not to say anything until Trubetskoy had finished.
Trubetskoy folded his arms nervously and sat back on the couch to
listen, but since Pašić said nothing he went on, speaking rather more
quietly, but firmly:

"Russia regards your intention to attack Bulgaria, apparently to
forestall her attack, as a crime. As much of a crime as a Bulgarian attack on you would be."

"I never dreamed, Your Excellency, that now, when Bulgarian
troops have moved to attack Serbia, Russia would demand that Serbia
give up Macedonia."

"That's the one way in which the Bulgarian mobilization will lose
its raison d'être in the eyes of Bulgaria and the world. The only way,
Mr. Pašić."

"Since it's so obvious that Bulgaria is on the side of Germany and Turkey and is preparing for war against Serbia and the Allies, do you, her liberator, still consider our defensive war against Bulgaria a crime? Doesn't Russia see we must prevent Bulgaria from capturing Niš and the railway line which connects us with Salonika and our allies? Are we to let them and the Germans surround us and annihilate us, Prince?"

Pašić's voice made Trubetskoy jump up from the couch. He walked over to the window with his hands behind his back, returned to his seat, and met Pašić's opaque glance.

"Bulgaria won't attack you if you give her Macedonia immediately. The powers of the Quadruple Entente, and Russia in particular, guarantee that. We therefore demand that you stop the movement of your divisions toward Bulgaria. I must tell you frankly, Prime Minister, if you don't comply with our request, you can no longer count on our help."

Pašić looked at the floor: fourteen months of war, hundreds of thousands of lives sacrificed, half the country destroyed—to no purpose! Absolutely everything had been in vain. He didn't hear what Trubetskoy was saying as he paced up and down in the office. He stopped him with a dry whisper: "What will we do when the Bulgarians attack us? What if they arrive in Niš in two days? What then, Prince?"

"That won't happen—we guarantee it won't. But you mustn't provoke them!" He shook his finger menacingly.

Pašić asked in Bulgarian: "I ask you, Prince, what do we do if the Bulgarians attack us, notwithstanding your guarantee?"

"You must withdraw! Avoid any clash! Your army mustn't offend the Bulgarians, or do anything to provoke them to open fire."

"What if the Bulgarians *do* open fire? What then, Prince?"

"You mustn't shoot. The wisest course for you is not to enter into any conflict with the Bulgarians."

"So you advise us to flee from their approach?" stammered Pašić in Serbian. "How far, Prince?"

Trubetskoy leaned toward him and spoke in Russian, softly and deliberately: "Don't be afraid—Russia cares about you. The Allies have guaranteed that Serbia will extend to Split. You'll have a long coast."

"What if they drown us in the Nišava and Morava rivers, Prince?"

"That won't happen. The French will land in Salonika in a few days. We're taking steps to send a large Allied army to Serbia's assistance. The Bulgarians won't dare attack you."

They were now both silent. Pašić got up and went over to Trubetskoy: "Why doesn't your fleet take possession of Varna and Burgas right away? Then Bulgaria and Serbia and the Balkans would be saved for the Allies."

Trubetskoy was offended. "Russia will never occupy the lands of her Slav brothers. Russia liberated Bulgaria!"

They were interrupted by Jovan Jovanović: "An urgent telegram from Athens, Prime Minister. And the English ambassador is waiting to see you."

"Please read the telegram."

"Venizelos considers that if Greece comes to the aid of Serbia in the event of a Bulgarian attack, Serbia is under an obligation to cede the area between Dojran and Djevdjelija to Greece immediately, and after the war to hand over Strumica."

"Reply that we agree to that."

Trubetskoy looked out the window and thought, *Yes, indeed. God made man and the world imperfect. The epitome of that imperfection was seen in the sacrifice of His son. Man works against himself.* He turned around to face the two men: "And we too, gentlemen, are compelled to act against ourselves. Against our conscience and our reason. But what can we do?" He gestured with his arms and walked to the door, bowing as he left.

Sir Charles de Graz came in and waited sternly for Pašić to ask him to sit down. Pašić asked Jovanović to interpret. "Prince Trubetskoy has informed me," he said, "that the Quadruple Entente is again united against Serbia. It's hard to believe that now, Your Excellency."

They looked at each other in silence. Sir Charles spoke:

"Lord Kitchener takes a hostile view of the intention of your High Command to attack the Bulgarians. He wishes me to inform you that this is the most dangerous course the Serbs could adopt, at the time when we're arranging to send troops to Salonika and trying to persuade the Greeks to help the Serbs. My other instructions are to advise you to cede Macedonia to the Bulgarians immediately."

"What you mean is that England advises us to capitulate. You don't want to see that Bulgaria has mobilized to help Germany defeat England in the Balkans and the Near East. Surely the famous English diplomacy has not altogether succumbed to Bulgarian cunning and hypocrisy."

Sir Charles de Graz returned his pipe to his pocket and asked sarcastically: "What is Serbia's advice to us, in view of our inexperience?"

"To issue an ultimatum to Bulgaria to demobilize within twenty-four hours. If she refuses, to declare war on her and immediately send at least a hundred and fifty thousand troops to the Balkans."

"We're convinced that such a sudden and violent gesture would be disastrous. An ultimatum from us to Bulgaria would certainly lead to war with her."

"And you think that more dangerous than an ultimatum to Serbia?"

"Great Britain has an obligation to save the pride of King Ferdinand. He's the king of a nation and our honor demands that we scrupulously respect his decision."

"King Ferdinand, the heir of the Coburgs?" hissed Pašić.

Pašić looked incredulously at Jovanović, then at Sir Charles, who continued: "In politics we behave as circumstances dictate. I don't think, Prime Minister, that we're to blame for your unhappy fate in history." Sir Charles rose and remained silent for a few moments: "I think I understand you, Prime Minister. I'll interpret your ideas and feelings faithfully to my government, as I have always done. Good-by."

About ten minutes later the French ambassador arrived. After stating his support for the positions of Russia and England, he expressed himself even more firmly and forcefully against a preventive attack on Bulgaria, asserting that Bulgaria wouldn't dare attack Serbia. Auguste Boppe promised substantial military aid, should Bulgaria attack Serbia, then concluded: "If Serbia doesn't take our advice, she'll be to blame for the consequences. In which case France disclaims all responsibility for the fate of Serbia."

Pašić and Jovanović were speechless.

That night Pašić refused to answer two telephone calls from Putnik. The next day he sent the High Command the following telegram through the Ministry of War:

SINCE BULGARIA WISHES TO COME INTO CONFLICT WITH US WITHOUT AP-PEARING GUILTY, WE MUST AVOID PLACING TROOPS TOO CLOSE TO THE FRONTIER, WHERE THEY MIGHT QUARREL WITH THE BULGARIANS. SINCE THE ALLIES HAVE CONSISTENTLY GIVEN US THIS ADVICE, AND SINCE THEY ATTACH SUCH GREAT IMPORTANCE THAT THEIR FUTURE BEHAVIOR TOWARD SERBIA WILL DEPEND UPON IT, I MUST REQUEST THAT THE HIGH COMMAND GIVE THE STRICTEST ORDERS TO THE TROOPS DISPATCHED TO THE BULGARIAN FRONTIER THAT ANY SOLDIER OR COMMANDER WHO PROVOKES, ATTACKS, OR QUARRELS WITH THE BULGARIANS WILL BE PUNISHED BY DEATH.

PLEASE CONVEY THESE ORDERS TO EVERYONE BY THE QUICKEST POSSIBLE MEANS.

OCTOBER 3, 1915

TO FIELD MARSHAL VON MACKENSEN:

THE SERBIAN ARMY MUST BE DECISIVELY BEATEN AND CONNECTIONS WITH ISTANBUL VIA BELGRADE AND SOFIA OPENED UP AND MADE SECURE.

WILHELM II

OCTOBER 5, 1915

WRITTEN INSTRUCTIONS FROM FIELD MARSHAL VON MACKENSEN TO THE GERMAN TROOPS ASSIGNED TO ATTACK SERBIA:

SOLDIERS! YOU ARE NOT GOING TO THE ITALIAN, RUSSIAN, OR FRENCH FRONT. YOU ARE GOING INTO ACTION AGAINST A NEW ENEMY, A DANGEROUS, TOUGH, COURAGEOUS, FIERCE FOE: YOU ARE LEAVING FOR THE SERBIAN FRONT. THE SERBS LOVE FREEDOM AND THEIR FATHERLAND; THEY WILL FIGHT AND SACRIFICE THEMSELVES TO THE LAST MAN. MAKE SURE THAT THIS SMALL ENEMY DOES NOT DIM THE FAME OR COMPROMISE THE SUCCESS OF THE GLORIOUS GERMAN ARMY.

OCTOBER 6, 1915

REPLY OF THE COMMANDER OF THE BELGRADE DEFENSE FORCE, URBAN SECTOR, COLONEL DUŠAN TUFEGDŽIC, TO THE DEMAND OF THE AUSTRIAN PARLIAMENT THAT BELGRADE SURRENDER:

BELGRADE WILL NOT SURRENDER! COME AND TAKE IT!

4

The battalion commander's orderly hurried through Ram on horseback to order the commander of third-draft men to line up his platoon
immediately, except the observer under the walls of the medieval
fortress towering on the bank of the Danube. So, instead of going to
the cauldrons for their lunch, the older men lined up with their fur
hats down to their eyebrows, staring at Second Lieutenant Levi as he
walked up and down in front of them in great agitation, waiting for
the battalion commander. Periodically, he scanned the other bank of
the Danube.

Above the trees already touched by autumn, smoke from an army
encampment was drifting in wide, blue tufts. The previous night's baggage trains had been busy there until dawn. One could hear muted
trumpeting, like the baying of a deer, and the clanking of metal.

The men were afraid. They expected a German attack every hour;
the lining up of their platoon was surely being followed through the
field glasses of German observers linked by telephone with artillery
batteries. Just a few shells and the platoon would be pounded to
pieces.

Bogdan Dragović stood at the head of the first squad and looked at
the Danube through the golden tops of the poplar trees. The gray river
reflected the sky, and was frighteningly silent to those who had been
straining their ears day and night to hear it under the early morning
cries of the herons and wild ducks. Some of his soldiers had doubted
whether the Danube was really flowing, so they left the trenches at
dawn and crawled to the water. They threw leaves into the river to see

if they would float, turned east, and crossed themselves. Their fear of the Germans—the terrible, unknown enemy who might ford this great river in iron boats to kill them and leave their bodies to the fishes—this fear that made them think the Danube had stopped, had descended on Bogdan last night like the chill of the autumn dawn.

Although for ten days he had been expecting an enemy attack to end the long lull, only last night had he felt afraid for himself. Not even thinking of Milena would drive away the memory of his first battle on Bačinac: he had been overpowered by a fear he didn't know existed in him, and his commanding officer Luka Bog had caught him in that fear and humiliated him to the marrow of his bones. Not even the recollection of battles in which he had vied in boldness with Aleksa Dačić, or the feats on Suvobor for which he had received a medal for bravery, could remove the pain and shame of that first battle. From that crack in his memory trickled a stream of doubt. He no longer had the strength to withstand fear. What would happen to him when the attack began, when the Germans moved off in their boats from the dark shore? Might not this first battle since he was wounded, taken prisoner, and ill with typhus also be a defeat?

That defeat in front of Ivan Katić would remain a secret between them, since Luka Bog was dead. But a defeat in front of these wretched old men, targets of the first blow struck by the Germans—men who looked to him as a father figure in the war beginning on the bank of this terrifying river, although in age he could be their son—would be a great misfortune. He would feel particularly humiliated in front of Kakaši, a Hungarian who had fled from the Austro-Hungarian army because of injured dignity, that imperial officer who last summer had swum across the Danube and now stood in the humble ranks of the Serbian third-draft men, peasants who he believed had more honor and dignity than his fellow citizens. He looked at Kakaši, the only man in his squad wearing a new uniform. That was because he was a Hungarian and an officer, but also to distinguish him so that his movements could be followed—in case he was a spy. Kakaši smiled at Bogdan gently, as if aware of his thoughts. Bogdan wanted to apologize to Kakaši, who had to stand hungry in the ranks in the name of some "military virtue" of the battalion commander Major Dunjić, who was more concerned about the correct way of addressing an officer than about the state of the trenches and the solitary machine-gun nest on the river bank that he was defending. Dunjić would no doubt conduct one of his inspections with flogging, when he peered into the soldiers' knapsacks to see whether each contained a needle and thread, and whether the rags for cleaning their guns were folded. Bogdan's eyes sought his comrade from Suvobor, Sava Marić, the sergeant of the second squad, who invariably foresaw Major Dunjić's actions and punishments.

Sava Marić was looking thoughtfully at the Danube, and at the reddening forest where the smoke was twining around the treetops. That was where *they* were. For Sava Marić all enemies were *they,* and the Germans most of all. But the flattened clouds of smoke, calm and beautiful above the Danube woods, now made the Germans seem closer to him and more ordinary than he had imagined. Sava, a peasant from the hills, was always refreshed and cheered by smoke from a forest, even when he was really troubled. A fire brought people closer. Nothing was so human as a fire. Fire and smoke were more intimate than house or sheepfold. These people now lighting their fires, warming themselves and breathing in the scent of wood and smoke—why should they be any more dangerous than the Serbs?

The platoon commander paced in front of the ranks in a state of agitation, and frequently looked over at the Danube. The soldiers swayed on their feet, so weak were they from hunger. Jackdaws cawed in the gloomy silence, took flight, and landed on the high stone tower. Two German airplanes flew low over the tower, one behind the other, and the whole platoon fell down beside the walls as if struck dead. But the airplanes droned off to Požarevac to drop their bombs.

Two hours passed before Major Dunjić appeared on horseback accompanied by an orderly, a clerk from the staff, and two peasant women. The platoon commander barked the order to stand at attention. Major Dunjić stood with his entourage in the middle of the ranks and stared at the old tower as if seeing it for the first time. At last he began to speak:

"Heroes! Last night two new pairs of men's socks and a big piece of bacon were stolen from these peasant women. Will the thieves step out in front of the ranks?" He dismounted slowly, threw the reins to a groom, stood between the peasant women, pulled his cap down to his eyes, and scrutinized the platoon. "Once again I order the thieves to come out from the ranks! One, three, five, seven! The thieves have obviously decided to remain thieves." He walked over to Bogdan, at the head of the platoon. "Sergeant, search all the knapsacks! We're looking for new socks and bacon!"

Bogdan looked at his commanding officer, Reserve Lieutenant Levi, expecting some protection, but Levi looked straight ahead and said nothing.

"Why are you dawdling? Get on with it!" yelled Major Dunjić.

Bogdan looked at his old men, gray-haired peasants wearing sandals, breeches, and fur-lined jackets, and carrying multicolored peasant rugs. All had moustaches, some were mourning dead sons and had grown beards. Apart from their guns and bayonets, they had nothing that belonged to the State or the army. Since the Germans were expected to disembark near Ram, the regimental commander had thrown this platoon of third-draft men into the first line of defense on the Danube. That morning an order had arrived that the old men were on no account to withdraw from their positions without personal instructions from the commander of the regiment. The men looked puzzled. They've probably taken those bloody socks and bacon, he thought. He would find them, Dunjić would order a flogging, and that night or the next morning these disgraced and beaten men would be killed for their country.

"You're a bunch of fucking thieves! Search their knapsacks, Sergeant!"

Pale and trembling, Bogdan muttered: "I won't search their knapsacks, sir."

"What did you say?"

Bogdan turned his eyes away. When he had been transferred to Dunjić's battalion at the beginning of August, the major had summoned him and said: "I hear that you've been prattling against the State and talking nonsense about justice and the workers." Bogdan had not replied, but had thought to himself: Who's spying on me in the platoon? "And I hear that on the First of May in Belgrade you carried a red flag at the head of some demonstrating workmen." "Yes, I did, sir," he had answered at once. "Don't grin. Just disappear into the platoon, and if I hear you've been talking against the King and the State to those old men, I'll have you hanged on Ram tower!"

"I asked you what you said!" Dunjić banged his saber on the ground.

Bogdan said firmly, "I can't search the knapsacks of hungry men, sir."

"I'll take care of you, you wretched scholar. All of you empty your knapsacks!"

The soldiers shook out their knapsacks, producing pieces of corn bread, onions, green peppers, salt wrapped in bits of paper, bandages, a dirty shirt, or a pair of underpants. Major Dunjić walked behind the peasant women who were after their property. The one whose bacon had been stolen walked quickly through the rows of men without looking at the contents.

"My bacon isn't here," she stammered.

"It must be! If it isn't, I'll give you twenty-five strokes on your behind. Now look for it!"

The woman halted in front of two bags with large pieces of bacon: "I sold them that bacon."

"So you're merciful to thieves. Come out in front of the ranks, you two who bought the bacon. And you, woman, look for those socks," he said to the other woman.

"That's my blouse!" cried the peasant woman. "I didn't know it had been stolen." She lifted it up and spread it out.

"I took it for bandages, sir," said the bearded soldier calmly, a red blanket folded over his shoulder.

"You stole this woman's blouse to bandage your hero's wounds, did you?"

"Yes, sir, I took it for my wounds."

"You'll have them right away, hero. Now, woman, look for those socks."

The woman soon found her two pairs of socks. The thief burst into tears.

Bogdan could hardly look at Kakaši, he was so ashamed, but he would have liked to ask him if there was a Major Dunjić in the Austro-Hungarian army. He went up to the woman who had found the socks: "Who will you complain to tomorrow about the Germans, when they take everything from you, you bitch?"

"Shut up, Sergeant. Go into that poplar wood and cut off three rods, regulation size!"

Bogdan looked despairingly at Kakaši, who nodded encouragingly: did that mean that he should or shouldn't go for the rods? He couldn't understand Kakaši's glance, but he raised his voice: "I won't carry out that order either, sir!"

They looked straight into each other's eyes, in a silence broken only by the sniffles of the weeping soldier who had stolen the socks.

Afraid for Bogdan, Sava Marić called out, "I'll go and cut some good rods, sir!"

"Why you, Sava?" cried Bogdan, dumbfounded.

Marić ran off to the woods and came back with three young poplar branches.

"Now those with medals, come forward!" commanded Major Dunjić.

Two soldiers stepped forward hesitantly. Major Dunjić dragged out another, then handed them the rods and ordered the thieves to take off their pants and lie crosswise on top of one another. Among the thieves, only the man who had stolen the blouse took off his pants and remained in his torn, dirty underpants.

"Down with your pants, too! What are you four waiting for?"

The man with the beard at once took off his pants, and two others stripped slowly and put their hands over their private parts. But the fourth, a man with a pointed gray moustache, took only his pants off and said: "I won't take off my underpants in front of so many people. You can kill me first, sir."

"Oh, yes you will!" said the major, who hit him hard on the shoulders with the flat of his saber. "Do it!"

"You can kill me, but I won't."

Dunjić struck him again and knocked him to the ground. "Lie down! You three on top of him! Crosswise, I said!"

The soldiers who had stolen the bacon lay on top of the soldier who had stolen the socks, with the soldier who had stolen the blouse for bandages collapsed on top of them.

"Now, you heroes, let's see what this country gave you your medals for. You're to hit those thieves' bare bottoms twenty-five times and that bastard in his underpants thirty times. Hit hard and count aloud. Change over after ten strokes!"

The soldiers decorated for bravery began hitting in a manner worthy of their medals.

"Hit harder, you weaklings!" shouted Dunjić.

The rods swished. The men groaned. The soldiers in the ranks looked smitten. The woman whose bacon had been stolen ran away wailing. The one with the blouse stood next to the major and watched the flogging. Bogdan noticed her malicious smile: she too was one of the "people" for whom they must give their lives. What was it they must defend from the Germans? For whom must he and the beaten men be killed?

From the other side of the Danube came the sound of cannon. A few heavy shells flew overhead and plunged into the slope above the village. The soldiers wavered, about to run away, but Dunjić yelled: "No one is to stir! Go on, hit him—that's only sixteen!"

The boom of shells was again heard above the tower, then a thunderous rumble followed by a shower of more shells. "Let the platoon go to the trenches—run for it! And you go on hitting! Twenty-two . . . twenty-three . . . Harder, you weakling! Don't shirk the job!"

Bogdan led his squad into the trench on the bank of the Danube.

It was the funeral of "a father who had collapsed and died after his only son expired from war wounds," as the obituary put it, and Belgrade turned out for the funeral as if it were burying itself. From Vasina Street, across Terazije, and then along King Milan Street walked the longest funeral procession Belgrade had seen since the war began. All the shops and street stalls were closed and the cafés empty, and all the women and those men not called up into the army were walking behind the hearse and the kinsfolk of the dead man. People who hadn't even heard of Voja the hardware dealer, the wholesale trader in Vasina Street, joined the funeral procession or watched from the sidewalks. In the tense expectation of an Austro-Hungarian attack on Belgrade, everybody was burying someone today. As if taking advantage of a unique opportunity, people hurried to join the dark procession which, weighed down by numbers, crawled along as though it had no wish to reach the cemetery. The people at the end of the procession couldn't hear the funeral chants being sung by the three priests in front of the hearse.

Bora Jackpot had loved only his mother more than this uncle behind whose coffin he now walked. In this town of Belgrade, in the defense of which he felt he would soon be killed, nobody had done so much for the fatherless boy or offered him so much joy and pleasure as his Uncle Voja. Not only had he helped his mother to such an extent that "his nephew should not know what poverty was," but he had bought him bicycles and fashionable suits in Vienna, taught him poker and other games of chance, and given him the nickname "Jackpot" when he was still in primary school. And when Bora had completed high school, Uncle Voja had said to him, standing behind the cash register in his shop:

"Listen, my boy, study something that the Serbs don't usually study. You know what that is, and I'll pay for it: from now on this cash register is yours for women and cards. So spend—enjoy life." Afterward, in situations where money might have stopped Bora Jackpot in his tracks and confused him, he had felt calm, as if the wholesale hardware dealer's cash register really had been his.

The mob of mourners trailing him aggravated his pain. The sense of horror he felt since he had kissed his uncle's dead hand never left him. He had not felt death in any man killed on the battlefield as he felt it from the touch of his uncle's hand. The death of men on the battlefield was murder, which aroused in him a different pain, mingled with disgust, hatred, and rage against the enemy. His uncle's death made him suddenly aware of the futility of life. He couldn't weep. He couldn't, although he desperately wanted to.

The priests fell silent, the procession halted, the hooves of the horses pulling the hearse clattered on the cobblestones. An airplane droned in the cloudy sky, flying low over the roofs and trees. The mourners looked up: they could make out the black cross on each wing of the airplane, and two airmen leaning out of it. The airplane circled overhead and disappeared. In its wake, patches of white fluttered to the ground. Someone handed a leaflet to Bora Jackpot. It was a death notice bordered in black:

WITH A BLEEDING HEART WE HEREBY ANNOUNCE THE INCONSOLABLE LOSS OF OUR DEEPLY BELOVED SON BELGRADE, WHO AFTER A SERIOUS ILLNESS OF MANY MONTHS, CAUSED BY OVERINDULGENCE IN AUSTRIAN BUCKSHOT, SHELLS, AND BULLETS, HAS PASSED INTO THE BETTER WORLD OF THE AUSTRO-HUNGARIAN EMPIRE.

THE EARTHLY REMAINS OF OUR UNFORGETTABLE DECEASED WILL NOT BE LAID TO THEIR ETERNAL REST, BUT WILL WAKE UP TO A NEW AND BETTER LIFE UNDER THE RULE OF AUSTRIA-HUNGARY.

"What is this?" asked Bora Jackpot, waving the death notice.

No one heard him. The mourners' attention was fixed on the airplane, which had climbed high in the sky. The priests were singing "Holy God" at the tops of their voices, the hearse was moving slowly, the female relatives following; Bora stood alone between his relatives and the rest of the funeral procession. He began to sob, the crumpled death notice of Belgrade in his hand. Someone called out sternly: "Move on, Sergeant!"

Bora threw away the crumpled death notice and hurried forward to catch up with the hearse, swaying on his feet. A sudden flaming crash knocked him to the pavement.

The procession halted and stood transfixed, looking at the airplane, which was now flying low, now ascending once more in a gentle arc toward the Sava. A shell had exploded at the rear of the funeral procession, tearing it apart and stunning them all. No one ran for safety until three hundred Austro-Hungarian and German cannon simultaneously showered shrapnel and incendiary bombs on Belgrade.

The earth shook under Bora Jackpot. He felt sick. There was a dull roaring sound in his head. The street heaved and whirled around him. Buildings were collapsing. His father's watch! He took it out of his pocket and pressed it firmly to his chest. Let them blow up his heart with the watch. He could not and would not run away. He stared at the blood and bowels of the horses, at the wrecked hearse. Bora rose to his knees and caught sight of his uncle's corpse, without head or arms, sprinkled with broken glass. Bora fell to the ground and began to vomit as he crawled along. Just before he lost consciousness, he caught sight of a heron flying in the mist above the Danube.

He came to and managed to stand up. The explosions merged into a thunderous rumble which made his ears ring and took his breath away. The street was now deserted and blocked with dead horses. His aunt, helped by two women, was returning his Uncle Voja to the splintered coffin, placing the torn-off limbs and head at one end. Had he actually kissed the severed hand in farewell? Not even death came only once. He was vomiting again and everything turned black. Again the explosions brought him to his senses. What they had been waiting for had begun. He watched as the three women covered the dead man with a bloodstained blanket, then he helped them tie up the coffin with girth straps and reins from the dead horses. Several people emerged from a crumbling shop and disentangled three wheels and axles from the carcasses of the horses. They helped Bora Jackpot load the coffin into the remains of the hearse and secure it. Then he and another man seized the shaft and pulled it by three wheels up a steep street toward the cemetery, followed by the surviving relatives. The effort of hauling steadied him. He felt he was paying back something of what he owed his uncle, and would have liked to prolong the effort until dawn, as long as that airplane with black crosses on its wings circled above them, as long as the shells burst around them. They continued up the torn street until they reached the cemetery. Shells were falling there, too, scattering tombstones, skeletons, skulls, rotten planks, rags, and dead bodies. Overwhelmed by the stench of sulphur and human flesh, Bora Jackpot leaned against a large black tombstone. He looked up at the sky: above the smoking city of Belgrade the airplane with black crosses was flying in wide arcs.

When the people who had helped him to take his uncle to the cemetery realized that the shelling would continue, they scattered. He didn't call them back. He didn't need them. He didn't even need the women who had helped him drag his uncle to the open grave in which two old gravediggers were crouching, holding their spades over their heads. His aunt handed them a ducat each, and they quickly lowered the corpse into the grave and piled on the earth. The women couldn't keep the candles burning on the low mound. It began to rain.

Bora took his father's watch out of his pocket and held it to his ear. The voice and footsteps of time were expiring, moving toward the end. He pulled his cap down to his eyes and set out slowly in the direction of his platoon at Little Kalemegdan. There shells were whistling, fires raging, roofs blowing wide open, holes gaping. Smoke and stench. Again he was overcome by nausea. His head felt so heavy, he could hardly support it.

While the German shells thundered above them in a dense shower, and struck the villages and hills above the Danube, Bogdan Dragović stared at the river from his hole behind a fallen poplar tree. *What is my country now?* he thought. *Must I defend Pašić's state and Dunjić's army? For what freedom, for whose freedom, must I give my life? Why did that Hungarian Kakaši swim across the Danube? Senseless and shameful!*

Suddenly the German guns were silent, and the quiet of dusk settled over the Danube, undisturbed by even a bird. The wind carried the smell of smoke. Bogdan turned toward the fields and slopes. Throughout Podunavlje, as far as the eye could see, villages were burning. To his left some old men sighed. Good God, there were tears in their eyes! There was no weeping he found harder to bear than the weeping of an old peasant. He couldn't comfort them. What kind of a choice did they have? They faced poverty and floggings on one side and murder and arson on the other. The old men were defending their poverty and their floggings. Not because they feared a court-martial. Dimitrije Tucović, the socialist revolutionary, had died defending what was his although he opposed the war. The same was true of many of his socialist friends.

Bogdan went up to Kakaši and told him in faulty German that Major Dunjić was a swine, but that most Serbian officers were not. Kakaši replied that officers were the same in all armies. Hungarian peasants were beaten to make them kill Russians and Serbs for the emperor in Vienna; Russian peasants were beaten to make them charge the Austro-Hungarian machine guns without rifles; and Serbian peasants were beaten because they stole bread and socks when they were hungry and barefoot. He didn't regret crossing over to the other side of the Danube to defend it against the Germans. Bogdan wanted to believe him. Sava Marić called him. He was leaning against a fallen poplar, rolling a cigarette.

"They've set fire to our villages, Bogdan."

"Yes, I can see our poverty going up in flames."

"It's our life that's burning, Bogdan. We have no other. You should have carried out Dunjić's order."

"I don't understand you, Sava."

"I'm a peasant, and you're a student and my comrade in arms. So I'm telling you again, you didn't behave right."

"You mean I should have searched the bags of those poor bastards who receive only half a ration of hardtack? I should cut rods to beat people who'll die for their country tomorrow?"

"I'll tell you something else you won't like. Even on Suvobor I noticed that knowledge and intelligence didn't help you students to save yourselves. Most of you seem to think that it's a man's duty to die as soon as something bad hits, and that it's great to die for pride and honor. I've heard your friend Ivan Katić talk like that. What put such ideas into your head, Bogdan?"

Bogdan watched the sure movements of Sava's fingers as they rolled the cigarette. The strength of this peasant in everything he said and did stirred his admiration but also made him rebel. He said scathingly: "It's disgusting and futile to live just for the sake of living. What is life worth under Dunjić's whip and saber? What kind of country is it in which you have to strip naked in front of a hundred and fifty people and be flogged? Why are you defending a country that sends to the front boots made of cardboard and half rations of hardtack mixed with sand? Why?"

"Bogdan, we'll just have to figure out how to get boots and bread, how to avoid Dunjić's stick and saber. If you can't make the man who's beating you have pity, then naturally you must deceive him! If you can't manage that, then you must bear it. The saber won't cut off the head that doesn't rebel, Bogdan."

Bogdan reflected for a moment, then said, "I won't let them beat me, Sava! I won't take that!"

"They'll break your bones if you don't give in. What honor is there in suffering at the hands of criminals and fools? Be proud among those who are proud." He handed him a cigarette and lit it.

A man groaned in the cornfield behind them.

"Do you hear him, Sava? That's the thief who was ordered five more strokes because he was ashamed to take off his underpants in front of the platoon. You cut off the best poplar rods, regulation size, for the beating. I saw you. Shame on you!"

"That's nothing to be ashamed of! It would be no easier for those men sentenced to a beating if I put myself under Dunjić's rod, too. As you did. You think you did something heroic, something honorable? Or that your soldiers will have more respect for you?"

"I did what I felt a man should do: I didn't help those who did the beating. But you . . .! I remember some of our conversations on Suvobor. I remember when you said the finest thing in the world was respect. Don't you believe that any more?"

"Yes, I do. I still think that in our struggle for life nothing gives more satisfaction than respect. You need nothing more—no greater freedom or higher rank or bigger property—than respect. But if you don't have it, if it's not possible? I seek respect as long as it's expedient. As long as it won't cost me my head."

"That's cheap respect, Sava. Very cheap. In our struggle for life, respect must be earned—and sometimes defended—with one's head. There's no respect or dignity without paying the price."

"Ordinary people call folks like you hotheads. No one really likes a hothead, Bogdan. Nobody. Hotheads drive people too far, make them do things they can't do."

Bogdan was offended. Since his childhood, everything in him had rebelled against such folk wisdom. He didn't want to live by it. When he had grown up and begun to read and think about the world, he had wished with all his heart for a life in which such complacency had no validity.

"The people only love dead heroes, Bogdan. And dead champions of justice."

"Then why are you decorated with the Karageorge Star, Sava?"

"To tell the truth, Bogdan, I've been brave only when I had to be. When I couldn't save myself any other way. When I saw that the other fellow would kill me if I didn't kill him. When they attack us tomorrow, I'll aim at them only as long as I see that it's the best way to defend myself."

A horseman was riding toward them through the corn. It was an orderly from the battalion staff carrying orders. They were anxious. Fires were spreading over the hills and valley of Podunavlje, smoke covering the clouded sky. The orderly came up and called out: "Sergeant Bogdan Dragović!"

Bogdan could scarcely answer.

"I'm sorry, Dragović, but I have to take you to the battalion staff, bound and under guard."

"I won't let you tie me up!"

"I must tie you up."

"I'll jump into the Danube!"

"Don't be a fool, Bogdan." Sava Marić pinioned his arms to his chest. "I'll tie you up. Don't worry. There's no time for a court-martial. We'll be attacked at dawn. You go there and keep quiet. Keep quiet, regardless of what they say to you! Do you have some rope I can use to tie up Dragović, Sergeant?"

Bogdan trembled and his eyes sought his old men: would one of them come to his defense? The old men were looking at the Danube in silence.

"I have a belt," said Sava. Taking off his belt, he tied Bogdan's limp hands lightly. He also assigned him a guard. Bogdan stood there, too numb to protest.

Kakaši came up to him and said in German: "Hold your head high —dignity costs more than freedom!"

"I'll run away," muttered Bogdan, first in Serbian and then in German.

The platoon commander appeared and ordered someone to act for Bogdan. The orderly rode off, telling Bogdan and his guard to follow. Sava whispered, "Keep quiet!" and pushed him forward. The wind blew through the corn. The air smelled of burning. Bogdan felt as if the field, the trees, and the underbrush were all moving against him. He thought of Milena, and of his mother and sister. He felt pain for them, then shame that he had let himself be tied up, that he had no strength to pull his hands out of Sava's belt and run away. He would flee to the hills and fight on his own against every army! He looked at the burning village of Zatonje. The fires lit up the trees and houses; cattle were bellowing, women and children screaming, soldiers running through the village lanes, orderlies carrying the wounded.

The major received him in front of the staff headquarters, the one building in that small hamlet which had not been hit.

"So you're still alive, you bloody rebel! Yes, our anarchist is still alive. The enemy has destroyed our *Débange* artillery and flattened half of Rečica and Zatonje. Can you see the houses and stables going up in flames? While *you* are inciting a riot, you bloody socialist bastard! You're to go before a court-martial at seven o'clock tomorrow morning. You'll squeal all right! Shut him in the pigsty and put him under guard!"

Bogdan trembled and couldn't utter a word; he looked angrily at Dunjić, whose face was lit up by the flames from the neighboring stable.

"Forward march, you idiot!" yelled Dunjić.

With shaking knees Bogdan set off behind the soldier, who led him to the pigsty.

In the early evening, columns of smoke began to rise and a terrible fire spread through Belgrade. The first to catch fire was a mold and dye-stamp factory on the Danube, then the sawmill and the houses on Jevrejska Street. Then the docks on the Sava. Soon the whole town was enveloped in smoke and flames. The Danube quay was like a pan on the boil, and the fire spread to the docks on the Sava. We could see Gypsy Island in the distance. The flames reached up to the sky. The stench was so powerful that we began to suffocate, and the heat made us sweat violently. The telephone wires were torn down by shells. We were cut off.
—From the testimony of Captain Živko Kezić

Bora Jackpot shuddered: someone was calling out his name. It was as if once more a flaming beam was falling in front of him, as if children were screaming over someone being dug out from the rubble. Only this time he was even more frightened, because the voices were familiar and sounded close, yet somehow farther away. His legs were entangled in telephone wires and broken poles. He saw coming toward him, walking around a shell hole, his friends from the student platoon, Djordje Tričković, orderly to the battalion commander, and Mirko Durić, sergeant of the second squad in Bora's platoon, called Wren. He was nicknamed after this prettiest of birds in Serbia because of his good looks and gentle nature.

"Here you are. Šunto Zlatiborac told us the funeral was hit hard!" they said, greatly agitated. "Did you read that death notice of Belgrade? Nobody's ever seen anything like it! What happened to you?"

"Some swine nearby knocked me down," mumbled Bora.

"Are you wounded?" asked Wren.

"That's blood. The hearse was hit and my dead uncle mutilated, and so were the horses."

"Terrible! No one will survive this war—not even cowards," said Wren.

"Šunto Zlatiborac will, that Serbian imbecile," said Bora Jackpot.

"Where were you during the air raid?" asked Tričko.

"Looking at flying corpses, crosses, and tombstones. I saw . . ." Bora Jackpot bent over and retched.

Tričko grabbed hold of him and said as he held his forehead, "Šunto Zlatiborac is right. That's no ordinary airplane. It's a metal

---

monster, a German vampire or devil! It flies around, stops, and looks at us shivering. Then it shakes its wing, turns upside down, screams, and hisses."

"It's the dream of Icarus come to life, Tričko," said Wren. "A bird-man!"

"Shut up. I have a splitting headache." Bora Jackpot wiped his mouth with his sleeve. "Listen, I have to get some sleep."

"No time. Major Gavrilović has summoned all the commanding officers and sergeants to the battalion headquarters. We must be at the Golden Carp Café at eight o'clock sharp."

"Tell them you couldn't find me, Tričko. I must get some sleep."

"You'll get some sleep tomorrow, Jackpot," said Wren gently.

"If only I could go home to Bitolj tonight! I'd come back for the battle," sighed Tričko.

"Why are you such a crybaby?" shouted Bora Jackpot in the empty, shell-torn street.

"I was born in Belgrade, and I'll die in Belgrade."

"That's enough, Wren! Ever since we were transferred to Belgrade, you've done nothing but snivel. It's disgusting!"

Tričko took hold of his arm and led him into a nearby café. Bora made no attempt to resist. His house had been leveled a few days before and he had nowhere to go.

The café was full of soldiers, male civilians, and women. They found a table but there were no chairs, so Tričko carried in three empty beer barrels from the courtyard. They sat down and ordered tea, but the proprietor shouted angrily: "They're drinking tea in Budapest and Vienna this evening, gentlemen. But you know what we drink here in Belgrade!"

He brought them double portions of strong brandy and asked them to pay immediately.

"What's this?" asked Wren, banging his fist on the table.

"Pay for your brandy right away, and beat your breast in front of the Germans tomorrow, Sergeant."

Tričko paid him and ordered one more round. Bora Jackpot swallowed the brandy and shuddered. Tričko also drained his glass, but Wren only sipped his: "We're giving our lives for that café proprietor and his property—this, too, is part of Belgrade. How disgusting!"

"Enough of your exalted feelings!" cried Bora Jackpot.

Tričko regretted having persuaded Jackpot to come into the café. Its closeness stifled him. He had a fear of all enclosed spaces. That day's bombardment had caught him in the prison cells of the Belgrade fortress. If he hadn't been in Belgrade, between walls and houses, he wouldn't have been quite so frightened. He'd have liked to confide in Wren, but Wren was too absorbed in his own misery to listen. How excited he had been at the thought of fighting in the war, when he decided to volunteer! There had been only a few volunteers from Bitolj and he'd been the first. He was disappointed in his comrades and contemporaries who had not remained loyal, and had exaggerated his own achievement. When he had been on leave last summer, Bitolj had seemed too small and cramped for him. But the defeat of Serbia which everyone expected, and the fear that the Bulgarians would capture Bitolj and kill his family because he was in the Serbian army, dimmed all his patriotic ideals.

"Why are you so down, Tričko?" said Bora. "You're an orderly working for the staff. I'm in the front-line trenches."

"Yes, I am an orderly, but I'm also a Macedonian."

"Why is it any easier for me because I'm from Belgrade?"

"Do you realize what my family is in for, if the Bulgarians capture Bitolj?"

"And if they take Leskovac, Tričko? What will happen to my folks?" asked Wren with a sigh.

"There's a big difference between Bitolj and Leskovac. It's the hardest thing in the world to be a Macedonian. In peacetime you're a migrant worker, in war you don't know whose side you're on. Whoever wins, it's all the same to us."

They fell silent, each thinking his own thoughts. Then Tričko said, "Bora, have you got that pack of cards which Dušan Casanova gave you on Suvobor? The ones he didn't want to use until the war was over?"

"Should we play the first postwar game now?"

"No. I just wanted to know how many cards were missing from the pack."

"I haven't counted them."

"You know, for two nights running I dreamed that I picked up those cards from the snow around Casanova's dead body. But they weren't cards with the usual numbers and pictures. Instead, there's the wedding photograph of my father and mother that hangs on the wall in their room, a crucifix, an exceptionally beautiful naked woman, and our Don Quixote from Skoplje on horseback. And some meaningless words instead of figures. Let me look at Casanova's cards."

"Please, Tričko, don't bother me tonight with your memories of the Cadet Battalion! I don't want to remember it. I grew up here in

Belgrade, went to school here. Everything in my life has been in Belgrade. I don't want to sigh over bloody memories. Such banality makes me sick!"

"That's just what I want to do," said Wren excitedly. "Yesterday I visited the ruins of my house—it was destroyed last year—and sat on the doorstep. My God, the hopelessness and the pain of it all! Black leaves were falling from the walnut tree in the backyard. I sat there until an old woman invited me to have some jam tarts at her house."

Bora interrupted: "That old woman made them for the Fritzies, you idiot! To soften their hearts."

"Why do you always spoil everything?"

"I do it out of love for the human race. What happened after you ate the jam tarts?"

"I walked through the streets and stopped in front of the houses of my friends and relatives. I strolled along the main street, and stared into the closed windows of all those fine houses. I whistled an aria from Mozart's "German Dances." Then I sat in Kalamegdan Park on all the benches where I had sat with Zlata."

"Wren, the thing I hate most in the world is banality. And sentiment."

"And you don't think you're banal?"

"I am. That's why I often despise myself, why I'm often sad. I no longer dig up things from the past."

"I'll relive my whole life tonight, when I'm alone."

"Do you really think your lofty feelings are worth it?"

"Well, they're life, Bora."

"They're junk, shit! There's much more to life."

"What do you mean?"

"The hard things. The times when you were hurt, when someone beat you, when you got syphilis."

"Yes, when I believed that you were the only person in whom I could confide. And you said without hesitation, like a professor of V.D., 'a classic case of syphilis'! Nothing to worry about. In Latin it's called *lues*. I was much more ashamed than frightened. I couldn't button up my trousers. What happened after that, well, it's best not to talk about it." Wren took his head in his hands and leaned on the table, his eyes filled with tears. If there was one person he adored, to whom he was devoted, it was Bora. He followed Bora around like a dog. And here he was, spitting on all his feelings!

A soldier took a sturgeon out of his bag and offered it to them: "The last fish of freedom, gentlemen. I caught it last night while on sentry duty. You won't eat such fish again until the war's over, or maybe never. Of course everything costs twice as much this evening, and I'm not taking paper money—it burns too easily, gentlemen!"

Tričko shooed him away. A woman by the name of Dara came up to him. Tričko had described her to Bora and Wren once as a colonel's wife, a beauty, and "a real European lady."

"Tričko, my darling, you're alive?!" She sat down between Tričko and Bora Jackpot, whose face darkened at the sight of this heavily made up old hag draped with furs. So this was Tričko's marvelous "European lady"!

"I was in the fortress prison cells," muttered Tričko, turning red.

"Thank God you survived. I've endured all the air raids in Belgrade. I can't go to a village, even for a wedding. In fact, I can't live outside Belgrade, so let them blow me up with my poor cat. Just think, Tričko, poor Cica was killed on the street. She got scared, rushed outside, and that was it. That gray airplane with the black crosses, flying up there peacefully like a bumblebee and turning around as if waltzing, with Belgrade on fire—simply horrible! I hear the Fritzies are crossing over tonight."

"Who told you that, madam?" interrupted Bora Jackpot sternly. "Don't you know that I could shoot you for blabbing like this?"

"Stop acting like Vojvoda Stepa, Sergeant! If they don't cross the Sava and the Danube tonight, they will tomorrow. I'm no less patriotic than you, gentlemen. That's why, on this last night or last night but one, I want to offer you the pleasure for which crowns have fallen. You're nice, slim, young boys." She smiled.

Tričko was ashamed, and Wren frowned in disgust. This lady reminded Wren of Fanika, the singer who had ruined his life. But Bora suddenly changed his tone: "Are you offering us blondes or brunettes?"

"I've several wonderful friends who are afraid to be alone tonight. All women from good families. Their beds are in the cellar so you needn't be afraid. They'll be saved tonight, and you'll be lucky. No one in the world can hug like a frightened woman. Why are you frowning, little one?" she said, holding out her hand to Wren.

"How can you think of such things, madam?" asked Tričko. "We have to be in the trenches tonight."

"The Fritzies attack at dawn. Until then, why, have a good time. You don't get much out of life from your head. Life is best tasted in the dark. Isn't that right?" she said, smiling at Bora Jackpot.

"Madam, I'm from Belgrade. Please don't make me hate my own birthplace tonight!" interrupted Wren in genuine anger.

"Why are you so sensitive, for goodness sake? It's for kindhearted, sisterly reasons, because you're pals of Tričko's, that I want you to enjoy yourselves tonight. It might be your last night. You have a fine head on you." She stretched out her hand to caress Wren, but he moved away from the table.

"Leave him alone, madam," said Bora." "He's madly in love and engaged to be married. But we two could do with something."

"We have to be at the battalion headquarters at eight, Bora, and from there we go straight to the trenches," warned Tričko, who was anxious to get away as soon as possible.

But Bora Jackpot waved his hand and began to talk with Dara about the ladies who were afraid of spending this night alone.

The café proprietor brought them coffee and brandy. Tričko paid and urged Bora to leave. Bora drank his coffee and then asked Dara, "Do you have someone who can fall in love before daybreak? Don't lie to me! I'm a gambler and lies don't sit well with me!"

Smiling broadly, Dara moved closer to him, pressed her knee against his, and told him about a widow who could "fall in love in a flash."

A voice rose above the clamor: "I tell you, my fellow citizens, no one can survive in Belgrade!"

Wren thought of the last night in Skoplje just before they left for the front, when in a drunken state he'd taken the singer away from his friend Danilo and contracted syphilis, but had been too ashamed to consult a doctor. He had lied to Bora, told him that he had seen the regimental doctor and was taking medication. In fact he was treating himself with various infusions, but without success. He was in such despair that on a number of occasions it had seemed easier to die than to have his family and fiancée find out about the disease. And since he hadn't cured himself, that summer he had broken off his engagement to the girl he had been in love with for three years. Recently the disease had suddenly become worse. He imagined himself full of pus and suffering from progressive paralysis and insanity. "Well, Nietzsche went mad and died of syphilis. Even men of genius go mad, you idiot!" So Bora had said in his characteristic fashion, trying to comfort him. Two days ago Wren had sent farewell letters to his parents and sisters in Leskovac, and to his comrades and friends. They were short letters, written in the heroic vein, saying how proud and happy he was that history would let him give his life for Belgrade. But today he had been terribly frightened that he might be killed; of course he must die in a charge, so that all who knew him would hear how he had been killed. His thoughts dwelt pleasantly on how they would recount the story of his death. Perhaps what moved him most was the thought that after the war his professor at the Prague Conservatory, Vaclav Prohaska, would talk about his best pupil, a Serb of genius who had died a heroic death for his country. In the past few days he had often delivered this speech to himself, embellishing it with grandiose and moving words.

A woman came up to them with a suitcase she could hardly carry. She said in a hoarse voice: "Gentlemen, I'm buying watches, rings, knives, cigarette cases, and all the objects that warriors and martyrs don't need. The army warehouses are burning. No more rations. For those objects you don't need, gentlemen, I'll pay you in homemade sausages, bacon, sugar, coffee, and canned food from England."

Tričko pushed the woman away, but he couldn't put off Naja, who told his fortune whenever she met him in a local café.

"Now, children, let me see what happens to you tomorrow. God would bring live worms out of my eyes and ears for charging you tonight, if I didn't have to. Now a whore won't show herself till she gets paid, so toss it in my bosom, the smallest change you have. Do you want the cards, or shall I read your hand?"

"Read my hand," said Wren, stretching out his palm.

The gypsy stared into his eyes and then at his palm: "You needn't be afraid, my boy. You're going to have a long life. And money and fame and love and power. You'll have everything. And you'll get married three times, you billy goat!"

Wren laughed disbelievingly and pulled his palm away from Naja's hand. "That's enough!"

Tričko refused to have his fortune told and grew despondent. Naja promised all the soldiers long life and many children. She was lying this evening to comfort them.

"I'm looking for a third for poker," cried an officer from another table. "Ten dinars a chip!"

"Shame on you! Children are whimpering under the ruins, and you're getting drunk here!" shouted a woman with a scabbed face, holding a child in her arms.

Wren could stand it no longer. He had barely crossed the threshold of the café when he stopped and shuddered, sensing the presence of the invisible Danube, that immense, dark, icy stretch of water which tormented him with a fear he hadn't yet felt during the war. Wherever he was during the last few days, he felt the river's breath and the chill of that water with its abundance of fish, shot through with decaying matter from the forests on the Banat shore. "I'll drown, that's for sure!" he muttered to himself. The wind blew through him, bringing with it the horror of the turbulent water. "But we aren't crossing the Danube, we're waiting for them on this bank! Why am I afraid?" He walked slowly into the darkness, toward the Danube quay.

Lieutenant Kirhner came into the café with Lieutenant Kezić and two soldiers. Kirhner, formerly a second lieutenant in the Austrian army, was now commanding the Srem volunteers. One of the soldiers with him was carrying an armful of rifles, the other a case of ammunition. As the noise died down, Kirhner shouted: "Here are rifles and ammunition for you civilians! The army will defend the Serbian capital. You defend your homes and your backsides!"

Some of the civilians came right up for the rifles and ammunition; even the woman with a child in her arms took a rifle, but then she threw it down. A young boy picked it up and filled his pockets with ammunition. Lieutenant Kirhner clapped him on the shoulder encouragingly.

After taking the addresses of those "wonderful women" from Dara, Bora Jackpot and Tričko set out toward Little Kalemegdan. The street was full of ghostly light from the fires. The air smelled of burning wool. Women moaned and wept.

They reached the Golden Carp Café. Bora Jackpot tried to slip into 26 Dobračina, the first door on the left, the address given him by Dara, but his platoon commander, Lieutenant Jevtić, seized him by the arm: "Luković, I told you not to go into town tonight!"

Wren piped up: "How can you think of whores when Belgrade is burning!"

"I'll die of grief, you idiot! I'd betray Belgrade for someone's embrace tonight!"

"You buried your uncle today. It's disgusting!"

"My uncle would have loved me for it."

Wren pushed him through the open door of the Golden Carp. The battalion commander, Major Dragutin Gavrilović, was standing beside a table spread for a banquet, gravely greeting the officers. Behind him was a band whose singer was sadly watching the officers whom the commander invited to sit down without regard for rank or seniority.

"A funeral feast for the living—that's a good joke!" whispered Bora to Wren, sitting down between him and Lieutenant Jevtić.

Major Gavrilović stood at the head of the table and tapped his glass with a knife:

"Gentlemen, I haven't invited you to a funeral feast, although the enemy issued a death notice for Belgrade today. I've invited you to a social evening, to eat well, drink, and be merry. Tomorrow will bring glory for some, disgrace for others, and a day of trouble for all. You know what your duties are tomorrow, and I know what mine are. For this evening at the Golden Carp I issue the following orders: no talk of the dead or the enemy; complete freedom to joke and sing, without regard to rank. We'll start with hot brandy. And I'll ask the band to play in turn the songs we agree on." He took off his cap and sat down.

"Splendid!" said Bora Jackpot, jumping up. They all looked at him sternly. "Simply splendid!"

"Let's drink to each other's health, Sergeant!" said Major Gavrilović, walking toward him with a glass. "Your name's Luković, but you're called Jackpot, aren't you?"

The café owner and two soldiers set down trays with glasses of hot brandy. Bora Jackpot took a glass, remembered his Uncle Voja and his funeral, rose, and said with deep feeling: "Thank you, Major. There's nothing more moving than going under in style!"

The music began to play softly.

"If you go under in style, you don't go under, Luković. People who can do that go on living."

"Am I allowed to contradict you?"

"Yes, but only with a better joke than mine."

"I don't know how to joke, Major."

"Say it seriously and quickly, then we can empty our glasses!"

"Seriously?" Bora reflected for a moment, but didn't dare continue.

"One thinks seriously in quiet and solitude," said Major Gavrilović.

"I'm fighting for quiet and solitude, sir."

"Tonight you must decide on some greater war aim. Yes, Luković, you must strive for something greater than quiet and solitude. Cheers!" he said, clinking Bora's glass. "Cheers!" he repeated, turning to the whole company. Then he downed his hot brandy and returned to his seat.

The music got louder. Bora Jackpot pondered his war aim. It was banal! Patriotic ideals meant little to him, but he didn't want to admit this to anybody.

Wren was despondent, suddenly bothered by those letters about dying for Belgrade which he had sent to his parents and friends. Weren't they simply lies? Did he really have to die because he couldn't bear that his father and mother would find out that their ideal son was infected with syphilis and would die in pain and madness?

Lieutenant Jevtić whispered to Bora: "We've known each other for nearly a year, but I never knew your goal was quiet and solitude! A typical petit bourgeois ideal!"

"I'm sorry not to have disappointed you sooner, sir. But would you answer an important question for me? Will there be fear under socialism?"

"What kind of fear?"

"Fear of living. Real fear."

"If you want to discuss the subject seriously, Bora, fear is our constant companion because our lives are not free, they are threatened. When social conditions change, man will change, too. Fear of living will disappear."

"Can you socialists offer stronger proof? Proof from man himself, not from society?"

"Proof doesn't matter if we don't think of man dialectically, Luković."

"I hate thinking. I was joking. I understand it all." Bora drained his glass.

"I don't get it," said Jevtić. "Belgrade is burning like a hayloft, people are wailing in the town, and here we are having a good time. I'm ashamed."

Bora Jackpot fell silent, because in fact he didn't feel ashamed. The café owner served chicken broth, followed by stuffed cabbage, roast meat, and pumpkin pie, and constantly refilled the glasses with wine. The band played without pause, the singer sang hoarsely. The noise grew louder. Those who were cheerful plied with drink the people who weren't. Bora Jackpot looked at them all and wondered who would be killed the next day—the cheerful ones or the gloomy ones? This distinction didn't correspond to that between courage and cowardice; there were cowards among both those who were singing and those who sat in dejected silence. In any case this dinner at the Golden Carp wouldn't provide matter for poetry. There was no Christ or Judas here, no Prince Lazar or Miloš Obilić. Fate was not sitting at this table. All that could be said was that some were having their last supper, cramming themselves with stuffed cabbage and gulping down red wine for the last time. Perhaps he himself was gnawing a rib of suckling pig, his favorite dish, for the last time. "Last time" gave the succulent ribs great significance. The same words made life both important and meaningless. What had he to regret at age twenty-two, when he hadn't cared much about anything except a future which he would never experience? Who would mourn him except his mother? His few friends, if they survived, would forget him in peacetime. He could certainly have loved Dušanka—he couldn't forget that face on which everything was visible—but not even she would remember one wounded man she had made happy. Apart from fear of pain and the most commonplace instinct for life, what was there to prevent him from performing some brave deed tomorrow which would merit a street being named after him in Belgrade? Stupid, banal vanity! Because of those shells aimed at the funeral, because of the mutilation of his dead Uncle Voja, because of the death notice of Belgrade, for banality one had to fight and kill. And be killed? No lies! There was no such thing as a good reason for dying.

Major Gavrilović raised his glass to Bora with a smile. Bora smiled back and drank, wondering what Gavrilović's aim in the war was. He stared at the singer: for some, this old hen would be the last woman they would look at. *This slut represents the feminine part of our country,* he thought, *the so-called more beautiful half of the world for whom we will give our lives tomorrow. Yes, this tired, frightened whore has in her what all the women we love and adore have; the thing for which we would betray, kill, and die; for which I would swim across the Danube tonight, if Dušanka were waiting for me on the other side.*

The merriment sounded convincing; there were fewer gloomy faces. The officers joined the singer and she grew more lively. The musicians played with greater fervor.

Lieutenant Jevtić changed places with Bora to show Wren a photo of his wife and little girl:

"The day I fled to Serbia they took my wife to Tuzla and put her in prison. I don't know if she's still alive. My wife's sister took my daughter Senka, she's five years old. This is her sock." He took a little white sock out of his wallet and gazed at it tearfully. "The evening the news came that Princip had killed Franz Ferdinand, I fled across the Drina. But first, I stood over my sleeping child, looking at her long enough to last me a lifetime; the room was airless and the bed was swimming in my tears. I couldn't move. Then I saw this sock on a chair and took it."

Bora Jackpot was disgusted by Jevtić's story about the sock. He turned away from him and thought that soon a big shell might fall on the Golden Carp—a direct hit! He emptied his glass and turned to his commanding officer:

"Forget about the war tonight, sir. Be a good socialist and let me return to the platoon by twelve o'clock. They won't attack us before midnight."

"What do you plan to do in town tonight? It's chaos."

"I have a date."

"A date tonight? With the dead and wounded under the ruins, fires blazing, and people wailing! Are you serious, Bora?"

"Why not? What's more human than love, or more honorable than tenderness? What's more courageous in Belgrade tonight than the fervent embrace of a woman from a good family."

"You're drunk, Bora. You're not to go anywhere."

Bora Jackpot emptied one more glass of wine and went up to Major Gavrilović: "May I, sir, as a sergeant, ask you a question? What is your aim in the war?"

Gavrilović reflected for a moment, then said: "Among other things, Sergeant, it's to conquer people who believe that their name, religion, and power give them the right to despise my name and religion and everything I am."

"That's indeed admirable. But that goal is unattainable, sir. Those people are much stronger. We can only sacrifice ourselves."

"You're not suggesting that we should allow the Austrians and Germans to stroll into the ruins of Belgrade tomorrow?"

Bora summoned his courage and said: "Surely, sir, you don't think people are contemptible for all they do in war?"

"No, I don't. Your thinking is brave on this occasion, Luković."

"I think my thoughts are sadder than yours, sir."

"What do you mean?"

"Only that we deserve scorn for what we're doing. Just imagine, sir, what people will think of us a hundred years from now."

"I don't believe our descendants will find us ridiculous. No, I don't."

"You believe our descendants will admire us?"

"Perhaps they'll envy us because we suffered so much. Perhaps they'll also envy us because we died nobly. How do you know?"

Bora was confused; never before had he heard such ideas from an officer. But he wouldn't give in right off, so the words flew out of him like a counterblow:

"Do you really believe that we'll win, sir?"

Gavrilović put his hand on Bora's shoulder: "Only the weaker side can be victorious in war, my boy. Do you understand?"

"Not really. I'll think about it tonight. I certainly won't understand you tomorrow."

"You and I both carry our jokes a bit too far, Luković. Come on, drink and be merry. What song would you like?"

Bora leaned toward him and whispered: "Give me permission to go into town, sir. I'll come back to the platoon by midnight."

"Off you go. But see you're in position at the sound of the first cannon."

Bora wanted to squeeze his hand gratefully, but his joy suddenly clouded: *He's being generous because he sees death in my eyes,* he thought.

"Listen, young man. You can survive this war only through hope or by sheer pigheadedness. I mean, survive honorably. Now go wherever you want to."

For a moment Bora remained motionless behind the commanding officer, who summoned the band leader and began to sing:

> Oh my sweetheart dear,
> My fountain of delight,
> I left behind my saber
> Where I stayed with you last night.

Bora Jackpot walked out slowly into the rain and darkness. The sky above Belgrade glowed with a restless, sweeping light. "I'll be killed," he said aloud. Lenka. Dobračina 26, first door on the left. Panting, he struck a match, found the number, and entered the passage. His heartbeats would blow the house to bits. What if she was ugly, repulsive, and dirty? It was dark, he would run away. No, he would not! He lit a match and knocked at the first door on the left. Not a sound. He knocked more loudly. Perhaps she had fallen asleep? He knocked really hard.

"Who is it?" shouted a man's voice.

Bora Jackpot's legs gave way under him.

"Who is it, please?"

"I'm looking for Lenka."

"You're too late, brother. Lenka will be busy until the Fritzies arrive."

These words brought him to his senses. "Fuck you, brother!" he cried.

He sat down on the stairs. He was disgusted. After a while he pulled himself together, sneaked out into the street, and set off toward his home in Kosančičev Venac. Encountering a fire, he turned back. He leaned against a tree and stared at the flames: on Suvobor and on the Drina he had been defending his homeland. Here in Belgrade he was defending himself. Was he a worthy war goal for himself? He set out into the wind, walking toward Little Kalemegdan, slipping downhill on the muddy cobblestones. The fires lit up the shell holes. He stopped dead. The wind was carrying the sound of quiet music from the Danube: violins and double basses. He couldn't believe his ears—it must be the wind. He set off again, his knees shaking. The music came closer. It was the song that Major Gavrilović had sung that night. Was he making the rounds of the trenches? No: it was only his memory of the music in the Golden Carp. A sentry challenged him: "Stop! The password!" He had forgotten the password. He gave his name, explained himself, implored. It was no use. He'd have to lie down in the mud and wait for the change of sentries. This mud too was Belgrade, something of his. As a child he had run barefoot over these cobbles to swim in the Danube. He would never tread on them again. The music grew more distant, carried down the Danube by the wind.

Vojvoda Putnik was drawing rosebuds on a piece of paper and thinking about hatred as a factor in survival. The sheet of paper was full of sprays and branches of rosebuds, perfectly drawn and shaded. *Brave men will fight for love, but, driven by hatred, all men will fight. In times of storms and tempests which pull up a nation's roots and destroy a man inside his own skin, hatred is the force which gathers and unites all energies, the force which makes survival possible. Hatred is our strongest defense in the face of great evil. In a fighting man, only hatred is not shaken by either disparity of strength with the enemy or the conditions of the fight. Or by the outcome, for that matter—and that's the most important thing of all. With hatred there's nothing a man dare not do, no limit to his endurance. But do I dare summon the Serbian army to hatred?*

Colonel Živko Pavlović clicked his heels in front of him. This man, the most sensible in the High Command, looked thoughtful. Putnik again lowered his eyes to the paper on which he was drawing rosebuds, and said:

"Have you received reports from all the divisions?"

"Yes, sir."

"Give me a summary." Putnik did not look at him, but stopped moving his pencil.

"All our positions from Višegrad on the Drina to Golubac on the

Danube were pounded by the enemy today with at least a thousand cannon. Forty-two-caliber cannon. The bombardment lasted three and a half hours. Belgrade and Smederovo have been leveled, as have all the villages along the Danube, the Sava, and the Drina. Shrapnel from the shells has driven the soldiers crazy."

Putnik laid down his pencil, pushed away the cat with the tip of his boot, and looked attentively at his anxious assistant. "Have they crossed the Sava or the Danube anywhere?"

"Not yet. But troops and landing craft are massed all along the banks."

"That means they'll cross tomorrow. Today they were sizing us up. It was a test of strength, a psychological attack. That's what you must say in our statement for the Allies and the newspapers. Do you have today's report about the landing of the Allies in Salonika?"

"No news since yesterday's landing of some French and English battalions there. But I have a report about preparations to receive the Allies in Serbia: from Djevdjelija to Paraćin they're putting up triumphal arches in all stations and town centers. Meanwhile, Mr. Pašić ignores the deceptions by the Allies and continues to betray Serbia. That's what he's doing for our defense."

Putnik frowned: until now none of his subordinates had ventured to oppose the government and complain about Pašić to his face. He looked out the window: the reddening crown of a pear tree was lit by the electric light bulb. He looked for a long time at that lovely autumnal fire, then turned back to his assistant: "Colonel, do you remember how the Greeks defeated the Persians?"

"Yes, sir."

"Good. Then tonight please tell the officers of the High Command how the Athenians, though weaker, defeated the invincible army of Xerxes. Wake me up as soon as they cross the Sava and the Danube."

Putnik was alone once again. He thought of the frontiers of Serbia and saw a garland of fire. Black darkness pouring forth from Bulgaria and from the heavens. That day Heckendorf and Mackensen had infused the Serbian positions with dread. *My soldiers don't fear any man, but they're afraid of machines. That fear, too, can be overcome by hate. Yes, hate. And by a fear greater than fear for one's own neck. The hour has come to use the children to strengthen the hearts of the soldiers. Tomorrow male children must be gathered together in the regional command post, and brought out in front of the army. Every fighting man must bear in mind that, to the last Serbian trench, he*

will be defending his descendants and everything he has. And that
every foot of Serbian soil is his hearth and home.

Putnik wheezed—the onset of an asthma attack. He took some medicine, thrust back his head, and summoned the strength to pull the telephone toward him: "Get me the Prime Minister at once. Good evening, Prime Minister. Yes, I know it's late, but we no longer have time for formalities."

"I hear that Belgrade has suffered a terrible blow. Do you have precise information about it, Vojvoda?"

"They were only sizing us up. Testing their artillery and our spirit. We're expecting the real attack tomorrow."

"Today we broke off diplomatic relations with Bulgaria, Vojvoda. You must be prepared for that war, too."

Putnik fell silent, hoping to hear something more, but all that came through was the tinny echo of the wires. He took a deep breath: "Well, you know what I think about the outcome of that war."

"Yes, I do. But England and France are asking us only to hold out for three weeks, until their armies arrive. They've promised us fifteen divisions. The Russians are preparing to attack Bulgaria. Please tell the army that."

"Do you believe those promises, Prime Minister?"

"I must believe them, Vojvoda. What will happen to Serbia if the Allies don't come to our aid? What would you and I do without that faith? So please tell the army before daybreak that the Allies are on their way, that the French will arrive in Niš in three days. I've ordered the civil authorities to prepare a reception."

"The worst suffering comes from deception, as you well know. Prime Minister, today we have the right to call upon the army and the people to make the supreme sacrifice. But we have no right to lie to them."

"We aren't being judged today, Vojvoda."

"Yes we are, Prime Minister."

"Those whom Fate has ordained to lead a nation are judged only at the end. And by only one judge. Victory justifies even the greatest crimes committed in its name. In the face of defeat we can't redeem ourselves even by wise and good deeds. That's the way it's always been."

"I've called you to suggest a complex course of action, for which the two of us would have to take responsibility. . . . Prime Minister?"

"If it's something complex, Vojvoda, it would be better if more of us shared it."

"There's no time to share our burden, Prime Minister. We must do something immediately that will convince every Serbian soldier that he's defending his own family and possessions. That as soon as he stops fighting, he loses everything."

"I didn't hear you clearly, Vojvoda. The wires are buzzing."

Putnik doubted Pašić would see things his way. But he coughed, paused for a moment, and continued: "We must do everything that our enemies cannot do. I shall immediately order all male children fourteen years of age and over to be gathered in the regional command posts in the next twenty-four hours and taken out in front of the army. Can you hear me, Prime Minister? Hello, Niš!"

"I hear you very well, Vojvoda. I think we should collect all the children, female as well as male. Everything that can move should be brought out in front of the troops—people, animals, institutions, government, and property—anything that can move or be carried."

"That could cause chaos, which would be a disaster, Prime Minister. Disorder in the rear is a worse enemy than a hostile army."

"Never mind chaos. Today it must be made clear to every Serbian man and woman that in this war we can only vanquish or perish. So as I say, bring out everything. Food and property, museums and libraries, books, icons, archives. And let the convicts and lunatics be brought out, too, to meet the enemy."

"What did you say, Prime Minister?"

"Convicts and lunatics, too. The government will issue an order to that effect tomorrow. Let me know as soon as the attack begins," he said, hanging up.

Putnik was frightened by Pašić's intention and his firmness. Courage would be impossible in such disorder. He imagined the roads leading to the south thronged with people in flight. A solid mass that had come to a halt. Where would the military baggage trains go? He dialed a number on the telephone:

"Get me the commanding officer of Belgrade. . . . Did the walls of the Belgrade fortress hold out, Živković? Yes, I know. They were only sizing us up. At dawn they'll shell Belgrade to cover their crossing." He was defending his country and freedom, but must he nourish the army with hatred?

"Many large buildings have been destroyed, and factories and warehouses set on fire. They destroyed a third of our artillery. They've cut our communications. I must tell you, Vojvoda, that they've smashed all our searchlights and we can't see what's happening on the other side of the Sava and the Danube. Belgrade has seen the end of the world this afternoon."

"That, Živković, was simply the Germans testing our spirit, our strength. Please convey this order to all the officers and men in the Belgrade Defense Force: 'The enemy who is destroying and burning Belgrade . . .' " He paused. How could he formulate an order about hatred? "My orders to the Belgrade Defense Force for the seventh of October, 1915 are as follows: 'You are to convince our enemy that Belgrade is a greater city than Vienna, Budapest, or Berlin.' Yes, write that down. One sentence. Keep in contact with Živko Pavlović. I hope you have a quiet night, Živković. . . . Operator, get me the commander of the Third Army. . . . Can you see the Danube tonight, Šturm?"

"All you can see in the valley are fires, Vojvoda. They've set Smederovo ablaze, too. The wind is blowing hard and spreading the fire. If it doesn't stop soon, I don't believe that my compatriot and schoolmate Mackensen will cross the Danube tomorrow."

"Believe me, he will. And you must wait for him in the wind. Your schoolmate Mackensen is a military leader who wins glory by defeating his foes in both good weather and bad. Now I want to make the following addition to today's orders to the Third Army: 'The bank of the Danube is to be defended with hatred.' No, wait a minute, Šturm."

"I understand, Vojvoda. I've got the third draft entrenched on the bank. I've told Kajafa not to withdraw a single platoon without my consent."

"I'll dictate it from the beginning. Write this down, Šturm: 'I order the Third Army to defend the first foot of Serbian soil with the same perseverance and strength as if it were the last.' Full stop. Tell the troops this before dawn. Take care of yourself in the wind, Šturm! . . . Now get me the commander of the First Army. . . . Putnik speaking. Our uncertainty is at an end, Mišić."

"Yes, I'm relieved. Where do matters stand with the Allies, Vojvoda?"

"Are you asking me that question for the men in the trenches or for you people at headquarters?"

"I want to know how long Pašić can deceive the High Command— and the Serbian people."

"Mišić, you and I, not the Allies, are waiting for the enemy. I called to give you the following orders: 'The First Army must prove to our enemies that the Drina is now three times as wide as it was last year, and that the Sava is the biggest river in Europe.' That's all."

The smoldering fire in the stable and hayloft of the neighboring courtyard was fanned into flame by the wind, and illuminated Bogdan Dragović as he stood in the rain. He wanted to move closer to the pigsty, where it was dry, but the soldier wouldn't allow it:

"You're a suspicious character, Sergeant. I have to keep you where I can see you."

"What were you in civilian life, soldier?"

"I was a peasant. What else?"

Doesn't it matter to this peasant that I'm tied up because I tried to protect his fellow peasants from being beaten? In the reflected light of the fire Bogdan looked at his guard, a man ready to kill him. Did his opposition to Major Dunjić mean nothing? If he were shot, would these people regard him as a hotheaded fool? Did they think that way because of military discipline, because of their oath to their country, or because of fear for their own necks? Surely people didn't think that this oath justified everything? It was Sava Marić who had tied up his hands, a brave and sensible man, whom everyone considered honorable. He had cut the rods for the beating, too, and then tied Bogdan's hands, all in the name of that cunning which for him was the greatest power of all and could never be dishonorable if it saved one's life. Maybe it wasn't dishonorable to confront force with cunning, perhaps it was a life-preserving wisdom. How he hated this world.

Heavy shells fell above the village. The wind blew with great force, accompanied by rain. He asked his guard: "Do you know why I'm tied up in this pigsty, soldier?"

"I've heard something, but I don't know. It has nothing to do with me."

"Why not?"

"My orders are to make sure you don't run away. It's none of my business why you're here."

"I'm here and will be tried by a court-martial tomorrow because I tried to save your hungry, barefoot companions from being beaten by Dunjić. That's why, soldier."

"Sergeant, I'm on guard duty. Even if you were King Peter, I'd shoot you if you tried any funny business."

"For God's sake, soldier, I'm not a spy. I haven't embezzled the regimental funds. I haven't killed a Serbian soldier or betrayed my country."

"Sergeant, I don't give a damn about what you have or haven't done. You're under arrest. You may be as innocent as Jesus Christ, but I'll put a bullet between your shoulder blades if I have to."

Bogdan shuddered. This was a man who could crucify Christ and murder a child. Yet he was downtrodden—a peasant, a poor man to be fleeced by landlords and beaten by officers. He himself had become a socialist believing in men like this one, in their feeling for justice, their readiness to fight for their freedom! He remembered Gavrilo Stanković and the pipe he carried in his pocket. He wanted to smoke that pipe which had belonged to the aristocrat-revolutionary Anatole Žarov. Žarov had been cut to pieces with a saber by the son of Žarov's coachman, a member of the Czarist police, during the St. Petersburg uprising. He remembered Gavrilo's story about the pipe. And every word Gavrilo had spoken before he committed suicide on the big, white bed in that filthy hospital full of wounded men and typhus patients.

"How can you talk like that? Aren't you my comrade? Do you really think it honorable and decent to shoot a fellow man, a brother Serb whose only crime is trying to defend his hungry, barefoot soldiers from Dunjić's rods? Why, they'll be killed for the fatherland tomorrow, along with you! Doesn't that mean anything?"

"What would happen to our country if we soldiers started to question whether the orders given us are wise and honorable?"

"If you did start to question the orders given you and those who do nothing but give you orders, you'd get full rations of hardtack and you'd have boots and overcoats. You wouldn't be giving your lives for bloodsuckers!"

"God forbid that we start questioning the people who rule us! Then the State and the army and everything else would go to the devil. So don't talk to me against the State."

"But I told you, man, I was defending innocent people!"

"There are no innocent people in this country. My orders are that you're not to talk with the guard on duty."

Bogdan fell silent. Yes, Sava Marić was right. All the evils of this world were eternal. This peasant didn't want to think; he believed that it was easier to endure than to resist. Confronted with Sava's wisdom and his experience with the guard, what were science and philosophy? Where was their validity? His own great faith in the people, in the poor, was all delusion. *I'll run away,* he thought. *Yes, I'll run away. Let them kill me in flight. I'll jump on this vile creature, hit him hard, knock him down, trample him!*

"Don't take a step, Sergeant! I'll kill you!"

Bogdan swore at the man and vowed to remember this night. He decided to wait for the guard to be relieved, then run away. Perhaps the next one would be less disgusting, perhaps he might be a man who could think.

The new guard was no better. Still, he did suggest that Bogdan take shelter from the rain and get some sleep, since it was after midnight. The guard then sat down by the door of the enclosure with his rifle between his knees and soon began to snore, although shells were exploding above the village every ten minutes. Bogdan walked over to him, bent down to see whether he was really asleep, then walked slowly out of the pigsty.

"Halt! The password!" yelled the sentry in front of the battalion headquarters.

Bogdan rushed down the lane into the darkness. The sentry fired three bullets, one of which buzzed past his ear. He disappeared behind a bend and fled through the village toward the fields, slipping on the muddy road. He stood still and listened: no one was pursuing him. There was a smell of smoke, a dog whined, the wind rattled the fences. Where could he go? First he must free his hands. The worst punishment of all was to be bound. He went into a courtyard and knocked on the door with his boot. A woman opened the door at once, as if she had been waiting for him, and let him into a room with a fireplace. She poked the fire in the hearth and the light showed a bed on the floor on which lay a boy and two little girls, fully dressed with their shoes on. He asked the woman to cut the belt with a knife and free his hands. She quickly released his hands and offered him some milk. Sitting down on a three-legged stool, he drained the bowl of milk, then said: "Why don't you run away with the children? Tomorrow the Germans will cross the Danube and destroy the village with their cannon."

"Where would I flee to? If it's our fate, we'll die in the house."

"Where's your husband?"

"My husband and my brother are at the front, near Belgrade. I have some cheese and bread if you're hungry."

Where could he go from here? He must flee the village before it got light. But first he would write a letter to Milena. This woman was goodhearted, she would mail it as soon as the mails restored service.

He poked the fire to fan the live coals to flame, took a notebook out of his pocket, and began to write on a kneading board. Not a single word he knew seemed right for addressing the girl he loved.

I don't know where to go. I've run away from a court-martial. They'll condemn me because I couldn't humiliate my own soldiers. Before dawn I'll decide whether to be an army deserter or agree to be shot as a patriot. It's after midnight and I'm thinking of my mother and you, deeply unhappy that you have to live in such a cruel world. I want to cause you as little pain as possible. Is there such a thing as an honorable death in this land of death? I no longer understand anything. Everything I knew and believed has been obscured, and the faith I had on Suvobor, and as a prisoner and in the hospital in Valjevo, is extinguished. From the other end of the world I hear advice from Gavrilo Stanković, but I can't put it to use. My whole life is pain. A slave is free to dream and use his imagination. He can fight and struggle, he has hope. He can be cunning and wise. But a man who has been humiliated can only hate. Hate and be a traitor.

As he wrote the last word his hand grew rigid. The windows shook from the explosion of a shell nearby.

"Have some food and then do your writing," said the woman.

Her gentle voice made him tremble. He turned around to see her face. It was full of anxiety. Anxiety and kindness. She was the people, too. That was the other truth. She was the country. He wanted to touch her hand, to caress her, to embrace her like a sister. He shivered.

She put some bread and cheese in front of him and covered up the little boy, who was kicking in his sleep and grinding his teeth.

Bogdan put his head in his hands. Where could he go from here?

What he had written to Milena wasn't true. Nothing of this night should be hers. Let her remember their convalescence and their mutual delight in the spring. Their hair had fallen out while they were ill, and every morning they'd measured each other's hair with pieces of thread to see how much it had grown in the night. But this night was his alone, his torment at being branded a traitor when day dawned.

Close by a shell exploded.

"Why do I exist, and why is there such torment?" whispered Bora Jackpot as he dragged himself through the darkness and the wind toward the Danube. The commander of the guard had recognized him after he had lain on the cobblestones for nearly two hours, and had allowed him to go to his platoon beside the railway.

One has to wage war and kill for senseless principles. What kind of people are we? First there's the national, political, territorial questions, the real reason for a European war, and then the question of under what flag, under whose crown, I should gobble my food, shit, and make love to Lenka. And be free not to do what somebody wants, to swear at a man who swears at me, and to despise fools. To be what I am, as that good-natured Major Gavrilović said this evening. Was I born to be killed defending my country? Do we need a country where everybody born in it must perish? That's the question my war aims depend on, and my hope, and my endurance of suffering before death. Yet what really troubles me is which second in all eternity is mine— which? "But it's your country, all Serbia is yours!" you exclaim with patriotic fervor. What can I do if I don't feel tonight that Serbia is mine? Mine is what I feel belongs only to me. You patriotic gentlemen must accept that. I don't want to suffer and perish for the land of my fathers or for the freedom of somebody's descendants. Who sentenced me to that? Who made death my fate, convinced the entire Cadet Battalion that they must go singing to their deaths? In this land of plum trees, what apples of sin have we eaten knowingly?

I know what you'll say: we didn't start the war, we're defending ourselves, we aren't attacking Vienna but defending Belgrade. And with that fact, my dear sir, my intellect must come to rest. I must think no further. What if I can't do it? Not what if I won't, but if I can't. Then you'll smile at me in pity as you did tonight and say: "In that case, young man, you're a traitor and a scoundrel!" Ah, one can betray only something one believes in, you wily patriot. As a traitor and scoundrel I can think logically and ask what you want me to remember, when things are going so badly for me. I put to you this logical question: Should we defend ourselves even when we can't? Must we die simply to demonstrate dignity and honor? Is that our national duty? To whom do we demonstrate this dignity, confirm this honor, under the shrapnel of forty-two-caliber shells? The German gunners? That can only strengthen the enemy's satisfaction in killing and make their victory more significant. If, among the subjects of Franz Josef and Wilhelm who carry toothed bayonets and have "Gott mit uns" written on their belts, there's someone who sets a high value on honor and dignity, then I suppose our suicidal bravery will arouse in him a deep respect. Must thousands of soldiers—my companions—be blown to bits by shells on Gypsy Island and the banks of the Sava and the Danube, just for national vanity? Why should the Fritzies tear out my guts with their toothed bayonets and fling them onto the Dorćol garbage heap? You can't answer that one, Major! All you have to offer is hope, and mulishness, and your joke that only the weaker side can win. It's poor hope that under a salvo of three hundred guns not a single splinter will split my head open, and that in a rain of bullets not one will hit me.

Pigheadedness in the face of the inevitable is pitiful and ludicrous. With what other hope am I to perish, if I have no hope of life and victory? Hope in the future, if a piece of metal only chops off an arm, a future among survivors with murder in their hearts, or among scoundrels behind the lines, in the cafés and the park in Niš? Or am I to place my hopes in our unification with the men in German uniforms who translated the death notice of Belgrade into our common language, and are ready to hang their flag on King Peter's palace again? I spit on union with them, and on that Great Serbia of the future, that Great Yugoslavia! Or could you be thinking, you old fox, of hope in kings, politicians, generals, and vojvodas who'll rule me again in peacetime according to their laws and rules of military service? Excuse me, sir, but I'm not playing that game! I have no desire for a peace in which one must know their password. Oh, how good it would be, how it would save me, if I couldn't think! Or perhaps you thought, Major, that I'd trust in God and hope for his mercy? Well, I've had some experience of life, and I don't need fifty years to convince myself that the easiest thing of all is to believe in something impossible and senseless. So what are we left with now? There's no great war aim, old man—it's all futile and meaningless.

He stood in the wind under the Prisoners' Tower: reflections from the fires lit up the foaming surface of the Danube and the shore opposite. In that chasm of darkness Austrian and German divisions lay dozing, waiting for the order to attack Belgrade. In that chasm gaped the barrels of their cannon, ready to blow him to pieces. Toothed bayonets were pointed at him. They would tear out his entrails and fling them into the mud. A splendid human invention, the bayonet. The general staff had introduced it into the armaments of a great European nation, whose poets he had studied so he could be a cultured Serb. He mustn't think of that either. If only the prospect of death wouldn't torment him with its secret, with its chill rising from the darkness, from the howling of the wind. This lashing wind, had it slithered down the warm gun barrel, or along the cold surface of the toothed bayonet? It stank of iron. It really did smell of gunpowder and the cutting edge of steel, the breath of the Austro-Hungarian Empire. It was revolting, horrible. But he wanted to breathe it. Yes, he did. It was because of this smell that he wouldn't run away from Belgrade. What drove him to breathe it? What was dragging him to his death?

"Is that you, Sergeant?"

He started as if he had been fired on from the darkness, and shouted: "Who's there?"

"It's me, Šunto Zlatiborac. Lieutenant Jevtić sent me to look for you and bring you to the platoon."

"What's going on?"

"We're waiting for them."

Bora couldn't see him in the darkness. Šunto Zlatiborac was all but mute. He pronounced only a barely comprehensible word now and then and he always stammered. Bora took a closer look at the man: he was tall and bent and looked like Šunto Zlatiborac. He asked him cautiously:

"When did you start to speak properly, Šunto? Without stuttering?"

"I stuttered when I thought I ought to, Sergeant. But not anymore."

Bora continued on his way toward the railway embankment, doubtful whether this man was Šunto Zlatiborac, a soldier who dressed in rags, had neither rifle nor bayonet, and whose real name no one knew. Because of his inability to carry out any order he was called Šunto, "the dumb one," and as he had come from a village on Zlatibor, he was given the surname Zlatiborac. Lieutenant Jevtić, the platoon commander, had taken him as his orderly about two weeks before, so as to rescue him from molestation of various kinds—an action inspired by his socialist sympathies. This thin, lanky, lop-eared man with fair hair had never succeeded in standing at attention properly. And when the order to count off was given, he could never answer correctly, which had caused sergeants to hit him with their sabers and one corporal to give him a broken nose, while his faulty steps on the march had earned him more beatings than the rest of his regiment. So he was labeled an idiot and ordered to chop wood, light the fires, clean the latrines, scour the kitchen cauldrons, wash Corporal Jeremij's feet, and hunt up whores for the soldiers. Šunto Zlatiborac performed these services for his country without a word of protest, with humility and devotion, smiling his broad, foolish smile, even when Second Lieutenant Barjaktarević ordered him to show his cock to his cronies playing cards and drinking, which Šunto did with an even broader smile than usual. This really infuriated Barjaktarević: "See this wild animal from the woods?" he cried. "Damn you, Šunto, where did you get such a big panhandle? God has really loused up. What do you want with such a tool, you old motherfucker? I'll chop it off before the Fritzies take Belgrade, or my name's not Miloš Barjaktarević!"

God knows who I was talking to, thought Bora Jackpot. That blow on the head and the cemetery experience had thrown everything into confusion.

The wind blew from the Danube with a pelting rain. Heavy shells fell on Ram and the surrounding hills, as if carried by the storm. While waiting for the order to take his squad to the Danube, Sava Marić sheltered his old men under a barn in the yard of a peasant house with a high stone wall, which provided protection against both bullets and the wind. They were dry there and they were free to smoke or doze or talk. Sava sat on a sheaf of cornstalks, leaning against a wooden post. He worried about whether his folks at home had brought in the cornstalks and hay from Fox's Hollow, which couldn't be reached with a four-wheeled cart once the rains started, and where the corn, lard, and salt had been hidden so *they* wouldn't find them. His folks wouldn't flee when *they* arrived. While he was on leave last summer he had provided them with a sack of salt and a can of gas, and he agreed with his father and his wife that they shouldn't leave their home whatever violence and misfortune befell them. If Serbia were enslaved, they'd bow to foreign law until a Serbian government was set up again. So he worried about his house, and was torn with grief for his children and the knowledge that his wife wanted him.

Meanwhile the old men were talking:

"Listen, if we have to die, let's die like men. It's been a dog's life, but it's been a man's life, too. We're being sacrificed—no question about that. How can our platoon of old men and two squads of second-drafters defend Ram and the land around it? We'll finish them off! What do you think, men, how much do those shells cost that they fired at us yesterday? Why, my little wound from a splinter, just a little splinter that grazed my shoulder, cost a million! What do you think, how much does a cannon cost? I'll bet you that in one battle our platoon of old geezers burns up more in ammunition than the price of two good grape harvests in our village. Plain as a pikestaff, old man. After the war our taxes will be three times higher than before the war. Somebody will have to pay for the weapons and ammunition, and who but us peasants? The majors and colonels and generals, they all have to be paid for. That freedom, as they call it, is going to mean backbreaking toil and sweat! Never mind that; I want to look at the sun and the plants. To hell with the sun, Obrad! I want to spread a woman's legs again. Whichever way you look at it, there's nothing better or cheaper than good food. You're right about that. Pickled cabbage, say, and young turkey with potatoes, after lamb broth. And young lamb roasted on vine leaves with some good wine, now that's something! And grilled suckling pig on a spit, cooked over an oak fire. Ah, well. We won't taste these things any more, damn it! Oh, but I will! I'll survive even this country. That you will, old dog! We'll finish them off, I tell you!

"I counted the shells up to a hundred, then suddenly I lost track. Lots of them hit, but not all. Not even God can destroy man. When Adam fled from the garden, God grew angry and let loose wild beasts and sickness on us, hunger and fire and floods and all these wars, but he couldn't do us any harm. There's more and more of us. That's right. There's no god or devil under heaven can finish off mankind."

A shell whirred past them and exploded. A dark shadow blotted the searchlight on the opposite bank. A tile in the eaves clattered in the wind.

"We have to die, but let's not just tumble into the Danube like shit. I tell you, we'll finish them off, damn them!"

Sava Marić listened to them with only half an ear. He was thinking about Bogdan and how he, Sava, had cried while tying Bogdan's hands.

God grant that they cross the Danube before dawn, and that the major, that bastard, won't have time to court-martial him. It's disgusting to live just for the sake of being alive, that's what that hothead said. But what should one live for? You last as long as you can, then carry on through your children. My father and mother lived for me, and I live for my children. And so my property will get bigger, with the help of my children. And my meadow, my wife, and my words, they all exist because of life. Why does Bogdan find this disgusting? Where does he get such ideas anyway? Even if he gets out of this scrape tonight, he won't get out of the war. Even if he survives the war with them, he'll be fighting a war against life in peacetime. And when has a man ever won that war? That's what I'll ask him, if God lets me see him again.

Another shell flew past, then still another.

"Listen, since we have to die, let's die like heroes! We're going to finish those bastards off! Yes, we will! Shut up, that's enough for tonight. Oh no it isn't! Play a tune on your flute, Vidojko. But don't sing! Yes, sing as much as you want. Shut up, Čedomir, I'd rather listen to the wind. What are words compared with the wind? And what is man, poor creature, compared with the Danube or a star? A tiny piece of iron! We're nothing. I tell you again in plain Serbian: We're going to finish those bastards off!"

The wind wailed above Wren and, wetted by the icy Danube, sent a shudder through him. Wren crouched down by the edge of the trench—his last, powerless barrier and protection, perhaps only until dawn. So it was with everything—until dawn. He didn't want it to be that way. He was weeping for himself and his life. Shame had killed him, not the war. Shame that prevented him from going to the regimental doctor and asking for medication in time. Along with shame there was the discovery that man was such a wretched, vulnerable creature that he could be destroyed by a single act of sin, a drunken moment of mad craving for a woman. That prostitute in Skoplje had been his first woman. He had kissed Zlata only a few times, and before that had held Christina's hand. Bora Jackpot slept with a different woman every Saturday. What hideous injustice! He had been full of anger at this injustice even when fighting on Suvobor, and had wished to end it right there. But this hadn't happened, and he was left with nothing but his sin. Until that supper in the Golden Carp, he'd believed that he could atone for his sin by a heroic death, recover his self-respect, and deserve the grief and pain of those who loved him. But that too was an illusion. He no longer had the strength for an honorable death. And so he wept.

But when he set off from the Golden Carp for the trenches, in his skin, his bones, his clothing, he felt a desire to live. An irresistible desire to live, even with his shameful disease which would end in madness. And even with his parents' disappointment and with Zlata's —Zlata whom he had shamefully abandoned, supposedly because she hadn't written him more often at the front. Shame had killed him long ago. The Germans were only pushing him into the darkness. He had inherited this shame from his father, that poor wretch who was always ashamed in front of everybody, including his children, always stammering apologies, a sickly, miserable creature who "couldn't tread on an ant," as his mother had said on a number of occasions with angry tears.

My poor, wretched father, how could you create me when you couldn't even tread on an ant? It's from you that I've inherited this shame, this soul torn to pieces, this pack of cowards within me. Who gave you the right to create me?

Bora Jackpot was lying between the railway tracks with his bag under his head. He curled up on the ties and the gravel, and tried hard to complete in his sleep the scene of his uncle's funeral, and to forget that unknown whore. But he was also kept awake by the memory of his father's murder, which, until the battle on Suvobor, had made him feel a violent disgust and hatred for all the peasants in the trenches and their idle talk.

"Why don't those bloody bastards come across? The Germans are gentlemen. They don't attack until they've had breakfast and coffee. Those women gave themselves for nothing last night, Milenko. Just like that. We're Serbian men, and they're Serbian women who felt sorry for us because we're going to die. Don't tell fairy tales, whores don't give themselves for nothing. Only honest women do that. I tell you, I made mincemeat of those two Jewesses. Don't you give me that shit. I know they're sisters. It's because they're sisters that they gave themselves to me, you blockhead! First the younger one, then the older. That younger one, she was really white."

Bora couldn't stand it any longer. "Shut up, you ass!" he yelled. "Stop lying!"

But the talk resumed before long:

"What do you think, Vuja, will the schools be open under the Fritzies? If they meant to educate our children they wouldn't have destroyed Belgrade and hurled so much fire and iron at us. I'm worried about the schools, too. My Ranko is of school age, and if there aren't any schools until the war's over, he won't learn anything. Don't worry, Svetozar, if he doesn't learn to read and write, the women will teach him something much better. His cock has been growing, too. You're right, Veljko. What if these youngsters are sleeping with our women? Well, boys, those little rotters will really have a time with our widows! Better that the neighborhood children keep our wives busy than bosses and convicts. Well, I hate it. I'd shoot God himself if I thought he was having my woman while I was dying! When I think of it, I could kill the lot of them, and with more pleasure than I'd kill the Fritzies!"

They're my brothers too, thought Bora Jackpot. *We speak the same language, take the same oath, and sing the same national anthem—we're all Serbs. But is that enough for brotherhood? Perhaps one of those jealous men is the son of that criminal who murdered my father* with an ax and chopped off his horse's head? What kind of kinship do we have? In peacetime everyone is somebody's enemy and everybody is corrupt. Everybody is afraid of somebody, but envies him at the same time. Everybody cheats and humiliates. We kill each other for half a glass of brandy, for a foot of plowed soil, for a head of cabbage eaten by a neighbor's cow. Are we really brothers?

"And when I think of her lifting her skirt for those thieves, I feel like going to the village right now and having it out with those two, then returning to the platoon and bashing the Fritzies as long as there are any left to be bashed. What are they waiting for? Why don't they come over, for Christ's sake? Are you eating, Marko? Yes, I am. If they kill me, they're not going to get my half-ration of hardtack."

Is he my brother too? thought Bora Jackpot. *No, he isn't. I'm alone. Alone in a trench on the bank of the Danube. Quite alone.*

Tričko Macedonian was standing next to the battalion commander, Dragutin Gavrilović, and another orderly, behind a pile of rocks under the Nebojša Tower. A big barge was floating slowly toward them, clearly visible in the bright reflection of the Belgrade fires. There was no sound except for the wind and the waves breaking against the sandy shore of the Danube.

"That's a cavalry detachment!" cried Major Gavrilović. "Where did it come from? It can't be! Are my eyes deceiving me, Tričko, after all that wine last night?"

"No, they are not, sir. It's cavalry."

"How can they cross the Danube and attack a fortified town with cavalry? What joke is Mackensen playing on us, damn him? Stojanović, run to the second platoon leader and tell him not to fire without my instructions!"

Tričko was happy to be at the major's side. Next to him he'd face a whole squadron of cavalry and a regiment of infantry.

"Are you sure those are horses, Sergeant?"

"Yes, sir, I am. It's cavalry all right, sir."

"I studied at the Military Academy. This is my third war. When did they ever send cavalry to attack in front of the infantry and before a preliminary artillery bombardment? Our eyes aren't playing tricks on us, are they?"

"No, sir, they aren't."

The big barge full of horses, as if driven by the wind, was drawing near the Serbian shore, lit up by a brighter glow from the fires.

"Can you hear motorboats, Sergeant?"

"The horses are jumping into the river, sir!"

"I can see that. Are there any men there, any soldiers?"

"No, sir."

The horses were jumping into the water from the barge and swimming toward Belgrade. Their heads made dark patches among the foaming waves.

"Perhaps we're dreaming, sir."

"What kind of a dream is that, Sergeant?"

"I don't know, sir."

"Open your eyes!"

Several soldiers on the barge were jabbing the horses with their guns and forcing them into the water. Then they lay flat on the deck of the barge, which was slowly carried toward the Danube quay by the mainstream while the hundred or so horses swam ashore.

"Are you sure there are no soldiers hanging onto the horses' tails, Sergeant?"

"I can't see them, sir. Perhaps they're under the horses."

"But they'd drown if they were under the horses!"

"Our eyes must be deceiving us, sir."

The horses emerged from the river, shook themselves, snorted, and, as if directed by invisible riders, formed themselves into a close pack ready to charge. Then they galloped toward the Belgrade fortress.

"There's another barge, sir!"

"Don't shoot!"

The horses jumped over the trenches full of soldiers and rushed into the shadow of the fortress, the wind carrying the sound of their hoofs and of rifle fire.

"They're revealing our positions, damn them! The Fritzies have pulled off their joke."

"There's another barge coming, sir!"

"Yes, but it looks empty. Can you see anything on the barge, Sergeant?"

"No, sir. It's black."

"There's nothing black about it, Tričko. They're trying to draw our artillery fire in order to reveal our positions. I hope to God our gunners aren't taken in by them!"

The sound of rifle fire reverberated through Kalemegdan. *They're killing them like mad dogs,* thought Tričko with a shudder. Then, above Zemun and along the Danube, he saw red and yellow lights bursting high in the sky, while searchlights gleamed in the darkness, lighting up the Serbian shore and the walls of the fortress and Kale-megdan: Belgrade seemed to be wavering and stepping back from the Sava and the Danube into the darkness of Serbia, quivering in a milky haze.

"Look, their gunboats, and a whole string of barges! They're coming across!" said Major Gavrilović, giving Tričko a powerful hug. "Run and tell the gunners not to open fire until I say so! The infantry are not to make a move until the barges get to our side!"

Tričko reluctantly tore himself away from the major's fatherly embrace and ran off through the murky light and the wind, as if in a dream.

There was a thunderous crash behind the railway tracks and the trenches. A roaring current of hot air flashed above Bora Jackpot, lifting him high up. He came down with a thud, clutched the rails, and pressed himself against a tie that heaved under him like a fright-ened animal. Remembering his father's watch, he took it out of his pocket: half past two. They were off to an early start. Well, the sooner, the better.

"Into the front trenches! Into the front trenches!" shouted Lieu-tenant Jevtić behind him.

Bora Jackpot slowly straightened up and stood rigid in the light of the searchlights and fires on the embankment. The platoon ran across the railway tracks and knelt in the shallow trenches by the foamy Danube, staring at the row of cannon in the dark depths of Banat. Shells exploded above them. Bora looked toward Kalemegdan: in the wide expanse of light which had thrust its way crosswise into the sky, explosions were cutting through the walls as if they were dough. He looked down the Danube: the slaughterhouse, the power station, and the sawmill were crumbling, and smoke was billowing out into the yellowish light, twisted by the wind. That was where Wren was, but where was Tričko? The searchlight made it impossible for him to flee from the tracks. There was nowhere to go. You could see everything clearly before death. He felt no fear, as he had previously in battle or under artillery fire. Everything was unreal. Suddenly Šunto Zlatiborac came running toward him from the Danube.

"The C.O. is calling for you, Sergeant," he yelled.

Slowly Bora descended the embankment and joined Šunto, who had never before been in battle or even in the trenches.

"What'll you do in this mess, Šunto?" Bora asked gently.

"What'll I do, Sergeant? If I don't win the Karageorge Star defending Belgrade, how can I do it retreating all through Serbia?"

"Why do you want the Karageorge Star, Šunto?"

"Because I'd like to ride back into my village on a white horse."

"You? On a white horse? What did you drink last night?"

"I must ride through Zlatibor on a white horse. Run, Sergeant, or the rocks will kill you!"

Shrapnel whizzed above them and gravel was falling from the embankment. To protect his head, Bora ran over the sandbank behind Šunto Zlatiborac, still unconvinced that he really was Šunto Zlatiborac.

"Have you decided to get killed, like Wren?" said Lieutenant Jevtić from the trench.

Bora jumped into the trench, which the waves were filling with water, then jumped out again even more quickly. He was wet and angry: "I don't intend to get killed, or to stand in water!"

"I see their boats! They're coming! Lie down!"

Bora felt a sudden urge, a strong desire for a rifle to shoot at that dark mass of men. He couldn't miss now. As soon as one of his soldiers was killed he'd take his rifle. He looked down the trench at his squad, then at the motorboats, barges, and gunboats racing across the Danube toward them. The Serbian artillery fired, tearing the barges apart and sinking them. The rest sailed faster and faster into the light. There were bursts of rifle and machine-gun fire on the quay. Bombs too. Now poor old Wren must be catching it! Bora thought.

Jevtić seized him by the hand: "We must kill them! We must defend ourselves, my friend! Bugler, sound the note to fire! Fire a salvo!"

The bugle gave a despairing cry which was soon lost in the roar of the guns: the platoon hammered at the barges, and at the soldiers who were falling, groaning, jumping into the water. The gunboats opened fire on the platoon from the right with shells. Šunto Zlatiborac fired at the Austrians, shouting:

"Here we go! Here we go!"

"What are you doing, you idiot?" yelled Bora. He looked down the trench for a rifle. The cap flew off a man nearby. He knew that meant a direct hit on the crown of the head. He took the dead man's rifle and unfastened his cartridge belt. To avoid the water, he knelt down on the dead man and shot at the mass of men who were advancing. They were in water above their waists and held bayonets. He was unmoved by the thought of a toothed bayonet plunging into his stomach. In fact, he had no feeling of any kind. He fired quickly, mechanically, surely, and heard someone saying: "Here we go! Here we go!"

Then there was silence; *they* were plunging through the light with their toothed bayonets.

"They got that one, too!" said Sergeant Denča, but Wren didn't look at the metal windmill from which Austrians were hurtling to their death in the shallow water of the Danube, brightly lit as they fell. He heard the lowing of cattle between shell explosions. Before he caught sight of the enemy firing line approaching him from the side, densely packed, and his squad shot at a boat heading straight for him, he again heard the roar of cattle from the burning slaughterhouse. The pain of those animals left him senseless. The chimney of the slaughterhouse swayed, then tottered and collapsed in flames from which leaped burning oxen with huge, redhot horns. The oxen seemed to fly up over Belgrade, trailing smoke behind them. When he recovered consciousness and looked around, the Germans were only a few paces away. He heard Sergeant Denča yell, "You motherfucking Fritzies!"

"Shells!" he cried.

Once more he looked at the Danube in the firelit haze of the gunboats and motorboats, while the broken German line fled behind the railway embankment, pounded by machine-gun fire from Platnara. Sergeant Denča sang in a hoarse, moaning voice, as if crying for help:

> My wife is a rifle,
> A fast-shooting gun.
> Come with me, comrades,
> Fighters for freedom!

Just to live, to be alive, thought Wren. He wanted to embrace the man who was singing. What did disease matter? Or insanity? What did syphilis matter, or disgrace, or disappointment? All that mattered was to be alive, to live—here on the Danube quay, under shells, in the middle of a fire, in a burning slaughterhouse, but to live!

Denča shouted again: "There's another Austrian falling from the windmill—the motherfucking Fritzie!"

Wren looked up: shrapnel was exploding above the metal column, on whose rungs the dark form of a man was suspended, until a second shell blew him to pieces and he fell into the shallow Danube.

"Go on singing, Sergeant!" cried the soldiers.

"Go on singing, Denča!" cried Wren.

An explosion blinded and deafened him. The burning oxen with their big redhot horns flew noiselessly into the sky. Then Wren came back to his senses, drenched in sweat from the smoldering heat. Sergeant Denča was silent as bullets whizzed around his head. The Germans ran from the burning slaughterhouse to surround him.

"What should we do, Denča?"

Denča didn't reply. Wren reached out to touch him, and felt blood on his hand. He started, straightened up in terror, and cried out: "Retreat to the fish pond! Crawl there on your hands and knees!"

"When he realized that barely half his squad had escaped from the trench, he wanted to order them back. But the Austrians had already jumped into the trenches, waving their bayonets.

Tričko Macedonian stood in a corner of the cellar, against the wall, which shook from exploding shells. He never took his eyes off the commanding officer. As long as he was next to him no shell would hit him. If the headquarters was hit, in this corner he wouldn't be completely buried, provided he wasn't blown to pieces. But his turn must come: he'd be ordered out to a position and he wouldn't come back. Like Spasojević. And Vojić. He watched every movement of Major Gavrilović, who was going outside. As if pulled by a magnet, Tričko followed him. The officer looked at his positions, listened, then came back to the cellar, and sat down between two lamps at the table to cross out something—probably the losses—while Tričko retreated to his corner to await the order to go to his death.

Captain Grujić ran into the cellar: "Things are boiling on the Danube quay, sir. I think the first and third platoons have been forced back."

"Is this a guess or are you sure?" asked Gavrilović.

"I'm judging by the flames in Banat Street."

"Banat Street? What are you saying? An orderly must go there at once!"

Tričko held his gaze steady, to show his readiness, but there was a sparkle in Gavrilović's eyes as he said, "Jeremić, run there and get reports from the commanding officers!"

He was flooded with relief. But what if Jeremić didn't come back? He knew from the way Gavrilović had looked at him that he too would be sent to a place from which orderlies didn't return. His life was now in Jeremić's hands, and Jeremić was well known for timidity. He'd hide in a cellar, stay there half an hour, and return only after the commanding officer had sent him, Tričko, to his death. Where was Jeremić? It didn't take more than a quarter of an hour to get to the quay. When had he left? Why hadn't he timed him? When he'd joined the army his uncle, an old guerrilla fighter, had said to him: "When you're in a place where people get killed, never look at your watch—never! Don't make your life a hostage of time." Since noon yesterday, when the first shell had exploded, he hadn't looked at his watch. Perhaps it had stopped. A bad sign. If he looked at it now, they'd all know why. Was his mother still asleep? he wondered. The first thing every morning she prayed for him.

Major Gavrilović looked at his watch, then at Tričko. Stick it out, Tričko thought to himself, and gave the officer a grateful smile. Gavrilović nodded in agreement. Or was he shaking his head? He wouldn't send him there—or would he? Three orderlies hadn't come back. Why had he thrown away his grandmother's amulet a few nights ago, when he was drunk and that cynic Jackpot had goaded him? People don't believe in the impossible. They believe in what helps save them. He felt suffocated by the smell of sulphur and gunpowder which the wind blew into the cellar from the battle zone. An explosion nearby made the plaster fall from the ceiling. Gavrilović wiped his face with his sleeve and went outside. The minute he returns he'll send me off, thought Tričko.

"Do you know what Napoleon said about courage, Tričko?" whispered Korać, another orderly.

"No, I don't."

"The most difficult time to be brave is three o'clock in the morning. The bones are asleep."

"That's not the point."

"Which of us will be the first to go west, Tričko?"

"Me," he stammered sincerely and at the same time insincerely. He was tempting fate, confirming his readiness.

"Let's bet on it! He'll send me first."

"What's the bet worth if nobody's going to win it?"

"Never mind. Let's bet a hundred dinars, without paying anything down, just our word. The money stays with us, and whoever survives can spend it on his friends."

"You mean spend it for a wake."

"He can treat fate."

Major Gavrilović came back, sat down at the table, bent over the map, crossed something out, and looked at Tričko. Now you must go, he thought—Tričko could see it in his eyes!

"Korać, you're a brave man. Run along and see what's happening there. Get back as best you can, and fast."

"I can go, too, sir," said Tričko resolutely, stepping in front of his commanding officer.

"You've lost, Tričko!" snapped Korać.

"Your turn will come," said the officer.

"What did I tell you? My magnetic needle doesn't lie. We'll make it a hundred. So long, Fatface," said Korać with a frozen smile, pinching Tričko's cheek as he always did, just like Napoleon, when he took leave of his friends. "Napoleon was a sergeant, but I won't be an emperor," Korać would say. "Still, I can at least pinch people's cheeks like he did."

Tričko pressed his hand in a brotherly fashion. Forgive me, it's not my fault, he said to himself, and leaned against the wall to stop his trembling. He looked at Gavrilović, to whom an orderly had brought coffee. He thought of Korać's approaching their battle position. He saw him running between explosions, jumping into shell holes, weaving among burning houses, falling, running, then not getting up. *But he is getting up. Run, Korać, brave Korać, run, you've won the bet!*

"What happened to Korać, for God's sake?" asked Gavrilović.

"He should have been back by now, sir," said Tričko firmly, though he didn't believe that Korać had even reached the third platoon yet. His mother must be up by now. It was cold. She'd have to get up early to light the stove and make coffee for his father. His mother had deep faith, she was a saint. But people only believe in what helps them.

Gavrilović walked outside. Now he'd order Tričko to go. But perhaps Korać would come back. A man never dies when he thinks he's going to. How many times had he been sure before a battle he'd be killed!

Gavrilović came back and said softly, "I can see from the flames that they've landed on the quay and smashed our positions."

"I'm sure you're right, sir," said Captain Grujić.

That Bigwhiskers doesn't like me, thought Tričko. When he heard that Tričko was from Bitolj he had frowned: "I've nothing but unpleasant memories of that place!" he had said.

Šunto Zlatiborac ran in and stood at attention, thrusting out his chest in parade-ground style: "Sergeant Luković wishes to inform you that our commanding officer, Lieutenant Jevtić, has been killed, sir. We've withdrawn to the first row of houses."

Tričko looked at Šunto in confusion. He didn't believe that he knew how to stand at attention, let alone speak. The officers looked at Šunto in astonishment: "Aren't you the battalion idiot?" asked Captain Grujić.

"I was, sir. I was also orderly to Lieutenant Jevtić, and there never was a better man!"

"What about the third platoon, soldier?" asked Gavrilović.

"The Fritzies have pushed them back over the railway tracks, sir." Gavrilović wrote two notes and handed them to Zlatiborac.

"Give this one to Sergeant Jackpot Luković and that one to Sergeant Wren Durić, and return with their answers as soon as possible."

I'm saved, thought Tričko. He would have liked to send messages to Jackpot and Wren, but what would he say? He saw a string of onions at his feet. Should he send them each an onion? No, that would never do! Jackpot would laugh at him.

"Sergeant!" said Major Gavrilović, cutting through his train of thought. Tričko stood at attention. "Yes, sir?"

"Run with this order to the commander of the Srem Volunteers, Lieutenant Kirhner. Tell him our situation is critical and he must hurry! Good luck."

"I understand, sir." He broke off an onion from the string and clenched it in his fist. He stood at attention, trembling, until he thought he saw a smile in the commander's eyes. His mother would be up. He was sure he'd get through to Lieutenant Kirhner.

. . . Our Srem Volunteer Brigade, composed of young soldiers and old chetniks from all parts of our heroic land, numbered 360 rifles and was sheltered in the prison cells of the Upper Fortress, in front of Sahat Tower. At two o'clock in the morning an orderly got through a hail of bullets and informed our commanding officer, Lieutenant Kirhner, that the enemy had crossed the Danube and taken possession of the embankment of the Jalija-Klanica railway line, capturing two squads from the Tenth Regular Regiment and the Seventh Regiment of the second draft. The Srem Volunteer Brigade was ordered to move up as soon as possible to the Danube-Jalija quay, to attack the enemy and wipe them out. The brigade reached Great Kalemegdan, then, keeping close to the King of Serbia Café and Realka, reached Czar Uroš Street and proceeded downhill through a rain of gunfire toward the Jewish Quarter. We suffered some losses, but the wounded made no sound. We ran into some wounded men who were unbandaged. In front of us the roof of a house caught fire and fell in. The flame enveloped a wounded man. He tore his clothes off and, naked and bruised, fled from the inferno.

When we reached the Café Jasenica, all the houses around it were in flames. Beams were splintering, chimneys falling; walls, fences, and furnishings—everything was turning to ashes. From the cellars of ruined houses we could hear the cries of women, children, and old men.

We passed them by, unable to offer any assistance. When we reached the first houses at Jalija, everything was in flames. We rushed into a courtyard overlooking the railway track and re-formed to attack like tigers. We tore off the bayonets from our rifles, took our daggers out of their sheaths, unscrewed those square hand grenades, and at a sign from the bugler . . . There was a flash, a dull rumble. The earth shook, then the whole Jewish Quarter. We heard a short but audible "Hurrah!" The slaughter began. Then suddenly everything was quiet. We were masters of the railway line from the Golden Carp to Knez Mihajlov Crescent. Defense lines were realigning to the left and right of us. We made contact with them, and then there began a frightful, unprecedented battle.

—From the testimony of Captain Živko Kezić

Ram and the surrounding heights rose clear from the fog, painfully and briefly, just enough to show Sava Marić and his old men that dawn had reached the bank of the Danube, and to convince the German gunners that there was more in front of them than fog. Sava and the old men continued to stare at the river from their holes behind poplars. A flock of wild ducks swam toward them, then stopped. The drake straightened his yellow-crested head, listening intently. *I'd rather take one of these beautiful wild creatures home to my children than a bag of ducats,* thought Sava. The ducks circled the drake, then pressed on toward the shore, clean and free. *What lovely creatures! Bogdan said that there was no God. How else could such a beautiful bird be created on this earth, how else those beautiful trees that flowered and bore fruit—dark purple plums and rosy apples?*

The ducks fluttered their wings, then were motionless. Some fifty cannon fired over Ram and the riverbank, their thunder reverberating through Podunavlje. The ducks dove into the river. In dread, Sava crossed himself three times. In that dread there was no sense of helplessness. He felt he could do anything to save his own life. But against a fellow man? Perhaps this had nothing to do with him: both salvation and death were decided by some power on high in the universe, the same power that made beautiful birds and beautiful trees. And which also plagued them with storms. He knelt next to an old poplar and looked down the shore at the position of the squad over toward Ram. Shells were felling the poplars, uprooting willow trees, scattering tree trunks, blowing the old men to pieces or burying them alive. He turned his face to the river. Some ten meters from the shore two landing craft were emerging from the fog. His breath curdled. Those blue figures with their pointed iron helmets were more terrible than anything he could imagine. He heard the drone of their motors, and he yelled: "Fire!"

He threw a grenade, but not far enough. Then another, again not far enough. Only when he saw the Germans falling into the river, when he had assured himself that they were men and were dying, did he pull himself together and hurl a grenade at the second motorboat. Their cries and groans were the same as other people's, they fell and sank into the water like any other men. The boats were slowly obscured by the fog and swallowed into the bloody river. He stood up and shouted to his men: "Don't be afraid!"

The boat emerged again from the fog, and the old men pounded it with gunfire and grenades. Its dismembered, groaning cargo shed yet more blood into the river, then it was again obscured by the fog and borne along by the river.

To boost his confidence, Sava fired two bullets after the sinking boat, then set off down the bank to encourage his soldiers, jumping over dead bodies and begging the wounded to endure with patience until the attack was over. From the rattle of machine guns and the buzzing of bullets it was clear that the enemy had landed under the walls of the tower and was moving along the shore to attack.

"Fire from the flank!" he shouted.

His right arm gave a jerk; sparks flew before his eyes. He dropped his rifle but quickly picked it up again with his left hand and knelt on the sand; something warm and wet poured down his arm, and numbness spread through his body. It wasn't a bullet but a shell splinter that had smashed his right arm, he thought. The fog thickened, and from among the poplars and willows there appeared the quivering firing line with pointed iron helmets, bright and shining, like those on warrior saints. But these saints shot at his soldiers, knocking them down one by one. He crawled to the water to plunge his hand into it and extinguish the fire. Two landing craft emerged from the fog, like two ducks; he would cut off their heads and crawl back to the tree trunk. "A hit! A hit!" he yelled, and threw his last grenade with his left hand. The grenade lit up the fog, and he again saw the upright trees and *them* behind a fallen poplar, firing at his squad. He saw his old men pounding them with rifle fire as they jumped out of the boat, up to their chests in water, shooting even as they went under. There was a burst of yellow light and the sand flew everywhere. Painfully, from far away in space and time, suffocating under the earth, he realized that here he was safest of all: he could breathe. He wasn't sure whether it was a memory, or whether there was still the sound of thunder somewhere, and the muffled firing of guns. Everything around him grew small and still. It was as if sleep laid hold of him on a carpet of dry clover.

What kind of a soul did he have? Was he really such a coward? Wren was filled with self-hatred as he crouched down with two soldiers in a shell hole into which muddy jets of water streamed from the nearby fish pond and the ice ponds of the Belgrade ice plants. Even when he wasn't fighting, a ceaseless battle raged inside him. How long would it last? Was this shameful, hopeless life worth so much? Was it better to end up in a madhouse than to perish here defending Belgrade with his brothers and companions?

Through the spring and summer he had wished only for death. He had prepared himself for death, died a thousand times. He had in fact long been dead, he had perished the moment Bora Jackpot had said in an icy tone, "A classic case of syphilis!" On Maljen he had rushed out to meet death. Why couldn't he do so now? During the summer he'd been the only Serb who had secretly hoped for an attack, who had felt a thrill of excitement when he was transferred to the Belgrade Defense Force. He imagined himself charging down Kalemegdan, or perishing in a counterattack in Terazije. But to die for this fish pond, to be killed defending this stinking puddle!

Šunto Zlatiborac leaped into the shell hole, and, straightening up as far as the rim, stood bent over at attention: "New instructions from the battalion commander, sir! And greetings from Sergeant Tričko, who was alive a while back."

"What do you mean, 'a while back'? Is he alive or isn't he?"

"I left him alive at headquarters, sir."

"Don't play the fool, Šunto! Don't you see what's happening?"

"Things are bad, sir, very bad. Have you had a report from the new platoon leader, Sergeant Luković?"

"Since when has he been the platoon leader?"

"Lieutenant Jevtić was killed, sir, the best man in our regiment. Now that things have started, you might be the C.O. by midday and battalion commander tomorrow. May I go, sir?"

Wren motioned him away with an embarrassed wave of his hand, then immediately regretted it. Šunto Zlatiborac would be killed. He was running off amid shrapnel and torrents of water unleashed by the shells falling on the fish pond. He remembered Jevtić's story about his flight to Serbia and the little white sock in his pocket. They'd been together almost a year, but only last night had Jevtić shown him the sock. He too had had a feeling he would die. He must read the battalion commander's instructions:

"Please send at once a written report of the enemy's landing to date." To date? Nonsense! "The fish pond is our battalion's key position. It mustn't be abandoned unless there's no further possibility of defending it."

How could you determine the point of "no further possibility"? Who would know that now, unless he was a coward? Denča would certainly have known, but he was dead. Sergeant Medarić would have known, but he'd been killed a while back. Corporal Stanko would have known, but he'd fallen into the pond wounded and had drowned. Like Stanko, Wren too would fall into the icy, stinking water and it would turn red from his blood. (From the beginning this man had gotten on his nerves. When he wasn't firing his rifle he'd crack walnut shells and pry out the kernels with a razor blade. Wren hated him for it.) How could he judge the moment of "no further possibility"? Waiting for "no further possibility" was certain death.

"They're coming again, sir!" said a soldier who was eating bread spread with plum jam.

He jumped back from the pond into the bottom of the shell hole, and leaned against its muddy side: three hundred meters away the Austrians were forming firing lines and advancing toward him in a dense column. They'd encounter unexpected pools of water, and would have to break their line and advance along the narrow strips of land between the ponds. That would be the time to open fire!

"Gašić, run down the squad and tell them not to fire until they hear my whistle!" he ordered. Then he turned toward the position of Bora's squad, where grenades were reverberating. What was Bora doing? Bora always knew when there was "no further possibility." Bora was now his commanding officer, he'd wait for his order to retreat. He wouldn't think any more. The Austrians were advancing slowly toward him, sometimes shrouded in fog, sometimes exposed by a gust of wind. They certainly wouldn't take cover at his salvo—there was nowhere to go. They'd charge with bayonets, so he must meet them with bayonets. But their numbers were five times greater. He'd fall into the water, stabbed by a bayonet. Shells flew over his squad and crashed down in the courtyard of the sawmill. Beams, rafters, and planks flew up in the air and scattered over the fish pond. He might be killed by a beam. There was no such thing as a heroic death! Death was a humiliation—the worst, final humiliation. It didn't really matter whether it came in a madhouse or in this fish pond. Oh, but it did! He might be rotting away and going mad, but he was alive. He could see and hear! What was that smell coming from the Danube?

The Austrians had reached the first pools. They tried to go around them, when the officers yelled, *"Vorwärts! Vorwärts!"* He thought he heard revolver shots from behind the firing line, which dispersed. Then four dense columns began to run along the strips of land between the pools.

He bit his whistle. It still wasn't the moment of "no further possibility." Not yet!

"Pull the position back a little, sir!" said a soldier, offering him his brandy flask.

Greedily he swallowed a few gulps of strong brandy, and the Austrian columns grew misty. He'd let them get as far as those overflowing pools, then drown them. That would be the moment of "no further possibility" for them.

"Give the order to fire, sir! They'll cut us down like pumpkins!"

"Not yet! Let them come closer." Into the pool! *Now* was the moment of "no further possibility"! He dragged himself out of the shell hole to his waist and blew with all his might on his whistle, setting off a volley of gunfire. The Austrian columns collapsed. Most of the men fell into the pool, but those still standing opened fire. They feared death by drowning and were fleeing from the pool toward his position. They were fleeing, but many didn't escape. The fleeing men grew more numerous. Now they were near. Now his moment of "no further possibility" had come! He jumped out of the shell hole and glimpsed the Danube. Something high up drew him irresistibly into its depths, urged him to plunge into its muddy current, foam-flecked by the wind, to find salvation.

"Charge the bayonets!" he cried, and fired his revolver into the blue shapes fleeing from the pool. Suddenly the firing stopped. "No further possibility." Now there was only wrestling and groaning on the narrow earthen bridges crisscrossing the green, yellow, and red water which was extinguishing his shattering pain.

From the high slope of Gorica, Bogdan Dragović looked toward Ram and the Danube. An invisible battle was raging in a sea of fog. Yellow smoke spewed from every shell, until the wind dispersed it and it merged with the fog. Below, his old men were fighting and dying—those old men who had implored him to watch over them, to protect them because of the "hungry mouths and feeble hands" they had left at home. Sava Marić was down there, Sava who had bound his hands to save his "hot head." Sava had been good to him and Ivan Katić on Suvobor. But Major Dunjić was more troubled now by Bogdan's flight the previous night than by the battle in which his battalion would be wiped out, sacrificed in advance to the first blow of the German army. The old men and Sava, if they thought of him at all, would envy him because last night he had been led away from the shore of the Danube. But he was a deserter, overcome by despair. What could happen to a living man that's worse? Where could he go now? To his mother in Valjevo? He would be seized by the Serbian military authorities, or by the Germans when they occupied the town. To Milena in Prerovo? Natalia was there, it was her village. He would have to meet her, and cause her pain. He couldn't hide. Should he seek out his political comrades in Kragujevac? That was the seat of the High Command! And if he went to Kruševac, who would dare conceal a deserter? Should he go to Skoplje, to his first commanding officer, Lieutenant-Colonel Glišić, who had placed him under arrest, hit him in the face with his whip, and threatened him with a court-martial, from which he had been saved by his departure for the front? That gloomy, fanatical nationalist, who had suffered terribly because of the irresponsibility of students in preparing for war, was perhaps the only man to whom he could turn for help, to whom he could tell the truth.

A horse came galloping toward him along the path—he must take refuge in the brush. A battalion orderly rushed by: Sergeant Petković, who had taken him to Major Dunjić last night. He wanted to stop him, but Petković might tell Dunjić where he had seen him. Withdrawing further into the brush, he sat down on a mound of grass and glimpsed a blackbird just above his hand: it was fluttering from the noise of the guns, and flinching. It was afraid. They were both the same now. The same instinct drove it and himself to run away and hide among the thorns. That was what troubled and humiliated him all night: that fluttering like a bird, like an animal. But only that. After that, nothing. No, not quite. Someone would remember him: Milena. But he wouldn't know it, so it was nothing.

A shell burst nearby; the whistling of the metal shook the leaves. The blackbird gave a cheep, swooped down, and cowered next to his boot. He picked it up and wanted to release its warm, soft trembling, this one thing in the face of nothingness. He pressed it against his cheek, listened to its heart. When it stopped, it stopped forever, for all time. Their tremors mingled, unbearably painful. One must get rid of this fear of annihilation. Surely that was easier than the struggle for life? Gavrilo Stanković hadn't wanted to cower, to live a life that was a burden. He wouldn't accept the life of this blackbird. A blackbird and a deserter. He wouldn't have been a deserter, that was certain. He took the major's pipe out of his pocket and gazed at it, remembering how he had taken it from Sergeant Pepi in the hospital on Suvobor and given it back to Major Stanković. Bogdan had been beaten up and tossed on a snowdrift to die. He remembered how Milena had given him this pipe as Gavrilo's posthumous gift, when his typhus broke. Gavrilo Stanković would run now to the position, to be with his comrades. He had chosen either life or death, he had been free for the one and the other. He had always been free, right to the end. "I will not live under all circumstances. I will not, I can refuse to do so, and I dare to!" These were the words he had shouted at Doctor Sergeev when Sergeev tried to persuade him to have his leg amputated. Should he be a blackbird, a mass of tremors? For how long, and to what purpose?

No, I won't, he thought. *I won't hide in the thornbush with the blackbird while they're dying. I don't want the comfort of the blackbird. I must be with my downtrodden old men, my soldiers and comrades, down there in that yellow smoke, I must be with them now.*

He came out of the underbrush carrying the blackbird. The fog had broken on the heights along the Danube and cleared on the Serbian shore above Ram, where his platoon had been positioned; yellow smoke was seething through the valley, the ground was shaking from the shells. Gavrilo Stanković wouldn't have hesitated; he'd rush into the thunder. Bogdan slipped the blackbird into the pocket of his overcoat, put some tobacco in Gavrilo's pipe, lit it, and inhaled greedily.

An airplane circled above him and flew toward Banat. Bogdan stopped smoking and rushed down the slope into the yellowish fog, into the thunder, then halted in front of a huge shell hole: houses, already collapsing, rose out of the fog. The Danube was visible for about half its width, on which black barges full of Germans were floating noiselessly. But he felt no fear: the unreal light on the great river, like light in a painting, enchanted him. He sat down and watched it until he caught sight of some orderlies carrying wounded men. He began to run. Bullets and shrapnel whistled around him but nothing would stop him, so overwhelming was his desire to be with Sava Marić, his old men, and the Hungarian Kakaši.

A few old men wearing fur hats ran out to meet him; they looked comical. He was delighted to see them: "Where are you going?"

"We've fled, Sergeant! We've all fled!"

"Where's your commanding officer? Where's Sava Marić?"

"Both dead."

"Where's my squad?"

"Those still alive are making off through the plum orchard!"

Bogdan rushed through the underbrush and met his soldiers, among them Mileta, the one who had stolen a blouse to make bandages. The soldiers stood still, stunned. He tried to smile at them, but wasn't sure he succeeded. "What's happened to our squad?"

"What you see here, that's your squad. The Hungarian's gone off with the first draft."

"But the battle's still going on!"

"That, sir, is a first-draft squad which arrived just a short while ago."

"Then we'll go join the first draft."

"But look at the Germans over there, sir!"

"Never mind—don't be afraid!"

"It's pitch black! And the Germans would fill a churchyard!"

"The more Germans there are, the easier it is for us to find them! Take two grenades each and follow me! Anyone who has more than two, hand them over!"

Mileta cried out: "That's right, we can't run away! We'll do something to make the people back home remember us." He handed Bogdan a grenade.

Bogdan smiled at him, formed some of the old men into firing lines, and led them down through the village, which was littered with shells and filled with blue haze mixed with wisps of yellow smoke.

All hell has let loose on the Danube quay, such as the human mind can't imagine. The smoke is terrible, and rocks, bricks, and bits of iron are pouring over us like rain. Heavy artillery batters us mercilessly. The small, shabby Jewish houses are lifted into the air almost intact. The air is rent with the screams of innocent children. We're powerless to help them. Enemy planes are circling over us like birds of evil omen, coming down quite low. We can hear them, but can't see them for the dust and smoke of the ruins, nor can we aim our guns at them. After they circle over a certain place, a veritable rain of light and heavy cannon fire immediately follows. The Austrians and Germans are transporting their army by all conceivable means, from ordinary fish-

*ing boats to steel gunboats with barges alongside. The entire surface
of the Danube is crowded with floating objects. Their dark shapes on
the water look like wild ducks. Our artillery pounded them until it
was itself destroyed. The defense now rests on narrow-bore rifles, bayonets, and hand grenades. The defenders aim and fire at the barges,
motorboats, and small craft transporting the enemy in massive numbers. But a bullet is powerless against steel. Wooden boats and barges
are being sunk, the Danube carries them away full of corpses, but our
powerful enemy keeps on coming. Heavy shells are scattering pieces
of the railway track like bits of straw, showering rails over the neighboring houses and slicing people up like worms. One charge after another. No sooner does a detachment land on the shore than the order
is given to charge. We drive them into the mud and kill a good number
of them. But numbers are misleading. There are fewer and fewer of us,
more and more of them and their artillery. Our strength is giving out,
we're suffocated by smoke and possessed by a terrible thirst. The Danube is in front of us, but we have no water.*

—From the testimony of Captain Živko Kezić

Although Major Gavrilović had given orders that no more wounded
were to be carried from the battlefield, Bora Jackpot did attempt a
charge on the fish pond in the hope of saving Wren, who according to
his soldiers had been wounded and left lying in a pool of water. But
Bora was thrown back by the Austrians and withdrew the remains of
his platoon into the ruins of the Jewish quarter. With his orderly Šunto
Zlatiborac he took shelter behind the synagogue, into which elderly
Jews were coming with rifles, and small baskets full of ammunition
and grenades, to defend their homes. Apart from thirst, Bora's only
clear feeling was pain for Wren. If he hadn't been platoon commander,
he'd have crawled to the fish pond with Šunto Zlatiborac in order to
save the saddest and most unlucky member of the Cadet Battalion from
a hero's death.

A few boys with rifles came running toward him. They heard shells
and hit the ground. Three others who had attached themselves to the
platoon that morning had been blown to bits by a shell on the railway
embankment. He came out of his cover and yelled: "Where are you
going?"

"To our position!"

"The position is here. Lie down against the wall and fire toward the
Danube!"

The boys obeyed. Some Chetniks hurried past, carrying their

wounded commanding officer, Lieutenant Kirhner. The volunteers wouldn't defend the street nearest the railway track for long. He too would have to retreat before the first German charge, despite orders not to withdraw across Dušanova Street on any account. The firing from his position subsided. By nightfall the killing in Belgrade would be over.

"Police!" cried Šunto Zlatiborac. "First time in my life I'm glad to see them! They're like bluebells—you can see them from the other shore. The Fritzies will make mincemeat of them!"

"Shut up unless I ask you something!" said Bora Jackpot. He turned around: a platoon of policemen was indeed approaching in firing lines behind an officer with a drawn saber, marching according to parade regulations. Just before they reached the exposed positions in front of the railway embankment the enemy spattered them with machine-gun and artillery fire. Their blue firing line was thinned, but not destroyed.

"What did I tell you, sir?"

"Get me some water."

"What'll you drink if there isn't any water?"

"Anything wet."

Šunto ran across the street and quickly returned with a bottle of cherry brandy. "You've got food here as well as drink."

Bora drank almost half the bottle and felt thirstier than ever. Shells burst around the synagogue. The two of them took cover in a corner of the stone wall.

"Are there any wounded here, soldiers?"

Bora trembled at a voice that sounded just like his mother's and turned around. Two middle-aged women with Red Cross bags stood on the other side of the wall. Šunto answered them: "There are many wounded, ladies. There's three of them behind that broken pole. But let me warn you that two other ladies went there a short while ago and didn't come back."

The women ran to the place Šunto had indicated. Bora felt like boxing his ears: ever since the battle had begun, Šunto had infuriated him by his free-and-easy behavior, his chatter, and his tootings on a horn that he'd taken from a dead bugler. Right now he was playing something that sounded like both a song and a command to charge. The right wing of the platoon was moving back toward Dušanova Street. He sent Šunto to the battalion headquarters to inform the commanding officer that he would have to withdraw to Dušanova Street, then ran down Banat Street through a shower of bullets to halt the platoon. The soldiers stopped in their tracks, behind walls or heaps of ruins. He too crouched down under the steps of a ruined house. The bullets spattered the remnants of the wall, showering him with plaster. He could hear long-drawn-out cries in the cellar under the ruins and fled to the first shell hole. This was no time to save oneself, but to kill! Šunto came running through the dust and smoke and he went out to meet him: "You're ordered to withdraw the platoon to Czar Uroš Street at once!"

"Who'll take over our positions?"

"Nobody! Can I sound the retreat?"

"Where did you learn to sound the retreat?"

"I know how to play for a wedding, too!"

He played the retreat correctly. Bora could not believe his ears, and as he waited for the platoon to assemble, he asked:

"Are you a devil, Šunto, or have you gone crazy with fear?"

"I'm not a devil and I haven't gone crazy, sir. To tell the truth, sir, when I was on leave this summer I gave my solemn word to my wife that I wouldn't come back home without the Karageorge Star. My neighbor Ognjen, he has one, and his wife taunts my Ruža. Ruža doesn't like it, and she's ashamed that all I do is wash cauldrons and clean latrines. So I told her straight that I'd decided to become a hero. I'm not going to be a nuisance any more."

"Is that what you've been doing?"

"I was pretending, sir."

"Wonderful, Šunto, wonderful!" He led the platoon up the steep Czar Uroš Street, refreshed and delighted. "Šunto, why don't you become another Napoleon? Do you know who he was?"

"Not exactly, though I've heard he was an old joker who trampled empires like a drunk man on a box of seedlings. But a clever fellow, even so."

Bora Jackpot laughed, then felt embarrassed and alarmed. He hadn't laughed like that since he came back from his leave. His knees buckled at the thought that from noon yesterday to noon today—a full twenty-four hours—he was the only person in Belgrade who had laughed!

Šunto called out to the platoon to take cover in a courtyard, then led Bora into a workshop where Major Gavriolović sat behind the counter drinking coffee, while some women bandaged two wounded officers.

"Sit down, Luković," said the commander. "Are you hungry?"

"No, only thirsty, sir."

"Yes, that's a soldier's torment. Thirst—false thirst. Let me tell you something. You fight better than you talk about fighting. That pleases me. Today in Belgrade an honorable man shouldn't utter a word he's not sure of. Silence is best of all."

I'm falling asleep, Bora said to himself helplessly.

"The Austrians have taken Gypsy Island and broken through to Čukarica. They've broken through from the Zemun side as well. They've destroyed our artillery. The situation is critical. But I can see your eyes are closing. Get some sleep."

Even if sleep means death, I'll go to sleep. This was Bora's last conscious thought.

He was jerked awake by Šunto Zlatiborac: "Get up, sir! The troops are assembling for inspection. The C.O. is calling for you."

Bora couldn't remember where he was. He spotted a pitcher of water on the counter, drank nearly all of it, and went out. Across the road in a courtyard some two or three hundred soldiers were lined up, and Major Gavrilović was talking to them. Tričko Macedonian motioned to Bora to stop. He was happy to see Tričko through the smoke of rifle fire and shell explosions.

"The High Command has crossed our regiment off its active list," said Major Gavrilović. "Our regiment has been sacrificed to the honor and glory of Belgrade!"

"If we've been crossed off the list, how'll we get our rations tomorrow, sir?" Šunto asked Bora.

Bora didn't answer. He was tired, and struggled to grasp the meaning of the order given by Gavrilović.

"Soldiers! You needn't worry about your lives any longer! Your lives don't matter!"

"You don't say! Well, I'm alive and I suppose I'll stay that way, Major Gavrilović, sir."

"Forward to glory! For king and country!"

"What would Vojvoda Putnik do if he knew our major was blasting us to hell?"

"Listen Šunto! If you don't shut up, I'll break your jaw!" snapped Bora. He hurried off toward Tričko. Gavrilović intercepted him: "We're going to charge, Luković! We must push them into the Danube. Don't you think we can do it?"

"Yes, I do. Today a man can do anything," he replied, sincerely but indifferently.

"A man can't do anything. But men can do almost anything, Luković. When we go down Dušanova Street, you lead the right wing and push them toward the Danube as far as the embankment. Leave the wounded. We'll pick them up tonight, when we've finished the job."

"I understand, sir." He saluted the commanding officer, who went on ahead. *If I push them on toward the fish pond,* he thought, *I might find Wren alive.*

"You've heard what happened to Wren?" said Tričko. "He's been cut to pieces with a bayonet!"

Tričko seized Bora by the arm and was startled by his bloodshot eyes and sweaty, sooty face. *Now he looks just like Bora Jackpot,* thought Tričko; *I wonder what I look like to him.*

"You're covered with blood!" exclaimed Bora, looking at his friend's bruises and bloody forehead.

"If you knew what I've been through since we left the Golden Carp! You could never guess. I feel two hundred years old!"

"You'll feel five centuries old by midnight. And tomorrow you'll be a god, Tričko."

"Don't be a fool! If we survive this honor and glory, I'll come over this evening."

"I don't believe we will. Do you want Casanova's cards?"

"No, you keep them."

Tričko embraced him and ran off after the battalion commander. Bora was overwhelmed with sadness. In a faltering voice he ordered his platoon to set out, keeping a distance of five paces between each man, then moved off himself to the killing. Shambling downhill into the even denser buzz of bullets and the stench of battle and fires, he formed the platoon on Dušanova Street, thinking of Wren, cut through by a toothed bayonet, but perhaps still alive in a pool even now.

"If you can, sound the notes for a charge," he said to Šunto.

"I can do that!"

He took the bugle from his shoulder and blew with all his might: the signal for a charge broke toward the end into the rhythms of a folk tune. Bora tapped him softly on the back with his saber, then resolutely led his platoon to the slaughter.

Making his way through whizzing bullets, through wrecked buildings and courtyards, and past shattered trees, burnt-out sheds, and overflowing toilets, Tričko frequently crossed himself, quickly and stealthily. He prayed that he wouldn't be wounded. He concentrated all his efforts on not falling behind Major Gavrilović, who was marching forward, guiding his firing line to a shortcut through the gardens of Dorćol. He ordered Trićko to follow him. *He's rushing to a glorious death,* thought Tričko, sensing that soon darkness would come. He had already died several deaths the night before in the cellar, when the orderlies were being killed one after the other, and when he ran to the headquarters of the Srem Volunteer Brigade under fire. Once more he crossed himself, praying that he wouldn't be wounded, that this glory might cease and darkness come. He stumbled over dead policemen, jumped across wounded men, and thought of God. He was drawn on by that possessed man in an unfastened overcoat who was shaking his fists, urging them to run, to cry out in fear and help-lessness, as that darkness cut through these yells of charging men, scattering them amid burning beams, crushed chrysanthemums and dahlias, and overflowing outhouses. But *he* did not heed any of this, the man who had proclaimed his battalion dead and ordered it to perish for the honor of Belgrade at exactly three o'clock; he was hurrying madly to that glory. Tričko was suddenly transfixed by some-thing stronger than fear: why did it have to be three o'clock? Why not four or five? Why not six? A loud bang and searing heat felled him. He called out, or perhaps thought: What time is it? A flash dissipated the darkness: he was lying next to a bloodstained cat and a broken door. He felt the animal. Yes, it was a cat, warm and staring with glassy eyes, blood trickling from its mouth. He grasped the doorknob and rattled it. Yes, it was a doorknob, and a door. He moved his arms and legs and stood up. He wasn't wounded. No, he wasn't! He shook violently. Was it after three o'clock? He took his watch out of his pocket: a quarter, seventeen minutes past. *So I'm alive again,* he thought. But where was his C.O.?

Major Gavrilović was crawling between shattered box hedges, bare-headed, with bloody shoulders. Tričko ran to him and grasped his wounded chest to lift him up. Blood poured from his neck.

"Leave me alone! Who are you?"

"Your orderly Tričko, sir. Lie down, so I can bandage you!"

"Follow my orders! What time is it?"

"Seventeen minutes past three. Twenty past."

"Find Captain Grujić. Tell him . . . my orders still stand. At three o'clock sharp. To the last man. Three o'clock."

"Let me take care of your wound, sir," said Tričko, extracting a bandage from his bag.

"My orders are that the wounded be picked up tomorrow night. Do your duty, Sergeant."

Tričko couldn't leave him. He tried to bind up his neck with a bandage and stanch the blood:

"Go! Go do your duty," gasped the major. "I'll shoot you, damn you!"

"What'll I do?" Tričko asked himself aloud. Bombs were exploding at the railway embankment and the quay, and he could hear the yells of charging men from both armies. Where could he find Captain Grujić? He wouldn't—he'd be killed. He would save himself and his commanding officer. Who would know what orders the C.O. had given him now? And if Gavrilović survived, he wouldn't accuse him of cowardice because he'd have saved his life. Quickly he bound up his neck to stop the blood. The firing got closer. *Those are our boys retreating,* he thought. How could he carry this giant of a man? He ran toward Dušanova Street and saw two women carrying a wounded soldier in a blanket. He asked them to put the man down and help him carry Major Gavrilović, who was seriously wounded. The women obeyed and ran with him. He remembered the door he'd lain on, tore it from its frame, and with the help of the two women placed his commanding officer on it. The jolting revived the major. He groaned and looked at Tričko with hatred: "How dare you disobey my orders? Damn you. March . . ." he stammered, then lost consciousness again. Tričko said timidly, right above his bloodstained face, "I understand, sir!"

With the two women he carried him into the town, to save him, to save himself. He'd take him to the military hospital, do anything to carry him as long as possible, to be far away from the Danube and Dorćol. He replaced the women with two boys, but he himself remained: he wouldn't have laid down his burden if the hospital had been on the top of a mountain—it was atonement for what he had done. Jackpot and Wren were still down there, in the thunder. He wanted to weep, yet at the same time he felt a sweet, choking pleasure.

Under constant artillery fire we reached Dorćol in the early evening. We made contact with our firing line with the help of policemen. I went to the station to which I'd been ordered: the position of the Srem Volunteer Brigade in Banat Street, with its one surviving officer, the courageous Lieutenant Živko Kezić. Only remnants were left of that brave garrison that withstood the enemy attack for fifteen hours. The Srem Brigade was wiped out, as was the Second Battalion of the Tenth Regular Regiment. The police who hadn't perished were scattered. There were masses of dead in the streets, courtyards, and trenches, and those who were alive looked like ghosts. As I made rounds of the trenches, I came upon the remains of a platoon under the command of a seriously wounded sergeant. It was surrounded on three sides but still fighting bravely. In a narrow trench the dead and the fatally wounded were lying on top of one another, while the living continued to fight.

—From the testimony of Zdravko Vesković, commander of the Pioneer Platoon

It was getting dark and it had started to rain, but there was no let-up in the battle at Dorćol and throughout Belgrade: the enemy artillery pounded with great ferocity from the shores of Banat and Zemun, and from the gunboats on the Sava and the Danube, as if the attack were just beginning. Bora Jackpot didn't see this simply as a sign of the enemy's strength. This destruction of what was already destroyed, this setting fire to what was already burning, this killing of dead men he saw as an immeasurable hatred, more intent upon the degradation of the Serbian opponent than a military victory. And since, after a second charge, he didn't get through to the fish pond, where he might perhaps have saved Wren, Bora concentrated all his efforts on one objective: that the war which he had viewed as inevitable the previous evening should not lose its meaning—the war to kill the killers.

Šunto Zlatiborac brought him a can of meat, some bread, and a bottle of wine. He took a bite of the meat, ate a piece of bread, and drank at a gulp half the bottle of wine. He attached the remnants of his platoon to what was left of the Srem Volunteer Brigade, placed himself under the command of Lieutenant Živko Kezić, and waited for his orders. He sat down against the last remaining wall of a burnt house, seeking warmth. If Lieutenant Kezić had not disturbed him with his preparations for a charge with grenades and bayonets, timed to start exactly at midnight, he'd have fallen asleep there. As he breathed in the stench of fire and battle, he told himself firmly that tonight he mustn't fall asleep, he must do his duty. He must do it because he was a man, and for some compulsive force which was higher than national and moral obligation, higher than honor and dignity, higher than the war goals of Major Gavrilović, his hopes, and his obstinacy. Right now he had neither the capacity nor the will to clarify for himself the meaning of this compulsive force. But why all this fuss? He should enjoy the warmth of this burnt-out human dwelling for a few more moments, and not think about anything. How much suffering and stupidity, how many lies were there in these embers? He dozed off.

Šunto Zlatiborac was asking Lieutenant Kezić what a soldier must do to win the Karageorge Star. Kezić believed that only those who died defending Belgrade deserved it, and asked anxiously whether the enemy had taken the villages of Čukarica and Senjak.

At exactly midnight they made a futile attack with grenades and bayonets. The slaughter left ten of their men dead, and the wounded crying out pitifully. Bora moved to another spot along the wall, which was now just barely warm. Tormented by his passion for vengeance, inflamed by every casualty among his men, Kezić renewed the charge with grenades and bayonets at three o'clock, but they were again thrown back. At dawn the enemy attacked ferociously, but they were forced back, too. Soon thereafter an orderly of Colonel Tufegdžić, commander of the defense of the urban sector, brought orders that the enemy was to be driven out of the city and into the Danube with the greatest possible speed. This, Bora thought, would give Kezić an inviolable right to run desperate charges for vengeance all day long. Yet Bora felt no fear, and no longer saw any reason to retreat or flee from Belgrade. It made no difference when and where he was killed, though now and again the thought flashed through his mind that if he wasn't killed, he'd be the last to leave Belgrade.

At dusk they could no longer withstand the powerful frontal attack by the enemy and withdrew toward Knez Mihailova, behind barricades prepared by detachments of Moslems from Novi Pazar and the Vardar region. He recalled that half a kilometer downhill was Dobračina 26, first door on the left. Perhaps Lenka was alone tonight? He trembled. Should he slip away and collapse into bed beside a strong, warm woman? And at dawn go on with the killing? Suppose some "fellow Serb," without shedding a drop of blood, had conquered the dominating point of his Belgrade tonight, his Terazija, his Slavija? That little bit of the fatherland which for a few hours would belong only to him, just the space of a bed, one warm bed out of a million beds, for a few hours of one night. Of all the people for whose freedom he must perish, of the millions of bedworthy Serbian women, was it possible that he didn't even have the right to Lenka, a whore who used as an enticement her fear of sleeping alone and at the same time raised the price for her customers? If he went there for the night, Kezić and all the soldiers would think it a shameful betrayal of the fatherland, worse than surrender to the enemy. *Ah, you poor, weak, degraded animal, killing other degraded animals who'll scatter your guts on the Belgrade cobbles!* A rocket fell, lighting up the barricade and the people on the sidewalks. A machine gun began to stutter: a battle was starting up, saving him from himself. He pulled himself together and with about ten soldiers and Lieutenant Kezić approached the Czar of Russia Café, where they spied several Austrians sitting around candle-lit tables. The lighted candles reminded him of the vigil for his dead uncle—the café seemed like a huge mortuary. In a state of uncontrollable excitement, without waiting for Kezić's orders, he fired through a large pane of glass, right at the candles. Groans echoed in the darkness as he fled to the barricades. Fighting was building up in the streets; along with the remains of several platoons that had converged on the center of the town, they withdrew to the Flower Market and Tašmajdan.

As dawn approached, the enemy artillery pounded the center of the city with increasing ferocity. Charges and retreats continued through the day. Šunto Zlatiborac could hardly wait to sound his bugle. Bora's one fear was that he might sit down and at once fall asleep. He was so tired that the street battles didn't seem nearly so fierce as the day before. He felt less and less fear. The charging and retreating, the panic-stricken flight and frenzied counterattacks seemed like scenes from a French war film he had seen in Niš. People and buildings had no clear outlines, they were floating in mist and dissolving into space. Nor did the explosions of shells and grenades have the terrifying impact of the previous two days. The falls and last movements of men who had received fatal wounds no longer aroused horror in him. Killing had become a nightmarish, senseless, ugly task. Barricades were being constructed from cooking stoves, china cabinets, beds, and barrels. The streets were choked with ruins. It was easy to find cover, easy to steal up to the victors and throw a grenade. Šunto did this often, each time shouting: "Let's get going!"

Before night fell it began to rain heavily. The rain smothered the cries of both armies. No one issued orders, everyone did what he had to do. They're all using their last ounce of strength to kill one more before being killed themselves, thought Bora. They didn't do it out of hatred. Then at dusk the Austrians surrounded them in the Flower Market on three sides, with immensely superior numbers. Šunto saved Bora by leading him past a bakery through a courtyard to Alexandrova Street. There they met a column of Austrians, so they slipped into a cellar with a carpenter's bench and a pile of white pinewood crosses. The dry air and smell of pinewood made Bora so sleepy that he barely managed to tell Šunto to wake him up at midnight, before stretching himself out on the crosses.

Waking up was so painful that he began to wail as if stabbed with a bayonet. "Let them kill me!" he cried. He embraced the crosses and fell asleep again, but felt Šunto lift him up. Suddenly, by the light of a flickering wall lamp, Bora found himself face to face with an Austrian officer, rushed in terror to the door, and collided with an old man who was leaning against it, and who then collapsed with laughter.

"Don't be afraid, sir. It's me, Šunto Zlatiborac. I'm just play-acting."

Smiling the smile of a victor, Šunto related how he had killed an Austrian officer and two soldiers in an ambush, captured the officer's white horse, and dressed himself in the officer's uniform. "It's long past midnight. Now I'll take you to our positions, then I'll parade around Belgrade on a white horse, like an officer. Fuck the imperial army."

Bora sat down on the crosses to light a cigarette and make sure he wasn't dreaming: it was indeed Šunto in the uniform of an Austrian officer, and the old man in the sheepskin coat was probably the owner of the cellar and the wooden crosses. Why he made crosses didn't interest him now, nor did he have the will power to oppose Šunto Zlatiborac's crazy idea; but he refused to be taken away from Belgrade. The old man gave him some grapes, which he ate, and a packet of tobacco. Bora then picked up a bag of grenades which he had taken from the Flower Market the previous night, and went out into the street and the darkness.

No light anywhere, no sign of life. He was alone, yet not alone within himself. Inside him was someone who could do things he had thought he could never do, someone who had killed even when he didn't have to kill: that person had shot at people sitting around tables with lighted candles in the Czar of Russia Café. His teeth chattered as he leaned against a wall. He didn't know how long his heart had pounded against the stone—but whose heart was it anyway? The heart of the person who could kill a man sitting at a table in a café, or the heart of the man whose teeth were chattering? He felt a sudden desire to hold the hand of that girl Dušanka in the park in Niš. And to hear someone's footsteps. And a voice—anybody's voice—in this infinite silence. He couldn't move a step; there was nowhere to go. The silence filled him with such horror that he wanted to shatter it with a grenade. He'd have done it, if he hadn't heard an invisible Šunto mount an invisible horse, and clipclop off in the direction of Terazije. The clipclop roused him; he moved.

He walked along the sidewalk, stumbling over corpses. His knees shook. One needed some idea in order to kill. Those banal, grandiloquent words. One must have a war goal, one must accept a large-scale fraud. He encountered Austrian patrols and fled into Ratarska Street. Once more he walked on corpses: soft, yielding objects obstructing his purpose, stiffening piles of horror, nausea, and futility which in a few hours would begin to smell. Defeat and victory smelled alike. Why didn't people know that? Suddenly he heard a bugle sounding reveille. He pressed himself against a wall and held his breath. The reveille overflowed into a shepherd's song: it was Šunto. He was playing for the dead Seventh and Fourteenth Regiments, for the men from Srem and Banat, for the police. Bora walked slowly, scarcely moving his feet, then stopped. Now the bugle was close at hand, again sounding reveille and ending with a shepherd's song. He set off boldly, stumbled over a broken cart, and fell into a shell hole.

Near the Kamenović Café he caught sight of a big fire with some Austrians around it. A white horse carrying a rider in a black cloak trotted past the fire and the Austrians. It was him! Moments later Bora heard reveille being sounded at the Red Cross and set off in that direction. Perhaps he would meet Šunto and go down to Marinko's Pool with him. The bugle now sounded a charge. There was a salvo of rifle fire, and a machine gun. Šunto would be killed. "Belgrade will be taken," he said aloud, and hurried downhill. The charge ended near Slavija. He heard someone crying pitifully in the darkness for his mother. He felt fear and joy. He listened; it was as if the man's breathing was forcing its way through to him. He went up to the cry.

"What regiment are you from, comrade?"

The wounded man didn't reply. Bora struck a match, but it wouldn't light. It was damp. He tried a few more: no luck.

"What's wrong? Why don't you say something? Is it your jaw? Come on, say something."

There was no reply. Rain was falling. What on earth should he do? How could he leave a wounded man to be killed by the Fritzies? He couldn't save the battle for Belgrade by such a betrayal. He knelt down. "Get on my back! What are you waiting for?"

The man didn't stir. Bora cursed him loudly and lifted him onto his back, then set off downhill through meadows and vineyards. Ahead of them some Austrians were sitting around a fire. He would have to make a detour. The wounded man grabbed his neck.

"Don't squeeze so hard, you'll strangle me!" he muttered. The wounded man squeezed harder. "Let go of me, you coward!" He rushed down to the stream. The Austrians fired a few shots; the wounded man groaned and nearly suffocated Bora. He threw him onto the ground and barely restrained himself from crushing him. But the fall silenced the wounded man, who lost consciousness. Bora lifted him onto his back again and carried him out of the stream. A bugle sounded a charge. There was a thick burst of rifle fire, with grenades. He halted with the wounded man on his back, waiting for Šunto to get killed. The firing went on and he continued uphill into the rainy dawn, tottering under the burden that was squeezing his neck. "I'm saving you, you idiot, and you're strangling me!"

"But you haven't saved me—I'm not on your side," said the wounded man with a long-drawn-out groan.

"Whose side are you on?" He bent over him: in the dawn light he saw the Austrian uniform and jumped away in fright. "You're one of them, you bloody bastard!"

"I'm a soldier of the Emperor."

"You're one of our Fritzies, damn you! Why didn't you tell me?"

"I was afraid you'd kill me. I was wounded in the chest, and my men abandoned me last night to rush after yours."

"You mean ours, you idiot!"

"You don't have any doctors or hospitals. What'll happen to me? I'm finished. What'll I do?" The wounded man was weeping.

"Wait until your men arrive!" said Bora. He spat at him, then set off along the slope. Soon he was stopped by a Serbian sentry. He gave his name and asked for headquarters. The soldier pointed to a white building above a plum orchard. After some ten paces, Bora turned around and told the soldiers that an Austrian was lying wounded on the other side of the forest and should be taken to the first aid post. "He deserted to us," Bora said, despising himself.

Early in the morning an officer from the staff of the Belgrade Defense Force took him to report to General Mihajlo Živković on what had happened in Belgrade the previous night. Bora was the last of the defenders to escape alive.

The splotchy-faced general stood next to a map of Serbia, looking suspiciously at Bora.

"So you were the last Serbian soldier to leave Belgrade this morning, Sergeant?"

"No, sir. While I was extricating myself from the stream at Čubura a band of our men made a charge from Veliki Vračar toward Slavija. The fight lasted till dawn."

"Do you know whose detachment that was?"

"Yes, sir. It was the platoon of Šunto Zlatiborac."

"Magnificent! That's how the Serbian capital should be defended!

Captain, bring me a form to recommend Šunto Zlatiborac for the Karageorge Star, first class."

Bora smiled.

"Do you think this hero deserves the highest award for bravery?"

"Yes, I'm quite sure of it, sir."

"Thank you, Sergeant. Get some rest, then report to the regimental command."

Bora saluted and went out to look for a dry place to sleep. But from under the eaves Tričko Macedonian leaped and hugged him: "You're alive, damn you, you're alive!"

"I'm not sure. But I got the Karageorge Star for Šunto Zlatiborac. Find a dry spot for me. I want to sleep."

5

Since dawn King Peter had been looking at the Bukulja and Rudnik mountains. He was full of apprehension. He walked through the heavy rain and entered his church, where the workmen and stonecutters had gathered. The King had ordered work stopped on the sarcophagus, which had come out seventeen centimeters too short. Some of the marble slabs were two to three centimeters wider than the space designed for them. The three rows of slabs leading to the main door were laid down unevenly—people would stumble. Wrapped in his soldier's overcoat, the King stood on the top step of the nave, his architect, Jovanović, beside him.

"I gave them precise measurements, Your Majesty. You can check the plans."

"What use are precise measurements to illiterate people? Why didn't you check what they were doing?"

"But I did, Your Majesty, whenever I was in the quarry. The workmen can't concentrate. They are upset by the approach of the Germans."

"Nonsense! Two weeks ago you asked for a raise, and I acceded for the third time this summer. *Pillards sans scruple!* It's impossible to deal with such architects. Well, it's all my fault. *Dans ce pays il aurait fallu être inspecteur de police, et pas roi.* Where's the material for the church? When will the material for the caretaker's cottage be here? The building site is chaos, and the Germans are on their way, Mr. Jovanović!"

"What can I do, Your Majesty? People can only think about how to save their skins. In fact, several workmen fled last night."

"Don't use the enemy as an excuse! Manasija and Kaknić were built while the Turks were in Kruševac. If you had worked harder, you'd have finished the church and transferred Karageorge's bones by the feast of the Assumption."

His adjutant, Colonel Todorović, announced that the High Command was on the telephone.

"Tell the High Command to leave me alone! The Germans will be here in three days. What can we do before then? I won't be able to bury Karageorge. The Germans will capture my unfinished church. It's a disaster!"

"His Royal Highness Prince Alexander wants you to come to the telephone immediately," Colonel Todorović said firmly.

"Tell him to call me at seven." The King turned around and saw builders and stonecutters gathered in the narthex. "Are you gentlemen waiting for coffee and cognac?" he asked.

"It's pouring, Your Majesty."

He walked quickly to the door, stopped under the portal, and stared at the heavy rain coming down on Topola. "A disaster," he said, and went down into the crypt. He leaned against the sarcophagus: it was the worst debacle of his life. A king was king through the privileges he ensured for his subjects and the churches he built. The privileges were never exactly what he would have wished for Serbia, but now she was losing everything. And he wouldn't finish the church; he would never finish it. You couldn't build a holy place with people who weren't holy in their hearts. He was thinking of God and eternity, while those around him were thinking of themselves and the present. The debacle of one more Karageorgevic. Why hadn't he remained Pierre Kara, an officer in the French army?

The sound of rain and artillery vibrated through the domes.

Since the time of the pharaohs no one had built any temple, church, or monastery from his own savings and a monthly allowance doled out by an Assembly. Tyrants built for eternity. But this was impossible for the constitutional king of a poor country, who in ten years could not save more than five hundred thousand dinars, and who had to buy lead for the church roof by economizing in the kitchen. No, he could not build for eternity.

The King looked up and saw Todorović.

"His Royal Highness Prince Alexander has ordered our evacuation from Topola. Two trucks will come for us at daybreak tomorrow. Prince Alexander will expect you in Kragujevac tomorrow evening."

"Tell the High Command not to send any trucks. I'm not leaving Topola."

He waved him away and walked to the door. Above the door, where the wall joined the ceiling, he saw a leak. The King dropped his stick and walked around the church, staring at its domes. Then, spotting a damp patch on the central dome, he stopped dead. His powerful, autocratic ancestors would have cut off heads as punishment for leaking domes! Freedom builds only for today. It builds only what is useful. Did he regret that he wanted human freedom to be his memorial?

Doctor Simović and Zdravko came in with a lamp and took him back to the house. He refused supper, but asked that a cup of herb tea good for rheumatism be brought to him in bed. He lay down. Apart from using force and taking from the state treasury, was there any way he could complete the foundations for his church and his hospital in a free country? Perhaps the unfinished church was punishment from God for a terrible, unrepented sin. Or perhaps his fate was decided by the fate of Serbia—all that he had begun would collapse with his country.

Colonel Todorović announced that Vojvoda Putnik was on the telephone. He would have to talk to him, the first vojvoda of Serbia.

"Good evening, Vojvoda."

"The enemy is advancing on the northern front, Your Majesty. We must retreat as fast as possible to avoid the encirclement and annihilation of the army. In three days Topola will be under fire from long-range artillery."

"Let them fire. How is the army taking the retreat?"

"Military reasons and reasons of state require that you withdraw to Kragujevac tomorrow, Your Majesty."

"I won't withdraw from Topola, Vojvoda, until I've transferred Karageorge's bones to my new church. The roof needs repairs."

"The High Command can't leave Your Majesty in danger. I beg you, tomorrow at the latest—"

"Worry about the armies and the munition supplies, Vojvoda, not about an old king. Withdraw the supply dumps in good time, and let royalty take care of itself. That's my advice to you."

"My oath obliges me to protect my King."

"Then the King releases his Vojvoda from that oath."

"Forgive me, Your Majesty, but a ruler cannot be released from his royal duty to the country and the army. I must ask you to permit the evacuation of your property tomorrow morning."

"My property is my church foundation. And it is being built,

Vojvoda, so that there should never be any withdrawal in the face of any enemy of Serbia. Since I haven't completed the church, I have no right to retreat. Good-by."

The King spent the night in fitful sleep broken by anxieties, disappointments, and regrets. Several times he got up to see whether it was raining. The church was shrouded in misty darkness. Under no circumstances would he withdraw until he had interred Karageorge's bones in the church. Karageorge's murderer, Prince Miloš, had sent Karageorge's head to Istanbul as a sign of his loyalty to the sultan. For decades he had been tormented by this incontrovertible fact of Serbian history, and asked himself whether it had been necessary, when the Serbs were already defeated, to send the head of the leader of the uprising to the Turks as evidence of their devotion.

At dawn he went into the church with Zdravko to inspect the leaks. There were new water stains in the apse. He then visited his hospital in Topola, where the central heating installation was full of water. On the way home Zdravko said: "I can hear artillery, Your Majesty."

"I didn't ask any questions. Do your duty."

When the King arrived Jovanović reported that three stonemasons and a tinsmith had fled during the night.

"I'm not interested, sir. I'm now giving you orders, not as your employer, but as King of Serbia. The leaking roofs and walls are to be repaired by tomorrow evening. And remember this: my grandfather Karageorge shot at his own brother. And I am—we are—now at war!"

The King went into his private room. Before adding up his extra expenses, he set aside the money for the poor, which he noted in his account book under a variety of symbols. He did this to preserve the dignity of the King and the honor of the recipients: the royal assistance must remain a secret. He considered reducing aid this month, but quickly decided not to. These might be his last royal benefactions.

Colonel Todorović announced the arrival of the Valjevo priest Božidar Jevotević. The King was as delighted by the arrival of his faithful companion from the Bosnian uprising of 1875 as he would have been by a clear day or a lull on the front. This priest and platoon leader was the man with whom he had escaped from Bosnia after the failure of the uprising.

The priest bent down humbly to kiss the King's hand, but King Peter would not allow it. Instead he embraced the priest and kissed him on the cheek.

"I'm delighted to see you, Božidar! Only God can have sent you on such a day. Sit down. Don't worry about sitting in the King's chair.

You're wet and muddy. Zdravko, bring some hot tea and breakfast. What brings you here, Božidar, at this unhappy time?"

"People are running away. Serbia is in flight once again, sir. I too have set out, in the wake of our male children. I've dropped in to ask you what's going on."

"I don't believe the Russians and the French will allow Serbia to be overrun. I have faith that the Allies will land a large army in Salonika and strike at the Bulgarians from the south."

"I'm afraid, sir, it might be too late for that. But first let me ask you about your son George. I hear he has been wounded in Belgrade."

"Yes, that's so. But thank God he's alive."

"That's right, sir. May his wound heal in the shortest possible time, with God's help. I've lived a long time, and can remember great trials and misfortunes. But I've never felt such fear for Serbia as I do now. Serbia is being pulled up by the roots."

"I know, Father," the King said, "but as always in our past, there'll be people to seize the banner and rush forward against force and power. As you did in 1875. The Turks were stronger, but didn't we give them a beating? Were we ever so hopelessly surrounded by stronger forces? But we charged and we survived."

The priest drank up his tea, looked the King straight in the eye, and asked sternly: "Do you think, sir, that it's good for the future of Serbia to bring all the male children over twelve out in front of the army? Abraham taking his son Isaac onto the hill of Moria—that's how I see it."

"Everything must be sacrificed to God and country, Father. That is our fate."

"God stayed Abraham's hand and saved Isaac. But you haven't stayed the hands of Pašić and Putnik, sir. You don't get around to it because of your involvement with your church."

The King trembled. So that was what he thought, this rebel leader and famous patriot from Hercegovina! He looked at the priest in amazement. "I can't do everything. If we're in God's hands . . ."

Colonel Todorović announced that Prince Alexander was on the telephone. The King went out to answer it.

"Why such urgency, Sandra?"

"Father, you must withdraw from Topola without delay. I cannot allow the King of Serbia to be taken prisoner."

"No one can take Peter Karageorgevic prisoner, my boy. I shall withdraw from Topola when I've finished my work here. You concentrate on your own problems." He hung up and rejoined the priest.

"I know there will be a terrible vengeance for our victories on Suvobor and the Kolubara," the priest went on. "The Bulgarian vengeance for Bregalnica will be even more terrible. But sir, whatever lies ahead, the people should not be separated from their homes, their sheepfolds, and their meadows. That's where they are strongest."

"The enemy will crush our people in revenge, Božidar. All who can must flee."

"The people cannot save themselves from their fate, from what God has ordained for them. A man must wait for every evil on his own doorstep. The evil which outlives him there has still deeper roots. The scythe strengthens the roots of the grass, sir."

"But we're only withdrawing until the Allies arrive, Božidar. And they must arrive, because otherwise the Germans will take Istanbul and the Bosphorus before Mitrovdan.*

"And if the Allies don't arrive, what will we do with our children then?"

The King stood by the window, stared out at the rain and at the workmen on the main dome of the church, and then turned back to the priest. "I don't know, Father."

Vojvoda Putnik was weakened by the latest bout with his illness; breathing was becoming very difficult, and his conversations with the commanders who telephoned twice a day even more so.

"Mišić, what is it you wanted to tell me this morning?"

"If I send Živković the regiment which the High Command instructed me to send last night, I'll have to evacuate Valjevo in three days."

"You must give him the regiment. If we don't hold the enemy at Kosmaj, they'll rush down the Great Morava valley."

"Yes, sir. But with a weakened army I can't hold a three-hundred-kilometer front and keep the Germans out of the Western Morava valley at the same time."

"I know, Mišić. But I still believe that the best course of action is to slow down Mackensen's breakthrough along the Great Morava, because of the Bulgarian offensive and the Allied help we're expecting."

"Which isn't likely to come."

"We'll have no more discussion about that!"

"But I must ask you, sir, to listen: our defense is unpardonably passive. We must take a decisive initiative."

* St. Demetrius' Day, October 26. [Translator's note.]

"What initiative? And where, Mišić?"

"By striking a blow at Mackensen's flank with my army."

"Where can we get the men for such action? A big attack would exhaust our strength."

"Defensive strategy and protracted resistance can only increase our difficulties."

"Perhaps someday you'll have an opportunity to demonstrate this in the Military Academy. But now, Mišić, carry out my orders."

Putnik hung up. Mišić wanted to repeat the Suvobor action, so he was pushing his own idea: attack, attack! This was no longer a strategic plan, it was desperation in which there was an illusion of courage. He had saved his honor as a commander and won fame and glory, but behind him he left graves. Yes, graves. Putnik closed his eyes to compose himself, but the telephone rang again. It was General Živković. "If I don't get new reinforcements today, sir, I can't hold my present positions until tomorrow," he said.

"Fight with what you have. Our military reserves are in our hearts, Živković, and in our will to hold out."

"The spirit of the army is powerless against Mackensen's heavy artillery, sir."

"Don't listen to the German guns. Listen to the hearts of your soldiers, Živković."

"I'm convinced that it's strategically necessary to maintain today's position at all cost."

"No position is to be defended at all cost now. Positions are to be defended as long as our soldiers believe that the enemy's losses are no less than our own. Our army must never feel defeated."

"Have the Allies moved from Salonika? What should I tell the soldiers, sir?"

"The Allies have promised help. We're waiting for it."

The telephone rang again. It was Šturm: "The state of my army is critical, sir. There have been more surrenders. The army has lost faith in the Allies."

"We are defending ourselves with our own faith, and can expect only help from the Allies. Low morale among your men is your fault, Šturm."

"Why, sir?"

"In an unequal war, it's the commanders who lose the battles, not the soldiers. An army must feel that it can and must do what it's being asked to do."

"How can we convince them of this when one naked, barefoot

platoon of ours is attacked by a battalion of theirs, clothed and shod for mud and cold? When we have only one piece of field artillery with a range of six kilometers, against five of theirs which can fire thirty? What can they do?"

"They can do their utmost, Šturm. What counts is the skill of our commanders, and knowing how to use our troops to the limit of their capacity. And that limit is in the soldiers' hearts. Find it and guard it carefully."

"Can I have at least two batteries of field guns, sir?"

"Who can I take them from, Šturm? Work with what you have."

Putnik was dripping with sweat. Supported by his orderly, he walked over to his bed, but the telephone rang again. It was Vojvoda Stepa, who was holding crucial positions against the Bulgarians.

"This morning the Bulgarians made a powerful thrust toward Skoplje, sir. They're attacking with three armies. If I'm to hold them back at all, I must have at least one division."

"All I can send you, Stepa, is the High Command guard, a platoon of third-draft men, our last reserves."

Stepa hung up. How could Putnik defend himself from his commanders? How long dare he oppose facts and logic by force of will without destroying the army's faith? And would he, in his bed, know when the critical hour for the Serbian army had come?

As evening approached, his anxiety increased along with his difficulty in breathing. Colonel Živko Pavlović brought him disastrous reports. Putnik didn't want his subordinates to see his face, so he had his orderly place only one flickering lamp on the table. Night filled his room with an unpleasant, disturbing smell, the smell of chrysanthemums and new graves. Twice he rang for his orderly to close the windows tight and stuff the cracks with rags, but the smell seeped through the walls, the wooden ceiling, and the floorboards. His orderly brought incense, but it only made his cough worse. He was anxious for his children. He would take his eldest daughter, Radojka, with him, but what should he do with Milica, the youngest? He was less worried about his sons. And the night life in the High Command made him angry: he was aware of disorder, of laxity in discipline. He shuddered. Discipline was not only the essential quality of an army, an indication of the level of its organization, but also the visible form of all great laws, the sense of direction, shape, and beauty of every manifestation of energy. Only the weakest human material resisted discipline. He didn't have the physical strength to prevent the chaos in which the vital axis would be broken—the axis that, along with faith in this order and a sense of its purpose, kept the human community in order. If his spirit and will didn't prevail here, in the High Command—if he couldn't maintain discipline and military order within himself and around him—how could he command an army in an unequal war, in the daily defeats before the final one?

Before midnight he summoned the section chiefs, checked that all his instructions were being carried out, and gave orders that officers who had been slack in their duties be sent to the battlefield in the morning. He threatened demotion and punishment for every failure to carry out orders, for every breach of the rules of military service. All this in a whisper. He ordered his assistant, Pavlović, to call together the staffs of the armies, divisions, and regional commands to check whether his latest instructions had been carried out; he wanted to stretch out his hand to the battalions, to have his whisper heard in every platoon, and have every soldier in more than a thousand kilometers of trenches feel his eyes upon him.

Once he was left alone with his sleeping cat, his breath short and wheezing, his head lying limply on the pillow, he asked himself if his illness hadn't made him ridiculous in people's eyes, if he wasn't ridiculous because of his faith in victory. To be decrepit and old, but have great authority—that was the most painful and hideous thing in the fate of a man of power; the final, shameful descent, the broken end, the undignified fall of a lofty arc. A sick and aging military leader: what was more wretched and pathetic, where strength and will should be dominant? This weakness of old age was disfiguring his whole life. Success, reputation, great deeds—all were now in question in himself, in his subordinates, in Prince Alexander, and in the politicians. Any attitude which he held tenaciously was exposed to doubt, and his firmness was subject to pity, his severity to concealed scorn. The more he stressed his faith in victory, the less convincing he was to himself. He sensed that people had little confidence in a belief that was overemphatically expressed, because faith could conceal fear, too. It was long past midnight: he ached from the feeling of the futility in this war in which the forces were so unevenly matched; it was madness that upheld him and the Serbian army! Yes, it was great and honorable, heroic and holy, but madness all the same! He wanted to groan aloud but he dared not, for he knew that Doctor Stojadinović, his orderlies, and the sentry were nearby, listening to his breathing. And some of the chiefs of the High Command stood there against the wall for hours. He was afraid of himself, so weak and invisible in the darkness of a great battlefield in which one small army was being crushed in vain resistance to three great armies attacking from three points of the compass. And the commander of that army lay in bed between pillows, with wool socks on his feet, suffocating. A fish on dry land. The veins in his neck and temples were swollen from the effort of breathing; the whistling and creaking in his chest were intolerable. His hands were sweating and trembling. And that dull pain in his chest: it was as if some merciless victor had trampled on it in a wrestling match. He asked his orderly to take out the cat and bring him some elderflower tea. He hated this tea but it would lessen the stench of wet graves, which seemed to emanate from everywhere. Rottenness, autumn, death.

"Forgive me, Vojvoda, for waking you," said Prince Alexander, standing next to his bed. "But last night's reports from the fronts are extremely disquieting. Can you hear me?"

"I'm listening, Your Highness."

"Mackensen has made a powerful thrust into the Great Morava valley. In a few days our army will be split in two, surrounded in central Serbia, and wiped out."

Putnik looked resentfully at Alexander, who was always ill at ease, and who persisted in attempting to command an army with the knowledge of a lieutenant, refusing to accept his official rank of Commander in Chief as titular only. But Alexander's fear was justified. The Serbian army was in a crisis. Still, what gave him the right to that reproachful tone, that dark and angry expression? He was passive and lacking in initiative, unfit to command the army, yet perhaps he was waiting for him, Putnik, to resign.

"If yesterday's penetration continues," the Prince went on, "they'll be here in Kragujevac in three days. Stepanović won't be able to hold out in Niš. We must do something, Vojvoda!"

"Permit me, Your Highness, to get up and get dressed," he said crossly. "Then I'll give you my opinion."

Putnik rang for his orderly and told him to dress him and put on his boots. He had never in his life felt so humiliated, struggling to dress in the presence of Alexander, who stood by the window with his hands behind his back, berating Pašić and the government for the national comedy of preparing a welcome for the Allies. After he had washed, dressed, and drunk his tea, Putnik sat at the table and began to speak.

"What kind of action do you have in mind, Your Highness? What hasn't been done that should have been?"

Alexander turned pale. "We must do something more significant and decisive. We must be in constant touch with the commanders on the battlefield. Panic is spreading."

Putnik understood this as a reproach against himself, directed at his illness. Alexander would replace him in a minute, if he could, but Putnik wasn't going to let him. No, this was *his* war. "What do you propose, Your Highness?"

"Strengthen our defenses in the direction of the Great Morava. Immediately."

"With what troops? We have no reserves, not even a platoon. Mišic protested yesterday because we took another regiment from him. From whom can we take a battalion today?"

"They'll split us! They'll surround us!"

"That was their intention from the start. But I won't let them break us and surround us. Colonel Pavlović and I are prepared to forestall that. The enemy won't capture a single battalion by military skill. Only cowards and those who've lost hope . . ." His cough prevented him from finishing.

Alexander paced up and down the room, complaining about the Allies, especially the English, who so far had landed only four infantry regiments and two battalions of artillery at Salonika.

Putnik grew calmer, wiped the sweat off his face, and lit a cigarette to relieve his asthma.

"Yesterday I sent the Allies new requests for help," he said. "I repeated that we must retreat southward, and fast. But Great Powers don't always behave sensibly. Even when it's to their own advantage."

Živko Pavlović came in with telegrams. His face was distorted from lack of sleep.

"Good news, I hope?" Alexander said anxiously.

"We haven't had that kind of telegram yet, Your Highness. Allow me to give you the news on Salonika. Here are the telegrams from Paris that General Bayou has received: 'Do not cross over into Serbian territory. Occupy the Strumica area.' And then: 'Remain in Salonika until you receive an additional division.' "

"The French general staff must be drunk!" cried Alexander angrily.

"When our military attaché proposed to General Saray in person that a strong offensive be launched, he replied: 'I'm a Frenchman and a general in the French army, and I won't become a pawn of the Serbian general staff.' General Saray's reply to your next to last telegram, sir, is: 'With the best will in the world, I cannot undertake an offensive until I have sufficient troops.' "

Putnik felt a burning sensation mounting in his throat. He couldn't bear to see Pavlović and Alexander looking at him with pity and condescension. When the burning subsided, he nodded to Pavlović to continue his report.

"The Russians have informed us that they can't help with their Bessarabian army in the foreseeable future. They don't have enough boats to cross the sea and the Danube, and the Rumanians won't let them cross their territory."

"Surely the Russians aren't washing their hands of us?" said Alexander.

"The worst news yet is from London. Lord Kitchener replied to our military attaché yesterday as follows: 'You Serbs find yourselves in such a situation today, because you obstinately refused to make the concessions demanded by Bulgaria. You maintained that you would rather perish than give the Bulgarians eastern Macedonia. It is logical that you are in such a difficult position now. We will help you, but we need time.' "

"Disgraceful! England is on the side of the Bulgarians! The world will be appalled by this injustice to Serbia. We'll bear it, but we won't forget it. There's still Russia, and God." Tears came into the Prince's eyes.

Putnik didn't care for emotional reactions to great issues. He found it odious to hear Serbs wailing about the injustices of the world. All that noise and protest against the mighty order and eternal laws was for him a sign of inferior intelligence, of sheer human folly. But he was deeply worried by Lord Kitchener's message, not because of the injustice toward Serbia but because such an attitude might lead the Balkans to surrender quickly to Germany and Austria-Hungary. He asked Pavlović to instruct the armies to begin immediately a gradual withdrawal to a shortened defense line, but when Alexander left to call the Allied military attachés once again and ask for help, Putnik sank back in exhaustion.

This faintheartedness did not last long. He must think: had he really done everything possible? No: there was still fear. He had the power and the right to use it—it was his final military reserve. Fear was both the destroyer and the builder of men. Fear was all-powerful. It was time to strengthen the vacillating and despondent spirit of his army with fear. He tried to write an order to all the commanders for the introduction of court-martials, but his hand shook so much that he could hardly hold the pencil. He summoned Pavlović and dictated it: cowards, insubordinates, looters, and all who show distrust in the government and the Allies, or poison people's hearts with pessimism, were to be shot without mercy.

Vojvoda Mišić was shocked by Putnik's order to withdraw to the banks of the Western Morava. He saw it as a psychological blow to the Serbian army, the beginning of the end for Serbia. He immediately telephoned the High Command and demanded to speak to Putnik.

"What is it that you don't find clear, Mišić?"

"Your instructions about withdrawal, sir. If we withdraw to the banks of the Morava, what's left to defend?"

"Serbia, Mišić."

"There's not much of Serbia beyond the Morava, and on that remnant we can't defend the country."

"And where can we defend it?"

"Where we are now. We must consolidate our positions and offer decisive battle. If we retreat, we'll get weaker and they'll get stronger."

"With that strategy and without allies, we'd be defeated in a week."

"In your withdrawal toward nonexistent allies we'll be annihilated and disgraced."

"Vojvoda, I order you to implement my decision."

At dusk the army staff set out toward Mionica and Gukoši. Mišić sent his wife and daughters with an escort to Arandjelovac, while he remained in the deserted district court with his adjutant, his orderly Dragutin, and a few soldiers, without a telephone or any contact with the High Command or his troops. He ordered the sentry not to admit anyone, then told Dragutin to light the stoves in the empty courtroom, in which a year before, at that fateful meeting of the government and the High Command, he had taken the first step toward his greatest military victory: his resolute opposition to Putnik's proposal to initiate peace talks with the enemy. He wanted to have the stoves lit not so much because it was wet and chilly outside, but because he wanted to spend this last night in his native district gazing at the fire, roasting apples, breathing in the fragrance of winter, and remembering his childhood. It seemed to him that more than a decade had passed since last year's victory over Potiorek. He felt great sorrow over that victory and the fame he had won as a commander. He'd felt sorrow since that night in Struganik when he had sat by the fireside of his family home with Vukašin Katić.

The noise he heard from the street—the rumbling of carts, the local people calling out to one another, the barking of dogs—he took as the end of the world in which he had lived. With every step he took in the empty courtroom, he felt he was going away, and forever. Every cigarette he lit seemed to be his last.

"Your apples are burnt, sir."

"Bring some more, Dragutin. And another cup of lime tea."

There were tears in Dragutin's eyes, but Mišić couldn't comfort him. He couldn't comfort himself. He was tormented by his inability to do anything or change anything. This war was so unequal, the struggle for survival so unjust. His role had become a secondary one, determined for him by the incomprehensible Austro-German strategy of attacking Serbia, which Putnik's defensive strategy was confirming.

Last autumn, when they had debated in this very courtroom whether Serbia could be saved from Potiorek's armies, he had opposed Putnik's conclusion that the Serbian army had done all it could to defend its country. He had countered this by challenging everyone to have faith, with his conviction that in the people there was an inexhaustible will to survive. This will was not the same as Putnik's present belief in victory, a belief in a miracle. The will to survive was deeper and more fundamentally human than any belief in victory; military victory, or for that matter any other victory, wasn't the only possible means of survival. With this will they could survive military defeat and bondage if this meant less suffering and death, less destruction of the nation and the individual. This will sought survival under any circumstances and by all means necessary: by courage, by saving one's neck, by submission, or by stubborn resistance.

Pašić, on the other hand, strove for victory through faith in the Allies, lying to and deceiving both the people and the army. Pašić and Putnik were prepared to sacrifice everything for the creation of a Greater Serbia and some kind of Yugoslavia. What nonsense! The most difficult objective, in the most difficult circumstances. In this hopeless situation only an insatiable desire for fame and self-love—only the vanity of a vojvoda and the political grandiosity of that aging, power-hungry Pašić—could present to the people aims which were beyond their power and outside their vital needs. As for Putnik, he wouldn't relinquish command even on his deathbed; he considered himself anointed by God, and believed that Serbia would collapse without him. A commander who served the people, not his own ambition, would have passed the command to a younger, healthier man. Unfortunately, the Serbian people, too—down to the last baggage-train attendant—believed that the Serbian army couldn't exist without Putnik. Serbia seemed doomed to have faith in leaders who in fact were not leaders; that faith might be their downfall. Could a small nation survive in these evil times, a nation hated by all its neighbors?

What could he do in this hurtling progress of events, in the face of inevitable catastrophe? He had spoken his mind to the High Command, to the government, and to King Peter, risking the reputation he'd gained from his victory on Suvobor. Perhaps he too would be disgraced and ruined in this national calamity.

"Your apples are burnt again, sir," said Dragutin as he made up the fire.

Mišić's spine ached. He sat down by the stove and stared at the fire: flame would always end in smoke, and embers in ash. Why resist the inevitable?

At first light Mišić, accompanied by his adjutant and Dragutin, left the Valjevo courthouse and got into his car. He told the driver to go slowly and to sound the horn only as a last resort. He wanted to overtake as few as possible of those oxcarts full of children, maize, and household goods; he didn't want to frighten the animals, women, and old men fleeing to some unknown destination. When they had left Valjevo and set out along the road to Mionica and Ljig—a road along which weak and helpless people, the survivors of typhus and enemy reprisals, were creeping from hedge to hedge—he was seized by the memory of the refugees he had seen along the same road last year. He alone had been going in the opposite direction. Then he had been in the Prince Regent's car, recently appointed to the command of the disintegrating First Army, and from Kragujevac to Mionica he hadn't met or overtaken anybody. Now he was going in front of his army, at the head of the terrified and despairing refugees, and he had no words of encouragement and comfort for either them or his soldiers. He couldn't say, "Where are you fleeing? Go no farther. I'll stop the Austrians and drive them across the Drina and the Sava." He couldn't speak a single kind or cheerful word to them; he had none.

The car stopped behind a flock of sheep and a herd of swine that refused to stir from the road while some women and children hit and pushed them in vain. The driver asked whether he might sound his horn. Mišić nodded, and with great difficulty the car pushed its way through the animals. Just short of Mionica they stopped again: the road was blocked by people, animals, and an army baggage train. Dragutin, his face pressed against the car window, groaned aloud.

"What's the matter, Dragutin?"

"All this misery, sir. And rain to boot."

"That's our fate, Dragutin."

"I understand, sir."

"You must understand and endure." Mišić warned the driver not to sound his horn, curled up in a corner of the car, and lit a cigarette.

Elderly peasants crowded around the car and recognized him. Some raised their caps and cried, "Where are we going, Vojvoda? What's going to become of us?"

Mišić looked at them: no, he wouldn't deceive them with hope in the Allies. "This isn't the first or last time we've taken to flight. We're struggling for our lives and our freedom, and with that in mind we must endure everything. We've outlived many a mortal foe, and we'll outlive this one. I'm sure we will."

"Can't you promise us anything else?" asked an old man with a forage cap pulled down to his eyebrows.

"Only that I'll work hard for our survival, and endure together with you. Right to the end."

"Thank you, Vojvoda."

Mišić saluted them and told the driver to move on. In front of the town hall in Mionica an officer from his staff stopped the car to hand him two telegrams. One was from Pašić, attacking the lack of faith in the Allies which now undermined the army, and asserting that the Allies would come to the aid of Serbia with strong forces, and soon, to help defend his "great and holy national aims." The other was a public statement of Nicholas II of Russia, condemning the "Bulgarian betrayal of the Slav cause"; for this reason, the Bulgarians could expect "the just retribution of God." Mišić read both telegrams hastily and handed them back to the officer.

"Put them in the archives!"

On the bridge at Mionica, where last autumn he had halted an army in flight and, risking everything, affirmed his will over the chaos of defeat, he told the driver to stop. He got out of the car, leaned against the stone parapet, and stared at the turgid Ribnica, the river of his childhood, the river from whose banks he had begun the action leading to the victory on Suvobor. Could so much suffering and sacrifice have been in vain? The rain was pouring down on the unharvested fields, knocking dead leaves from the yellowing willows and poplars. Mist and cloud enshrouded his homeland in sadness. Some people came up to him, raised their caps, but maintained a strained silence, waiting for some word from him. He didn't know what to say.

"We've a terrible autumn in store, brothers. Prepare for great hardship."

"Will the Allies help us, Vojvoda?"

"They will if they're sensible. But don't put your trust in someone else—put it in yourselves, as you always have. And share good and ill like brothers. Meanwhile the army will do its duty."

He got back into the car, which then moved off toward Gukoši, slowly pushing its way through the fleeing populace. He didn't look at his village of Struganik as they passed by.

"Last autumn these ditches were full of Austrian munitions carts and gun carriages," said Dragutin, his face pressed against the window.

"Do you believe we'll come back to Valjevo, Dragutin? Do you think we'll pass this way, as we did when we came down from Suvobor?"

"Yes, I do, sir. We'll come back as we did that time when some officers met us at a bend in the road and handed you a vojvoda's baton, and you told me to stuff it in my bag."

"Does anyone else believe this?"

"Not everyone, but there are a lot that do."

Mišić fell silent.

"There's the plum orchard where you rescued me from that lieutenant—who was killed ten days later, God rest his soul. There's the plum tree I was tied to," Dragutin concluded.

As soon as they reached the inn at Gukoši, where the staff of his army had established itself, Vojvoda Mišić and Colonel Hadžić worked out a plan for a flank attack against Mackensen's thrust, which he told Hadžić to propose to the High Command. Within half an hour Živko Pavlović approved the plan. Mišić was surprised by this affirmative response from the High Command, and the speed shown by Putnik. Was something significant about to happen? Why shouldn't a miracle occur? In man's struggle for life, miracles were possible.

Adam Katić was dozing in the saddle, hanging on to his horse. The squadron was marching through the dusk. Just before the German attack he had bought his mare Lasta for her speed and beauty from a captain on the division staff, paying in ducats. Although she was more timid than a hare in battle, on the march she carried him perfectly: her step was so light that he could have slept peacefully even with the rain trickling down his neck. But he was tormented by something more than fear for his life: the fighting which had begun some three weeks ago filled him with shame.

Yesterday there had been a short battle with German cavalry near Vodice, ending in defeat—a battle in which more Serbs had surrendered than had been killed, and of those who had been killed, more had died from the blows of rifle butts and sabers than from bullets, because they had been waiting to surrender with upraised rifles. In the first village they had come to, his squadron had looted without mercy and beaten women and old men as if they had captured a German village. When the looting was over they had come upon King Peter standing beside his car; he had greeted them by raising his stick and crying out in feeble tones, "Forward, my boys!" "Long live King Peter!" the soldiers had responded. "Long live Uncle Peter!" But Adam couldn't join in. He was amazed to find that the King was a poor old man who couldn't even mount a horse. Afterward he had felt sorry when Sima said, "Now that we've seen our oath, boys, tell me why half of Serbia must perish for the court and the sons of that man whose kingdom is being looked after by Pašić?" Adam didn't want to eat the bacon which Uroš Babović had stolen from a poverty-stricken house. He couldn't bear to feed his horse with stolen food, let alone himself, yet the squadron rarely received their rations, and then only half the regulation amount. So far, only cowards and men of bad character had deserted, but now everybody in the squadron was saying aloud that Serbia was collapsing and the Allies had deserted her. And tonight his friends Sima Pljakić and Uroš Babović, riding beside him, were grumbling:

"Where are those French and English troops? When will those Russians arrive to attack the Bulgarians? Don't talk to me about our allies, we don't have any! Pašić is lying, and Putnik, too—they're all lying and taking us for a ride. The rich are saving their skins in Greece, but we have to die for our country. Our homes are deserted, our barns and sheepfolds empty, they've driven our children to the army command posts, and we go to our death hungry. They won't even let us be taken prisoner—did you see yesterday how they beat up those who wanted to surrender? Why surrender when you can hide? I could hide where a whole division wouldn't find me. Listen, you've just got to save your skin while the enemy is passing through, and until they set up a government; afterward, you pay double taxes, cross yourself for Franz Josef, and go on toiling the same as you did under King Peter. You're right, Sima. To a peasant and a poor man all kings and emperors are the same."

"No they're not, Sima," snapped Adam Katić.

"Yes they are, Adam. And if there's any difference, it's still us who suffer."

"That's not true. *They're ours!*" he said, spurring his mare to get ahead of Sima, who was an Opposition supporter and stopped "pushing politics" only when he was asleep or firing his rifle. Sima found fault with everyone—Pašić and the State, the rich, the army contractors, thieves and generals. These complaints about the collapse of Serbia were painful to Adam, not because he believed that Serbia could be saved, but because it emerged from Sima's talk that one could save one's life only by desertion and disgrace, for which Adam was not prepared. His best friend Uroš Babović came up alongside him; as always when they were alone together, Uroš began the same story: "I can't help wondering whether Vida made it home, Adam."

"Of course she has!" Adam replied crossly. "She left two weeks ago. She could have reached Istanbul by now, let alone Trnava!"

They were indeed close friends, like brothers, but he couldn't bear to listen anymore to Uroš's daily worrying about Vida. Uroš had gotten married while on leave last summer and had been unable to part from his wife; he had brought her to the front at Mačva, hidden her in the village near their encampment, and with Adam's help had gone to her every evening, returning at dawn. Although only a few of the soldiers had seen Vida, the whole regiment talked of her miraculous beauty. Few knew that she was Uroš's wife; most thought she was Adam Katić's fiancée. Adam had neither confirmed nor denied it and although he envied Uroš, he enjoyed helping him in his secret married life. Adam had been punished with imprisonment and ran the risk of a court-martial, but because of the pleasure it gave him and for friendship's sake, he didn't flinch from any danger. The night the Germans crossed the Sava he and Uroš had left the column on the march, so Uroš could take leave of his wife and say to her: "Vida, tell the godfather that I wish our son to be called Miloš. If it's a girl, name her Milica. Leave for home at daybreak, and Adam and I and the men will take whatever fate assigns us." Vida had groaned aloud in the dark. Adam, thinking of Natalia, had stretched out his hand to Vida, but she hadn't touched it. He'd have liked to embrace her simply because she was beautiful, like Natalia, and because he might never embrace another woman. He stood there, his hand trembling, and he was ashamed. Then he got on his horse. He could hardly bring himself to move off behind Uroš; he didn't want to catch up with him and didn't speak a word to him: sadness and envy hurt like a physical pain.

"Do you think such a good-looking woman can hide from the Fritzies, Adam?"

"Your Vida isn't the only good-looking woman in Trnava, damn you!"

"I didn't say she was. Just think, though, what'll happen if some of those officers set eyes on her."

Adam fell silent and once more rested his head on his horse's neck to doze, but in vain. He was thinking about Prerovo, his grandfather, and his father. He remembered those mild nights full of the sound of frogs or crickets when, light as a cat, he had jumped over fences and hidden in haylofts where grass widows and young hired girls waited for him.

At dawn the squadron halted in Lapovo.

"So we'll have to plunder the poor again because of that bastard Pašić!" muttered Sima Pljakić, tying his horse to a fence.

Adam tied up his horse between Sima's and Uroš's, then went up to Lieutenant Sandić, the officer commanding the squadron: "Why don't we buy oats and hay for the horses, sir?"

"You must fend for yourself, Katić!"

"I won't steal from the people."

"Shut up, Katić!"

"The army ought to receive its rations, sir."

"Talk to the commanding officer—don't bother me. It's my job to make you give your life for your country. And to shoot you if you run away, according to the latest order from Putnik. You yap about something every time we stop."

Adam looked at him with contempt. Ever since he had taken this good-for-nothing lieutenant's pay at a game of cards and then lent him two thousand dinars, Sandić wouldn't play cards with him; and every time Adam spoke, he threatened him with beatings or imprisonment, and now with a firing squad. *That bastard will shoot me simply to avoid paying his debts,* thought Adam. He gave a thin smile but saluted correctly, then set off with Sima and Uroš to go from house to house, asking the women for food: "Can't you give us a bag of oats and an armful of hay, ma'am? And a bit of bread and cheese? I'll pay whatever you ask. We've lived on grapes and apples for two days. Tomorrow the Fritzies will take it all anyway."

"You're the third person since last night who's taken from me. Look at my sheepfold and my granary! And my hearth and my kneading trough! Empty! The Serbian army is taking everything. Who are you fighting for anyway?"

The three of them continued through the village, trying to beat the other members of the squadron to the richer households. Sima was happy because the women and old men cursed the government and wouldn't sell food, whatever money they were offered. Then Adam spied a pile of yellow corncobs under the roof of a shed. He gave Uroš ten dinars to buy a bundle of hay and a bagful of oats, while he himself slipped into the shed, lay down on the pile of corncobs, and breathed in the fragrance of meadows and autumn. At home now his corncribs would be full to the brim, and under the roof of the shed would stand a hillock of corn. The entire village of Prerovo would be yellow from husked corncobs. Was there anything in this world more beautiful than corn? How many times, coming back from being with a woman, had he fallen asleep on a pile of corn, his face against the ears, breathing in their ripeness and dry corn silk? Then just before dawn his father would cover him with blanket or send him off to his room. He had left for the war from Višnja's corncrib; the corn had buried their naked bodies.

Prerovo wouldn't be preparing for flight now, as the Germans were still a long way off; they'd be harvesting the corn and picking the grapes. His grandfather and father would be sitting on the porches of their old houses, drinking coffee and smoking, and sighing for him. They'd be quarreling about whose fault it was that he'd run away from the Valjevo hospital where his father had found him a job, by generously greasing a few palms. But how could he, a cavalryman decorated for bravery after Suvobor, hang around with medical orderlies and cripples? He'd written them frankly that he'd rather charge under fire than carry slop pails and clean up the hospital garbage. During those two weeks in the hospital he'd felt such disgust for his hands that he couldn't pick up a piece of bread. Sometimes he still thought his hands stank of the hospital. But hospital orderlies don't get killed. If the Germans reached the Morava and Prerovo, if they conquered Serbia—which they would—where would he go? Not to a prison camp—never. He'd take to the hills and live like an outlaw. The corn smelled of Prerovo and of the Morava at dusk. And of Natalia when she was bathing with her sister in the rapids by moonlight. He'd hide in an old corncrib, and bury himself deep in corn until the war was over.

"We're moving on! Hurry up!" Uroš shouted, slipping a piece of cornbread in his hand. Adam put the bread in his overcoat pocket, then ran to mount his horse. Lasta understood the command and knew where to go, so he dozed as the squadron passed through the village.

"Those bastard officers are going to shoot the men who are tied up!" Sima Pljakić yelled.

Adam opened his eyes wide: they were standing between empty railway tracks, facing hundreds of lined-up infantrymen. Next to the station lavatory, seven bound soldiers swayed in front of three officers. The bugler blew the call to stand at attention, which the cavalry also obeyed. A colonel climbed onto the platform of the station warehouse and said in a hoarse voice:

"Soldiers! Take a good look at what happens to deserters—the filthy cowards, the rotten traitors, the monsters who defile the sacred name of Serbia! And remember that the same fate is in store for every deserter, every coward, and every looter! Captain, carry out the punishment in the name of our country!"

"Ready! Aim! Fire!"

Ten rifles fired discordantly, and Adam suddenly became aware of the squad of infantry that was shooting the deserters. Only one deserter fell. The one next to him keeled over, dragged down because they were tied with the same rope. One of the men not hit cried out: "Brothers, I've a medal for bravery!"

The colonel waved his arms at the captain: "Go on, fire! What are you waiting for?"

A breech clicked, a word of command was given. More discordant shooting. The deserters still didn't fall, but blood trickled down the face of one, who appeared to be wounded in the ear. The colonel jumped from the platform and rushed at the firing squad: "I'll shoot the lot of you, you traitors!"

"Long live Serbia!" shouted two deserters wearing peasant breeches and torn military jackets.

The captain again gave the order to fire. The only man to fall was the one who had been wounded in the ear. The horses grew restless. Adam gripped his saddle to steady himself; he was trembling violently.

One of the deserters cried out: "Aim well, brothers, don't torture yourselves!"

Lieutenant Sandić stammered: "First squad, dismount!"

Adam and Uroš looked at each other in bewilderment. Sima Pljakić said softly, "Fire above their heads!" They slid down from their horses and, following Sandić's orders, took the place of the squad that had failed to carry out the shooting. Adam's knees shook: he had never felt such fear. Sandić called out the command. After a brief pause, Adam fired at the roof of the lavatory. The colonel threatened to shoot him for mutiny. A prolonged volley followed. Only two men were hit, one of whom cursed:

"Damn you, you fucking colonel! You'll be exposed, you murderer!"

Again there was a command to fire. This time Adam didn't fire. The only man still alive was the one with the medal for bravery, and he was bent double under the weight of the dead men on both sides of him, staring into the pools of blood in front of him, cursing. Adam couldn't hear him. He was deafened by the sound of firing, his hands shook, and before the colonel came up to shoot the deserter with a medal for bravery, Adam closed his eyes. He went back to his horse and was the last to mount. They left the village and rode through a field alongside a road filled with refugees and a medical column with a doctor riding at the head—an Englishwoman wearing a black coat and a yellow helmet.

"We're going to the front again!" Uroš Babović said suddenly.

"What difference does it make whose gun kills you or whose shit you spill your blood into?" said Sima Pljakić.

"It matters," Adam said, listening to the thunder of the cannon toward which they were riding.

"You're not going to run away from these heights, you bastards! You've been showing your asses to the Bulgarians for three days, you cowards! It's because of you that I've lost all the battles with the Bulgarians!"

Lieutenant Colonel Nešić, regimental commanding officer, was shouting as he passed the entrenched battery of field cannon in which Corporal Aleksa Dačić was serving. The commander halted next to Aleksa's field gun.

"You're to stay where you are! Better alive than dead. Just get this into your head, Lieutenant Smiljanič! We're defending Niš, the capital of Serbia. Vojvoda Stepa has given me this order personally. The position is to be defended to the last man! Otherwise, Lieutenant, I'll shoot everybody right down the line, from you to this corporal here. And you're to shoot every man who turns his back on the Bulgarians. On the spot! Why are you squinting, Corporal?"

"I'm looking you straight in the eyes, sir," said Dačić, confidently standing at attention.

"I'll be watching you tomorrow when you squint at the Bulgarians. Before nightfall you're to supply yourselves with ammunition for a whole day. Have I made myself clear, Lieutenant?"

The regimental commander rode off to inspect the infantry who were digging trenches on the heights above Niš. Lieutenant Smiljanić turned to the gunners: "You've heard the orders. If you have any food in your bags, eat it. Don't leave it for tomorrow. Then say the Lord's

Prayer and go to sleep. The first gun crew is to keep watch until midnight, the second until the Bulgarians appear."

Aleksa Dačić didn't want shelter from the rain or supper until he and Gojko, the volunteer who loaded the shells, had cleaned and polished his cannon fit for a parade or inspection. No fatigue or darkness could make him go to sleep under a dirty gun, no danger could make him flee without having cleaned his fieldpiece. He might be dirty, but his gun must always be fit for a parade. He loved this gray monster more than he had loved any horse or cow before the war. He delighted in the way it could smash several baggage trains at a distance of six kilometers, blow up a house like a pile of cornstalks, and mow down half a squad of Bulgarians. When he pulled the firing mechanism he felt a sweet sense of power, and the gun, like a stallion, would roar with flame and leap after the shell, then shake its hot body and smoke as if it had fallen upon a fiery mare.

He oiled the firing mechanism by the light of a lamp, sold his companions a few measures of strong brandy and some tobacco, decided not to sell his cheese yet, had a bite to eat, then crawled under the gun to sleep, covered with a tent flap. Ever since he had been reassigned to the artillery last summer, in response to his request as the holder of a Karageorge Star, he had slept under his gun even in the heaviest rain; he felt more secure there, and he was alone. His whole body was numb with fatigue, yet he couldn't get to sleep. There was the rain and cold, the threats of the commanding officer, and the rumors that Serbia was finished. Even if they retreated to Niš, there was nowhere to go from there. It was said that the Bulgarians killed the wounded and prisoners. First they tortured each wounded man by lighting a fire on his chest, then they gouged out his eyes and finally cut him up with a bayonet. Aleksa listened but didn't believe it. Yes, it was true that the Bulgarians were treacherous, that they had sold themselves to the Germans and betrayed the Russians and the Serbs. But he knew Vasil and Stojanov, frontier guards with whom he had traded. He had become friendly with them, made vows of brotherhood, and exchanged presents. They had vied with each other in cursing the Germans and exalting the Russians and the Czar of all the Slavs, who would wring Ferdinand's neck in Sofia. Bulgaria and Serbia would attack the Germans jointly, as brothers. Vasil and Stojanov weren't any different from Serbs, he thought—maybe they were even more kindhearted. How could they be roasting wounded men and gouging their eyes out? Since his first day in the army he had hated all the stories officers told to frighten the soldiers, just as he'd despised the cowards who believed those tales. He wasn't fighting because he was afraid of the enemy, but because he wouldn't let anyone conquer him. He was Aleksa Dačić, a Serb from Prerovo, and that was that.

Yet he could see that the situation was tough. They were heading for a precipice, but this wasn't the first time for the Serbs. Last fall they had been sinking, too, when suddenly Živojin Mišić, a great man and a general, saved them. Mišić had broken Potiorek's backbone on Suvobor and started the stampede to the Drina—you could hardly wade through, there were so many dead Fritzies and Austrian baggage trains. *If Živojin Mišić and Stepa Stepanović dig their heels in again our wagon won't lose its four wheels and we won't be crushed. No, we won't. You don't fall from heaven, you fall on the earth, and even in the Sićevac ravine there's brush on the rock, there's a lump of earth and a thistle that you can get hold of and hang on to. We can hide there like hares, like lizards. Then we'll go on again and get further than we expected. That's how things have been for as long as the Morava's been flowing.*

Aleska had gotten these ideas from his father, from Aćim Katić, from the schoolmaster, and from the old men of Prerovo—millers and ferrymen, monks and beggars: no one could beat a Serb! Not a living soul! Even Ivan Katić, a half-blind student, could bear those terrible hardships on Suvobor. He had written in his notebook: "I must stick it out. If I fled, how could I ever live among my people? Who dares flee from the trenches while Aleksa Dačić is fighting?" While *he* was fighting! Ivan mentioned him in six other places in his notebook. Yes, it was a big disaster, but there would be bigger ones: every evil was outdone by another, greater evil. Every man in Prerovo knew that, had that firmly impressed on him by both war and peace.

As for those whom that bastard colonel called cowards, let them worry until daybreak about how to save their skins. He himself had made his decision: he would never be a slave. He had refused as a hired man, and now he would refuse with such a good dowry from Jelka at stake—land and property in Prerovo. What he had in his sack would bring a nice sum of money: four flasks of strong brandy, three kilograms of tobacco, and some cheese. He'd acquired it all since his arrival on the Bulgarian frontier, while staying with his battery in a village adorned with garlands of tobacco, and full of livestock, cheese, and kindhearted women. He and some baggage-train men had bought and stolen mutton and suckling pigs, roasted them, and sold the meat to officers and infantrymen. He had earned good money this fall trading brandy, cheese, and tobacco. He had sewn some thousand-dinar notes into his belt. He'd never had so much money. When he went home, he'd say to Jelka: "Here you are, my girl. I didn't come back empty-handed!"

He placed the knapsack containing the tobacco and a change of clothes under his head, put the sack with the rest of the stuff next to him, and covered his head with the other end of the tent flap. Then, wondering whether his wife had gathered the grapes and corn before the rain came, he quickly fell asleep.

He was wakened by a dream: his wife Jelka had been offering him some grapes near a well, with a sad expression on her face—he could remember that quite clearly; then suddenly she had pushed him so hard that he fell headfirst into the darkness, waking up just before he hit the water. He was trembling. The rain was drumming on his field gun. He could hear roosters. Was it midnight or dawn? He didn't usually dream, and didn't remember his dreams when he did, certainly never a dream like this one. What misfortune could befall him, other than to be killed? A fitful wind moaned inside the barrel of the gun, the rain beat on the tent flap. He felt the horror that comes before great danger. He shuddered, grasped the spokes of the wheel, and said aloud: "I'll be killed!" Just then some Bulgarian shells exploded around the gun, illuminating the darkness and the bushes, scattering the bushes in all directions, and spraying the gun carriages with bits of iron and rock.

"Take cover! Take cover!" shouted Smiljanić. Aleksa tightened his grip on the iron spokes, as if dangling over the well of his dream, incapable of a single movement to save himself: *I'll be killed,* he thought—*damn it, there's no way out!* He was transfixed and only half-conscious, but aware that he'd never felt such fear. He tried to convince himself it was simply the dream. Could Jelka be the cause of his death? He had married her for her land and property, as she had said through tears at their parting. God wouldn't allow him, a hired man, the son of Tola Dačić, to have a servant after the war.

Shells exploded again, setting fire to the hornbeam trees. Aleksa clung to the iron wheel; Gojko Kninjanin urged him to take shelter under the rock, but he couldn't move, he dared not. What had happened to Aleksa Dačić, whom the battalion had unanimously elected to receive the Karageorge Star? Shells were falling farther away, then nearer. The Bulgarian gunners were seeking out the Serbian guns on the hillside and among the hornbeam. Aleksa lit a cigarette to show those who had taken cover—and himself—that he wasn't afraid: something he had never done before. He had never tried to convince anyone of his courage. He had behaved courageously when he had to and when it brought advantage to himself and the platoon.

A shell exploded nearby, covering him with pieces of rock and earth. He regretted that he hadn't taken cover. No, he wouldn't leave his gun. He'd be blown up with it, if that was his fate. He took a flask of brandy from his knapsack and had a swig. Everything he had in Prerovo, and the money under his belt and the goods he had in the sack—he'd lose it all. He'd never thought of this while buying and selling and stealing, and smuggling on the frontier with the Bulgarians. He wanted to have more than he had, and the more he had, the more he wanted. Why, when any minute a shell could crush everything to powder? An explosion nearby made him drop his brandy flask; he clung to the wheel of the gun carriage. He listened to the rain falling on the gun and to the wind in the barrel. What about his brandy flask? He jumped up to retrieve it: the brandy was trickling out! Five dinars lost! He swore violently. Gojko Kninjanin called to him, so he crawled out from under the gun, still angry.

"Do you believe in dreams, Gojko?" he asked.

"I sure do, Aleksa. A dream is halfway to the truth."

But there was no time for chitchat: the Bulgarian artillery began to pound the infantry in the trenches with redoubled force. Lieutenant Smiljanić gave the command: "To your places!" Aleksa stood by his loaded gun. As he waited for the commander to determine the distance, angle of fire, and type of shrapnel to be used, he passed a flask of brandy among his companions and brought out the cheese. They looked surprised and smiled maliciously, because he was giving them something for nothing. He felt both offended and ashamed. Let all his belongings go to hell. He didn't want anyone to have them—not a soul! He fired a few shells at the Bulgarian infantry who were moving over the rocky heights toward the Serbian trenches, singing their national anthem, "The Roaring Waters of the Marica," as they went. The Bulgarian artillery fired again. Aleksa turned to Gojko.

"If they get me today and you survive, Gojko, help yourself to my knapsack and my sack. But swear in the name of your father and your child that you'll unpin my Karageorge Star and take a notebook from the inside pocket of my jacket. The notebook belongs to my sergeant, Ivan Katić, whom the Fritzies took prisoner. When this bloody mess is over, take it and my Star to my father, Tola Dačić, in the village of Prerovo—near Palanka."

"But they won't get you, Aleksa."

"I know, but just in case. As you said, a dream is halfway to the truth." He turned back to his field gun and continued to mow down the Bulgarian infantry, even while debating whether to say anything to Gojko about the thousand-dinar notes in his belt. The Bulgarians stripped a dead man naked, so they said, and took anything of value— even cut jacket buttons off. Ten days ago he had bought an overcoat, jacket, and breeches from the regimental quartermaster. The Bulgarians would strip him and find what he had sewn into his belt. Wouldn't it be more decent to leave Gojko the money? On the other hand, if the Bulgarians found the thousand-dinar notes, even if they were swine they'd have to say: "Well, this Serb was a man of property, God rest his soul!" This praise from the Bulgarians sounded sweeter than the thought of Gojko's gratitude. He fired one shell after another. The Bulgarian infantry wavered, hit the ground, and returned the fire. He heard the command to increase the angle of fire. They must be seeking out the Bulgarian artillery. He had done well not to entrust his belt to Gojko.

"Well done, Corporal—that's the way to fight those sons of bitches! Three more hits like that and you'll get a medal!" The C.O. was standing next to Lieutenant Smiljanić, who was watching their target through his field glasses. "Those Bulgarian bastards will remember the way to Niš!" cried the C.O.

Aleksa wasn't pleased by the regimental commander's praise. Right now he wasn't interested in getting a medal, only in surviving the day. He sighed with relief at the command to cease firing.

The morning had passed. Mist lay along the Nišava valley. Rain drizzled from the glowering sky. The gunners were talking to each other, moving away from their dead companions and horses, lighting cigarettes. Aleksa sat down on the field gun with Gojko.

"What's in that notebook?" asked Gojko.

"All sorts of things. The difficulties people have who work with their heads. Instead of occupying themselves with the land and animals, or some such occupation fit for a man, they study books. Books and bits of paper."

"I know. I've a brother who's a student in Zagreb. I've seen his head just about burst from a book."

"The notebook also tells you how to be a man. Racking your brains about that is harder than climbing to the sky." He fell silent and thought about his dream: why had Jelka pushed him into the well?

The Bulgarians renewed their infantry charge and intensified their artillery fire against the trenches and the battery. Both sides warmed up. For Aleksa it was the hardest battle yet with the Bulgarians. Two guns in the battery were destroyed and more than half the men and horses killed. Numbed and deafened, Aleksa worked hard on his gun and waited for his shell.

At dusk the Bulgarians drove the Serbian infantry down the bare mountain slope and opened fire on the two remaining field guns. Lieutenant Smiljanić was wounded in the hand, and the crew of the second gun fled through the hornbeam grove. But Aleksa wouldn't leave his gun. He implored Gojko not to run away, took aim through the barrel, and blasted the Bulgarians closing in on him. Their swearing angered and encouraged him, but at the sight of their bayonets he began to yell as if wounded. He pulled out the breech, put his sack on Gojko's back, and rushed with him down through the hornbeam trees into a field, where they joined the infantry and the wounded. But the Bulgarians pursued· them, killing them without resistance, driving them into a flooded field, into pools of water up to their waists. Behind roared the swollen Nišava; ahead, the Bulgarians raked them with machine-gun fire and drowned them in the mud. But the night saved them: darkness fell and there was silence, as if not a single shot had been fired. Then the voice of the regimental commander broke the silence: "Where are you, you cowards? You've turned into frogs, you shit! Forward, onto the road! Come on, this way!"

They dragged themselves out of the mud and onto the road and the foothills of the heights from which the Bulgarians had driven them. They did so in silence without looking at one another, with despair in their hearts, humiliated by the Bulgarians and by their own commander, as though they had lost their last battle and everything they had been fighting for.

Aleksa passed his flask of brandy to Gojko and the others, treating them because he was still alive. He had survived the dream, though just barely. He had paid with his field gun. He thought of bringing out some cheese, but decided the occasion didn't quite call for such generosity.

The regimental commander rode past a group of men, shining a light in their faces. With curses and threats, and blows from the flat of his saber, he ordered them to line up in platoons. He reached Aleksa:

"Where's your gun, Corporal? So you left it for the Bulgarians to shoot at Niš with, you cowardly piece of shit!" He hit him hard on the shoulder. "You've deprived me of my colonel's rank, you bastard! You've torn up Stepa's application for my promotion! I'll shoot all of you if you don't get those guns back. Form a firing line and start uphill!"

The blow almost caused Aleksa to drop the breech, but if he was going to fall he'd fall holding it. He was offended by the blow and the injustice of it. Since he'd been in the army he'd been struck only once in the face, and that was by the platoon commander, Luka Bog, who paid for it with his life. But the colonel was right: they must get the field guns back. He told Gojko to carry the breech and fixed a bayonet on his rifle. When the command was given for the regiment to scale the heights and drive the Bulgarians from the trenches, he ran alongside the hornbeam trees. The mutual slaughter of Serbs and Bulgarians by grenade and bayonet began in the darkness over the rocky ground, each side cursing the other in its native tongue. Aleksa plunged his bayonet into the chest of a burly Bulgarian and himself fell down, remembering his dream. He heard the blood gurgling in the man's chest and thought: should I bandage him? Then he heard Gojko: "Where are you, Aleksa?"

"Vasil, is it you, my sworn brother?" whispered Aleksa. "Stojanov, my brother, tell me if you're here. Don't be afraid, it's Aleksa!" He leaned over the dying man, but didn't look at his face or at his wound until he heard his final death rattle. He could hardly drag himself to the gun and Gojko, who had fixed the breech in position and was happily clapping his hands. They began to clean the gun in the dark. The battle on the high slopes was drawing to a close: the Serbian infantry had recovered the trenches and were collecting their wounded and plundering the dead Bulgarians. The two of them finished cleaning and oiling the gun, then sat down in silence to smoke and drink some brandy. They had just barely finished their cigarettes when they heard wounded Lieutenant Smiljanić giving an order:

"Hurry up and take the guns down to the road. We've been ordered to retreat toward Niš. We've given our lives in vain! For a colonel's rank! But what can we do? That's war!"

Aleksa and Gojko dragged the field gun down the rocky slope. Aleksa felt calmer now that his dream had not come true; he was exhausted by the most protracted fear he had ever experienced.

TO THE MILITARY ATTACHÉS IN PARIS, ST. PETERSBURG, LONDON, AND ROME:

OUR SITUATION IS GRAVE. TO THE NORTH AND WEST WE ARE HARD PRESSED BY AUSTRIAN AND GERMAN FORCES OF THIRTEEN TO FOURTEEN DIVISIONS.

THE BULGARIANS ARE ADVANCING WITH STRONG FORCES FROM THE EAST. ALONE WE WILL NOT BE ABLE TO HOLD OUT FOR LONG SINCE OUR RESIST-ANCE, THOUGH HEROIC, MUST INEVITABLY COME TO AN END. THE ONLY HOPE IS THAT OUR ALLIES WILL COME TO OUR AID AS SOON AS POSSIBLE. PLEASE TAKE ACTION WITH THIS END IN VIEW.

VOJVODA PUTNIK

ORDERS FROM FIELD MARSHAL VON MACKENSEN TO THE THIRD AUSTRO-HUNGARIAN ARMY AND THE ELEVENTH GERMAN ARMY:
THE MAIN BODY OF THE SERBIAN ARMY IS TO BE DRIVEN INTO THE CENTER OF THE COUNTRY AND DECISIVELY BEATEN.

TO THE AMBASSADORS OF THE KINGDOM OF SERBIA IN ST. PETERSBURG, PARIS, LONDON, AND ROME:
PLEASE INFORM ALL ALLIED GOVERNMENTS THAT IF THEY DO NOT SEND FROM 120,000 TO 150,000 MEN TO SERBIA'S AID WITHIN TEN DAYS, SERBIA WILL. BE DESTROYED.

PAŠIĆ

From noon on, sounds of battle were heard throughout the north. King Peter too heard the howitzers, but not even the priest Božidar could persuade him to leave Topola until the essential work on the church was completed. That night the tomb must finally be put in order. The next day he would inter the remains of Karageorge, then carry out his remaining duties as king, in the order dictated by the war and his honor. Just before dark everything that the enemy would confiscate as court property was taken to Kragujevac. The King kept nothing in his room but the bust of Karageorge, having resolved to part with this only when he went to the battlefield. His suite and servants went with the court furniture and household goods. Only Božidar, the officer on duty, and Zdravko remained behind.

The King would not allow Božidar to leave Topola: he was to

perform the service at the interment of the remains of Karageorge. King Peter was convinced that in this way he was conferring the greatest honor upon him. The priest submitted to the King's will more out of pity than a sense of duty as metropolitan of Serbia. Actually, he wanted to set out for Kragujevac with his grandchildren and a battalion of boys from Valjevo, to help them in the hardships of flight and to strengthen their spirit. After Valjevo, God alone knew where they would go. There was no duty more sacred for him than this one on which he had suddenly decided, without hesitation. Although he sympathized with the King's suffering, he could not refrain from voicing his own anxiety: if the children were driven out of Kragujevac, how could he catch up with them and find them?

As soon as darkness fell, the battle subsided. The workmen lit the church with lanterns and carbide lamps and continued to work. Now and then one of them would stop and listen to a baggage train passing on its way to the battlefield, or a man's hands would stiffen at the sound of the wind moaning through the domes, and he would look fearfully at the King, who was standing in the middle of the church with Božidar. "Don't be afraid, my children," King Peter would say. "I'm here with you tonight. God and the King will reward your work."

When his back grew numb with pain, he returned to his empty house and sat in the wicker chair beside the bronze head of Karageorge. His face darkened: Serbia is falling into bondage, he thought, God knows for how long. Everything he had accomplished was being destroyed. And he had accomplished much less than he had aspired to. There had been no time for freedom to build up virtues in his people, or for democracy to become a government of wise and honorable men. No time for anything great and lasting. War had filled the greater part of his reign. The victory over the Turks, the people's dream for centuries, had been transformed by politicians and generals into an overmastering drive for power and glory. Nor were his children bringing peace to his declining years. George, with his difficult nature and public scandals, had forced upon him the hardest of all acts for a father: depriving his first-born son of his right to the throne. Alexander, always hot-tempered and hasty, was downright vicious the moment he sensed insubordination, and he readily suspected even the best of men. Even if a time of freedom should come while he was king, that unhappy man would never feel free.

Božidar tried to turn the conversation to their joint experience as guerrilla fighters in Bosnia and Hercegovina, but the King cut him short.

"How much am I to blame for what my people have to go through now? Tell me like a brother, Božidar. Be my judge."

"When the night is long, one shouldn't sit in judgment on any man."

"You're my friend, but your office requires you to judge me according to God's law. When did I sin?"

"God judges a king also for what he hasn't done. But the people, well . . ."

"The people judge me, too. And you, Father. Because I took the crown forged from cannon used in Karageorge's uprising."

"Well spoken, Your Majesty! No king wears a heavier crown!"

"I longed for it when I lived in exile. And I committed some wrongs to get it. Although I wanted the royal crown because of the throne and the title, I wanted it just as much because of freedom and justice. But I sat on a blood-stained throne, Father, as you yourself reminded me at Žiča on the eve of my coronation, when you said: 'Things won't be easy for you, Peter Mrkonjić. You're mounting the throne after bloodshed and an unhappy, evil reign.' "

"But you found it distasteful, sir. To those who had fallen from power you owed magnanimity and justice, and to those who put you on the throne, an enormous debt of gratitude."

"That's true, Božidar. But gratitude for the throne was harder for me than magnanimity to my opponents. That gratitude, that debt to one's supporters, is a very hard thing for an honest man in a position of power."

"But you must have known, sir, that a debtor's authority is a hard thing for the people."

"Do you think I didn't see that?"

"Not the way you should have."

The King's face clouded and he stared at the floor a few moments. Then he grasped the arms of his chair and asked sternly: "In your opinion, Božidar, where I did make my great mistake?"

"You made your great mistake, Peter Mrkonjić, in believing that what the people needed most was freedom. The people need justice much more than freedom."

"I'd make the same mistake again, Božidar. Yes, I would. Where there's no freedom, there's no justice. For freedom, Adam renounced Eden."

"That was the beginning of our endless sufferings, sir."

They both fell silent. Božidar crossed his hands over his stomach and dozed. King Peter was engaged in an inner struggle over whether to confess the terrible sin he had committed against the mother of his children.

"Listen to me, Peter Mrkonjić. Serving the people is only half of a king's duty. The king is also responsible for the way in which the people serve their country. Few have served your kingdom honorably and zealously in peacetime."

"Although I'm aware of all that a man on a throne can do, I wouldn't use force, even to make the people serve the country."

"There was an English king who didn't learn what human misfortune was until he experienced his own unhappiness and ruin. The poor man went mad, so they say." Božidar sank back in the wicker chair and dozed.

The King placed his hand on the priest's shoulder: "What is it that a king must not do now, Father?"

"What your grandfather did after the defeat of the uprising," he answered, his eyes closed. "What you and I did when the Turks rushed at us."

"I think so, too. A king must not save himself when a war is lost."

"Nor should he return to the place from which he fled. As your grandfather did."

The King was silent: if only he could bury his grandfather, so the bones of the unfortunate rebel might rest in peace in one place forever. He got up abruptly and went to the church with Zdravko, who lit the path for him with a lantern. Once more he implored the workmen: "Stick it out, my children. Your brothers at the front aren't sleeping tonight either. Who can sleep tonight?"

He stayed there a long time, moved by the sight of them hard at work. On the way back to the house he clapped Zdravko on the shoulder:

"What do you hear now?"

"The roads and footpaths all over Šumadija are burdened with suffering, Your Majesty."

"You don't hear rifle fire?"

"The darkness is stirred up as if vampires were running through the forest."

"You know I don't like your fairy tales."

"Some little girls in the village are wailing as if they were being slaughtered, Your Majesty."

Wakened by his own worries, Božidar asked the King, "What's been hardest for you on the throne, sir?"

"What's been hardest? Protecting myself from toadies. And being poor."

"I can believe that, Peter Mrkonjić."

"I've had only two days of happiness. When I arrived in Belgrade from Switzerland to mount the throne, and when I came to Topola to bow down before Karageorge's grave, and the people wept for joy. Since then it's been nothing but anxieties, and no one to share them with."

Božidar leaned toward him. "There's been much lawlessness and thieving in your kingdom, Your Majesty."

"And in what country has there been less, Božidar?"

Božidar didn't reply, but walked over to the window. The wind roared in the forest above them.

Upset by the priest's insight, the King thought hard about what he had done for law and honor. "There were times when I was sorely tempted to use powers not assigned to me by the constitution—for the good of the people."

"You should have done so. Those in authority have done little good for our people."

"I did so once."

"It's a great pity indeed that God didn't help you to do so more often."

"Thank God that he didn't, Božidar. Respecting the law is more sacred to me than righting injustices. Tyranny begins when those in authority think that they're more competent than the law and wiser than the people."

"One of your ancestors, Njegoš, once said, 'The multitude is one great, huge animal.' "

"It's hard for a country whose king has no faith in its people."

"You, sir, were more worried about what was being said in the Assembly than how the *people* judged your performance."

"I read only Opposition newspapers."

"Did you really believe what the newspapers said?"

"What else could I believe but what was publicly spoken, Božidar? Only a tyrant believes informers and people in his court."

"If you knew the people as I do, well . . . I didn't envy your being King." Božidar dozed off again.

Just before dawn the King finally fell asleep. Soon thereafter, however, he was awakened by his orderly, who announced that some officers from the headquarters of the Belgrade Defense Force had come to evacuate him. It was expected that Topola would be bombarded that morning. The King immediately went to the church. He found a single workman there, hurriedly collecting his tools, but didn't ask when the others had fled. He went into the altar, stood at attention, then bowed his head.

"Lord, I know I've sinned by not doing more. Am I also a sinner because I didn't agree to do less?"

Then he went outside and with tears in his eyes examined the church, damp and gray in the clouded sky of early morning. In front of the house a group of officers waited for him beside a car with its engine running. He had no wish to flee. He walked into the nearby wood and placed his hand on the damp trunk of an oak tree. In this wood he had once looked after the flocks with the shepherds of Topola, picked acorns, and been happy. Why hadn't he remained a shepherd? Why had he left this beautiful wood to go after his father's crown? As an old man he could have gathered acorns. He picked up a few fine large ones and put them in his pocket.

"Your Majesty, we can't wait any longer."

He waved the orderly away with his stick and slowly walked behind him to the car. The officers helped him in, handling him as gently as if he were wounded. Božidar sat next to him, crossing himself. The car sped off. Although he felt with a shudder that he'd never again see his church or the little house below it, the King didn't turn around to take a last look. He couldn't: the pain of his unfinished task was harder to bear than any he had yet experienced.

The road was full of baggage trains, soldiers, and refugees. The King looked into the distance limited by the low, clouded sky. He felt no sympathy for the suffering soldiers, women, and children on the muddy road, nor did he return the officers' salutes. He passed through the wartime confusion of the Kragujevac streets in the same absent-minded state. At the frequent, choked cries of "Long live the King! Long live Uncle Peter!" he grew even gloomier. Božidar clasped the King's hand and said:

"You're a lucky man, Peter Karageorgević! You've progressed from king to Uncle Peter. That's the greatest thing you've done on the throne. Forgive me for the hard things I've said to you. They were said out of devotion. If I don't find the children here, I'll have to ask for your help. Good-by!" He told the chauffeur to stop, and got out.

The King saluted him.

At headquarters Prince Alexander greeted his father in a high-pitched voice: "Did you want the Germans to take you prisoner in Topola?"

"I had to carry out one of my duties. And now, my son, I place myself as a soldier under your command."

"You must leave for Niš immediately with an escort, on the royal train. Pašić will meet you there and tell you what to do next."

"As soon as I've written my will, I'll go straight to the battlefield. I want some paper and need to be left alone for half an hour."

"Father, a king may do anything except be ridiculous."

"My son, a king is king only if life is harder for him than for his subjects in times of national misfortune."

"It's the king's duty to transform defeat into victory."

"That's only part of the king's duty, my boy. I must also suffer for the suffering of my soldiers. I bear the guilt for their suffering."

Alexander walked quickly to the window, turned to look at his father, then folded his arms. "You know I won't flinch at any danger or at anything which your soldiers or mine must suffer. But you're old, Father, you're a sick man."

"But I'm still the king. And now I must write my will!"

Alexander walked despondently out of his office. The King felt sorry for his son, but there was no time to clear up matters with him now. An adjutant brought him paper and ink. The King wrote rapidly the dispositions which he had thought through long before: except for a bequest to his foundation, he left his entire estate to his children, to be shared equally. After signing the will he added: "Please pay five thousand (5,000) dinars to Zdravko (my personal servant). Peter." He and the adjutant sealed the will and deposited it with his personal papers. Then the King walked over to the office of Vojvoda Putnik. After they had saluted each other, the King asked: "What's the situation with the Allies?"

"They've told us to hold on until their help arrives."

"I don't trust them."

"Mr. Pašić says we must trust them."

Some enemy airplanes flew over Kragujevac. The Serbian artillery fired at them, as did riflemen in the streets and around the High Command. The King and Putnik waited for the firing to stop.

"Vojvoda, what sector is the enemy attacking most heavily today?"

"Our entire front is retreating, Your Majesty. And we've been pounded by artillery. As regards morale, I'd say the Belgrade Defense Force is having the hardest time. Their numbers have been halved while defending the capital."

"I want a staff officer to take me to whatever regiment's having a hard time today. If possible, to a trench nearby. I feel stiff these days."

Putnik looked at him calmly. The King was standing like a cavalry officer, with his hands on his hips.

"Your Majesty, I venture to say that it's extremely difficult to behave rationally today."

"This is no time to be rational, Vojvoda. Please do as I ask."

They could barely make their way through the baggage train and the division hospital as they advanced along the field path in the rain. Several times they had to be pulled out of a puddle by an oxcart. Just before dusk the King's car arrived at the eastern foothills of Rudnik. A regiment fleeing from the trenches was being pounded by enemy artillery. The King got out of the car, stood in mud halfway up his boots, and gazed at the fleeing soldiers, who were dirt-spattered, wet, and exhausted. He knew that for a brave soldier flight was hardest to bear. The commanding officer recognized him and, panic-stricken, reported the state of the battle. The King ordered him to halt the regiment and line it up under cover.

The soldiers didn't listen to the orders. The officers shouted: "The King is here!" and fired their revolvers in the air. More than half an hour passed before the remains of the regiment were finally lined up in square formation in a sheltered place. The King gave Zdravko his cane, and with great effort walked erectly over to the soldiers. He wanted to meet them eye to eye; he wanted them to feel his fear. He looked at them in silence, then said:

"God help you, soldiers! I can see you're tired. How could you not be, after so many battles? Things have gone badly for you, so you want to get back to your villages."

The heavy grumbling among the ranks was interrupted by shells that whined overhead and exploded in a stream nearby. The soldiers grew rigid, standing at attention with their eyes on the King, but no one broke rank. To conceal his emotion, the King raised his voice:

"Soldiers, you've taken an oath to defend your king and country. I release you from your oath to your king. But I've no right to release you from the oath you've given to your country. Whoever dares to release himself from that oath, let him leave his rifle and ammunition and go home. I wish him a good journey. Make up your minds freely. I'm waiting for you to step out of the ranks."

He averted his eyes so as not to prevent any man from leaving, or to frighten any waverer, or put a brave man to shame.

"But where can we volunteers go, Your Majesty?" someone asked. "Those of us from Bačka and Banat and Dalmatia?"

"Those of you who want to continue the struggle for freedom, stay here with me. We'll dig a trench and wait for the enemy. The rest of you, leave your rifles and hurry off home."

"We're tired and hungry, Your Majesty. Barefoot. In shreds. We're wet and cold. Where are the Allies? Where is that army from Salonika? Why do they lie to us? We aren't cowards!"

"You are heroes, my children!"

"Long live the King! Long live Uncle Peter!"

The King ordered the regimental commander to determine the fighting position of the regiment and asked for a rifle and fifty bullets. The regimental staff ran up the slope, while behind them the battalions dug trenches in the hills. The King, accompanied by Zdravko and an orderly who carried his rifle and bag of ammunition, looked at his soldiers, and for the second time that day his eyes filled with tears. On the surrounding heights stood the long, blue firing lines of the Austro-Hungarian army. The regimental commander gave the order to fire. The King took his rifle and knelt down in a shallow trench between two soldiers. Bullets whizzed around him. The soldiers looked at him. He smiled, then took aim and fired rapidly.

Nikola Pašić spent the night awake in an armchair, in his dressing gown and slippers. Silent and despondent, he watched his wife and daughters choosing clothes and valuables to take with them to Greece. His home was being broken up, his family was going off into an uncertain future. If there was anything in this world that could make him happy, it was his family, in which he would not permit himself any attributes of authority, over which he would not exercise the rights of seniority and hierarchy. There was no trace of severity in his attitude toward his children. He had never punished them or uttered a word of reproach. He always spoke to them softly and hesitantly to preserve their affection. His wife and daughters were now preparing for flight and exile, with blankets over the windows and low-burning lamps on the floor.

The inhabitants of Niš kept their eyes on his house, lest they be too late to flee before the Bulgarians arrived to exact vengeance for the war lost in 1913. Although he had advised everyone to leave quickly, and he didn't demand heroic sacrifices even from his ministers, he knew that the departure of his family from Niš would cause a general collapse of morale and arouse anger against himself. But he was certainly not going to endanger the lives of his wife and children. This second night spent in preparing a magnificent reception for the Allies —a French regiment would arrive from Salonika the following morning—provided a convenient opportunity: he felt sure that not even the most cautious and fearful would imagine that the prime minister's family was packing for flight to Greece on the eve of the Allies' arrival.

They went to bed at dawn, but shortly thereafter Pašić was awakened by the telephone. Jovan Jovanović, his assistant for foreign affairs, asked him to come to his office immediately; a fiacre had already been sent for him.

"Have the Bulgarians cut the railway line?"

"It's worse than that, Prime Minister."

"Yes, I know," he said, and hung up. He washed and dressed quickly. For the first time since they had been in Niš, Djurdjina did not accompany him to the door. He was further irritated by a group of people waiting at the gate: "Are they coming, Prime Minister?"

"Yes, they are!" he shouted crossly, and told the coachman to drive slowly along the main street to the railway station and then to his office: let the people of Niš think he had risen early to supervise preparations for the reception. He now felt what gave him the greatest satisfaction in his position of power: his always being first to know, and knowing the most, about a matter of utmost importance for the fate of the country and its people.

The cafés were already open, the sidewalks full of idlers. He had always shunned idlers, convinced that they were up to no good. He withdrew further in his seat to avoid acknowledging their greetings. But wherever triumphal arches were being raised—arches made from branches of box or fir, dahlias and chrysanthemums, with "Long live the Allies!" and "Welcome, friends!" in French—wherever women were decorating windows, gates, and fences with flowers, he would lean forward and greet them by raising his hat. When he heard cries of "Long live Pašić!" he shuddered, however. If the Allies didn't come, he'd be guilty in the eyes of the people. He'd be the one who had deceived them, an elderly traitor. He'd heard himself described that way ever since he'd entered politics over fifty years before. Bad press had never upset him; one could use it to one's advantage and rule more successfully. Anyway, he knew that no one gained people's confidence as easily as a man in authority, and that no disappointment was so short-lived as disappointment in those who ruled. People didn't expect good from their rulers. Any government that was better than the previous one by even a hair's breadth was good, and this wasn't hard to achieve. Certainly he had achieved it. But this unanimous demonstration of confidence from the people of Niš—the first since the expulsion of the enemy from Serbia the previous year—filled him with foreboding. He huddled in the corner of the fiacre.

The railway station was decorated with garlands of autumn flowers, its eaves weighed down with French flags and branches of box and fir. He stopped the driver on the pretext of examining posters with messages of welcome, and waited while some of the townspeople roasting rams and calves over huge fires behind the station warehouses came up to him with a pitcher of brandy.

"Let's pray for our safety, Mr. Pašić, and welcome our saviors," they said as, raising their hats, they handed him the brandy.

He rose from his seat, took off his hat, crossed himself, and said quietly, "Remember this, my brothers: victory is ours! To your health!"

He brought the brandy to his lips but didn't drink it, then gave back the pitcher and told the driver to move off. "Long live Pašić! May God preserve you!" the people shouted.

In his office his secretaries and Jovan Jovanović greeted him despondently. Of all human feelings, he most despised burning patriotism away from the battlefield, and anxiety for the State on the part of its employees.

"Niš is decorated as if for a wedding," Pašić remarked.

Jovanović bit his moustache and said sharply: "The Allies aren't coming, Prime Minister. Here's a telegram from Salonika."

Pašić didn't pick it up. "The telegram needn't interfere in any way with our preparations to receive them. The Ministry of the Interior should telephone all the district chiefs along the Djevdjelija-Paraćin railway line and ask how the preparations are coming. As many people as possible should be at the stations and along the line today."

"Prime Minister, our military attaché in Salonika reports that the French General Staff has ordered Bayou to remove his troops from the train and stay in Salonika."

"That order doesn't concern us. We're waiting for the Allies and we must prepare a splendid reception. Let's show them how much we love them. If they don't show up, that's their disgrace and their military risk."

"I'd like to say, Prime Minister, that raising hopes in the Allies and their help could be fatal for Serbia."

"No sensible government has ever destroyed its people's misconceptions. A wise government uses them to achieve its goals. Tell those two secretaries not to breathe a word to anyone about the telegram from

Salonika. And you, Jovanović, make sure that tomorrow the newspapers devote the entire front page to our preparations for the reception."

Jovanović placed the telegram on the table in front of Pašić, who didn't read it. Instead he wrote to the ambassadors in St. Petersburg, Paris, and London, telling them once more to inform their respective governments that Serbia's collapse was inevitable and couldn't be delayed unless the Allies immediately came to her assistance and broke the Bulgarian attack.

He walked over to the window: women and children were decorating the bridge over the Nišava with flowers. People were swarming toward the bridge from all directions. He could hear a band playing—drums, cornets, and bassoons. Let them make merry, let them be full of hope and rejoicing. He exulted in his power to keep up their hope in salvation on this dark day. He would do his best not to destroy it. Let time and those who loved truth do that.

Although Kosara didn't want to go greet the French soldiers, Olga persuaded her to get dressed, cautiously recommending clothes suitable for the occasion and the gloomy autumn day. Olga herself got ready to go out with her, although she hadn't the least desire to see anyone. What had happened to Vukašin was proof to her of how unjust people were; they had also ignored the voluntary sacrifices that Ivan and Milena were making for their country. This was extremely painful to her. Devoted to her grandson, who every day seemed to her more like Ivan, she had little sympathy for Vukašin's gloomy silence, being was more concerned about whether, like his father, her grandson would be near-sighted.

So it was that the fall of Belgrade and the imminent collapse of Serbia gave Olga one overwhelming concern: how to protect her grandson. She even forgot about Milena, who had written only one brief letter from Prerovo: delighted with her grandfather and the village, she said not a word about returning to Niš. During the last few days Olga had been disturbed by a sudden change in Kosara's behavior and appearance: she had become taciturn and absent-minded, and her milk had almost completely dried up. If they had to leave Niš, how would they feed the child? Olga was afraid that she might have offended her in some way. She had bought her the most expensive clothes and shoes she could find in Niš, and introduced her to friends with affectionate dignity as Ivan's fiancée, and the child as her grandson. She made great efforts not to show in any way the shame she felt because of Kosara's origins and appearance. But it was no good: there was Kosara in front of the mirror, staring at herself, her hair uncombed, smoking. Olga put her hand on her shoulder; Kosara did not stir.

"Aren't you well, Kosara?"

"I'm all right."

"What's the matter?"

"Nothing."

"It's not nothing. Tell me what's troubling you. I think I've earned your confidence."

Kosara didn't answer.

"Hurry then, or we'll be late," she said, and stroked her cheek. Perhaps Kosara felt that Vukašin's gloomy mood was directed against her, thought Olga. She went up to Vukašin and whispered, "Do make an effort to be kind to Kosara. Don't you see how depressed she is?"

"I don't have to make an effort. She has borne me a grandson and that's sufficient reason for me to respect her."

"Still, do talk to her."

"Do you think I ought to go with you? Someone must stay with the child." He raised his voice, afraid that Olga would insist. Nothing would induce him to greet the French soldiers, not only because he doubted that the Allies would help Serbia enough, but also because he couldn't be part of the crowd that had so humiliated him in front of the Assembly. "Traitor!" they had shouted, "how much did they pay you for selling Macedonia?" All this in return for his efforts to save his country! His life seemed futile. He had long ago grown used to failure and defeat, but to be spat on by those for whose welfare he had fought so hard was unendurable. He had finally grasped that in the struggle for ideas and principles one must bear humiliation, too. One must suffer the revulsion of the mob and shameless words from fools. But he wasn't one to forgive and forget. He didn't love his neighbor. He wasn't another Pašić, who made use of his greatest humiliations to climb to power, who lulled and received his opponents by his patience, and, being cast down, rose up again just as they broke into victorious smiles. The conduct of the friends in his own party made his humiliation complete: many of them avoided him on the grounds that he had compromised his opposition in the eyes of the nation. He saw only one honorable way out: to join Mišić's army and serve in Ivan's regiment. He wanted to discuss this with Mišić, who was still his friend though he didn't share his opinions. He'd have done it long ago, had it not been for Olga, his grandson, and that unhappy girl, Kosara. He had become completely wrapped up in the child, excited by this gift of fate. Was it pure chance that the day he had been spat on by nationalist fanatics, he should find a grandson at home? Did this happen to comfort him, or to bring him new suffering?

Olga warned him not to smoke by the cradle and hurried out with Kosara. Vukašin sat down and began to read Montaigne. The book fell open at a page over which he had reflected often in the last few days: "There is in us less bad luck than worthlessness, less ill-will than stupidity." Nothing had more power to move people to evil than stupidity. Nothing. And so people were guiltless—including those who spat on others or killed.

"We are not so much full of evil as of futility; we are not so much wretched as insignificant." Was there any point in resisting this truth?

He shut the book: all this was familiar, well known. He stood over his grandson—an unknown factor. The cause of further suffering for Ivan in the prison camp. Vukašin hadn't written Ivan since Kosara had arrived. He must write him immediately, while the mail was still working.

My dear boy, I'm standing over your son, unhappy and at the same time happy that something of mine, of yours, will outlive this time of evil and shame. Kosara has gone to the station to wait for our friends.

He stopped: how could he say what he wanted to, without the Austrian censors' destroying the letter?

Olga and Kosara reached the main street of Niš and paused in front of the immense crowd which filled the sidewalks and spilled over onto the road with its triumphal arches and posters: children waving French flags; high-school choirs singing the "Marseillaise" in French; girls and women holding chrysanthemums and marigolds; peasant women with baskets of fruit and bread; peasants with pitchers of brandy and bottles of wine; townspeople, invalids, and officers exchanging the latest news from the front; a band with trumpets blaring and drums banging under the cloudy sky.

"They've reached Leskovac! They're at Vranje! They'll be here in an hour!"

Olga felt sick. She'd have stayed where she was and waited for the life-saving miracle to descend on these people, but she was afraid Kosara might think she didn't wish to be seen with her. Taking her hand, she led her through the noisy crowd. Kosara didn't utter a word; she clenched her teeth and looked at the ground. Olga was thinking of returning home, when she caught sight of Doctor Radić a few paces ahead of them. "Let's stay here," she said.

"I see a relative of mine I want to talk to. Please wait for me."

"Of course," said Olga, leaning against a fence. She remembered a cigarette spark in the darkness of a crowded train; a few flickers of flame illuminating an anxious face; a dark, weary voice offering her a seat; a hand stretched out to help her off at Valjevo; a tall officer in front of the hospital gates, leading her past a pack of hungry dogs into the hospital. The man who had helped her understand how small her happiness was, and how small Vukašin's great love. How easily she had loved Vukašin. Radić was thinner and less attractive, but finer. How could he spend a month, six weeks in Niš without coming to see her? She'd been waiting for him, though she wouldn't admit it to herself. Why hadn't he come in to say hello the day he accompanied Vukašin home? *You feeble creature! Were you afraid? Your heart is full of vanity. Valjevo, the nights on duty in the Warehouse of the Dead, the evening visits to Bogdan, the vigils at Milena's bedside, have you forgotten it all? Everything that happened in Valjevo was the death agony of typhus, the usual masculine yearning under inhuman conditions, something freakish, banal. That's all it was, Doctor Radić! I suffered such torments as I strove desperately to put my hand on your shoulder that night in Valjevo, to come close to you on the hospital steps and look into your tired eyes, desiring something else, something that was impossible. But I couldn't do any of these things. Not from any fear of the consequences—it wasn't that. I was simply ashamed of being unfaithful. Shame—that was what I felt. I couldn't give myself to myself. I couldn't.*

Mihajlo Radić lit one cigarette from another and squinted.

Surely he could feel her presence. She'd been looking for him all summer and fall. Was he suffering, or couldn't he see anyone beyond himself? Who knew what this man was like outside the hospital, away from Valjevo? Everything that had happened, everything she had felt for him had been from that part of life. Well, let what she had had from him remain in her heart. That was a great deal. *Thank you, Mihajlo.*

Tears welled up in her eyes and she decided to go home. After a few steps she remembered that she had promised to wait for Kosara—the girl would think she had abandoned her. She turned around and met Mihajlo Radić's eyes: he was astonished, embarrassed, delighted. She trembled as she had in front of the hospital gates, as she had when she held his hand during his illness.

"They've reached Skoplje! They'll be in Niš this evening! They'll be here in half an hour!"

Radić came up to her and tossed away his cigarette. "I was going to visit you this afternoon," he said, taking her hand.

"This is simply a chance encounter, Doctor," she said firmly.

"Sometimes happiness comes by chance, Mrs. Katić."

"And sickness too, Doctor."

"That's true. But also salvation." He lit a cigarette.

"What are you doing here in Niš? I can't believe that you've been here more than a month. That you aren't working in the hospital."

"I've been waiting for a post from the Ministry of War. I only got it yesterday. I'm now head of the medical service of the Niš reserve troops. The Niš reserve troops consist of children—boys between fourteen and eighteen; some are twelve."

"What are you doing with them?"

"They'll grow up for the battlefield under my medical supervision. For the trenches of some other war, I suppose."

"That's terrible—children as soldiers! In Valjevo you were fighting against dirt and death. What will you fight against with these children?"

He was embarrassed. Around them people were shouting: "They arrived in Djevdjelija this morning! They've left Skoplje. They haven't left Salonika. They'll be here in ten minutes! Long live France!" There was no sign of Kosara.

"You don't believe the Allies will save us? The people we're waiting for?" Olga asked impulsively.

"No, I don't. But let's forget about the war. How are your children? I'd love to see Milena."

"She's staying with her grandfather in Prerovo. Ivan writes once a month. He has a fiancée, and I already have a grandson."

"Really?"

"I never imagined what the child of my child would do to my life." She waited for him to ask about Vukašin. She felt offended that he'd said nothing about him.

Two wounded men were angrily denying that the Germans had taken Kragujevac that morning, the Austrians Valjevo, and the Bulgarians Bor. A group of high-school students sang a Serbian version of the "Marseillaise." Newsboys shouted: "Russian ships moving against Bulgaria! Czar Nicholas's advice to Pašić: the Serbs must hold out one more week! Allies declare war on Bulgaria! Panic in Sofia!" Several Austrian officers, prisoners of war, were flirting with women who spoke in halting German. A man wearing dark glasses was offering for sale a Serbian-German dictionary: a thousand German words for only three dinars. For three dinars you could save your skin!

Radić interrupted their silence. "You see and hear the depths of shame in our misfortune? A nation without hope is wretched. During the epidemic in Valjevo, suffering gave people some greatness, a sense of purpose. We had to cleanse filth, overcome pain, conquer death. To work, not to sleep. Even the mean-spirited were different then. There was great effort and seriousness. But now?"

"That's also a disease, Doctor," said Olga, upset by his last words. Could he be joking? She was blushing. "This celebration," she stammered, "what a great sickness it is. But where's my son's fiancée?"

"Olga, if what has been happening all over Serbia the last few days—I mean waiting for the Allies—if this were only a disease, we'd be justified in feeling some hope. But in this wretchedness there's so much humiliation and stupidity."

She replied reproachfully: "Surely you must feel pity for these poor people?"

"What we're looking at is shameful and humiliating, Olga—even ridiculous. Just look at those young gypsy belly dancers! Listen to them shouting."

"Ah, Doctor Radić! Good afternoon, Mrs. Katić." Major Paun Aleksić bowed to them, smiling broadly.

Olga inclined her head but didn't offer her hand.

"Delighted to see you. How's your daughter? I haven't the honor of knowing your husband personally, but please give him my greetings and convey to him my admiration for his political wisdom and courage. I'm not interested in politics, but regarding Macedonia and the fuss over the Allies, I'm on your husband's side. Did you know that as early as yesterday morning Pašić received a telegram saying that not even that one French regiment would come to Serbia? As for the three-day welcome celebrations, my dear compatriots, that's Pašić's shot of morphia for a patient whose condition is hopeless!"

Olga could no longer listen to this man, nor could she bear to look at Radić, standing there beside him, upset and embarrassed. Their meeting in this place, their conversation had become intolerable. She told them she had to go home, nodded slightly, and left. Pain and disappointment welled up inside her, disappointment in herself and him, but more in herself. She could hardly restrain herself from bursting into tears.

Paun Aleksić watched her receding from sight. He sighed. "A fine woman, that Mrs. Katić. Beautiful in her maturity, at the peak of her form. She'll crack up, though, at the first illness or a single pang of suffering. By March she won't be what she is now, and by next summer she'll have lost all her beauty."

Radić was startled by her abrupt departure. He hadn't said a word to her about how he felt. She could have no inkling of his torment. He hated Aleksić, who had entangled himself in his life and kept him six weeks in Niš to satisfy a whim.

"Listen, Mihajlo, what do you intend to do in this situation?"

"In what situation?"

"The present one. In five days the Bulgarians will be in Niš and the Germans in Kragujevac. I have a seat in Najdan Tošić's railway coach. I could squeeze you in, too. I suggest we slip off to Greece."

"I won't leave Serbia because of you or the Germans!" He moved away through the crowds toward the tobacco warehouses where the regiment of boys was assembled. Among them he could still be a man. They needed him. Somebody needed him.

"Long live our allies! Long live our great ally France! Long live Mother Russia!"

The band began to play. Trumpets and drums. Violins and double basses.

It was raining.

With considerable effort Olga told Vukašin about her encounter with Radić. Vukašin reproached her for not bringing home to lunch this kind man to whom their family was forever indebted. She was saved from further conversation about Radić by her grandchild's crying for his mother's breast; his mother wasn't there. Lunch passed, still no Kosara. Olga wondered what had happened, and whether she was responsible for Kosara's appearance and behavior that day. Meanwhile Vukašin was thinking about his unfinished letter to Ivan. The reasons Vukašin had given Ivan to be happy to have a son were not particularly convincing; it bothered him.

Just before dusk Najdan Tošić called on them. Since Kosara's arrival he hadn't crossed their doorstep. Disappointed in her appearance, he hadn't even wanted to see the "cuckoo in the nest," as he called the grandchild. He scolded Olga for taking in "that trollop" who had brought shame on Ivan and the family. But today Olga was glad to see her cousin. He was always helpful in difficult situations. Before he had even sat down she began telling him about Kosara. Najdan cut her short:

"I've no interest in Kosara. I'm here about a far more important matter. Where's Milena? Vukašin, hasn't Milena been in Prerovo for nearly two months?" He was addressing Vukašin for the first time since their quarrel over Vukašin's speech in the Assembly regarding Najdan's shady army contracts. "How can we go without her?"

"I don't understand. Where are we going?" asked Vukašin crossly.

"We must leave Niš by noon tomorrow. I have a railway coach reserved for Salonika. Our family can be fitted in comfortably. If you have a close friend without children, I can take him, too."

Vukašin bowed his head: once again Najdan was offering him safety. Once again the man who had robbed the State was fleeing from the fate of the people, using the state railway and a coach purchased for the purpose. Once again he had bribed a minister or general and come to ask Vukašin to share in his shame. Yet he was doing him a kindness in saving his family. Perhaps there was no honorable way to save oneself these days.

"Aren't the Allies coming?" asked Olga timidly, to break the silence. She was afraid that Vukašin might lose control.

"Don't talk to me about the Allies! We've been sacrificed, Olga. Sacrificed to Vukašin's Europe, Pašić's Slavdom, and dear old Mother Russia." Najdan waited for Vukašin to attack him, but Vukašin said nothing. "The Allies can't even defend themselves, let alone Serbia and the Balkans. You were right, Vukašin. For the first time since you've been heading that ridiculous Opposition, you've been wiser than Pašić. Macedonia is the graveyard of Serbia!"

Could Najdan really share his opinion? Vukašin interrupted firmly:

"The two of us have nothing to say to each other about politics."

"You're right there. I've had to mix with you politicians because of business and family affairs. As for politics—in which wise men and fools, the honest and dishonest lose equally—who wants it? Only those who have no real ability. Playing with the mob in the dark. A game of poker with fate, in which two people always have a stack of aces. A filthy and disgusting trade! Let's see. I must send my car for Milena immediately. How many kilometers is it from Palanka to Prerovo?"

Vukašin was silent. Again he was being tempted, crucified—forced to wage a painful struggle for honor and dignity. It would surely be a useless sacrifice. Was there any point in it after what had happened to him?

"Vukašin will decide about that, Najdan. And what shall we do with the baby, not yet three months old? We must discuss it with Kosara."

"Discuss it with Kosara? Nonsense! I'm trying to save the three of you. I don't care about Kosara and her bastard!"

"Thank you for your concern and help, Najdan," said Vukašin, but I won't leave Niš while the government and the Assembly are here."

"Listen, Vukašin, three days ago I loaned two ministers a truck to take their families and possessions to Salonika. Three deputies, and two from the Opposition at that, will join us. Don't be ridiculous! Patriotic duty and honor are subjects to be discussed after the war. Now it's time to save your skin!"

Najdan paced about the room, collided with a pile of suitcases, and sat down on the bed. The baby began to cry, so Olga went to him. Vukašin replied to Najdan's lecture:

"I know as much about what's ridiculous and pointless today as you and your fellow travelers to Greece, but I'll act in my own way. I'll join Mišić's army."

"Where are you going, Vukašin?" cried Olga from the other room.

"Where our son would be if he wasn't a prisoner of war. Naturally I have nothing against you and Milena going with Najdan. It would be foolish to stay in Niš."

Olga came up to him with the baby in her arms. "This is the first I've heard about your joining the army."

"I didn't want to talk about it until certain matters were settled. Now Najdan has provoked me. Anyway, it's high time we decided where to go and what to do in the face of this disaster."

"I won't go anywhere without you, Vukašin. If we must flee from Niš, we'll flee together. Milena, too." She raised her voice. "And this child and his mother come with us."

"I'm sorry, Olga, really sorry," said Najdan. "If there's anyone I love —surely I don't have to say it. Listen, Olga, I don't want to break your patriotic heart, still less your husband's. I don't want to save you if you don't want to be saved. As for that creature in your arms and his mother, I wouldn't go to paradise with them, let alone into exile. Do as you wish. My railway coach is at your disposal, and I'll give you my car if you don't want to come on the train with me. I'll be in Niš until noon tomorrow. Think it over. I'll call in the morning. Good night."

The child began to cry.

"What's going to happen to us, Vukašin? Oh God, why can't we save ourselves like everybody else? Why?"

Vukašin was moved. He walked over to her and placed his hands on her shoulders: "I don't know, Olga. I don't know what we'll do. But let's somehow preserve what we've always been. It's not only dignity. Let's go to Prerovo together. Do it for me. Milena is there, too, and we'll all three decide together."

Olga could barely restrain herself from groaning: why Prerovo, *now?* The sound of heavy footsteps was followed by a knock on the door as she stammered, "All right, I'll do anything you want."

Vukašin switched the light on and opened the door: a policeman saluted him: "Mr. Katić, Mr. Pašić asks that you come to his office at ten o'clock this evening."

Vukašin nodded. This was the first time Pašić had summoned him since the secret session of the National Assembly.

Three times Kosara came up to the gate but didn't dare enter, although she hadn't fed the child since morning. She went back to the inn for another strong brandy, then two more. She just couldn't feed Života for the last time. Yet she couldn't *not* feed him once more and hold him in her arms. She would die! Drunk like this, how could she get past *her,* and that gentleman—her mother-in-law and father-in-law? She just couldn't stand their play-acting, their pretense that they were happy to have a grandchild and a daughter-in-law, and that she was, so to speak, Ivan's fiancée. She'd die for Života, God would kill her. Should she tell them that she ran into some old friends in town, that in celebrating the Allies' arrival she'd too much to drink? The thought of his long look and her whimpering was too much. Where have you been all this time, my child? To hell with her! She who'd given birth to a half-blind idiot who didn't even know how to lie when he had to, or how to finish with a woman, or how much to pay! For him it was love, real feeling. And all because that pig Ćira didn't come from Niš as he had promised, the bastard. Bloody swine! Well, go on, you whore! What if they asked where she'd been and why she was drunk? Never mind. She'd just swear and look them straight in the eyes! But what if they didn't ask any questions? The train would leave before midnight. Good evening? No, no good. Not a word, then. Just look at the floor and hurry off to Života. She went into the house.

"For goodness' sake, Kosara, you haven't fed the child all day!"

"What do you mean, for goodness' sake? What if he had no mother? Thousands of children in this war have no mother, and they're still alive! There's milk and tea and the pacifier. And the pacifier is just like a nipple. I grew up sucking a piece of rag soaked in milk."

"Don't be angry, Kosara. We were worried about you."

"Why? What's all the fuss about? I don't want anybody to worry about me!"—*You're hungry, my pet, aren't you? All out of breath from crying. Now you'll get your lunch, if your poor mother's got anything, with all this worry. I'll go crazy, clean crazy! Go on, take a suck, have a good bite, my poor hungry little boy. Will you remember how upset your mother was before she left for Skoplje? I must go to our house, Života. The Fritzies are coming, and the Bulgarians. They'll take everything we have. Where will I put you in an empty house? I sweated blood to get every single thing, every rag. But now, Života, the trains don't leave on time, and they don't arrive on time, and God knows when your mother will come back to you. Go on, Života, bite it, suck hard, the milk's at the bottom. But you must remember, Života, how your mother cried over you, heartbroken because of what she had to do. So I must go. I must go for your good. I'll bring you a bunny rabbit and a kitten and a puppy. I'll buy you the nicest toys in Salonika and Istanbul. Suck harder, give a good tug. Ah, but it's hard for me, Života! How can I put you in your cradle? How can I? Maybe the Bulgarians will blow the train sky high, and I'm looking at you for the last time. How will I put you down and cover you up. What'll I do? I must go or I'll be late, Života, my son; you'll see, your mother will come back!*

She didn't look back as she disappeared into the night.

Kosara's drunken return and her hasty departure left them speechless. Vukašin went off to see Pašić without saying a word to Olga. She sat in the dark, stuffy room, wondering what would become of them and the child. Where could they go with this unhappy, drunken girl? Vukašin wanted to go to Prerovo. And the shock of meeting Radić! She'd feel pain for days on account of him. Perhaps she'd never see him again. Her eyes were dry, but she trembled.

The child began to cry; she jumped up and went to his cradle. He clucked his lips and then grew quiet. He was hungry. She sat down to listen to his breathing. This was how she used to listen to Ivan and Milena. For her there had been nothing more beautiful than the sound of their breathing in her arms. She felt as if she were holding the whole earth with its seas and rivers, woods and meadows. She held her breath to hear better the warm movement between the rising and setting of the sun; she saw and heard and knew that light and dark gently changed places with the rhythm of a child's breathing, that something of hers was reaching toward the stars, moving into the unknown and the infinite, and that it would last very long in hope and fear. She bent over her grandson. He began to cry loudly. He had a pain in his stomach from sucking the breast of his drunken mother. Where had that unhappy girl gone to? She switched on the light to take the child in her arms and make him some camomile tea; as she lifted his blanket she caught sight of a piece of paper.

Dear Mrs. Katić,

Života is alive and God grant I may never see him if I'm telling lies.

My heart is torn in two but I cant stay with you any more. You've just about been the death of me. It would be easy for me if you were one of these stuckup women or if you treated me like dirt under your feet or looked down your nose at me for me being what I am.

But I'm a mother and I cant be a loose woman and a whore. I cant look Mr. Katić in the eyes any more as he stares at my Života who isn't his grandson. A few times I've seen tears in Mr. Katić's eyes.

And because of you Ive felt like hanging myself. I'm ashamed and I don't want my son to grow up with my lies. It's better he has no grandpa and grandma than he thinks he has them and really doesn't.

Ivan isn't Životas father and that's why I'm running away from you.

I'll go mad, Mrs. Katić, you are a mother and you know how I feel when I must leave my child for you to worry about and look after while these bad times last because with nothing to my name I cant even feed myself and itll be worse when we are slaves again. If you look after Života for me God will look after Ivan for you. When the war is over and maybe before I know where I can find you and Ill take Života because its me that should look after him.

Goodby Kosara

Olga dropped the letter, gripped the cradle, and looked at the child who was out of breath from crying: oh God, was he really not hers?

Pausing often, Vukašin made his way through groups of invalids, poor people from Niš, and gypsies who were reveling drunkenly and shouting, "Long live our great allies!" By the light of an occasional lightbulb he could see French flags and flowers scattered over the cobblestones. The wind was tearing down garlands of chrysanthemums and triumphal arches made of pine branches and dahlias, and beating on the canvas signs bearing the words "Welcome, friends!" and "Long live our great ally France!" For more than twenty years he too had spread among the Serbian people faith in Europe, especially in France. *But where can we go now in our drunkenness,* he thought, *or in our despair when we sober up?*

On the bridge over the Nišava he stopped to let some fifty boys go past, bent under bags and multicolored blankets. They were accompanied by their mothers and grandmothers, who carried bags of food and bedding, and were preceded by old men. He stopped an elderly peasant at the head of the procession.

"Where are you off to, my friend?"

"I don't really know, sir. I'm the village mayor from Žitkovac, and I've been told to bring all the male children to the regional command. Where they'll go from there, and how far, God knows. Wait a minute, children, while I light a cigarette."

Vukašin gave him a cigarette and lit it. Some of the boys sat down on the wet, muddy bridge.

"So the Allies haven't come, sir?" the peasant said.

"No, they haven't."

"But there's people still waiting alongside the railway track. They've lit fires and they're waiting."

"No need to wait any longer."

"Surely Russia will defend us against the Bulgarians?"

"We're alone, my friend."

"Then what'll we do, sir?"

"We'll defend ourselves as long as we can."

From the other side of the bridge a driver shouted to the boys to get out of the way and let his fiacre through. The mayor thanked Vukašin for the cigarette and hurried across the bridge with his group. The fiacre pulled up next to Vukašin. Auguste Boppe, the French ambassador, greeted him:

"Good evening, Monsieur Katić. Would you like me to drive you home?"

"No, thank you, Monsieur Boppe. I've been summoned by the Prime Minister."

Boppe got out of the fiacre, told his secretary to wait for him on the other side of the bridge, and leaned against the parapet.

"Monsieur Pašić informed me that all embassies must be evacuated from Niš within three days. In response to my question, 'When will *you* leave Niš?' the grand old man said icily: 'When we hear the artillery.'"

"How did you comfort him?"

"By assuring him that France would live up to her commitment to Serbia."

"Only in formal words?"

"And by silence. I know what you'll say, Monsieur Katić. I'd say the same to you, if you were the French ambassador in Niš. However, there are times in politics when honorable men cannot behave honorably. This is such a time. Integrity, conscience, and virtue require specific conditions—lofty conditions. The same is true of beauty."

"I'd accept your lofty reflections, if I could use them to comfort these old men and boys who are walking past us, treading on the flowers intended for the French soldiers."

"We'll certainly help Serbia, Monsieur Katić. We won't abandon you!"

"Just look at those dark shapes, that procession of our male children! What's going to happen to them in a few days, Monsieur Boppe?"

"Don't take things so hard. You must preserve your faith in your sacrifice. It's a great purpose—a magnificent one, Monsieur Katić! What other nation in this war has such great goals!"

"But what if, after tonight, we doubt the worth of our sacrifice?"

"Then you've lost the war, Monsieur Katić."

"Maybe that's just how we'll lose it. But if you believe, Monsieur, that lofty conditions, as you so elegantly describe them, are necessary for honest policies and for the fulfillment of promises made by the Great Powers to a small nation, then proof is necessary to sustain that nation's faith in its sacrifice on behalf of the Allies. *Proof!*"

"I must repeat what I said to you on your return from Paris. You must solve the eternal problem of human survival, how to choose the lesser evil, the shorter *via dolorosa*. That's Serbia's problem now."

"For us the shortest road is the longest one to Golgotha."

Boppe lit a cigarette. In front of them the wind played with the signs hung on the bridge. Vukašin excused himself and left Boppe staring at the procession of village boys who were lethargically crossing the bridge, trampling the flowers into the mud.

Vukašin walked hurriedly past the offices in which clerks and policemen were packing official papers into boxes, and in Pašić's outer office found a number of ministers sitting in funereal silence. It was the first time he had seen them since the secret session of the National Assembly; he felt very uncomfortable.

The ministers slowly rose to greet Prince Trubetskoy and exchange a few words with him. Meanwhile a secretary took Vukašin in to Pašić, who greeted him with a nod as he talked on the telephone.

"Yes, Vojvoda, I know you don't even have a regiment of reserves. Five minutes ago Prince Trubetskoy assured me once again, on the

Czar's instructions, that Russia will help us. And this evening Boppe asserted that the French troops' not arriving was merely a technical matter. He begged us in the name of the French government to hold out for three weeks at the most. England guaranteed the same time limit for the arrival of her army. I believe them. Yes, I firmly believe them." He put down the receiver and said hoarsely: "Now everybody's asking me for proof we'll be saved. Why don't they turn to God?" He raised his voice: "How dare people be without God now? Take your coat off, Vukašin, and sit down."

Vukašin hung his coat on the stand, and asked as he walked over to the couch: "What are you planning to do with those children, Prime Minister?"

Pašić lowered himself into his armchair. "Save them from the German and Bulgarian bayonets, and use them to replenish our troops when they grow up."

"I don't know why the children are being sacrificed, Prime Minister. No god has ever accepted that kind of sacrifice."

Pašić shrugged. "There's cruelty at the heart of every religion. The greater the religion, the greater the cruelty."

Vukašin didn't feel like a political conversation, but Pašić asked him sternly: "What do you think about our situation?"

Looking straight into Pašić's gray pupils, Vukašin replied: "We could cease to exist."

This nation could never cease to exist!" Pašić was silent for a moment, then added: "If, God forbid, Serbia should lose the war, we can be sure that we've done everything in our power to prevent that misfortune. And if we don't do all we can, we won't have done our duty."

"To do everything today doesn't mean to sacrifice everything. Let us *do* everything, but without sacrificing everything."

"Yes, Vukašin, but how? I've always despised policies that encourage sacrifice as if it were some sort of virtue."

"First of all," Vukašin said firmly, "we must issue an ultimatum to the Allies: if they don't send an army to help us as soon as possible —if they don't attack Bulgaria—we'll make a separate peace with Germany and Austria-Hungary."

Pašić leaned forward and said in a confidential tone: "I've already let the Allies know that Germany and Austria have offered us a separate peace, but it's done no good. Anti-Serbian circles have even used this to pressure their governments to abandon the Balkans once and for all. If they sense now that we're wavering, they'll feel free of any moral or political obligation to help us. We'll just have to hold out."

For a long time they sat in silence. Vukašin wanted to smoke, but he knew that Pašić disapproved, so he decided to end the conversation. "What will you say to the people tomorrow, Prime Minister? The people who've been waiting for the Allies with music and flowers for three days?"

"I'll tell them the Allies will come. I'll do all I can to keep up their faith in the Allies."

"Even by telling them lies?"

"Yes. Since there's no truth that the people can believe in, we must make do with lies."

"How long do you think the army and the people can be led by deception?"

"As long as they believe it, Vukašin. Then we'll see."

" 'Then' is a matter of days, Prime Minister. A few days, perhaps."

"As I see it, it makes a big difference whether we collapse tonight or in ten days. If the government announced to the nation tomorrow that the Allies have deceived us, that would mean capitulation. It would be an admission that we can't be saved. I'm here to convince the people that we *can* be saved."

"I don't believe it's possible to save Serbia and keep up the people's spirit through deception. After so much suffering and sacrifice, after so many vain hopes, how will we be saved? Can you think of any solution, Prime Minister?"

"Yes, I can. But I also think there's such a thing as luck. Perhaps it will stray in our direction."

They fell silent. From the street they could hear music playing and people shouting, "Long live our allies!"

Suddenly Vukašin asked, "Why did you ask me here tonight, Prime Minister?"

"To offer you the opportunity of sending your wife and child to Greece with my family. They should leave the day after tomorrow, before the Bulgarians cut the rail line to Salonika. You yourself can go with the Allied ambassadors and be my link with them."

"Thank you, Prime Minister, but I'll take care of my family myself. I'll stay in Niš while the Assembly is in session, and then I'll join the army. It's true I belong to the third draft, but my contemporaries are fighting in the trenches. I consider it my duty."

Pašić twined his fingers in his beard, narrowed his eyes, and said in an icy voice: "You consider it your duty to differ with me on everything. Even when the government's collapsing, it must have an Opposition!"

Vukašin walked over to the window, but shrank from the music and shouting he heard. He turned toward Pašić and said: "Yes, it must! As long as a government exists, whatever it does, there must be someone to oppose it—in war as in peace, in defeat as in victory. You've convinced me of this tonight."

Pašić stood up and held out his hand. "Well, good luck to you, Vukašin. It's said God looks after drunkards and fools. Feel free to call on me anytime."

The strong wind and driving rain did Vukašin Katić good. He'd have liked to take off his hat and coat and walk along the Nišava all night, but he had to go home. Olga was alone, and who knew when that drunken Kosara would come back. He stopped at the bridge. A long procession of men in chains and fetters walked past him, accompanied by policemen. Convicts! Was it possible? "Who are these men, Corporal?" he asked.

"Convicts from Požarevac, sir."

"Where are you taking them?"

"Ask the government and the High Command."

Vukašin could think of nothing more to say to the corporal escorting the hundreds of convicts. He waited for them to cross the bridge and then, attracted by laughter and shouting in the main street, went over to see what was happening. People with garlands of flowers around their necks, some in white hospital coats and with cauldrons on their heads, wrapped in rugs and blankets, carrying chairs, buckets, saws, clubs, and roasting spits with sheep's heads, were trudging up and down the streets, tearing down floral decorations from gates and from the doors of shops, smashing triumphal arches, hitting the French flags, and crying: "Long live Uncle Peter!"

Some wounded soldiers stood on the sidewalk, laughing and shouting: "Long live the lunatics! Long live our crazy nation!"

"What's happening here?" Vukašin asked a group of civilians leaning against a wall.

"Can't you see? These are lunatics from the asylums in Belgrade and Niš. They're being moved somewhere so they won't be taken prisoner. Putnik and Pašić are saving the lunatics!"

"Long live our crazy government! Long live our crazy High Command!"

Vukašin hurried home, convinced that his place was in the trenches.

Olga was waiting for him, holding the baby in her arms: she handed him Kosara's letter.

He read it, and thought of the letter he'd begun to write to Ivan. Then Olga said calmly and with conviction:

"We should be grateful to her for her honesty. And we'll look after her child for her."

Before ordering the High Command to abandon Kragujevac for Kruševac, Vojvoda Putnik sent a telegram to all the commanders of the Serbian Army written in his own hand:

OUR DEFENSE MUST LAST AS LONG AS POSSIBLE. NOTHING DEMORALIZES A STRONG AGGRESSOR SO MUCH AS THE PROLONGED RESISTANCE OF A WEAK DEFENDER. YOU CONTROL A SMALL AREA: SEE THAT EVERY STEP THE ENEMY TAKES THERE IS LABORIOUS AND UNCERTAIN. YOU HAVE ONLY A LITTLE TIME: LET THIS TIME PASS SLOWLY FOR THE ENEMY, LET HIS DAYS BE LONG AND HIS NIGHTS EVEN LONGER. DEFEND YOUR POSITIONS AS LONG AS THAT REQUIRES LESS SACRIFICE THAN RETREAT. RETREAT AS SOON AS YOU SEE THAT THE ENEMY WILL WIN THE BATTLE.

The evacuation of the High Command, begun that morning, continued throughout the night and would be completed at seven the next day. In the morning Putnik, his adjutant, his doctor, and his daughters would retreat from this place where he had been born, gone to school, and grown up. He knew in his heart he would never return. The packing and removal of the archives were done as if they were being stolen: so they'd disturb Putnik as little as possible, Živko Pavlović had told the officers and soldiers carrying packing cases down the wooden staircase to take off their shoes. But it seemed as though their soft and cautious footsteps caused the staircase to complain even more loudly than usual. Feeling a sudden desire to see what he looked like, Putnik asked his daughter Radojka to bring him a mirror: his face was puffy, and the veins on his neck and temples were swollen. His eyes had become staring and ugly, his lips blue. Horrible! Even dead, he shouldn't look like that. He dropped the mirror and broke it. Radojka burst into tears and kissed his hand—she knew what the breaking of the mirror predicted. He asked her to turn the light out and bring him some tea. He felt sorry for her but not for himself. He had no fear of death. He had been preparing himself for it since he was a boy. It was not being unjust toward him. There was real greatness and beauty in its inevitability and something of the eternity for which he had been created. And until that end? That was now the only thing worth thinking about, on this night before his departure.

He had done all he could to leave recognizable footprints on this well-trampled earth, to be a spark of light in the darkness. He had always believed in God the Creator, but not in a life after death. This didn't bother him. When, as a young man, he had gazed at the clear expanse of the heavens and begun his vigil under those fires of inconceivable magnitude, which for man were only flickering sparks, he had realized the nothingness of man amid the infinite clusters of stars. Later he had come to believe that by power of will a man could separate himself from the mass of mankind in this nothingness and shine a little longer, and a little more brightly. He had chosen the longest road, never fearing the distance or loneliness ahead. From the beginning one must work toward some great objective, work seriously and passionately for eternity: this one effort justified all others.

Countless times his father had repeated to him one idea, from the work of some philosopher—that a man couldn't do anything which he didn't believe he could do. His father had talked often to him about the will, that power in man on which belief and purpose rested. The sweet, burning vision of what was greatest and most distant—the terrible desire to do what was most difficult—had taken possession of him and driven him into prolonged, tumultuous periods of solitude. At that time, in the Serbia of his youth, he had seen that the best opportunity for the exercise of will, for the greatest and most difficult achievements, lay in the army. There one could work to realize the centuries-old dream of liberating and uniting the Serbian people. But he had never thought of approaching his goal as a nameless soldier, or as an officer known by his decorations for zealous service and bravery. No, from the first, when he entered the Artillery School, he had resolved to become the creator of the Serbian army and its military leader. Unlike many of his contemporaries, he didn't believe Horace's claim that it was "sweet to die for one's country"; but he did believe, with Njegoš, that "the power of the mind rules the world." So at the Military Academy his models weren't heroic warriors and military leaders but Frederick the Great, for whom "war was knowledge," and those who had more faith in the human spirit than in weapons. He never desired the fame of a brave fighter, but rather that of an intelligent soldier, which is more difficult to attain.

He had no regrets: he had had good reason for believing what he had believed in. Everything he had striven for had been for the best. He hadn't engaged in politics, but had performed the most significant tasks of his time. He had made no great efforts to secure a position of power, but had nevertheless exercised power over people—the kind of power that increased because of his deeds, not because of his promotion in rank. In the army he had achieved all that could be achieved. He had become the first military leader of Serbia. He had served in a number of wars, but only in one had he shed his blood in a foreign land. He had always tried to be what he ought to be: to his contemporaries, a companion and nothing more; to his wife, a husband and nothing more; to his children, a father and nothing more; to the army, a commander and nothing more; to the State, a soldier and nothing more. He had never in any way exalted or exaggerated his achievements, and never shown anybody more than he should have. He wanted people to respect his work and his deeds; he didn't want them to love him. The concept of popularity was alien to him. Anyone who was prepared to lead armies to their death had no right to expect people's love.

His daughter offered him some tea and wiped his perspiring face with a towel. She took his hand, and he stroked her forearm.

What had he found most difficult in life? To be free within the constraints of army rules, regulations, and orders. This had been possible through the power of the spirit, by being occupied with what was great, distant, and eternal. Above the imperfection and paltriness of human laws were the laws of the universe; and while these didn't bring him comfort, they did arouse his wonder. If he couldn't organize the State, he could organize the barracks; if he couldn't introduce logical order into the life of the nation, he could do so in a platoon, a regiment, a division, an army. And, however insignificant it might be in the general disorder, the existence of that order, which was maintained in his will and consciousness, gave him the satisfaction of a creator. He liked the barracks because that was a world in which there was little dirt and few mistakes, and because it contained plenty of subordinate elements and pliant, unthinking human wills. It was true that the deadly futility of army life in peacetime troubled him. It was true that he had then sought consolation in women—women whose husbands were his superiors. He knew no human activity was so senseless as that of an army in peacetime—and that no human exertion produced greater evil than the exertions of war. Still, he always bore in mind that no one could work so hard for the life and greatness of a nation as a military leader. This was why that power conferred great rights over other people. If he had abused this power, let his grave remain unknown.

He asked his daughter for another cup of elderflower tea, and lit a cigarette to relieve his asthma.

What had he done and failed to do in this world of selfish wills and short-term aims, in this small nation which wanted more than it could have or deserved? Kings and princes had replaced one another, politicians had been cast down and trampled underfoot, merchants had grown rich, officials had grown fat from idleness, thieves had spat upon honest men, the corrupt had besmirched men of good conscience, fools had laughed at wise men. Meanwhile—slowly, invisibly, with painful effort—he had been building up the force to realize the aims of many generations. When things were going well with him, he had an untroubled faith that, thanks to his labors, the nation would become self-reliant and free, so that it needn't suffer at the hands of others. When things weren't going well for him, he convinced himself that he was struggling for some great objective. With these great ambitions he had mastered all the temptations of youth, all longings for pleasure and vice. And the satisfaction resulting from conscious, clean-cut renunciation had calmed the tumult of his passions. Even now when he lacked the strength to breathe, he knew that if he hadn't been strict toward his body—if he hadn't subdued it from childhood through regular exercise, tiring marches, and long rides; if he hadn't exercised restraint in food and drink, and mastered his longing for certain women; if he hadn't fortified himself with the Stoic virtues and toughened himself with moral vows—his passions would have driven his body from its uniform, and he'd never have endured the rigors of discipline, the commands of the hierarchy, and subordination to men who didn't deserve it. His life would have been ordinary, worthless. But had he been happy? Was he happy? He sighed, then coughed and lost his breath. Radojka brought him the tea; he felt better and decided not to reflect further on happiness.

What was the worst thing he had done, and how had he deceived himself? Like most men in a position of authority, he had on several occasions believed he could do more than he really could. Wasn't that the fate, the curse of all who believed that they were powerful and that they were working for great and lasting objectives? Among great and important people, those who desired less than they were able to do were rare—it has always been the other way around. He had long known that immoderation and the inaccurate assessment of aims were the most frequent causes of human defeat and lasting misfortune. Wasn't this military defeat—this great defeat at the end of his life— the punishment for overconfidence? Wasn't it just to balance his previous victories? Dare he comfort himself with this thought?

All that was happening to Serbia was not just a lost battle or a lost war; it might become the defeat of the historic aim of the Serbian people, the collapse of a faith held for centuries. And a nation always names culprits for such defeats. It finds them among its teachers, inventing proofs, then curses them and uses them as examples to frighten its subsequent leaders. Perhaps the Serbian people would blame him for this immense disaster. Perhaps this greatest of all wars, but a lost war, would be marked with his name. It wouldn't be King Peter, or the ambitious young regent, or the wily Pašić, or any of the generals. No, they'd blame Putnik, the real commander of the Serbian army, because he was a very sick man who commanded the army from his bed, who'd never once visited the front, never entered the headquarters of any army or watched any major battle. He'd never even looked inside the offices of the individual section chiefs in the High Command. He'd sat on his bed surrounded by pillows, gaping like a fish out of water, shaking with fear that he might suffocate. Yes, he was guilty, he'd be blamed for this great defeat. He gave a long, loud sigh.

"Are you in pain, father?"

"Yes, my child."

"Should I call the doctor?"

"The doctor can't help me."

She wiped his face again, and offered him more tea with honey.

What was there left for him to do? Should he refuse to accept defeat? Should he replace defeat with uncertainty? Yes, that was what he'd do. If the army believed in uncertainty, it could believe in victory. Uncertainty meant the possibility of preserving what was best in each man and in the nation. But how could that be possible in this war, under these conditions?

"Radojka, do you remember the names of the autumn flowers in our garden? I taught them to you, and I used to test you to see if you knew them."

"I suppose I remember some. This autumn our garden was full of chrysanthemums of all colors."

"Were there Michaelmas daisies?"

"Yes, and asters and marigolds, and emperor's eyes and dahlias."

"Go on."

"Well, there was sweet basil, and begonias, and . . ."

"You've forgotten the cabbage flowers, called zinnias in Latin. And you've forgotten the muscatels."

"Muscatels flower all summer."

"But they're autumn flowers, too. Then there's snapdragon and night-scented stock." All this made him tired; he fell silent.

There's feverish haste in all the towns of central Serbia, with immense numbers of refugees arriving from the areas near the frontier. The railway line is crammed with people. Highways, country roads, and fields are black with refugees. An endless string of farm animals blocks their passage. All the movable property of the Serbian nation is moving toward the heart of the country.

The cold autumn rain pours down on these bewildered masses. A heavy fog falls like lead.

The soldiers are causing panic among the townsfolk. All are preparing for flight, nailing up their shops and workrooms. Crowds are seeking information at the post offices: perhaps one tenuous telephone wire can still give information. The news keeps getting worse. One by one towns are being cut off; the railway line is growing shorter. The situation is desperate. The people and their leaders are being tested in a crucible. The enemy is attacking from the north, west, east, and southeast. Where will they break through? The whole of Serbia is encircled by a ring of iron! Yet hope and faith remain.

—From the notebook of the poet Milutin Bojić

7

At dusk the beating of a drum in Prerovo heralded an order from the regional headquarters that all boys between the ages of fourteen and eighteen should report to the district office at dawn, with a change of clothing and food for three days. Meanwhile, a wave of refugees from Šumadija filled the lanes and courtyards, the barns and kitchens; in a few days they would have to move on, but where to? Why were the boys being assembled in the regional headquarters? What was to be done with them, when the army was retreating on all fronts? All through the night the village was restless: fires kept burning in the houses and barns. Was it necessary to send the children off to war, when Serbia was on the verge of collapse?

Aćim Katić advised that the order be carried out; Djordje Katić said no. For the first time since the fighting had started, Tola Dačić agreed with Djordje; he refused to send his grandson to the headquarters, and told everybody that survival must come before the interests of the State.

The schoolmaster Kosta Dumović responded angrily to the women's questions: who dared not respond to the call of the country? He was resolved "to fulfill his duty as a teacher and take his pupils to the war," he told his wife and daughters. With Natalia's help, in the bell tower of the Prerovo church he buried the school records, the icon of Saint Sava, and the seal, all of which had to be preserved from the occupying forces.

Natalia couldn't decide whether to leave Prerovo with her father and the boys. She hadn't gone away to work as a volunteer nurse at the beginning of the war, as many of her friends from the university had done. This was her chance to come out of the military defeat on an equal footing with her contemporaries. And it would provide an honorable means of escape from Prerovo, which had changed for her since the arrival of Milena Katić, whose fame as a nurse had spread throughout Prerovo. But when she told her father of her intention to set out with him, he cut her short: "No, we can't have that. It's the duty of a Serbian girl to endure the time of bondage with honor. The people of Prerovo need you. Remember this: if you can't do it with honor, you must accept the fate of your brothers, for whom I've lit candles on the school benches."

At dawn Prerovo was steeped in thick fog. The refugees wouldn't have stirred from their shelters, if a dull, thunderous noise hadn't rolled down from the north, choking the road from Prerovo to the Morava ferry with a new wave of refugees. Kosta Dumović, too, was deceived by the fog. He looked at his watch: it was already after eight o'clock. Rushing out with his large bag, he stood on the steps of the district office with the village mayor; they listened in silence to the artillery and stared into the fog, which hid the lanes from which the boys emerged at infrequent intervals, accompanied by members of their households. Nine o'clock passed; instead of seventy-six, Kosta Dumović counted only fifteen youths. The mayor ordered the drummer to go through the village once more and threaten to court-martial all those who didn't report to the district office immediately. The drummer set off reluctantly through the lanes, beating his drum gently, then disappeared altogether. Kosta Dumović was angered by the slowness with which the boys were assembling; the mayor ordered the sexton to ring the church bells as he had done to announce the outbreak of war and mobilization in Serbia.

Aćim Katić stiffened at the prolonged ringing of the bells: they were announcing the capitulation of Serbia! He hadn't seen a newspaper for several days. Some army deserters had arrived in the village, and a stream of refugees was pouring through Prerovo. A group of Croatian students who had fled to Serbia told him that the High Command had abandoned Kragujevac and the government had left Niš. Only a disaster could bring Vukašin home after twenty-two years. Aćim had been surprised and frightened by Vukašin's telegram; it was two or three hours before he collected his wits and told his daughter-in-law, Zorka, to decorate the windows of Vukašin's room with garlands of corncobs, place the nicest quince on top of the cupboard, and hang wreaths of chrysanthemums on the walls and above the bed, so that everything would be just as it had been when Vukašin had come home as a student for Christmas vacation. The sound of the bells turned him cold with fear. He looked at the gate, then at the telegram on the table in front of him. If Serbia weren't on the verge of collapse, Vukašin wouldn't be coming. Aćim was consumed with anger: let him see Vukašin once more, then let the country crack up and all of them fall over the precipice! He opened the window and called to Djordje to go to the district office and find out why the church bells were ringing.

Djordje angrily refused: he had no time to go find out what he already knew. For the third night in a row he and his wife, the servants, and Tola Dačić were hiding away corn, fat, salt, sugar, and gas in pits under the rubbish heap, which had been lined with concrete during the summer. Now he was thankful to God for the fog, so he could cram his storehouses for the occupation without being seen by the neighbors. As soon as Belgrade fell he had begun to prepare for a period of bondage: he had made his peace with those he was on bad terms with; had postponed the payments of debts due him until the country was free again; had given the poor everything they asked for; and had helped the refugees generously—all so he could await the period of bondage with as few enemies as possible. He knew the time was at hand when one heartless man could mean nine headless ones! Vukašin's presence meant trouble, too. That brother of his, who hadn't even wanted to get Adam transferred to the telephone service, was arriving today to add to his unhappiness. He'd look after Vukašin''s daughter and protect her as he would Adam; but he wouldn't have *him,* an Opposition politician, under his roof during the occupation, nor would he have his wife, whom he had never met. He'd make this clear to Vukašin before he entered the gate. If God would only grant Adam enough common sense to flee, if only he could see him in the courtyard. Then let the Germans and the Turks grab all of Serbia—to hell with them!

Milena was awakened by the bells: was Bogdan still alive, she asked herself, was he? If she believed he was alive, then he would be. She hadn't had a letter from Bogdan since the German attack started. She had heard terrible tales from refugees about the slaughter of Serbian regiments on the Danube. Last night a Dalmatian soldier had told her on good authority that, because of the Bulgarian advance from the east, the troops of the Third Army, in which Bogdan was serving, would retreat through Palanka. She wanted to go to Palanka immediately, but she hadn't dared tell her grandfather. She would set out now. Her mother and father were coming today and would be in despair if they didn't find her at home.

She dressed quickly and went off to see her grandfather. He was staring out the window and didn't look at her. She greeted him and sat on the bed. She couldn't bring herself to say that she must go to Palanka. Ever since receiving the telegram from her father, he had gazed absently into the void and spoken disconnectedly. Surely her father knew how much her grandfather was suffering. Her father couldn't be so cruel or so deeply offended, that he wouldn't forgive. She had not learned from her grandfather what had happened between them when her father returned from studying in Paris. In their leisurely walks through the apple orchard and the meadows, he would rather talk about plants than people, about Adam rather than Djordje. Only occasionally, as if by chance, would he talk about Vukašin—as a child and a boy, before he left for high school. In answer to her persistent questions about him after his return from France, he replied reluctantly. Whenever the conversation turned to politics, he would say, "That was before the world took Vukašin away from me." She had become convinced that it wasn't some petty flaw in her father that lay behind their separation. This idea was essential for her, if she was to preserve her respect for her father. She looked compassionately at her grandfather and wondered how she could tell him of her intention to look for Bogdan in the retreating army. Without even glancing at her, he told her to go to the district office and find out whose death was being proclaimed by the bells.

Milena set off toward the district office: she'd be late arriving in Palanka, and at the district office she might run into Natalia. Whenever they met—and it was always in the presence of Milena's grandfather—Natalia never failed to sting her with some malicious remark, and offend her by her ill-humored look and smile. But was it her fault that she'd fallen in love with Bogdan while they were both recovering from the illness of which they had almost died? At that time she hadn't even known of Natalia's existence. Everything had been honorable and straightforward, on both her part and Bogdan's. He had written Natalia a letter telling her that he had fallen in love with the sister of his best friend. How could Natalia be jealous of her and hate her because the young man whom she had disappointed no longer loved her?

As Milena strode slowly down the muddy lane, some boys hurried past with large bags, accompanied by their families. She knew where they were going and would have liked to comfort them, but didn't know what to say. Preoccupied with thoughts of Bogdan, she didn't notice that the bells were no longer ringing. She stopped as soon as she saw Natalia's father on the steps of the district office. He was wearing a soldier's cap, and a belt across his civilian coat. Ever since the day she had met him—even before she knew he was Natalia's father—she had disliked this tall, thin, sullen man who was always calling the government dishonest, who blamed Pašić for all the evils of this world, and who considered all towndwellers thieves and bad Serbs. Now he was calling out the names of the mobilized boys from a list. As she approached a group of women to ask why the bells had been ringing, she caught sight of Natalia and stopped dead. Yet she couldn't resist looking at her: she was a beauty! And strong, too. Milena had always admired strong women. Had Natalia and Bogdan embraced? Milena trembled. Whenever they met, and whenever she gazed at Natalia's body, legs, and breasts, her blood tingled at the thought that Bogdan had embraced her. Her nose protruded, her profile was not quite angular, and her neck was short. Her voice was not pleasant. Milena met her glance: sharp and malicious, it crushed her completely. Milena shrank away behind a woman who was moaning for her son and holding him by the hand.

With her scarf, Natalia was wiping away the tears of some boys who were sobbing as they embraced their mothers and sisters. The pretty young lady opposite—a product of the drawing room—had spoiled the village for Natalia, filling the lanes of Prerovo with her presence, so that Natalia couldn't walk them freely; she had covered the fields with darkness and soured the night with an odious breath. Flowers were not beautiful since her arrival, the Morava was not her river; nothing in Prerovo was hers any more. She would *not* wait in Prerovo with Milena for the enemy occupation; she would flee with the army, simply to get as far as possible from this viper who produced a nagging pain in her chest and made her lips seem dry and bitter. And yet, driven by a feeling compounded of pain and rage, she had an irresistible desire to look at her, listen to her, touch her. Whenever they greeted each other in Aćim's presence, she would shake all over from the contact with her small, warm hand: she experienced a burning sensation from her glance and her deep voice, too deep for her body. That birthmark on her neck near her left ear, that dark spot on her white skin, obsessed her, as if all Milena's power to seduce and inflict pain was concentrated in it: when Natalia shut her eyes that dark spot moved, crawling around in her inner vision, flying through space and the blue of the sky. She would see this spot on a leaf, on an apple, on her sister's cheek. As if by some mysterious force, her glance was entangled in the dark curls which had fallen out from under Milena's scarf.

Natalia's prolonged staring made Milena shiver and avert her eyes. Natalia felt something akin to victory, but it made her want to weep aloud.

The air between them was filled with the sound of women wailing for their boys lined up in two rows in front of the schoolmaster, who was shouting: "I don't want to hear any more crying from you women. These boys have been my pupils. Now they're all my sons and I'll take care of them. Mourn for us if we don't come back. Now go home, there's work to be done. The corn hasn't been gathered in yet. Children, follow me!"

The procession of boys disappeared into the fog. Natalia was surrounded by the women and children of Prerovo. Slowly she led them toward the Morava after the boys, who now stood in front of Aćim Katić's house. That must be her father taking leave of Aćim. Then the procession wound through the fields in the fog. Not until the Prerovo children had boarded the ferry, and the ferry had departed, did Natalia and the women approach the Morava. The bare poplars seemed to sway with lamenting. Natalia couldn't tell whether her father was waving his hand in farewell, or threatening the women who were wailing for their children even while they were still alive.

In the wood surrounding the Prerovo monastery Adam Katić and Uroš Babović parted, having agreed to meet when the Germans occupied their part of the country. They had resolved to take to the woods rather than be captured. Adam sneaked into Prerovo late in the evening, not because he was afraid that someone might report him to the authorities, but because he was ashamed of being a deserter. His father was waiting in the apple orchard, as if he had known when his son would come and where he would jump over the fence. Choking with happiness, Djordje hugged his son, and in their exuberance they practically knocked each other over.

"So you're home, thank God!"

Adam took his horse to the stable, then sat down on the doorstep of the distillery and lit a cigarette. His father sat beside him and also lit a cigarette; his trembling body touched his son's.

"Almighty God," murmured Djordje, crossing himself.

Adam heard the hissing and gurgling of vats and barrels filled to the brim, and caught the familiar, intoxicating scent of fermenting must. He wanted to cup his hands and drink his fill. He wanted to go under the outbuildings and sprawl in the piles of harvested corn, just to smell it. He interrupted his father's prayer of thanksgiving:

"I ran away, father. I'm a deserter."

"Never mind that. Thank the Lord God that He gave you the sense to escape. We're done for. Don't worry, I'll hide you until the army has passed. Once we get some kind of government, we'll fix things up easily."

Adam stood up impatiently and ran down to his grandfather's old house. For a few moments he stood transfixed at the door: inside, sitting at the table with his grandfather, was a young girl with eyes even more beautiful than Natalia's. "Is that you, Adam?" his grandfather asked. Adam was startled. That must be his cousin Milena, about whom his grandfather had written him twice.

Embarrassed, he greeted her, then kissed his grandfather's hand.

"Where did you leave your regiment?" Aćim asked Adam, before the young man could even sit down on the chair which Milena had brought for him.

"I left the squadron near Jagodina." Adam frowned: if his grandfather questioned him now in front of Milena, he wouldn't tell him the truth. He looked sternly at his grandfather and asked: "Are you ill, Grandfather, or just scared of the Fritzies?"

"I'm not well, but that doesn't matter. Tell me, has our army dug in at Belgrade to halt the Germans?"

"No. They can't stop the Germans."

"What do you mean, 'they can't stop the Germans'? How long does Putnik think he can keep running away? What's going to happen to this nation if you keep on running away?"

"Don't ask me. I'm tired and hungry."

"Milena, tell Zorka to get some supper ready and bring it here for him." As soon as Milena had gone out, he leaned toward Adam and asked softly with fear in his voice: "You haven't deserted, my boy, have you?"

"Yes, I have."

"Deserted? My grandson, my Adam—a deserter from the army! Oh, my God!" He seized his forked beard in both hands and went off to Vukašin's room.

Adam felt like weeping from shame and rage. After what he had gone through, was this all his grandfather had to say to him? He cursed himself for escaping when everything was collapsing. He waited for his grandfather to come back—then he'd tell him the whole truth. He finished his cigarette, but his grandfather didn't return. Adam heard him sigh; he went in and shut the door behind him. A fire was burning in the stove. His grandfather was standing by a window that was decorated with bunches of corncobs.

"Listen, Grandfather, I didn't run away because I was afraid of the Germans. Or because we're going to be defeated. I'll go back if you think I should, as long as they don't shoot me."

His grandfather turned around and came over to him. "Why should they shoot you?"

"Because my friend Uroš Babović and I saved the life of our friend Sima Pljakić. He'd been sentenced to death by a court-martial, and the squadron commander detailed me and Uroš to look after him until the following morning, when he was to be shot in front of the regiment."

"What was Sima Pljakić's crime?"

"Spreading panic. He'd said publicly that Prince Alexander had fled to Montenegro, and that Pašić and all the ministers had gone to Greece. Ever since the fighting started, Sima has been cursing the government, damn him."

"So a man was condemned to death for cursing that thief and liar Pašić and his toadies? Are you telling me the truth, Adam?"

"They made all kinds of accusations against Sima. Mind you, he did speak out against the government much more than you do. But I couldn't guard a man all night, a Serb and a friend, and then shoot him in the morning."

"What happened to Sima?"

"We were guarding him in the cellar of a school. About midnight the three of us agreed to run away. Sima went to his uncle in Varvarin, and Uroš and I came together to the wood by the monastery."

Aćim returned to his own room and sat down at the table to smoke. "Adam," he said suddenly, "you saved that man's life. He was no traitor. You ran away from Pašić's toadies. Still, you must go back to the army tomorrow. Go to another division where they don't know you. Have a good rest, take some clean clothes, food, and money, and go back to the army and the people, and share with them whatever God wills. You mustn't do otherwise. If Serbia collapses now, no one knows whether she'll ever stand upright again."

Adam listened despondently and looked at his hands: he'd believed that he was more important to his grandfather than anything in the world, but in fact Serbia was more important. He shouldn't have come home until the Germans reached the Morava.

"Go with the people, my boy. You can't desire a better fate, even under the gallows."

"I don't know where the 'people' are, Grandpa. Everyone's running away, saving his own skin. They'd sell their mothers for an overcoat, and their fathers for a pair of boots. Serbian men are busting the ribs of Serbian women with their rifle butts, just to get a decent supper. I've seen that with my own eyes, this autumn and last. In this mud and fog, Grandfather, you don't know who's laughing and who's crying."

"The 'people,' Adam, are the best of us. In our present misfortunes, the best are brave and honorable. Go to them, my boy. You're a Katić."

"Don't push my son into the grave, you senile old idiot!" yelled Djordje, banging the door open with his foot.

Aćim dropped his cigarette. Adam jumped up and stood in front of his father; then, seeing tears in his eyes, he retreated and sat on his grandfather's bed, trembling between two loves and two hatreds. Ever since he could remember, they had wrestled over him. Why had he run away? Where could he hide?

"All this time you've been waiting for Vukašin," said his father, "never once thinking of Adam! Vukašin hasn't come. So now you want to crush my son, you old glutton! The people? What people? You aren't the people, and neither is Vukašin! You're just politicians!"

Adam caught sight of Milena, who stood dumbfounded in the open doorway. He went up to his father, seized him by the shoulders, and said: "If you don't shut up, I'll ride off and never come back!"

Unable to wait for her father and mother, Milena firmly announced to her grandfather that she was going to Palanka to look for Bogdan. Her grandfather was astonished: could she really want to see someone else more than her own father? He would certainly have reproached her, had he himself not felt offended by Vukašin's behavior. Vukašin had sent his father a telegram for which Aćim had been waiting for twenty years, but hadn't said when he would arrive. Aćim sent Adam to get Tola Dačić to drive Milena to Palanka and look after her. But Adam didn't find Tola at home: he and many of the old people of Prerovo had run off with wheelbarrows to grab what they could from the wreckage of some government warehouses in

Palanka. Because it was time to pour off the red wine, Djordje couldn't spare a single servant to drive Milena. Adam couldn't bring himself to go with his cousin, though he dearly wished to do her some kindness because of her beauty and her service as a nurse in Valjevo. She wanted to go alone on foot, but Aćim wouldn't allow this. Since his unsuccessful revolt in Prerovo, his last imprisonment under the Obrenović dynasty, and his rupture with Vukašin, Aćim had vowed never again to set foot in Palanka—that corrupt town, that den of thieves, that monster that sucked a peasant's blood and sweat, and took away his best children! Although he had remained faithful to this vow for twenty-two years, he now decided to break it for his granddaughter. He realized that world—that state which had taken away his son, made his wealth worthless, and damaged the reputation he'd risked his life for—was now collapsing. He no longer had any reason to hate it. Now, in this time of suffering, all he wanted to do was satisfy his granddaughter's every wish. That was how he'd always imagined his old age: as a time when he would satisfy the wishes of his grandsons and granddaughters.

Knowing of her grandfather's vow, Milena wasn't pleased by his decision. She tried to dissuade him from the journey, even offering to postpone her departure until her father and mother had arrived, but he simply embraced her and waited for Adam to bring the carriage around. Then, as Adam helped him into the carriage, a thought struck Aćim: let the village and Palanka see him today as they used to see him! He went back into the house and put on a new suit, new shoes, and a new fur hat—things he had set aside some ten years ago for his burial. Of the things he took into the carriage, only his old stick was familiar to those who knew him now.

Before getting into the carriage, once again he said to Adam: "Stroll around Prerovo today, my boy, then have a good sleep. Tonight when we come back, we'll all have supper together, and then, with God's help, you'll go back to the army."

Severe and formal, he seated himself next to Milena. As soon as they came out onto the road, he drove the horses at a fast trot for all Prerovo to see and hear. Once they had left the village, they encountered signs of flight: people, animals, and carts filled with belongings and children. He moved ahead slowly now, often slipping into the ditch, saddened by the woes of the people. When they left the fields of Prerovo, he began to talk to his granddaughter.

"It was on this road that Mika, Vukašin's teacher, and I took your father to the high school. He didn't want to go on with his schooling, and his mother backed him up. We were ready to leave for Palanka; the horses were harnessed and his trunk loaded, when Vukašin fled to the apple orchard. We just barely managed to catch him, pulled him into the cart, and tied him up like a wild boar. All the way to Palanka the schoolmaster held him between his knees. Yet later, when he went out into the world, he got different ideas in his head."

Milena wanted to comfort him, but didn't quite know how. The things her grandfather said about her father filled her with confusion. Why had her father made a secret of his youth to herself and Ivan? Was it to protect himself or them?

As they passed through the first village after Prerovo, Aćim again drove the horses at a trot, but the many mourning flags above the doors of the houses made him feel it was unbecoming to hurry. He continued more slowly, so he could raise his hat to every old man or woman in whose courtyard he saw a mourning flag. Most hesitated before returning his greeting. Some came to the fence to have a better look at him, to make sure their eyes weren't deceiving them. It was as if they were asking themselves: Can that really be Aćim Katić fleeing? He was moved by these silent encounters with his political friends and foes of long ago. He felt as if he were being put through a difficult test, as on the days when he was up for election as a deputy in the National Assembly. Only now he was not counting people up as voters, or classifying them as opponents to be won over or chased away. Now he divided them into those who would come to his funeral and those who would not. Accordingly, he raised his hat and spoke to some, but waited for others to greet him first before he raised his stick or nodded.

"That man won't come to my funeral," he said solemnly. "From that house the women will come. Now *that* house is a den of thieves—no one will light a candle for me. And the people in that new house, they're not worth anything. They always voted for the man the police clerk told them to vote for. See these people, they used to have quite a bit of property, but they've fallen on hard times. Still, they're my people. They supported the elections with their rifles. These poor wretches with two mourning flags, they'll come to my funeral with their children. And that old woman supporting herself on two sticks, they'll bring her to my coffin in a cart. As for those houses apart from the rest, the people there have been the toadies of every government. They only voted for me if they were sure I would win."

Milena listened attentively, wondering if her grandfather had done something very wrong when he was young and had power. Was it because Aćim divided people into friends and enemies that his son had broken with him? She protected herself from such thoughts with her anxiety about Bogdan, and her regret that she hadn't visited him at the front before the fighting started; many women and young girls had done this, but she had felt too ashamed in front of her mother.

"Please, Grandfather, don't talk about your funeral!"

"What else have I got to talk about, my child? I must make my peace then with mother earth. All I ask now is that God grant me an easy death. I think my eighty-odd years deserve it."

"Has it been a hard life, Grandfather?"

"Yes, it has. There're all kinds of people in the world, Milena. And they can harm you in ways you'd never expect. To tell the truth, I have at times aimed to shoot people, but never from an ambush. I've had a hard climb up, but I've never maimed or crushed anyone in my way. I've slashed at the mourning flags of villains, but I haven't disgraced their children. I've taken things from people, but I haven't stolen. I've said all sorts of things to a man and sworn at him, but I've never lied, Milena."

"You've had a terrible life, Grandfather!"

"Not really, my child. At least not until the world took Vukašin from me. After that, everything rotted and wasted away. With this stick and this beard I still looked like Aćim Katić, but I wasn't. Things around me hadn't changed, yet nothing was the same. Now I can die: if Vukašin doesn't come, you'll attend my funeral."

"Father is surely on his way. He wanted to come with me, but he was prevented by the Assembly."

"On the other side of this bridge," Aćim went on, "after an election I'd won, the Progressives ambushed me. My mare was killed on the spot by a bullet. If I hadn't had a breech-loading rifle on my lap, I'd never have escaped alive. Another time, on this same bridge, when I was bringing Vukašin from Palanka for the Christmas holidays, we found ourselves facing rifles. But their aim was poor, so we were able to escape—racing like the wind, through waist-deep snow. Only my servant was wounded, in the elbow. . . . And while I was driving pigs to the Budapest market with Djordje and Tola, twice we were waylaid by robbers. There was shooting, and blood flowed! All sorts of things happened. It was a real struggle to keep your head on your shoulders on these roads, my girl. And the bigger the head, the more vulnerable it was."

"Grandfather, did you shoot at those people who waylaid you?"

"Yes, I did, Milena. If I hadn't, it would have been the last time I felt the sun warm my back!" He fell silent and looked sad. He put his arm around her and continued. "You'll see, Milena, how many people from the Morava valley and the hill country will gather at my funeral. They'll ring the bells all through the district, as if for mobilization. The people will turn out like monks on a saint's day in a monastery. There won't be room in our courtyard to light the candles. I want you to throw a bunch of flowers on your grandfather's coffin. If it's winter, sweet basil; if it's spring, fruit blossom; but if it's summer, pick a few of every flower in the meadows."

They ran into Tola Dačić, his wheelbarrow filled with sacks and with buckets of oil and gas. His daughter-in-law and grandson walked behind the cart, carrying bags full of metal boxes. Aćim stopped his horses: "Whose stuff is that, Tola?"

"Ours. Our flour, our rice, our gas and oil, Aćim."

"What do you mean 'ours'? It belongs to the State! Where'd you steal it?"

"It belonged to the State while there was a State. Now the State is finished, so it's ours. Just as it was ours before there was any State."

"Two of your sons have given their lives for Serbia, two of them are fighting, and you're looting warehouses!"

"My boys gave their lives when that was necessary. Those who are left have to survive."

"Shame on you, you thief!"

"There's no such thing as thieves now, Aćim. No landlords either, or poor folks. Now we're all slaves of the Fritzies. People are doing what they can to keep alive."

Aćim looked at him scornfully: was the time approaching for Tola Dačić's wisdom? That would be worse than loss of freedom. He whipped the horses to a trot, but around the first bend they encountered a long line of carts and handcarts filled with sacks of rice and flour, accompanied by women, children, and old men, bent double under plundered goods. Milena suddenly realized that occupation didn't mean just bondage. It meant that the whole of life was overturned. She listened to her grandfather's sighs as they passed the looters, bewildered by his suffering on account of government property—he who had slashed the mourning flags of his enemies! That was her grandfather. These looters were the people. This was the road along which it was hard to keep your head on your shoulders. Was that why her father hadn't returned to Prerovo after the Sorbonne?

As they crossed the Morava and neared Palanka, they found their way blocked by a baggage train, field hospitals, and retreating artillery units. Aćim was amazed by the extent of the defeat. Suddenly he felt exhausted; a mist swam before his eyes from the horror of it all. There in front of him was the town he found so odious; the nearer he came to it the heavier his weariness grew. He couldn't go there, not even now: he didn't want to die with that pain, too. Just before the excise building and the first houses, he turned the horses off the highway and said dejectedly to Milena: "You go there, Milena. Go look for Bogdan. If you find him, bring him to meet me. I'll wait for you here."

Milena got down from the carriage and hurried toward the crowds of soldiers.

Vukašin Katić didn't want to leave Niš before the government and the Assembly had left, so he didn't leave for Prerovo immediately after sending his father the telegram. He didn't wish his departure to seem like flight, so he left with the town's last defense force, just before the Bulgarians arrived. The packs of dogs which had prowled around the hospitals and the new cemetery all summer had entered the half-deserted town, and the riffraff had taken over the town center, plundering everything of any value or beauty in Serbia's wartime capital. Olga didn't hurry him. She waited patiently, her suitcases packed, concerning herself with Života. The only person angered by the postponement of their departure was Najdan's chauffeur. Olga tipped him generously and begged him not to show impatience in front of her husband. She was afraid that Vukašin, if angered, might refuse the use of the car, which he had accepted only on account of the baby.

Everything that happened on their way from Niš to Prerovo—the rain, the road blocked by refugees and the retreating army, the mourning flags, and their own slow, dangerous progress through the tumult—made Vukašin's return to his native village a strange journey for him. Olga sat in silence with Života in her arms. Vukašin said nothing to her about his childhood memories of the places they passed. He didn't even tell her when they entered Prerovo. He didn't stop at the cemetery to visit his mother's grave, as he used to do whenever he arrived in or left Prerovo.

When at last they pulled into the courtyard, he stared for a few moments at the dead ash trees, black against the rain-soaked sky, and wondered what to do. Must he enter the house where he had been born? He got out and waited for someone to open the gate. Then he would traverse the longest distance of his life as he walked across the cobbled courtyard. Should he go back to his own life, or continue his journey into uncertainty? He would kiss his father's hand as he always did upon arriving, and ask after his health. Then he'd listen to him, let him say everything he hadn't said for twenty years. It was a good thing Milena was there: she could share the meeting with him and Djordje, and make it easier to introduce Olga. But he couldn't see his father or Djordje on the porch; some people he didn't know were busy in the courtyard. Where was Milena?

The driver honked his horn, which made him angry; he set off alone toward the gate. It opened. A tall, strong young man straightened up in front of him. He had a mild, serious face like his mother Simka, and Vukašin thought sadly of the beautiful sister-in-law who had inflamed his nights with desire when he was a young man in Prerovo. He held out his hand to her son: "Are you Adam?"

"Yes, Uncle, I am."

"Are you on leave?"

"Just passing through. I'm going back to the army this evening."

"Where's your grandfather? And Djordje and Milena?"

"Grandfather and Milena have gone to Palanka, and my father's in the distillery, pouring off the red wine."

"Why to Palanka?"

"Milena wanted to see her—somebody called Bogdan."

"You hear that, Olga?" he said reproachfully, then left them to greet each other and push the car into a shed. Moving with difficulty, as if sloshing through waist-deep water, he approached his father's house, which seemed smaller and lower than he remembered. The house where he'd been born and grew up, and where he'd spent that Christmas Eve before his break with Aćim. But he couldn't go into his father's house without him, nor into his own room. He'd have begun to weep if Djordje hadn't come up to him with a woman he supposed was Djordje's wife, Zorka. They greeted him crossly, as if they had parted only a week ago. Could these strangers really be his nearest relatives? He looked around the courtyard and walked back to the steps. This was no longer his house, nor was this courtyard his courtyard, nor his brother the brother he remembered. Nor were these old, black ash trees the same—these trees in which he'd always caught his first sight of the sunrise; they had rustled through the nights of his boyhood, and throughout his youth the elongated Prerovo sky had rested on them, but they weren't his any more.

Olga greeted Djordje and Zorka and told them that she'd brought a child abandoned by its mother, which she would look after until the end of the war. This softened Zorka, and her manner was warm and friendly as she led Olga into the large, new house at which Vukašin was looking with indifference.

"Is there no hope for the country, Vukašin?" asked Djordje, as he invited him to follow Olga and Zorka.

He didn't reply immediately, but went onto the veranda of the old house and looked hard at his brother, now an old man. He seemed much older than he remembered him from the previous autumn in front of the hospital in Valjevo, when he'd caught up with Vukašin on the highway in the darkness and asked him to have Adam transferred to the telephone service. *I'm an old man, too,* he said to himself, and turned to his brother:

"It's difficult, but I think we'll pull through." He went into his father's room and stopped dead: everything was as it had been—everything! Yet somehow it wasn't the same room.

"How will we pull through?"

"The Allies will help."

"When? When will they help us? Do you hear those guns? How long are you politicians going to lie to the nation?"

"We'll talk about this later, Djordje. Let me take my coat off."

He went into his own room: the stove was burning, just as it used to. The bed was covered with his mother's rug, arranged as Simka used to arrange it when he was coming home for the Christmas holidays. Corncobs at the windows, quince on the cupboard, garlands of chrysanthemums on the walls. The enlarged photographs of his father and himself, taken before he went to Paris to study. Everything was the same. His head spun from the familiar smell. Everything was as it had been, but it wasn't *his* any more. Djordje was grumbling at the government and the High Command for ruining the nation and the army. Blaming him, in fact—that was clear—but he couldn't answer. How could his father go to Palanka today? Why couldn't he have waited for him?

Olga came in and said excitedly, "Your room is lovely, Vukašin! Strange and beautiful, like a room in our stories about village life."

"Yes. It does look as if it's from a story—because it doesn't belong to real life."

Aćim Katić sat in the carriage, leaning on his stick, stricken with grief by the misery he saw. He was dazed by this collapse, which he hadn't grasped from the reports of Adam and all the refugees and soldiers who had passed through Prerovo. For hours he watched the women and children, the ragged, ill-shod soldiers and wounded men with mud-stained bandages, pouring in an unending stream into the town. From the front the rumbling came ever more loudly, and from the railway station came sounds of general uproar. It was pouring, but he didn't feel it. He even forgot to smoke as he watched a baggage train stuck at the entrance to the town, pushing toward the main street; it was as if the town's ribs were cracking, as if it was suffocating. Then two batteries came up from the Morava, stubbornly bent on entering the town; drawing their sabers, the officers mercilessly thrashed the baggage-train men who stood in their way. Unable to remove the carts or budge the animals, the men fled or hid among the oxen, infuriating the officers further. Aćim Katić rose from his seat and shouted:

"Don't hit those men! You wouldn't beat animals like that! Where are your rifles, you goddam baggage men?"

They didn't hear him, and no one took any notice.

By now the guns had gone ahead of the baggage train and were stuck in the crowd behind the railway station. An officer on horseback, accompanied by a sergeant, came up to the hospital train and ordered the drivers and orderlies to unload the seriously wounded men. The carts were needed to carry the archives of the State Council, they announced. The medical officer protested that wounded men should be saved before archives. Aćim felt a glimmer of hope that a man wearing the State's uniform might be considered more important than its papers, but some orderlies had already taken off two wounded men. In fact the drivers, along with the orderlies, were beginning to unload the groaning wounded onto the ground, which was covered with reeds.

"Villains! Heartless villains!" Aćim shouted, waving his stick. "You can't dump wounded men in the mud! To hell with the archives!"

No one heeded his cries or looked at him. Tears welled up in his eyes. As he was getting out of his carriage he fell into the mud. After picking himself up, he set off behind the captain toward the soldiers and refugees, scolding and threatening, until he got lost in the mass of carts and gun carriages. Why was he there? Where was he going? Ah, as long as he didn't lose his stick! Clenching it firmly in both hands, he ran in and out of courtyards, then across gardens and plum orchards. There was the railway line—now he knew where he was, thank God! His carriage wasn't far away. What had happened to him, he wondered. Had he been dreaming? Perhaps Milena was there looking for him. Perhaps someone had stolen his horses and carriage. What if someone from Palanka had seen him in the mob? He wiped the rain and sweat from his face, sat down on a railroad tie to rest, and lit a cigarette. Then he heard cries and violent banging: he turned around and saw people attacking a train in the station with axes and picks. He walked over to see what was happening. On a mound near the track, two soldiers and an officer stood behind a small, elderly man in a general's uniform who, resting on his stick, was watching the people smash up a railway coach.

"Can that be King Peter?" he asked a woman who was standing on the track with an umbrella and a suitcase. She nodded. Aćim set off toward him. When he reached the old man, who was weeping at the sight of the train's being smashed and plundered by the mob, he halted and took off his hat. King Peter stretched out his hand and asked him where he came from. Aćim Katić was overjoyed at this meeting, which he had always secretly desired, and he introduced himself confidently.

"Aćim Katić?" said the King. "Were you one of those who led the people in revolt under the Obrenovići?"

Overjoyed that King Peter remembered his part in the uprisings, Aćim replied with his old assurance:

"Yes, I was, sir." He paused, then added. "Until the world deprived me of my son."

An adjutant took the King's arm and led him to a car.

"There's no hope for you, Serbia, when your King weeps," said Aćim aloud, turning toward the railway line, where men and women were fighting over sacks filled with goods. A royal guard fired two bullets in an attempt to protect the royal coach, then fled down the line, pursued by some women brandishing axes. Wildly angry, Aćim ran toward the mob flailing his stick:

"What are you doing, you swine? That's government property! The property of the Serbian army! Leave it alone! Leave those sheets, you bastards! What do you want with those books and icons? God grant that those candles burn you up! And those medals, you filthy gypsies, you thieves! Why, that's the King's uniform!" He hit women, children, and soldiers on the head with his stick.

They rushed at him; reeling from their blows, he fell down onto the rails. The train caught fire and the flames climbed into the sky. Noiselessly, the coaches broke away. Human feet crushed his face and chest.

Milena now asked less often for Bogdan's regiment and division. Half-conscious, she felt as if some force were pushing her from one end of the town to the other, through streets choked with terrified people, distraught soldiers, baggage trains, artillery, and animals, all standing in the rain. She remembered Valjevo and the hospital during the retreat of the Serbian army. She remembered every movement in that petrified void of expectancy when they waited for the enemy to appear, every word spoken, every sound. The hearts of the wounded had beaten loudly, like wall clocks. She had been frightened by her own people that night—by the Serbs, whom she had never expected to wrong their own in defeat. Now, driven by a tormenting curiosity, she pushed her way through Palanka, observing and listening to what was going on: the smashing and plundering of shops, bakeries, and inns; the carousing of soldiers in wine cellars, where drunken third-draft men were thrown into vats of pressed grapes; the sale to civilians of objects from museums—old national costumes, uniforms, weapons, pictures, icons, flags from the Serbian uprisings—by soldiers who had looted a train. She listened to what the civilians were saying, and to the soldiers at the inns and on the streets: Pašić had offered to surrender, had fled to Greece with Prince Alexander and the government, so why suffer hardships any longer? It was time to throw away the rifles and submit to the victor calmly, without angering him by senseless resistance.

But when she saw three soldiers fighting over a stolen fur coat—jabbing one another with bayonets, until two of them lay motionless in pools of blood, as the third carried off the coat—she was filled with revulsion, and fled toward where she had left her grandfather.

When she failed to find him there she grew even more frightened. At the entrance to Palanka she asked whether anyone had seen an old man with a carriage. No one had. Perhaps he had broken his vow and gone to the town to look for her. She returned to the Kossovo war memorial, which was crowded with refugee children waiting for their parents. She pushed her way through the main street and cafés, asking every peasant whether he had met Aćim Katić. Again she ran to where they had parted, but didn't find him. She asked, whimpered, implored, but no one had seen an old man with a forked beard, a peasant with a fur hat and a stick. Drawn by the shouting and yelling to the railway line, she met peasant women and old men carrying loot, and asked them whether they had seen Aćim Katić from Prerovo. An old man with a packing case on his back stopped and looked hard at her:

"What relation are you to Aćim Katić?"

"I'm his granddaughter."

"Go to the station—you'll find your grandfather there. He's lying on the rails."

"Why is he lying there?"

"Everybody gets trampled on these days, my child."

She rushed to the station, where the plundering of the smashed coaches was in its final stages. Women were gathering into their aprons the rice and salt spilled on the platform and the tracks, and some young gypsies were fighting over scattered war medals while a wounded man tried in vain to drive them off with curses. Peasants were loading onto handcarts some torn, half-empty sacks, and an empty gasoline barrel and some buckets for oil and gas from the last coaches. The front coaches were already on fire.

"Grandfather! Grandfather Aćim!" She pushed her way through the crowd and the gathering dusk, until she caught sight of the royal coach: there he lay on the rails, without his shoes and coat, his head bare, his face swollen and covered with blood, his eyes closed. She knelt down and raised his head, then listened to his faint heartbeat. "What have they done to you? Who killed you? Can you hear me, Grandfather? Look at me!" With her fingers, she found wounds made with a blunt instrument on his scalp and on the nape of his neck; they were still bleeding. She tore up her scarf and bandaged his wounds, took off her blouse and placed it under his head, then called out to nearby peasants, asking them to take Aćim Katić to Prerovo. But they just kept on loading stolen goods into their carts. She said Djordje would pay them whatever they asked, her father would give them a reward, but no one cared about Aćim Katić now, there was no room for him on the loaded carts, no one recognized him any more. Milena ran down the track.

"Is there anyone from Prerovo here? They've killed Aćim Katić!"

Tola Dačić, who had come back with his cart to scoop up some more government property, was loading the last sack of barley when he heard Milena's calls for help. He couldn't believe his ears, nor did he want to. He was ashamed to be caught looting. But not until he had filled the cart did he walk down the track and see Milena crying over Aćim. He ran up to them, bent over his master and neighbor, and realized what had happened. He felt pity for Aćim, but he felt much more pity for Milena: he couldn't bear the weeping of a woman. He told Milena that her father and mother had arrived in Prerovo about noon. He shouted to his grandson to bring up the oxen and the cart, then with Milena laid the unconscious Aćim on the plundered sacks. Milena climbed onto the cart and placed her grandfather's head on her lap, holding it in her hands. She asked Tola to drive carefully. The burning train lit up their way out of Palanka. After they had crossed the Morava and were riding along the highway, Tola tried to comfort her: "Don't cry, Milena," he said. "It was your grandfather's fate to be brought back dying from Palanka. And my fate, his servant and hired man, to bring him. It could have happened many times and many years ago, but it happened today. Vukašin will be waiting in the house."

Vukašin paced up and down the porch, smoking one cigarette after another. His ears strained to catch sounds from the road. He was waiting for his father. He was struggling to separate his previous periods of waiting into distinct experiences, to differentiate between those nights when he had stayed awake with his head on his mother's lap, waiting for him to come back with Djordje, Tola, and the servants from Budapest or Zemun, where they had driven hundreds of pigs to market, or from sessions of the Assembly in Belgrade, or from meetings and elections in Palanka. All those times of waiting had been shot through with fear that his father would be brought home dead. And on all those occasions the dogs had been barking. He had recognized every dog by its bark, and he and his mother had filled in the time of waiting by talking about the dogs of Prerovo. Twice the horses had brought the empty carriage from which his father had jumped at the sound of shots from an ambush. Once, after a meeting, the horses had brought his father back wounded. Perhaps it was during those hours of waiting—when the dogs barked in time with the beating of his heart, and there was anxiety in the rustling of the ash trees—that he had begun to decide his own fate.

Because of the never-ending uncertainty about the harvest after every seedtime, about the fruits following every flowering, about growth after birth, old age succeeding youth, dawn following night, the uncertainty of every step taken by man on this earth and of every hope and joy under heaven—perhaps it was because of this that, on his return from Paris, where he had written his dissertation on Locke's conception of democracy, he had decided to dedicate his life to bringing about changes in Serbia, a land sunk deep in fear, split by rival dynasties, rent by the quarrels of political parties, and in some respects no less degraded by its own government than it had been by that of the Turks. He had parted company with the socialists because he'd become convinced that their aims couldn't possibly be achieved, and because they were spreading the dangerous idea that it was necessary to destroy in order to build. He believed that in Serbia it was necessary first of all to create a modern European state, to introduce democratic laws and institutions, education and machines, newspapers and books, shoes and coats. He believed in Progress, in what was New, in Europe.

But the world and Europe had taken an unexpected turn. Progress had set in motion great new evils, and given the old evils a strength and dimension the previous century had not seen. Under such circumstances what could he do with his ideas, his knowledge and ambition? He could have remained a university professor, written a book on civil or constitutional law, or edited a learned journal. He could have been the rector of a university, an academician. Would that have made him happy? What would such work have meant for Serbia? Very little—nothing at all, in fact. Hadn't all the Serbian scholars and writers been politicians? How could he follow his own star in this country and at this time? He had wanted at all costs to pursue his own course, in spite of everybody and everything. And not only because of the ideas in which he believed and the moral principles he championed.

His breach with his father, his brother, and Prerovo hadn't brought only suffering. That painful rupture with his father, a peasant tribune, followed by the break with his socialist comrades, also gave him a certain intoxicating pleasure, a joy in his own power and will, enabling him to do the hardest thing of all: oppose his background, his youth, his father, a part of himself—the "good" part. He remembered clearly those days when he had destroyed for the sake of affirming his own will, his own victory. He remembered that powerful excitement in face of the new and unknown, at the start of a life in which every step would be his own. But he had long ago realized—and indeed learned from personal experience—that great crimes are often committed for the sake of affirming one's own personal power, because of the delight caused by that power, that joy in oneself, a raging fire in the soul. He himself had been ruthless toward his opponents, sometimes without just cause. He had hit people harder than they deserved, much harder. Always he had covered it up with ideals and moral principles. For every personal attack on an opponent, every wrong and injustice committed in a political battle, for every untruth he told about the opposition, he had an excuse—the general good, the common purpose. What a terrible, filthy, murky battlefield was public life! Over all their differences in politics, science, and ideas, people attacked each other as mercilessly as the peasants attacked and killed each other with axes and cudgels over a boundary, a foot of plowed land, a broken corn-stalk. How much strength, how much time spent over nothing! And after all that, where were they? After all that, he was left with knowledge that no one needed, and the pain of his failure in life.

After twenty-two years he had come back to Prerovo. He had brought his disappointment to this darkness filled with the barking of dogs. He had striven after something great, but had in fact accomplished little. And he could do nothing more. What should he do now? Accept his defeats in a sensible manner, endure them? Everyone can endure. The capacity to endure evil was the most universal of all human capacities. He could refuse to soften his suffering or think of a way to justify it. That was what he should do. But again that was an idea, an idea about defeat. The reality was his waiting for his father, and the Prerovo darkness disturbed by sounds of flight. He strained his ears. One cart after another passed through the lanes to the Morava; all the sheds were filled with refugees warming themselves around fires; nearby, a field gun was firing at regular intervals.

He couldn't see the ash trees. He couldn't see the apple orchard. He hadn't gone around to the distillery or the stables, looked into the sheepfolds, the corncribs, or barns. Nothing interested him. Yet what great significance every change had once had for him here in this court-yard which had seemed like a large and powerful empire! His roots were in this place. Then why was it now so alien to him? He had indeed deceived himself with this yearning for a return to his youth. This love for one's native region which he had suppressed, this belief in the significance of one's origin—it was an illusion, a sentimental illusion, a tradition he had easily accepted. What part of his present condition had its beginning in his childhood? What was there in him that had its roots where he was born? What remained in the Vukašin of tonight of the boy waiting on his mother's lap for his father to return from a dangerous journey, or of Vukašin the student? Perhaps only fear—that was the same.

No, it wasn't. In tonight's fear there was no hope. The person who had been born and grown up here in Prerovo had died long ago. There was only the memory of him, no going back. Even if his father had been waiting for him at Palanka with the carriage as he used to, even if his mother had embraced him at the gate, and the whole neighborhood had gathered to hear his stories about Palanka and Belgrade, this still wouldn't have been a return. There are no returns in life, only departures. Change is irreversible. That's why it's so painful. But where could he go from here? Into Mišić's army, to put on a uniform just as the army was disintegrating? Or into exile with Pašić and the government, at the mercy of the governments of England and France?

Djordje came in, sat down on the couch, smoked for a while, then said:

"Vukašin, would you talk to Adam? He deserted the army and now the idiot wants to go back. He feels ashamed before his grandfather. You know our father. For him the yardstick for everything is: what will people say?"

"What did Adam say to you?"

"The same old thing: Grandfather told him to go back to the army. But I don't think he really wants to."

"I don't know what to say, Djordje. Neither you nor I should decide for Adam."

"Why shouldn't we? Isn't it all over? What more is there to die for?"

"It isn't over yet. Not for those who are still fighting. I wouldn't prevent my boy Ivan from going anywhere he wanted tonight."

"You would let him go and lose his life?"

Vukašin shuddered at Djordje's tone. How could Vukašin comfort his brother? He couldn't bring himself to touch him in a gesture of fraternal compassion. They had parted in so many ways, so long ago. He couldn't even continue their conversation.

A cart entered the courtyard, clattering over the cobbles. He could hear Tola calling Djordje and Adam. Shivering, Vukašin hurried out to meet them. Zorka ran up with a lantern.

"What happened?" cried Vukašin.

"Grandfather was injured!" Milena cried. "He's unconscious. They killed him!"

They carried Aćim inside and laid him on the bed. Milena and Olga washed and dressed his wounds. Tola took Vukašin onto the veranda and said:

"You know through how many ambushes your father kept his head on his shoulders. His enemies just couldn't get it off. They did it today. I'll tell you something, Vukašin: today for the first time in his life, Aćim Katić was against the people."

Djordje came up to them. "It wasn't the people who killed him! It was thieves like you!"

"Those people there at the station, Djordje, they were the real people today. Peasants and poor folks from the town. The very people on whose account Aćim hated the State. Because of whom he couldn't forgive you, Vukašin, and that's a fact."

"You've no right to talk like that!" said Djordje. "You've been looting the State for two days now!"

Vukašin left the porch and walked behind the house to weep under the eaves, as he used to do whenever his father beat his mother.

Olga and Milena applied all their nursing experience to Aćim's care, but they knew that Aćim had suffered brain damage and couldn't last long. Olga timidly mentioned this to Djordje and was amazed at his anger: "Well, he could have spared me this anxiety! With so much work to be done around here, with so many people scattered all over the place, how can I bury him properly? Zorka, get a candle ready and bring me some brandy."

Djordje stared hard at Adam, who was standing at the head of the bed looking at his grandfather. Adam had now realized he felt closer to his grandfather than to his father. Djordje felt even worse about Adam than he had yesterday, when he had begged him to hide until the Germans had passed through and set up their government, which would be his—Djordje's—government, since the ducat was stronger than the State. Adam had replied: "Father, how can I look Grandfather in the face as a deserter? How can I drag myself around Prerovo like a leper?" Adam would certainly have obeyed his grandfather, Djordje reflected, if God hadn't moved someone to break the selfish old man's head with a stick. Only the old man's death could save that young idiot. He took a good swig of brandy and set the flask between his feet. Yes, the Lord God had dealt thus with Aćim to save Adam. Aćim's head was the price paid for Adam's. *O merciful God, confirm Thy justice. And if our house has to have a mourning flag like all the others in Prerovo, then, Almighty God, let it be in the proper order in which we have been born and lived. Aćim, then me. Yes, him, then me, O God.* But what was going on in his son's heart to make him look at him that way?

Adam was offended by his father's drinking. It made him ashamed in front of Olga and Milena. After his mother's death he had grown up in his grandfather's lap. His grandfather had granted his every wish, forgiven all his acts of mischief, taught him which people in Prerovo would cause him harm and when, and which people he could trust and how far. He had taken Adam hunting and fishing, to saint's-day celebrations and church services, and he had never gone to sleep without first having a word with him. What Adam's father had said yesterday wasn't true. "Now listen to me," Djordje had said. "Tomorrow they'll write in the newspapers that Aćim Katić was a great Serb. He sacrificed his only grandson to the fatherland. But that selfish old man would have been willing to see you shot!" Adam's chin trembled. He frowned at the look of sympathy in Olga's eyes.

She was moved to see this large, handsome young man with a gentle face standing dejectedly at the bedside, tenderly holding his grandfather's stick. Ivan would be proud to have such a cousin. Why hadn't Vukašin brought Ivan to Prerovo? She looked at Vukašin, who was sitting close to his father, waiting for him to regain consciousness for a moment. She gave a start: Zorka had placed a large wax candle on the table, with a pan of flour in which to stick the lighted candle when Aćim had breathed his last.

The vigil reminded Vukašin of the silence in this same room at the family's formal dinner on Christmas Eve, when he had told his father, brother, and sister-in-law that he was going to marry Olga, the daughter of the Liberal leader Todor Tošić, Aćim's fierce political opponent—when he had told them that he wouldn't follow his father in politics but would pursue his own course. Between that Christmas Eve dinner and this deathbed, Vukašin's life and Djordje's had developed separately, linked only by the pain caused by the breach in the family. Now their father's dying made them brothers once more. As the night progressed, however, and Djordje drank and talked against his father, Vukašin realized that he and Djordje would be brothers only until their father died. It couldn't be otherwise: their lives were split at the roots. Even now, when their lives, their children, and everything they had was threatened, they couldn't share the anxieties and hardships of survival quite like brothers. Vukašin had only one last hope: that his father would see him beside his bed and feel what was in his heart, and forgive him for departing so rudely that Christmas. He looked intently at his father's pale and swollen face, listened to his shallow, labored breathing, and awaited his forgiveness, without which it would be so difficult for him to leave Prerovo, this time forever.

How can he tremble over Father like that, Djordje asked himself, *when for twenty years he never wrote him a letter?* Vukašin had never even told their father about the birth of his children. A son's sin was a sin that God would never forgive. Did Adam, his own son, know that? Vukašin was the only person who could talk Adam out of rushing to his death. Djordje took Milena's hand and led her out onto the veranda.

"Milena, you're still a child, but you're a woman, too, and tenderhearted. So your uncle begs you—"

"Don't cry, Uncle Djordje, and don't beg me. Tell me what you want and I'll do all I can."

"Ask your father to tell Adam not to go back to the army. You know what it's like in Palanka."

"I'll ask Father. And I'll try myself to persuade Adam to stay at home."

"Ask him, will you? And you and your mother stay here with the child, even if your father has to go. I'll look after you. All of you. I'll hide you here."

Shaken by her uncle's words, Milena went back into the house, embraced her father, and whispered in his ear:

"I've never asked you for much, Father. Please tell Adam not to go back to the army. That won't be a betrayal."

"Milena, I can't give Adam any advice tonight that I wouldn't give Ivan or you."

"But Adam is different from Ivan and me, Father. The life of the Katić family depends on Adam. We'd die out without him."

Vukašin got up, took her into his own room, and shut the door. "Milena, why do you say we'd die out? You and Ivan are my children, you're Katići."

"We only have the surname Katić. You've changed, you're not the same as grandfather. Adam and these people in Prerovo, they're the real Katići."

Her father took her hand, and she could feel him shaking. "What has your grandfather been telling you?"

"He hasn't said anything about your break. I've come to my own conclusions."

"What conclusions?"

"If I ever have a child, I shall try hard to love it more than you or grandfather loved your children."

"I don't understand. Surely you don't question my love for you."

"Father, every love that is superseded by something greater and more important is in doubt."

"Milena, I can't do something I don't consider right. Adam is a grown man. He must decide for himself."

"He'll go back to the army. The night before last, grandfather told him to have a rest, take what he needed, and go back."

"If that's what his grandfather told him, maybe he should do it."

"No, he shouldn't. And if you won't tell him so, I will."

She left her father and went to find Adam. She took him out onto the porch and told him what she had seen in Palanka; she told him that the army was disintegrating and there was no longer any reason for him to go back.

"It is disintegrating. But what if Grandfather regains consciousness and says to me, 'Haven't you gone yet, Adam?' "

"He won't say that. He can't. And if he does, tell him you've been to Palanka, you've seen it all, tell him."

Her mother came and urged her to go to sleep. She must rest for the next day's journey.

"You haven't told me yet whose child that is, Mother."

"A big misfortune drives out a small one," Olga said. "I've agreed to look after the child until the end of the war. I love him as if he were my own grandchild, Milena."

"What if something happens to the child?"

"Nothing can happen to him while I'm alive."

"These days it's impossible to take care of even your own child, let alone someone else's."

"I know. But now this child *is* mine and I must look after it as I look after you."

"I understand, Mother, I really do. I feel a hundred years old tonight."

Milena went back inside to stand by her grandfather's bed. Olga followed her.

Adam lit a cigarette: what Milena had said to him about the army and the general collapse was true. Yet only his grandfather's death would make him change his mind. So long as Aćim Katić was alive, desertion was impossible. In any case it would be a shameful, filthy life. If he returned to his squadron, he risked being shot because of Sima Pljakić. His father would die of grief, everything would go to pieces. What advice could his uncle give him? He was even more devoted to this country, or he wouldn't have let his young daughter work as a nurse in a hospital. Or perhaps he could talk with Natalia. If he asked her, he'd have to do what she said. He couldn't go on hesitating. When they had met yesterday, she had hugged him and his knees had begun to shake. She looked lovely—he'd never seen her so beautiful. She had looked at him like a real woman, and her smile had made him dizzy. He was supposed to meet Draginja, but decided not to. He was thinking about Natalia. He hadn't even gone to see Ljubica last night. *Good God,* he thought, *what am I doing?*

He put out his cigarette, then went back inside and stared at his grandfather's bandaged head. The wick in the lamp smoked and sputtered, struggling to keep alive. Olga lifted Aćim's head to ease his breathing, then moved away and leaned against the wall to look at Vukašin. She was bewildered by the depth of Vukašin's suffering, which was stamped on his face and was inhibiting his movements. He hadn't smoked all night. He was looking at his father. How could he have loved his father so much, and yet not have seen him for twenty years? He had never complained, or confessed his feelings to her. Was that because he was strong and proud? Or perhaps she hadn't loved him sufficiently to deserve to hear the truth. *My God, how depressing and complicated it all is,* she thought. Perhaps he had suffered over the breach with his father, been dissatisfied with her, and concealed it all with his seriousness and high moral standards. She saw his true nature in his need to be alone immediately on returning home. Perhaps he had had his Mihajlo Radić during that time—why not? She hadn't suspected this earlier, because she hadn't loved him enough to be suspicious. If what she had discovered in the hospital in Valjevo had destroyed her confidence in her happy married life—if it had made her view all her previous experience differently and see Vukašin as poor and insignificant, then perhaps by her failure to understand his break with his father, his brother, and Prerovo, she had changed him, too. And so a love which had seemed to him a deep love was no longer so—just as she had felt about his love for her after meeting Mihajlo Radić.

Yes, just like that. O God, has anyone in this world ever loved the person he wants to love and should love? That real, true love, does anyone ever experience it? Or do we all blindly set out along another's path, lose ourselves in outward circumstances and accept the solution as inevitable? Now and again some of us believe ourselves happy, then suddenly by chance we come up against ourselves and those we love and realize that they don't love us as we want and deserve to be loved. Nor do we love them as much as they wish to be loved and should be. Then we see that we live in distant worlds. We don't see or hear or feel each other, and yet we share bed and board. We conceal this truth by all possible means and deceptions. We feel we must accept this. We have no alternative, we can change nothing. We can't jump out of our skins. We turn round and around in our own circle, we justify and deceive ourselves and convince ourselves that this is our fate. Perhaps it is, and that's all that matters, not the illicit loves that cause us pain and make us draw the knife or swallow poison. All these miseries are the consequence of unwitting error—if error it was. Adultery is only the announcement of defeat. We realize this too late, if ever.

She wanted to touch Vukašin, but felt her desire was out of place. She blushed, but leaned toward him and placed her hands on his shoulders. He saw tears in her eyes, got up, and went into his own room. She followed him, shut the door, and sat next to him on the bed.

"You and I haven't lived as we wanted to live—as we should have lived," she said gently.

"It's too late for this conversation now, Olga."

"No, it isn't, Vukašin. It's only tonight that I've begun to understand you. I feel guilty."

"This evening I've been struggling to believe that love is free of guilt."

"There is guilt in love. If we don't know the person we love."

"Let's not open new wounds tonight. We won't be able to sleep."

"We should save ourselves first, to protect ourselves from others."

"Olga, tonight I'd like to talk only with my father."

"Can't you just tell me why you hid your suffering from me? This life you lived in Prerovo?"

"This isn't the right time to talk about it."

"We may not have another chance."

"That would be just as well."

They heard Djordje talking loudly: "Yes, Father, you're having trouble breathing. It isn't easy for you. But this is only the beginning. Listen to me, Father. God isn't going to let your soul fly like a swallow. Mother's got her foot on your Adam's apple—she's put it down good and proper. As you deserve. Yes, Father, you deserve to wheeze and moan for ninety-nine days."

"What are you talking about, Djordje?"

"I'm talking about our father, Vukašin. Remember how he used to beat Mother? Whenever he came back from Palanka—when someone there had angered him, or he'd lost an election, or something in the newspapers had made him angry—before he even got inside he'd notice something hadn't been done in the courtyard, or hadn't been done properly. He'd throw down his hat, take off his jacket, wet a piece of rope in the tub by the well, and shut our mother up in the kitchen. He'd strip the poor creature, shove her to the hearth, and beat her—and how! Be quiet, Milena. Ask your father if it wasn't just like that. Come in, Olga, and hear what a cruel man your father-in-law was."

"Shut up, Djordje!"

"I won't shut up! Remember how you and I used to cling to the wall like lizards and listen? Swish, bang! Swish, bang! The mighty Aćim, beating. You can see what a well-built man he is, what powerful hands he's got, even in old age. Imagine how he could strike with a piece of wet rope! Our poor mother didn't dare cry, she just whimpered like a puppy. Am I telling lies, Vukašin? Why are you running away? Don't shut the door. You've got to know everything when a man's on his deathbed, so his soul will leave us what's ours and take away what's his. But first it must pass through us."

"Be quiet, Father, do you hear me?"

"Why should I be quiet, Adam? What I'm saying about your grandmother Živana is true. You can see that God hasn't forgotten it. See, he doesn't want your grandfather's soul. Doesn't want it because of the pain Živana suffered, to say nothing of his other evil deeds. God grant that you and your cousin Milena don't have to pay those debts."

Milena rushed outside, and Adam went to comfort her. Olga retreated to Vukašin's room and shut the door. Djordje tottered to his father's bedside.

"You hoped—didn't you, Aćim—that you'd get out of bed like the wind. Straight up to heaven through the chimney. Like a swallow. Well, Živana won't let you—she's got her foot on your Adam's apple. It's hurting, isn't it? Yes, it's hurting, all right. And it's going to hurt for a long, long time!"

Adam burst into the room, seized Djordje, and dragged him outside. Djordje didn't resist. It was as though he'd been waiting for this chance to embrace his only son and never let go. Adam couldn't shake him off onto the cobbled courtyard. Meanwhile, Vukašin returned to Aćim, kissed his hand, and whispered: "Don't open your eyes, Father. You've no cause to. Just rest. And die, so I can go away."

Aćim opened his eyes—the bloodshot eyes of a dying man. Vukašin let go of his hand, straightened up, and stammered:

"I'm here, Father."

Aćim slowly closed his eyes; his breathing faded.

The sound of hoofs in the cobbled courtyard startled Adam out of his slumber at his grandfather's bedside. He caught sight of a sergeant leading his horse toward the old house, and thought for a moment this might be the patrol rounding up deserters. He heard a voice say: "Is this Aćim Katić's house? Is Milena here? I'm her friend Bogdan Dragović. Are you her uncle?"

Djordje couldn't be sure that this sergeant wasn't looking for Adam, so he gave him a perfunctory greeting. Milena, however, on hearing Bogdan's voice, jumped out of bed and rushed down the steps, then stopped suddenly. How could she be so delighted to see him, when it was on his account that her grandfather had suffered his fatal injuries?

Bogdan threw aside the reins and rushed to her with arms outstretched. Milena thrust her head against his damp chest and burst into tears. Olga went out to greet Bogdan, who hugged her warmly. "Have you heard from Ivan lately?"

"He hasn't written to us for two months. Have you heard from him?"

"I've written to him twice, but he hasn't replied. Probably the Austrian censors have destroyed the mail from our front. I'd love to read one of Ivan's letters."

"Let's go inside. I'll give you all Ivan's letters to read."

Bogdan took Milena by the hand and with brotherly affection led her into the house.

Natalia had just arrived to visit Aćim, having postponed the visit for over three hours because she dreaded meeting Milena. Opening the gate, she saw Bogdan mounting the steps of the new house, holding Milena's hand. Natalia froze, unable to breathe. She was overcome by a sense of injustice and envy. The multicolored cobbles on the path leading to the house rose up in waves. She wanted to run toward the two of them to see their faces, both their faces; she wanted to tell Bogdan why she had missed the train in Kragujevac, to explain once more what she had written to him about love when answering the short, abrupt letter in which he told her he had fallen in love with someone else. She clung to the gate. Then Zorka called her, and she rushed back into the road and ran through the mud and puddles toward the Morava. She didn't turn back when Djordje called out to her: "Wait, Natalia, I want to talk to you!"

He had seen her at the gate and thought: she could convince Adam not to return to the army. He took Bogdan's horse to the stable, told one of the servants to unsaddle and feed it, then went into the kitchen.

"Serbia's done for, isn't it, Sergeant?" he said to Bogdan challengingly.

Bogdan was of two minds, but Milena's glance determined his reply. "No, sir, Serbia isn't done for. Our army is still out there fighting gallantly. But of course, no one knows what's going to happen."

"How can we not know? Don't you hear the guns? Judging by the state of the front, the Germans will be in Prerovo tomorrow. They'll break through to the Morava. All you have left then are the mountains and Kossovo. That means another two or three days to the frontier. Where will you go then?"

Bogdan felt unable to convince him of something which he no longer believed himself, but would have been ashamed to agree with Djordje in front of Olga and Milena. "Serbia must fight on without regard for the sacrifices involved," he said firmly. "Without regard for defeat." He didn't complete the official dictum according to which patriotism meant dying unconditionally for one's country and carrying out orders unequivocally. Since he was in danger of being shot for defying this kind of patriotism, he had decided to save himself by performing heroic deeds. He had made suicidal charges at Ram and Rečica, and rescued the wounded Hungarian Kakaši. This had gotten back to the division commander, Colonel Kajafa, who praised him in his written orders to the division. However, in two days he'd probably be court-martialed because Major Dunjić had refused to grant him eight hours' leave from the platoon during the retreat, and he had failed to obey his injunction.

In the next room the child began to cry, so Olga went to him. Djordje was displeased with Bogdan. Not wishing to waste time on this fool who ran his soldiers ragged to gain promotion for himself, he went out to the distillery to pour off the red wine and decide where to hide Adam until both armies had crossed the Morava. Milena took Bogdan's hand and told him about her experiences in Palanka the previous day and her grandfather's injuries. For Bogdan the joy of their meeting was dimmed: he had risked his life to be with her for a few hours, only to find her unhappy and burdened with guilt over her grandfather. Gently he withdrew his hand from hers and asked to see Vukašin. She went along reluctantly and was surprised to see the affection and excitement with which her father embraced Bogdan beside her grandfather's deathbed. Adam stood rigidly at attention in front of the sergeant, afraid he might ask him what he was doing there. Bogdan shook hands with him indifferently, then glanced at Aćim's swollen, bandaged head. Bogdan always feared head wounds, and so turned away now. He asked Vukašin about Serbia's position and her betrayal by the Allies, and was himself commenting on the demoralization and disintegration of the army when Vukašin interrupted him:

"How far is the front from here?"

"About twenty kilometers."

"When are you going back to the army?"

Bogdan hesitated: "I must cross the Morava before dark."

Milena was alarmed: he'd go soon, and they hadn't spent any time alone together. She took him to a shed, where they sat down on a large pile of harvested corn. She thought of Natalia as she gazed into his burning eyes and at the deep contours of the thin, pale face that she had liked from the moment she saw it. She wanted to caress him. "Have you seen her?" she asked.

"No, I haven't. I'll see her on my way back."

"I'd like you to see her now. Adam will take you."

"Why, Milena? I ran away from the platoon to see you, not her. I wrote her a letter."

"I know. But I want you to go see her now. When you go, we'll say good-by." She called Adam and asked him to take Bogdan to Natalia's house. The minute they were gone she regretted having forced the issue. His voice had trembled when he talked about Natalia. Vukašin called from the veranda. He wanted to see Milena and Olga at once.

Vukašin lit a cigarette, distraught. For the third time Najdan's chauffeur came up to him: "It's high time we left, Mr. Katić."

"We'll leave when we're ready," said Vukašin gruffly, and went back into his father's room. Had his father been sufficiently alert when he had opened his eyes last night to grasp that Vukašin was there? Olga and Milena came in, and he gently dropped Aćim's limp hand. "We must leave now," he said.

"We'll go after lunch," said Olga timidly, looking at Milena, who wanted to spend time with Bogdan.

"You two get ready. And have lunch with Bogdan. Ask Zorka to bring me a piece of bread and cheese here."

"Father, I can't leave with you."

"Why not? Bogdan's leaving, too," said Olga.

"I'm not staying because of Bogdan, Mother. I can't leave Grandfather."

Olga wanted to cry out with all her strength, to shriek enough to split herself in two. Where could they go without Milena? She looked at Vukašin: why didn't he say something?

Vukašin buried his face in his hands. *Milena is going to pay my debt to my father,* he thought.

"Why are you both silent?" whispered Olga.

"Listen, Milena, I don't want you to stay here. You've been a volunteer nurse with the army, and you're the daughter of a politician who's written a hundred articles against Austria-Hungary. I'm afraid of the occupying army's vengeance."

"It's hard for me to part with you both, Father, but I can't do otherwise. Please understand. Grandfather got hurt because of me. His heart is still strong; he might regain consciousness. Who'll look after him?"

"Your grandfather didn't get hurt because of you. If it's anybody's fault, it's mine!"

For the first time ever, Milena saw tears in her father's eyes.

Olga broke the silence. "Milena, how can the two of us go off without you? Why would we want to save ourselves without you?"

"Then stay here. All three of us will take what comes."

"But how can we stay? You know that it's your father's duty to withdraw with the government and the Assembly. He dare not let himself be captured by the enemy."

"All right, Mother. Then let Father do his duty."

"You two stay," said Vukašin. "Winter is coming. How will you manage with that child, Olga? If the Allies don't arrive soon, our withdrawal will continue toward Greece."

Olga looked at Vukašin: she felt she had to follow him. But how could she leave Milena? She said gently: "What's going to happen to us, Milena? I couldn't leave this child that isn't mine, let alone you. Think it over. Ask Bogdan."

"I've thought it all over, Mother. I can't do otherwise."

"Ivan in a prison camp and you here. What'll I do, Milena?"

"Make the parting easier for me. That much you can do."

"I can't!"

"How can I leave Grandfather in his present state?"

"Olga," said Vukasin, "it'll be easier for all of us if I go alone."

"I can't spend a single night in this house without you, Vukašin. We must be together."

"Father, I think the most sensible thing would be for you two to leave right away. You need Mother more than I do. Who knows how long this war will last? Mother, please try to understand that if there's anywhere I can hide, it's right here in Prerovo. Uncle Djordje will look after me, and Tola. The whole village will look after me."

"Why don't you have lunch now? Then we'll talk things over. We have another hour to decide, Olga."

Aćim began to wheeze again. Bloodstained froth came out of his mouth.

"Please set us free, Father," Vukašin whispered.

It was as if the three of them had made a vow not to show how hard it was to part. They said good-by on the road, with restraint and without haste. The mother and father tore themselves away from their daughter, performing an inhuman but inevitable act. Milena stood in the mud in the road, watching the black car carrying her mother and father vanish in the distance. Bogdan took her hand and led her into the yard. Her whole body trembled as she looked at the black shapes of the dead ash trees under the weight of the low, rain-sodden sky. Bogdan thought of his father's death and his parting from his mother. Suddenly Milena cried, "My grandfather!" and ran into the house.

Bogdan felt hurt. In spite of Major Dunjić's threats he had left his platoon, stolen a horse from a cavalry regiment, and by mercilessly beating the weary animal had raced to Prerovo. And now Milena had to keep vigil beside her grandfather's deathbed. Twilight rapidly thickened into darkness, the guns at the front fell silent, refugees filled the courtyard for the night; it was time for him to go. He went onto the veranda to tell Milena that he was leaving. She came out of her grandfather's room and touched Bogdan's cheek: "Don't go yet. Please! Grandfather can't last long."

She went back inside. Aćim's death seeped into Bogdan like the chill of the autumn night, filling him with foreboding: Major Dunjić would certainly court-martial him. Still, he must return to his platoon, or he'd betray those few friends who had survived the battles on the Danube, and the young recruits who had made up the numbers of his squad, and who saw him as their father even though he was almost their contemporary. He'd betray Gavrilo Stanković, Danilo History-Book, Ivan, Jackpot, Vinaver; he'd betray himself. He must go back and stick it out, even under Dunjić's heel, right to the end.

Milena ran her fingers through his hair. "Please, Bogdan, don't go yet!"

"I'll go when you say."

"Never."

"I can't betray myself."

"Then go at the very last minute."

"That may be too late, Milena."

Bogdan remembered how, when they were recovering from typhus in Valjevo, they used to measure each other's hair every morning in his room. After their illness it had suddenly started to grow again, but slowly. When her hair had grown to the length of her hand, he used to stroke it and say: Milena, promise me that you'll never cut your hair again." "I promise. And you?" "Well, I'll have to have it cut." Touching his forehead with her lips she said:

"I'll know when the last minute comes."

She returned to her grandfather's bedside. Bogdan followed her.

Adam felt awkward in Bogdan's presence. True, he was a student and Milena's young man, but he was still a sergeant, who gave orders, carried a saber, and treated his men harshly. Adam took Milena out on the porch:

"Are you sure Grandfather won't recover?"

"I can't be absolutely sure, but from my experience with such injuries, I doubt he'll last past midnight."

"When is your sergeant leaving?"

"Why do you ask?"

"I might leave with him."

"Adam, you mustn't. It'll be the end of your father. The army is falling apart. Where will you go?" Bogdan called and she hurried off to him.

Adam listened to the creaking of carts, the voices along the road, the barking of dogs. He thought of all the deserters from Prerovo. Not all of them were cowards. But Tola's Aleksa hadn't deserted, nor had Blaža. But Aleksa—what did he have that Adam didn't? Only Natalia could advise him now. His father stopped him at the gate and begged him not to wander around the village: he must go into hiding. Promising his father that he'd soon be back, he hurried to the schoolmaster's house. Natalia was standing under the eaves in the dark.

"Where are you going, Adam?"

"I'm looking for you. How did you recognize me in the dark?"

"You move like a fox. How's your grandfather?"

"Milena says he won't last past midnight."

"Milena knows everything, including how long people will live."

"I was looking for you today with Bogdan. He wanted to see you."

"Has he left?"

"Not yet."

"What's he doing?"

"Sitting beside Grandfather's bed with Milena."

She dared not ask any more questions. The thought of them together was painful.

"I ran away with a friend who'd been sentenced to death for spreading false rumors in the squadron. I don't know what to do. If I go back, I might be shot. If I don't go back . . ."

But Natalia wasn't listening. Suddenly she felt possessed. She grabbed his hand in the darkness. "Adam, let's go ride our horses along the Morava the way we used to. Through the meadows. Remember the time I fell?"

Adam was bewildered. The last time they had ridden along the Morava in the moonlight, she had worn his breeches and a cap pulled down to her eyebrows, and they had held hands. When he had ridden Dragan right beside her and stretched out his arm to embrace her, she had forced her horse to a trot and fallen, breaking her arm. That was the summer before she went to the university in Belgrade. Adam had waited for her to come back for the holidays. But when she returned, she no longer wanted to dress up in his clothes and rush into the fields at a gallop. Yet it wasn't because she was a student that she had abandoned these games with him.

"It's raining, Natalia," he mumbled.

"Who cares? This is our last night before the time of bondage."

She led him into the darkness, hurrying so as to give neither him nor herself time to think.

When he had hidden away in the house of his most trustworthy neighbor the last of the looted merchandise, Tola Dačić sat down by the fireplace to rest and drink brandy. He was pleased with himself. In the last two days he had acquired more than he could have in ten years as a hired man. Why, he could open a shop! He took several good swigs from the pitcher. He scolded his wife and daughters for bemoaning Blaža's and Aleksa's fate, though he himself was anxious about them. So many folks from Prerovo, including Adam, had managed to escape the disaster, why not his sons? In the days when it was possible to defend Serbia, he had done so with three rifles and a field gun, but now that even King Peter could only weep while the people took what belonged to them, why didn't Blaža and Aleksa save their skins? Aleksa had acquired such a nice piece of property through his marriage. Tola went on drinking brandy until his ears whistled and he groaned so loudly that the whole neighborhood could hear: "At dawn tomorrow Prerovo will be in bondage. Tomorrow Serbia's troubles will begin, and we'll have to bend under the German scythe like a dry blade of grass."

He hadn't seen Aćim all day, but what did it matter? His master Aćim had had his day. All his life Aćim Katić had trampled the people of Prerovo—as merchant, employer, and deputy—and he'd lived to see those people tread on him! Like a herd of swine trampling on a flower bed, on reeds in the mud, that's how they'd trampled him! In this life a man had to pay for every plum he picked up from the roadside. Still, they were neighbors. Aćim had been his employer since he could hold a stick above the animals, and he'd done him many good turns—though he'd also made him pay through the nose. Still, it was only right and proper that a man should visit his fellow man on his deathbed and light a candle for him. Tola strode over to Aćim's house. Milena and Bogdan were sitting bent over Aćim, who was breathing hoarsely.

"Good evening to you, children!"

His strong, cheerful voice made Milena jump, and she stared at him resentfully. Tola sat down and began to roll a cigarette.

"Yes, you're wheezing—wheezing badly, old man," said Tola. "If you're wondering about what the dawn will bring to Prerovo, you'll be lucky if you don't wake up. He's lived out his time, children. He got everything out of life, indeed he did. I don't suppose anyone in Prerovo has lived like Aćim Katić. He's done everything, feared nothing. He has eaten and drunk the best in Prerovo. As for pretty women, the only ones he hasn't had are those his eye didn't catch. Aćim Katić has been all that a man from Prerovo can be. In good times and bad. Yes, he's done folks a lot of good, but some harm as well. That's how it is: whoever can do good, can do even more evil, much more. When it's all shoved onto the scales at the end, we don't know which way the scales will tip. Mark my words, children: the worst people in Prerovo are those for whom there's nothing to weigh up. But those for whom we don't know which way the scales will tip, those are the real Prerovo folk. Your grandfather was one of them, Milena."

"Tola, don't talk so loud."

"Why shouldn't I, Milena? I'm shouting so he can hear me. He won't hear the priest. He won't hear the bells announcing his death. But I think he can hear now, even if he's only skin and bone. Our brain and soul and eyes and ears, it's all one single nerve made out of the pith and marrow of every living thing on earth. God could have made it only when He was idle and spiteful. Milena, bring me some brandy. That's how things are, Sergeant: even death's no good to a man if he doesn't know what he was. If he could talk now, he'd say: 'Get yourself a drink from any barrel you want, and sit down next to me, you old thief. Tell me everything in proper order, and don't forget the time I scared the chickens away!' Nothing's harder for a man on his deathbed than darkness and silence. That's what's waiting for him—he's rushing headlong into it. A man who gives up his soul slowly and reluctantly, with the devils pulling it out of him like hair—more than anything, he likes to have people around him talking, so he can hear what we think of him and what he was to us, so he knows he's not forgotten. Zorka could have offered me better brandy. Well, there's nothing more bitter than the spoken word, and there's no other creature that talks, except we who have two legs and don't fly."

"Tola, please lower your voice."

"I won't, Milena. I was his most faithful servant and his neighbor, which is important in Prerovo. There's nobody a man can do more harm or more good to than the person nearest him. And I consider it only proper that the two of us should talk tonight. This is the first time ever that all *he* can do is listen, the first time I can say everything I want to him. That seems right. But not quite everything. A man should also be left with silence. You see, children, this Aćim, who's having so much trouble dying, was both a man and a dog. Yet he had plenty of sense, you've got to give him that—enough sense to deserve a bigger beard than this forked one with blood on it now. All the good he did for people, he did with his own hand, so it could be seen. And all the evil Aćim did around Prerovo and among the Morava people, that he did by another's hand and in the dark."

Milena rushed outside to look for her uncle.

"Well, Sergeant, only a man who has plenty in his head—and a full purse—can act like that. Don't frown because I'm speaking the truth about Milena's grandfather. I swear to you in the name of my two living sons, trusting that Saint George will bring them to Prerovo by dawn, that even now, Aćim Katić, with his soul hanging by a thread, enjoys having been a man people feared. A tyrant. One who needed only to point a finger at his enemies, without speaking a word out loud. There was nothing he couldn't do. He had people where he wanted them! If he hadn't been like that, he couldn't have got himself so much property and sent his son Vukašin out into the world like a prince, and—what's hardest of all here by the Morava—kept his head and his honor. Yes, his sacred honor! That's how it is with us in Prerovo: you can do evil, but do it so it's seen and talked about as little as possible. If you can manage to keep evil hidden, more than half is forgiven."

Djordje came in with Milena. "Now, Tola, what are you babbling about here tonight? You're drunk!"

"I'm just passing the time of day with this old devil and these children until Adam comes back. He told me to tell you he'll be back by midnight."

"Where did you see him?"

"I met him a short while ago in my plum orchard, with another person. They went off somewhere on their horses."

Djordje sat down.

"Cross yourself three times, Djordje, and keep quiet. Your son is in Prerovo. Serbia is bigger for my sons than it is for Adam and those Prerovo men who've tossed down their rifles and crept under the blanket with their wives tonight."

"Milena," said Djordje, "get some sleep. And you, Sergeant, take a nap in Vukašin's room and then run off wherever you can. Some soldiers who came across the Morava a while back told me that the Germans will be in Prerovo at dawn. Tola and I will sit here and wait for what comes."

Out on the porch Milena whispered to Bogdan: "I found my uncle nailing a white sheet to a lath. That's the beginning of our bondage." They sat down on the bench, trembling and clinging to each other. Meanwhile Djordje and Tola drank brandy at Aćim's deathbed, and quarreled about who was to blame for the collapse of Serbia.

Soaked to the skin, Adam and Natalia rode slowly through the meadows and along the Morava, their bodies close together. Their horses splashed through puddles, fell into ditches, stumbled over underbrush. The swollen river roared menacingly through the darkness. They were silent, each possessed by the same deep sadness: it was impossible that night to recapture the joyful spirit of their former nocturnal rides. But they continued to struggle on through the darkness and rain. Adam thought of all those women with whom he had met secretly at night; Natalia thought of her sleepless nights as a young girl, listening to the crickets.

They had different memories of the times when they had raced over freshly mown meadows and late-flowering clover, or stolen melons and come upon Prerovo lovers in hidden groves, or rushed their horses through the shallows to get wet, then dried their clothes on the sandbanks. Getting wet, then taking off their clothes to get dry, was their most exciting game. Natalia feared she would be left in her underskirt; Adam hoped she would have to take off everything, including it. For him that was always the last chance to pull her down onto the sandbank and carry her off into the willow trees, always that same moment which he would no longer deny himself, and for which time and again his strength failed him. For her too this undressing was the most dangerous and exciting part of their game: she enjoyed seeing him tremble, enjoyed watching this arrogant young lover twist his hands as he swore that he'd turn his back to her and shut his eyes while she took her clothes off, that he wouldn't touch her when she ran into the poplar trees. Once undressed and barefoot, she would scream from fear that he'd rush after her, and from a half-conscious desire that he'd do so and embrace her. He never did turn around, but, furious with himself for his weakness, he'd gather up pebbles and fling them across the river until his arms and shoulders hurt. And she, leaning against a tree trunk, would watch him from the darkness of the poplar wood, and listen to the dull thud of the pebbles as if it were the beat of his crazy heart, fearing at the same time that he'd run up and pull her down on the grass. She couldn't have run away. The river gurgled noisily. She would take to bed with her the memory of the moon-speckled river flowing between the dark shapes of the willows and poplars, take it from Prerovo to Palanka, from summer to autumn and winter. That river would be transformed for her into the vain outpouring of her girlish longing for an unknown youth who possessed in full what all the others she knew possessed in part. So it had been until she met Bogdan. After that, those Prerovo summers had settled down into memories of her native countryside. She slumped down over her horse, pressing her face against its wet mane: Bogdan was in Prerovo tonight. With Milena.

Natalia's silence threw Adam into a rage against himself. Again he had yielded to Natalia's senseless wish to urge their horses through the darkness and puddles, just as in his childhood he had always yielded to her wishes. And to his grandfather's, until the war and his army service. A feeling of remorse that he had left his grandfather struck him like a stab of pain.

He stopped his horse and said:

"How long should we go splashing through the puddles?"

"Just a little longer, Adam. It's not yet midnight."

He rode on, wondering what was on her mind, thinking about his grandfather. If his grandfather found out that Adam had abandoned him tonight, he'd never forgive him, he who'd forgiven him everything. What should he do? Should he be a deserter, when not even Aleksa Dačić had deserted? Or should he walk into a trap? He'd be shot for allowing Sima Pljakić to run away after being sentenced. Yet how could he not fulfill his vow to his grandfather? And if his grandfather died before dawn, what then?

"So you think we should splash about in the dark till midnight, Natalia?"

"Come closer. Don't talk."

He pressed his horse forward and touched her leg. She felt for his hand on the rein and squeezed his fingers, just as she had on that last ride before she went away to the university. She had let him squeeze her fingers, enjoying the way he trembled with desire, when suddenly he had come at her like a wild beast. She had spurred her horse and jerked the reins. The horse had bolted through the meadow, and she had fallen and broken her arm. She had fallen because he had pulled her over to him. Should she now pull him over to herself? Let *him* fall and break *his* arm? Then he wouldn't have to go back to the army —he'd stay in Prerovo. She would love him. Of all the young men she knew, he was the only one who deserved it. He had loved her since primary school, but didn't know how to tell her. He was handsome and somehow dangerous. You could sense from his excitement what he wanted. She'd never met a man who had shown so much desire for her. How many women he had embraced and broken under him! Now he was trembling. Did he always tremble when a woman held his hand? Should she spur her horse into a gallop, knock Adam down, and break his arm? He was like a baby chicken in her hand. She squeezed his fingers more tightly and pressed her leg closer to his. She wanted to embrace him, but was frightened by her desire. Yet this desire was the only thing that could save her. Then she thought of Bogdan and Milena embracing, and let go of Adam's hand.

Adam felt offended. "Where are we going now?" he asked, when they had reached the main road to the village.

"To your shed. As we always did in our games."

She thought of the hayloft next to the shed, where the two of them used to play: she would prepare supper for him beside a stack of hay and make a bed of straw, while he plowed and sowed the meadow between the stacks. After their imaginary supper they'd lie down in the straw, cover themselves up, and pretend to go to sleep.

Adam turned his horse toward the shed. He was overwhelmed by the long-felt yearning which had always been cut short, only to possess him yet more powerfully when she smiled at him again. They reached the shed and the hayloft on the river bank. He stopped his horse and waited. She stopped, too. Her indecision was quickly dispelled by the roar of the river, dark, terrible, fleeing.

"Now you prepare the bed," she said firmly, remaining on her horse until he called her.

She crawled under the straw and embraced him.

For those who were awake, dawn was marked by fear of the approaching daylight. Those who had been asleep were awakened by fear for their existence. Fear dripped from the eaves, gurgled through the ditches, moved restlessly in the darkness, slithered down from the walls and trees, hardened in the fences, drifted in from the sky with the morning chill, and broke through the dampness of the earth.

The inhabitants of Prerovo, and the refugees and soldiers who had spent the night in the village, heard the dull, unmistakable rattle of a machine gun. For Milena and Bogdan, the machine gun counted out their last moments together: their hands dropped slowly to their sides, and they stood still looking at each other, until Djordje ran out of Aćim's room crying: "Where's Adam?" Bogdan went to saddle his horse, and Milena hurried away to prepare some food for his journey.

Tola Dačić placed a candle next to Aćim's pillow, then hurried home to wait for the Germans in the kitchen with his grandchildren and women. He wondered what food and drink to offer them so early in the morning, since he knew he couldn't soften their hearts with words.

The refugees rushed toward the Morava. Djordje was in his large, empty courtyard with a white flag in one hand and an ax and some nails in the other, calling to Adam and praying to God. He didn't say good-by to Bogdan, who, accompanied by Milena, led out his horse; they rode off.

Natalia was lying with Adam in the straw. Tired and drowsy, she could hardly grasp that the machine gun was proclaiming the end of her first night of love. Reluctantly she woke up Adam. He got out of the straw, hesitated, kissed her good-by. He ran off to the shed, mounted his horse, and galloped away. Natalia went back to their bed of straw and burst into tears.

Bogdan and Milena reached the shed. He threw aside the reins, embraced her, and kissed her fiercely.

"I must go, Milena! I must!"

Natalia heard Bogdan's cry, crawled out of the straw, and saw them in the early morning light—a single dark, swaying shape on the sandbank. She remained kneeling, staring at them, until Bogdan mounted his horse and entered the Morava. Then she ran up to Milena.

In the middle of the river Bogdan turned around and stopped his horse. The machine gun started to fire above Prerovo.

"Go on! Go on!" Milena shouted.

He stood there looking at them. Natalia called out:

"There's a whirlpool lower down! Watch out, Bogdan!"

He waved to them with both hands, then rode his horse out of the river, and disappeared in the poplar wood on the opposite bank. The two women remained on the sandbank, gazing at the turgid, fast-flowing river; then, silently, they set off together for the village. They paused as Adam, now in his uniform, dashed through the field on his horse.

When they reached the gate with the white sheet fixed to a lath, Djordje cried out to them for help. He was wading in wine to his knees, as he and Zorka stuffed rags and tow into holes in the vats and barrels, from which old wine was squirting. The Serbian rear guard had shot at the distillery, so the Fritzies wouldn't get the wine.

Natalia stepped into the wine, and Milena followed. They were up to their knees in wine, when a squad of German Uhlans rode into the courtyard and unsaddled their horses under the sheds. The Germans stared in amazement at the girls, but Milena and Natalia ignored them and went on plugging the barrels and vats. Then Zorka came over and told the girls that the old man had died. Natalia ran into the house. Milena sat down on the distillery doorstep; she wanted to cry, but couldn't.

No church bells announced the death of Aćim Katić. Natalia was the only friend to attend his funeral, for the occupying power forbade any assembly of Serbs. His grave was dug by Tola Dačić and his grandson; Djordje and Zorka put together a coffin, but didn't have time to paint it. The staff of the Hungarian regiment, which had installed itself in Djordje's house that morning, ordered the dead man buried immediately for reasons of hygiene, but allowed the Prerovo priest to perform the funeral rites in front of the house. Zorka placed Aćim's stick and tobacco tin in the coffin, and Djordje closed the lid. They loaded the coffin onto a cart. Only Milena and Natalia walked to the cemetery behind the corpse of Aćim Katić.

8

An endless stream of fugitives preceded the retreating army along the roads leading south to Kossovo. At the head of it were the hospital units, then prisoners of war and lunatics, convicts, boys between the ages of fourteen and eighteen lined up in regiments, actors, writers, artists, musicians, gilded court coaches, and what was left of the state and museum archives. After them came English, American, Russian, and French medical missions, and Scottish and Russian nurses in white caps, closely followed by French doctors carrying sheaves of cornstalks and half-roasted sheep on spits. Hurrying in the wake of the French medical mission were French aviators dragging airplanes with tractors. Not far behind this column was an English naval detachment which had defended Belgrade, with two heavy guns; then came foreign journalists, South Slavs from Austria-Hungary who had fled to Serbia, and the Royal Guard band with shining instruments.

Everybody who could and dared to was on the road fleeing southward. Wherever the fugitives stopped for the night, the streets, courtyards, schools, and churches were filled. Shops were padlocked, and food was no longer served in the inns. Nobody would sell anything for paper money, only for silver or gold. No one knew what to believe; people simply hoped. They still placed trust in the Russians, who, they thought, would advance through Rumania and overrun Bulgaria; and they still had faith that the French and the English would push back the Bulgarians with armies from Salonika and Greece. They believed fortunetellers and gypsies as much as they believed ambassadors and ministers; deception was accepted as a matter of course. People talked of the crimes perpetrated by the occupying armies the previous year, and moved on in fear—to the end of the world, if need be.

"Let them conquer an empty land! Serbia is where her army is."

Mihajlo Radić was retreating toward Kossovo as head of the medical section of the Niš reserve troops, which consisted of boys aged fourteen to eighteen. The troops were commanded by a general who had retired long ago, and by officers still on the sick list. One boy in five was armed with an old rifle, a few had bayonets, some had no military equipment other than a belt or a soldier's cap, a flask or a mess kit. Many were accompanied by mothers, grandmothers, or grandfathers carrying baskets of food and bundles of bedclothes. In fact, there was no indication that the boys belonged to the army, except that every time they entered or left a village they were ordered to walk in a column four deep, singing, "Our Uncle Peter rides a fine horse, / Old Franz Josef rides on a donkey."

Radić rode in a carriage with General Nikodije Jovanović, the commander of the Niš reserve troops, and the general's wife. It was hard for him to sit still while this sick and hot-tempered old man complained that his army wasn't marching properly, and that none of these fifteen thousand boys knew how to stand at attention or salute correctly. Every morning he forced them to drill for two hours before they continued retreating.

Grumbling about his painful sciatica, the general gave Radić strict orders that at every overnight stop he was to conduct a medical inspection of the recruits so as to declare the "permanently unfit" to be "temporarily unfit," and the "temporarily unfit" to be "fit for military service." Radić doubted he was doing any good, but he followed orders. He couldn't save the sick and weak by any medical decision. If he declared those "temporarily unfit" to be "permanently unfit," and the general dismissed them from the platoon, they'd have to return home through two armies and the battlefront; they'd be either killed or captured. If he pronounced the "temporarily unfit" to be "fit for military service," he might well be sentencing them to death from hunger, cold, or disease during the retreat. He didn't believe they'd survive the defeat, become fit to fight, and someday reach their homes and freedom. These sickly boys weren't sure which of his decisions at the inspection could save them, either—rarely did anyone give him a grateful look or even a smile. They wept as they got dressed, and shivered as they went out into the rain. They saw him not as an army doctor but as a father. From his examination they expected not the truth about their health, but compassion. Some of the boys burst into tears after his decision, so he made them strip again, and with his stethoscope on their thin chests, he'd ask what they wanted him to say. And so it went till dawn.

Radić sat down to write a report on the results of his inspection. But his head sank on the table and he fell fast asleep.

One of the boys led Bogdan Dragović down the school corridor to Doctor Radić. The one man who could help him was sleeping. Bogdan decided to wait for him to wake—but soon it would be daylight. He must flee before this column left and the military patrols arrived to seize deserters. He touched Radić gently:

"Forgive me for waking you, sir. I'm Bogdan Dragović, one of your patients from Valjevo."

Radić gave a start and blinked in confusion.

"You used to come see me with Mrs. Katić. Milena was in my house when she was ill with typhus. I was thin then, and didn't have any hair."

"Ah yes. Hello, Bogdan," Radić mumbled, and held out his hand. "I wouldn't have recognized you. Delighted to see you. What's your regiment?"

"Ninth Regiment, Danube Division. But I'm not with my platoon."

"What difference does that make? The entire army has disintegrated. We're a nation strewn in the mud. Our prisoners of war are kept in classrooms. Bring up a chair and sit down." He lit a cigarette. "As you can see, there are young men drilling in the schoolyard. Children, in fact. I head their medical section."

"And I'm a deserter from the army, sir."

"We're all deserters, Bogdan."

"That's true. But me especially. I'm fleeing both the Germans and my commanding officer. I left my platoon for twenty-four hours without permission—to see Milena in her father's village. When I returned to my platoon, I was told that the battalion commander had proclaimed me a deserter and I'd be court-martialed once they caught me. So I took off, and last night I learned by chance that you were here."

"What happened to Milena? And the rest of the Katić family?"

Bogdan told him briefly about his visit to Prerovo, his meeting with Olga and Vukašin, and their departure for Kraljevo. Radić interrupted him: "Are they retreating along the Ibar valley? Then we'll meet!" He realized at once that his reaction was inappropriate. He addressed himself to Bogdan's problems. Bogdan proposed to change into civilian clothes and accompany him as far as Priština. From there he'd make his way to the front near Skoplje and look for Lieutenant Colonel Glišić, the commander of the Cadet Battalion; he was the one senior officer to whom he dared announce himself as a deserter and ask for protection.

"Are you sure Glišić will save you, Bogdan? I've heard terrible things about his rigidity and his nationalist fanaticism."

"I'm not sure, Doctor, but he's the only officer I can turn to. Even when he struck me in the face with his whip, I felt he didn't hate me."

Radić looked at him hard: "Have you no stronger proof that he'll help you?"

"I remember him as a very unhappy man. A man who's so unhappy can do good in a way that no one else can."

"That's true, by and large. But there are also unhappy people incapable of doing good. They can't see another person's suffering for their own."

"I've no choice. It's either that or surrender to the Germans. Then I would be a traitor."

"A traitor to what?"

Bogdan restrained himself from answering the question. Outside, the commands of the drill sergeants echoed through the murky dawn, reminding Radić of the report he had to submit at seven.

"What are we betraying?" cried Radić. "Defeat, suffering, and misery?"

"We're betraying ourselves, Doctor."

"Yes! If we have anything left in ourselves to betray."

"I think we do."

"All night I've been writing death sentences, although I'm a doctor and it's my duty to save people. While performing my duty, I've betrayed myself!"

"If that's how you judge yourself, Doctor, then we're all lost!"

"So we are! Why are the sergeants drilling those boys, when our army is falling apart? We're no longer suffering to achieve national aims! We're sacrificing ourselves for some senseless goal. What's happening now isn't history!" he said, banging his fist against the wall.

"It's part of history. The history of a world which must be destroyed to its foundations. Doctor, I don't have much time."

"What can I do to help you?"

"Get me some civilian clothes. And make it possible for me to go to Priština with your medical service."

"And you believe Lieutenant Colonel Glišić will save you?"

"It's worth a try. I can't save myself any other way."

"Your sense of shame is very strong—you still have something to save. Come with me. I'll do what I can."

In the center of Kraljevo the road was blocked by fugitives. Vojvoda Mišić's car couldn't move forward, despite the threats of his adjutant and the orders of Colonel Hadžić. Mišić shrank back into the corner of his seat and lit a cigarette. He didn't reprimand his escort. It had taken six hours to travel fifteen kilometers on a road crammed with refugees, confirming his conviction that this was not simply a retreat before a more powerful enemy. But he still shrank from drawing the correct conclusion about Serbia and her army. If he did, he'd have to withdraw with his staff to Mataruška Banja, so as to hold the enemy at the Morava for a few more days. For the first time since becoming commander of the army, he sensed no decisive resistance among his soldiers, or anger against the enemy, no will to battle. Everything he saw and heard indicated weariness, weakness, and hopelessness; everywhere there was disorder, disintegration, and fear. In fact, he himself had shown no resolute resistance to all this since his failure to strike a blow at the flank of Mackensen's thrust. Borne along by the mainstream of defeat, he had simply carried out Putnik's orders.

Now, engulfed by the mass of people, he listened to the threats they directed at passing cars. Was it possible that no one recognized him? Or did they blame him, too, along with Pašić and Putnik, for their misery?

"Go on!" he ordered the driver. "What are you waiting for?"

In vain his escort invoked his name, argued, threatened. People rushed at the car, their fists raised in anger; the windows filled with eyes and mouths full of hatred. He felt he was being strangled. He shrank back into his corner, and tried to light another cigarette. His life was threatened, yet he was helpless. A shot from his adjutant's revolver forced the angry crowd back; the car moved forward at full speed. Swerving around an oxcart, it headed straight for a flock of sheep and some children. He closed his eyes. "Stop!" he cried. The car stopped. He dared not look. Only when he heard fists and clubs banging on the car roof did he open his eyes. A voice shouted.

"Where are you off to, Vojvoda?" asked an old man. "To Greece? You're all running away to Greece! Where can I go with *him?*"

The old man thrust a tear-stained little boy toward him, while other men and women lifted up their children. Overcome with shame, Mišić got out of the car and tried to raise his voice, but could only stammer: "I'm not fleeing to Greece. I'm not fleeing."

"Why are you playing games with us? Why doesn't the government sue for peace? The war is lost, Vojvoda!"

Mišić set off on foot toward the bridge. The crowd quieted down and parted to let him pass. He remembered the bridge on the Mionica where he had halted the disintegrating army last autumn; slowly he stepped onto the muddy bridge and into another silent crowd. It was their silence that stopped him.

"We'll struggle on to victory. I guarantee that with my life!"

Resolutely he walked across the bridge and climbed back into the car. He refused to talk to anyone until later in the evening in Mataruška Banja, when Putnik telephoned:

"Mišić, I understand that morale in your army is low, that there's disorder and chaos. If that goes on, we're finished."

"That's true, Vojvoda. But do you know why the army's disintegrating?"

"Yes. Now listen to me. The Russians will arrive via Rumania by the sixth of November, and the French and English will launch a decisive offensive toward Skoplje. We must hold out for ten days."

"There's no way I can convince my army that the Allies will come to our aid, Vojvoda. I refuse to try."

"You must put a stop to this disintegration—without mercy and without formalities. Morale can be raised by fear, Mišić."

"If I start courtmartialing, I'll need a whole division to man the courts and carry out the sentences."

They were cut off, or Putnik hung up—it made no difference to Mišić. He remembered his journey through Kraljevo and felt a sharp stab of shame. Ten minutes later Putnik called again:

"What do you suggest, Mišić? I'm listening."

"I suggest we select the best positions, dig in, and confront the enemy with firm resistance. Tomorrow, not the day after. We're getting weaker every moment."

"What do you mean by firm resistance, Mišić? And what do we do if we lose this crucial battle?"

"That's a question from one of your examinations, Vojvoda."

"Every day we take those exams by which we became military leaders. Right now we're taking an examination which we can't take a second time. The members of that examination commission will be our grandsons."

"I'm not worried about that commission, Vojvoda."

"You're a military leader, Mišić!"

"I'm working for our survival, Vojvoda. I'm forced to defend myself with a rifle and a field gun. I feel like a calloused worker in a small, barren field while you, Vojvoda, are a military leader. Your models are Frederick the Great and Clausewitz, while mine are Czar Dušan and Karageorge."

"Well?"

"I believe in Montenegro, and you believe in Russia and France. That's why you require your subordinates to be an elite in officer's uniform."

"What do you require of your subordinates, Vojvoda?"

"That they be the first to get up and the last to go to bed. You want a place in history. I want to go home and see my children grow up in peace and finish their education."

"As a matter of fact, Mišić, what I want is a place in the universe, in that clear blue space—not a place in history. Everything in history is rotten. The dead squabble for places assigned them by fools still alive. I don't want that, Mišić."

"I know. But to gain entry into your universe, Vojvoda, you need to halt the Serbian army and attack the army which we beat to its knees twice last year. Otherwise, the people will trample us like dirt."

Again their conversation was cut off. He'd do his duty, he was determined. In his mind he selected the position for his army. He'd request the Montenegrin High Command to order the Sandžak army to secure his left wing. The telephone rang. It was Putnik once more:

"I'm ordering you to hold the enemy at the Morava as long as you can, and to defend the entry into the Ibar gorge."

"That's just what I intended to do, Vojvoda."

"Afterward, when faced with great superiority, you'll retreat toward Kossovo without engaging in any decisive battle."

"To Kossovo? Kossovo again? The glory of Kossovo already belongs to the man who died for it.* To us it can bring only disgrace."

* Mišić is here referring to Prince Lazar of Serbia, who was killed while fighting the Turks in the battle of Kossovo in 1389. [Translator's note.]

"At Kossovo, Mišić, we'll wait for help from the Allies. Then we'll move back across the Morava, toward the Sava and the Danube."

"We won't make it back from Kossovo. We'll be hungry, barefoot, and without ammunition. Why wait for the Allies in Kossovo? They won't come—they've abandoned us. We'll be wiped out in Kossovo and cursed by our people."

"I can't hear you, Mišić, which is just as well. My orders will reach you through the usual channels."

Mišić put down the receiver and extinguished the lamp. He didn't want to see anyone that evening.

When Mišić's adjutant announced Vukašin Katić, Mišić jumped up, ordered the lamp lit, and embraced Vukašin at the door.

"Where are Olga and Milena? Do sit down. How thin you are! Lieutenant, have some tea sent in for us."

"Olga's here. I've found us a room of sorts for the night. I left Milena in Prerovo with my father and brother. Where's your family, Vojvoda?"

"They're here in Mataruška Banja. I haven't seen them today. Today, Vukašin, I've experienced the worst defeat of my life: I've been defeated by the misery of our people. And Putnik is forcing me to accept a lie as truth."

"Fighters aren't the standard-bearers of truth, Živojin."

"What is truth for those of us who aren't fighting?"

"Perhaps the truth is too strong for us. It might burn up our souls."

"What do you mean, Vukašin?"

"For those who are fighting, the most important thing is their war goal. Victory. So they swallow deception easily."

"I can't make my men give their lives for something I don't believe will help us survive."

"I'm not sure that we can save ourselves if we continue to act on that premise."

"How else can we act? Against ourselves?"

"We're all being asked to do in the name of our country what we don't believe in. I don't know anyone except Pašić who believes in the Allies, but we all must behave as if we do. If we didn't we'd desert or surrender."

"I doubt that even Pašić believes in the Allies. He tells us he does, but he's not speaking the truth. He couldn't govern without that lie. That lie absolves him from responsibility for the collapse of Serbia, to which he's contributed a great deal through his indecision and his bending over backward for the Allies. I don't want any part in Pašić's deception of the people or in Putnik's cosmic ambitions. But I suppose you feel differently, Vukašin?"

"If I do, I'm no longer sure I'm right. We two haven't talked since that night in Valjevo. Meanwhile I've been to Paris and London. My political ideals were all wrong. Europe is a den of thieves, Živojin."

"Then why are you and Pašić tying Serbia's fate to Europe's wheels?"

"Better tied to her wheels than underneath them. Look, we can't ever be to Russia what Bulgaria is—Russia will always need Bulgaria more. In a sense, it's Russia who's forced us to rely on Europe."

"I can't accept that, Vukašin. We'll find no safety or future under the skirts of popes or emperors, lords or counts. We must stand on our own two feet, and survive through our own wisdom."

"If only that were possible! The Great Powers won't let you be yourself and stand on your own two feet. You've got to take sides and accept the consequences. A small nation has to guess which of the great brigands is the stronger, and whose boot presses less heavily."

"Only for those of you who want a state stretching from Trieste to Celovac—those of you who are fighting for Yugoslavia—is it essential to seek powerful protectors and allies. This unhappy nation, which now resembles an anthill struck by a rifle butt, needs a Serbia no bigger than the land of the Serbs. We don't need Yugoslavia; we don't need allies for whom we must give our lives."

"The fact is, my friend, that we must become great and powerful in order to be our own masters, to be free. There's no other way."

"That's your feeble-minded political notion! We won't be greater or stronger if we unite with military opponents who've never been our brothers in peacetime, who insult us because we're peasants and Orthodox, who shout, 'Serbian brothers, surrender!' with their bayonets pointed at us."

Dragutin brought in the tea, served it, and left the room. As he sipped the hot tea, Mišić asked crossly, "So tell me, Vukašin, what is going to happen to your Yugoslav idea?"

"That's an uncertain and painful subject. Our allies aren't really concerned about Yugoslavia, and among us Yugoslavs everyone has his own concept of what Yugoslavia should be. Pašić wants to be a Yugoslav Bismarck or Cavour, and hopes that in time the Croats and Slovenes will become Serbs. Our Croatian brothers want to free themselves from Austria and not end up tomorrow among the defeated nations. They want to unite with Serbia and indeed they must. Of course, however, they believe that in time they'll convert the Serbs to Catholicism."

"All very fine, I must say! What about the ideals we discussed last spring in Valjevo?"

"Those ideals? Perhaps the realization of any ideal means its destruction. Perhaps one must attain truth by way of illusion and error."

"Some comfort that is! If I understand you correctly, Vukašin, we will achieve this so-called unification by shedding our brothers' blood, and on the basis of mutual deception."

"Survival demands deception, Živojin. The Croats must unite with Serbia in order to liberate themselves from Austria-Hungary and save Dalmatia from the Italians. They have no alternative, because they're fighting against the Allies. And we Serbs must unite with the Croats and Slovenes in order to destroy Austria-Hungary, our biggest enemy. Together, we can create the strongest state in the Balkans and make the Bulgarians and Albanians draw in their horns. That's how our vital interests coincide."

"A very clever plan! And all in the name of our brotherhood, in the name of a single people with three names, who for the last fourteen months have been killing one another with their bare hands. What do you expect of tomorrow? What do you place your trust in for this Yugoslavia, Vukašin?"

"I place my trust in time and in reason. In progress. And in our descendants."

"Ideals again. A very strong guarantee, I must say!"

"It takes centuries for a new nation to come into being, Živojin. We can't think about that over gun sights."

"I see now why you've remained alone in opposition. With such hopes—with such a fabricated goal—no one can follow you today."

"I know. That's why I've been spat upon and called a traitor."

"To tell the truth, when I heard that you'd supported the surrender of eastern Macedonia in the Assembly, I was astonished and angry."

"Therein lies the problem, not to say the hopelessness, of our Serbian situation. If the two of us can't think alike, what will happen to the others? How will we ever agree on a solution?"

Mišić silently reflected on his clash with Putnik that evening, then said: "So, like Putnik, Pašić, the politicians, and all your fellow intellectuals, you think that you've got to save the people from themselves. There's no hope of salvation for this nation, with you people at the top! None at all!"

He sighed and walked to the window. Frightened by Mišić's attitude, Vukašin got up; he wanted to put his hand on Mišić's shoulder and beg him to begin this conversation all over again and conduct it along different lines. He knew Mišić's character and feared a rift. He walked over to him and spoke softly, almost in a whisper:

"All my life, Živojin, I've been in opposition. I've always carried my thoughts and feelings to their logical conclusions. I've dragged out my own affairs and those of others into the full light of day, on the knife edge of reason and the far limit of conscience. What I've achieved, as you said a little while ago, is to remain alone."

Mišić looked at him sternly, straight in the eye.

"While I had a firm faith in my ideals, I could stand alone," Vukašin continued. "From solitude I drew the strength to endure. But now I'm afraid—most of all of myself. I can't change. I can't adapt myself." Vukašin felt relief, and a desire to open his heart further to this deserving man. With deep feeling he said, "I've been defeated, Živojin. And I don't know where I've gone wrong, apart from breaking with my father and sticking to my principles."

Mišić was astonished: Vukašin Katić admitting defeat! He interrupted him: "With your knowledge and experience, Vukašin, how could you believe that one climbs to power through wisdom and virtue? Surely you know that power is won by cunning, and held by lies and the saber?"

"I can't believe that!"

Now Vukašin regretted having talked about himself. As a rule he didn't open his heart to others. Whatever troubled him personally he would transform into a general problem, a matter of principle to be discussed objectively. He'd done this even with his closest friends.

"How do you think we can be saved?" asked Mišić.

"If we don't distinguish between military victory and salvation in the historical sense, it'll be hard for us to be saved. Given the kind of people we are, who knows whether we can be."

"What makes you say that?" demanded Mišić, raising his voice.

"We're an unfortunate nation, Živojin. Because of the soil on which we live, because of our history, and especially because of the enemies we've had. A nation is shaped by its enemies."

Mišić walked to the other end of the long, empty room, past the bare dining-room table and the metal stove in which the fire had gone out. He was silent for a few moments, then asked suddenly:

"Do you think we should withdraw now to Kossovo?"

"I think we must."

"And if we're driven from Kossovo? If the Allies don't come in time?"

"Then we must go to them."

"While there's a single Serb still alive—is that it? So this is our salvation in the historical sense!"

"In history, as I see it, survival is not secured by military victory."

"Then how?"

"By peacetime goals." Vukašin dared not go on—Mišić too was silent. They were afraid of telling each other everything, and both had the same thought: that man makes the hardest decisions in life alone. For painful struggles of this kind there can be neither brother nor friend.

"Živojin," Vukašin said suddenly, "I've decided to join the army—the regiment in which my son was serving. That's the one useful thing I can do now."

"You mean you want to join in the fighting?"

"Yes. With a rifle, in the trenches."

"It's too late, Vukašin. The most honorable course now is to be what you've always been. Your trench and mine are not the soldiers' trenches."

Mišić made this pronouncement with a certainty tinged with scorn. Once again Vukašin felt his own futility.

OCTOBER 22

TO THE FRENCH AMBASSADOR, AUGUSTE BOPPE, KRALJEVO:
THE LADY* YOU'VE BEEN HELPING FOR FOURTEEN MONTHS HAS FALLEN GRAVELY ILL. RAPID HELP COULD IMPROVE HER CONDITION. PLEASE SEND URGENT TELEGRAMS TO FRIENDS IN PARIS.

JOVANOVIĆ

OCTOBER 24

TO THE FRENCH AMBASSADOR, AUGUSTE BOPPE, KRALJEVO:
OUR PATIENT'S TEMPERATURE IS 104°. PLEASE TELL DE GRAZ TO HURRY WITH THE ENGLISH MEDICINES.

JOVANOVIĆ

OCTOBER 25

TO THE FRENCH AMBASSADOR, KRALJEVO:
WE ARE WAITING AND HOPING.

JOVANOVIĆ

* Serbia

313

ORDERS OF FIELD MARSHAL VON MACKENSEN TO HIS ARMY COMMANDERS: IN VIEW OF THE POLITICAL AND MILITARY SITUATION IT IS URGENT THAT OPERATIONS AGAINST SERBIA BE BROUGHT TO A SPEEDY CONCLUSION. THE POPULATION MUST NOT BE SHOWN ANY MERCY.

Živko Pavlović was informed by the doctors and Putnik's adjutant that the vojvoda had had a bad night and had not fallen asleep until daybreak. Pavlović therefore asked Prince Alexander and Nikola Pašić to begin the meeting of the government and the High Command at nine o'clock instead of at eight, and to hold it in the vojvoda's sickroom.

Alexander nodded and continued writing his proclamation to the army, which he had begun the previous night in the bedroom of the district superintendent. He had stopped at midnight because of a lack of conviction, but had continued at dawn, forcing himself to believe his own words:

Heroes! Today the enemy holds a large part of our land. But you must know that this is not for long. The day is drawing near when both the German aggressors and those traitors to the Slavs, the Bulgarians, will bitterly regret that they invaded Serbia. Our powerful protectors, the Russians, French, and English, are sending us help on a vast scale—whole armies.

His hand stopped; he put down his pen and gazed out the window at the fog which had descended on Raška, enveloping the town and the mountain above it. Wasn't he writing his own abdication?

As was his custom, Pašić avoided any conversation with his ministers or the officers of the High Command before the meeting, so he could change his opinions if opposed by the majority. He set off toward the bridge over the River Raška to see the people fleeing toward Kossovo and learn what they were thinking. In his pocket was a telegram from Paris which he had received the previous night, and which he had shown only to Prince Alexander. The French government had decided that "the game with Serbia was over." This was the hardest blow since the Austrian ultimatum from Count Berthold. How could he continue to convince the nation and the army of France's good intentions? Should he end his game with France, admit defeat, and submit his resignation? Or should he go on as if he had not received this telegram, placing his trust in Russia and, by means of this trust, compel the French and English to help Serbia?

He had no right to disappointment and hopelessness—they were no use to him. He would have to conceal what was in his soul. People are like dogs: if they sense you're afraid of them, they'll tear you to pieces.

The local people greeted him by raising their caps: anxious, frightened shapes swaying in the fog, seemingly unreal. He raised his hat in return. He wanted to find out why they were silent, these people whose greatest concerns were their children and their property, and to find out what they would do in his position. Ever since he had entered politics he had never wanted to act beyond the range of the feelings, needs, and wishes of the majority of the people. As the leader of the Radical Party, he had never supported any objective not shared by the majority, and had never entered any battle in which the majority would not have participated, and in which victory was not certain. The free press, his opponents, and his supporters helped him gauge the climate of opinion, the thinking of those who kept silent. Now, they looked at him like beasts at bay. Between four walls they were submissive, deceptively so; only at elections and in a crowd did they show their true feelings. As opponents they were dangerous and vindictive. In politics one could do anything against the individual, but never against the majority.

He raised his hat and nodded to a woman who was emptying a bowl, and to peasants who were leading their cattle. He had believed in democracy for fifty years, but only in recent years—his years in power—had he realized that democracy was of less advantage to those who were ruled than to their rulers. But what was the point of this experience, if no experience of any kind could bring France back into the game for victory?

He leaned against the parapet of the bridge and stared at the turbid waters of the Raška, and thought how seven centuries ago Nemanja and his son Stephen the First must have looked at this same river. Since their time everything in the land had changed, only to become the same again. Yet not quite the same, just as this turbid water was not the same. For Nemanja and his son, pride and honor had not been more important than their objectives, yet they too had been betrayed by their allies. They too had concealed their souls in silence. The game wasn't lost, Monsieur Poincaré—it couldn't be!

A wave of refugees filled the bridge. The people recognized him and shouted: "Look at *us*, Mr. Pašić, not the river! Look what you've done to us! Where can we go from Kossovo?"

He turned around, took off his hat, and bowed slightly, looking at the people who continued to shout: "Where are the Allies? Who'll save us now?"

Slowly he raised his hand toward the sky.

"What are you doing to Serbia?" they cried. "May the earth spit out your bones!"

Pašić could almost hate these people, who hated him because their fate was in his hands. But only a fool would despise the people, only someone who didn't know how to deal with them. The crowd was now pressing onto the bridge and a column of refugees was emerging from the fog. They gathered to listen to those who were scolding, cursing, and threatening him. Sensing that the moment had come, he spoke:

"You're right. I deserve your oaths and curses."

"What's he saying?" shouted the people beyond the bridge, pressing forward.

"If I had accepted the Austrian ultimatum last year," Pašić continued, "and handed Serbia over without a struggle, wouldn't you have crucified me as a traitor? Wouldn't you have?"

They were silent.

"Do you want me to capitulate to the Germans? To surrender? I can do so right away!"

The crowd didn't answer, but looked at him angrily, imploringly, in amazement. People were still prepared to follow him—he could read that in their looks. *The game isn't over, Monsieur Poincaré!* With deliberation he again took off his hat and bowed with respect. Then he set off slowly, striking the cobbles with his cane, and made his way through the thick fog to the house where Vojvoda Putnik was staying. When he had walked about fifty paces from the bridge, he heard voices behind him crying: "We don't want to surrender! Long live Pašić! May God keep you!" He didn't stop or turn around.

Tormented by his struggle to breathe and worn by a rending cough, Putnik was unable to get out of bed. His daughter Radojka was washing him in bed with the help of his orderly, Zarubac. He was of two minds whether to cancel the meeting with Prince Alexander and Pašić. He didn't wish to share with anybody the responsibility for his decision. He didn't need anyone's advice, didn't want to hear the complaints of the ministers about the sufferings of the people; he couldn't stand anxious politicians and unhappy soldiers. Moreover he'd feel humiliated by this gathering of the government and the High Command around his sickbed. Their looks of pity were harder to bear than hatred. What he had always found most wanting in people was not bravery and wisdom, but dignity and silence. He needed solitude— he'd never needed it more. In solitude he would have recovered his health and would never have made a wrong decision. But he hadn't had a moment's solitude since leaving Kragujevac. Just murk and fog, dirt and mud—no clusters of stars anywhere.

"They're at the door, Father."

"Don't let them in yet, Radojka. Comb my beard and hair nicely. Move all my things out of the way, Sergeant, and straighten that rug. Arrange the chairs."

He felt that his hands were not as clean as he'd like them to be, so Radojka washed them once more with soap and warm water. Now he felt better, stronger, and on a more equal footing with the men who even at this moment were despondently entering the room with Prince Alexander, greeting him quietly, and sitting on the chairs around his bed. He only nodded, and when they had all sat down, he said: "Please begin, Your Highness."

Prince Alexander: "We're in Kossovo, gentlemen. And every soldier, every Serb, feels in himself the spirit of Kossovo. Our fate is being decided, perhaps for centuries."

Pašić: "It's true we're in Kossovo, but I would suggest, sir, that we not discuss the heavenly kingdom. That's certainly not where we want to go right now."

First minister: "In our history, Prime Minister, there have been defeats greater than victories."

Pašić: "So poets think. But the people can't live on the glory of defeats."

Alexander: "Naturally we don't want to die for the heavenly kingdom. But it's quite obvious, Prime Minister, that we might lose the war."

Pašić: "I propose that we hear a report from the battlefields. I call on Vojvoda Putnik to speak."

Putnik: "Colonel Pavlović will give you that report. He can tell you more than I."

Colonel Živko Pavlović: "The enemy has not achieved its objectives."

First minister: "What do they still have to do, Colonel?"

Colonel Pavlović: "A lot, sir. In spite of numerical superiority and attacks from three directions, the enemy hasn't surrounded and destroyed our army. That was their principal objective. We have saved the main body of the army and are withdrawing it to Kossovo."

Second minister: "Losing almost all our territory in the process!"

Pavlović: "Yes. But by its strategy and tactics the High Command has fulfilled the requirements of the Allies and the directives of our government. Perhaps we could have waged the war differently."

Alexander: "Keep within the limits of your competence, Colonel."

Pavlović: "I will, Your Highness. But there's another important fact which must be mentioned: the Allies haven't kept one of their promises, which has meant that our government has been unable to keep its promises to the army. Yesterday a telegram arrived from our representative in Salonika which says that General Saray regards us as lost, that he won't answer any further requests of the Serbian High Command."

Pašić: "We'll talk about the Allies later, Colonel."

Putnik: "We should talk about the Allies now. In the defense of Serbia I've submitted to the Allied strategy and your policies, Prime Minister."

Pašić: "I will talk about the Allies and our policies in a moment, Vojvoda."

Putnik was seized by a spasm of asthma. Everyone but Pašić looked at his pale, puffy face, bathed in sweat.

Alexander: "Go on, Colonel. Report on the troops and reserves."

Pavlović: "Since the last attack on Serbia, seventy thousand men have been killed, and the same number are prisoners or missing. The number of deserters has grown significantly, as the soldiers move farther away from their native regions. The army is in serious disarray, and its morale is low."

Summoning his last ounce of strength, Putnik whispered: "Our army is weak but not broken. Not beaten, gentlemen. And that fact guarantees us—"

They all waited for Putnik to finish, but he was shaken by a fit of coughing.

Pavlović: "The hardest problem is feeding the army. We've again reduced rations by half."

Pašić: "The situation is worse than you think, but we can still endure much more than you've anticipated. No one knows what a man or a nation can do when its life is at stake. That is our reserve, gentlemen, our unknown and inexhaustible reserve."

Alexander: "You needn't justify yourself, Prime Minister. We aren't sitting in judgment today. We're simply looking for a way out."

Pašić: "What I have to say, you already know. I want us to agree on a decision. It's a great misfortune that Greece has betrayed us, and that Rumania still refuses to allow the Russians to advance across her territory against Bulgaria. Nor is our position good in either London or Rome. The Russians would help us, but they need time. We must be patient."

Second minister: "Are we not being patient, Prime Minister?"

Pašić: "Russia will not abandon us, whatever happens to our front. However, we have something worse to worry about, gentlemen. Yesterday evening I received a telegram from Paris: the French government considers 'the game in Serbia as lost.' As a result Saray has to withdraw with his division toward Salonika." Pašić paused. All eyes were on Putnik, who was exhausted from his coughing. Pavlović went out to call the doctor. Pašić continued: "That's hard for us, Your Highness, but we must be prepared for something still harder."

Third minister: "So France has betrayed us! We're finished!"

Pašić: "We must not betray France. I repeat: we must remain loyal, and by our loyalty compel her to help us."

Third minister: "If that's how we must earn her help, then I doubt we'll see our salvation."

Alexander waited for the doctor to give Putnik an injection of adrenalin, then said: "Gentlemen, we dare not keep silent about anything or overlook any danger. It's our fate that we're deciding."

Pavlović: "Our powers are small, but our responsibilities are enormous. We dare not make a single mistake."

Pašić: "There's only one mistake we dare not make now."

Alexander: "What's that, Prime Minister?"

Pašić: "Capitulation."

Alexander: "We're surrounded. If the Allies don't arrive soon—and by all accounts they won't—we must leave Kossovo in ten days. The question is, where do we go?"

Putnik: "To the Allies, Your Highness. We must use our last ounce of strength to break out of Kossovo and make a common front with the Allies."

Third minister: "Can we do that, Vojvoda, after the French decision?

Putnik: "We must. I'll send General Bojović to Kačanik, to open up a way through to Skoplje. Stepa will attack the Bulgarians with the Second Army, to enable us to break through."

Third minister: "How can we join the Allies when they don't want us? When they've played around with us and left Mackensen and the Bulgarians to crush us in Kossovo?"

Pašić: "We must force the Allies to accept us. By our faith in them we must put them under an obligation not to abandon us."

Fourth minister: "We agree, Prime Minister. But what happens if we can't break through toward Skoplje and Salonika? That's the question we must answer today."

Putnik: "A man can't do anything that he doesn't believe he can do."

Pašić: "Don't strain yourself, Vojvoda. Nod your head when you agree."

Putnik whispered: "We won't be defeated as long as we keep on fighting. We'll lose the war if we capitulate in Kossovo. Please, Colonel Pavlović, open the other window. We must exert all our strength . . . to break out of the ring . . . through Kačanik toward Skoplje . . . and Salonika."

Pašić nodded. After the adoption of Putnik's proposals, Alexander adjourned the meeting. He asked Pašić to send the Allied governments renewed requests for help, to convince them of Serbia's readiness to fight on without regard to the sacrifices involved. Then he returned to his room and finished his proclamation to the army:

Heroes! If we are to see the day when we will deal the enemy a heavier blow than we gave the Austrians last year, you must heroically endure a little longer. You must understand, soldiers, that each moment you are nearer the victory which will crown your efforts and sacrifices with new glory.

Meanwhile, in addition to proposing measures to secure a road for the retreat, Pašić announced that since the enemy would soon capture the monastery of Studenica, orders were being given to move the bones of Stephen the First, the first Serbian king, from the crypt of Studenica to Peć. Putnik nodded, but some ministers protested.

"Let's not profane our sacred objects, Prime Minister! They've withstood the violence of the Turks for five centuries!"

"If we take our children with us, why not the sacred bones?" said Pašić. "Let the world know that although the enemy has conquered the territory of Serbia, they haven't conquered our spirit. We're taking our books and our sacred objects with us, we're taking our spirit!"

After leaving Mataruška Banja and spending several nights in the car along the river Ibar, Olga was overcome with anxiety for Milena, and for the small child she had so daringly taken along. She constantly thought of her last conversation with Milena, of Bogdan's reproachful silence as she and Vukašin went to the car to leave for Kraljevo. She recalled Milena's words: "I can't come with you, Father!" Had it really been necessary for Olga to follow Vukašin on his death journey? Would that save her from the guilt she felt because she couldn't forget Mihajlo Radić? The endless rain and fog of the Ibar gorge and the general gloom of Kossovo deepened her sadness, while the frequent sight of sick women and children, and wounded soldiers and old men dying in ditches, filled her with an ever-mounting anguish and remorse for having parted from her daughter.

Meanwhile the people walking along the road followed them with looks of hatred and envy because they were traveling by car. To absolve themselves at least in part, they filled the car with children lost at the overnight stops, or picked up from their exhausted mothers. But these acts of kindness brought her no comfort: she was so shaken by the bewilderment of two ill-shod little girls who sat shivering at her feet, that she felt like getting out of the car and continuing on foot through the sleet. And she would have done so, with little Života wrapped in a blanket, if he hadn't been crying all morning; perhaps he was ill. She still had two bottles of milk for him, but no more. They were crawling through a bare, mountainous region with no sign of a village anywhere, and if they did see a house here and there, the driver would return empty-handed; the people had nothing more to sell. Why had she set out into this death trap with a baby? What would she say to Kosara if the war ever ended, if she returned to Belgrade? And Vukašin was now more wrapped up in himself than ever, living more in his own world than in the one they shared.

Vukašin could feel Olga's reproachful glance on the back of his neck. As they got deeper into Kossovo and moved ever more slowly toward Priština, the pressure of her silence became intolerable, preventing him from thinking about anything else. She was silently reproaching him for having agreed to let Milena stay in Prerovo by Aćim's deathbed. It's true that he had offered little resistance to Milena's decision and easily accepted the fact that she should carry out his duty. But every time he saw a dead person in the ditch, or looked at the people trudging along the muddy road, whipped by the icy wind and snow, he believed that Milena had acted wisely. She would surely be safe in Prerovo. If only Olga had stayed with her, he thought. He had a feeling that his father had died, and this alleviated his misery a little. Death had saved Aćim from living in bondage. He would never go to Prerovo again. He had left that cemetery among the thornbushes forever and gone into self-imposed exile. Was it not exile from Serbia as well? Where could they go if they couldn't make their way to Bitolj and find shelter in Greece? After their recent political differences it would be difficult for him and Mišić to go on being friends as before.

Mišić was not yet defeated. Those damned ideas of his were so deeply entrenched in his head! Why was he so persistent, when he was no longer convinced that the retreat to Kossovo—the flight toward the allies who didn't want them—was the way to salvation for this people? On their migration back to Kossovo they were suffering more than they had suffered a century and a half earlier when they had fled with the Patriarch Čarnojević from the Turks, crossing the Danube toward Russia. *But is Russia, our eternal hope and support, waiting for us in the south? Are we fleeing toward her now to meet the old, familiar disappointment? And there is Europe again looking on with indifference, mercilessly driving us on and leaving us to perish in the eternal delusion that we belong to her because we are Christian, because we believe in freedom and democracy, because we have consciously, with the greatest sacrifice, agreed to be her frontier and suffer on her account.*

The river Sitnica and its swollen tributaries were flooding the Kossovo plain, cutting off the road and washing away the smaller bridges, bringing to a standstill a stream of people, oxcarts, soldiers, hospital units, and prisoners of war pushing from Toplica and the Ibar ravine toward Priština and Prizren. At dusk, halted by a snowdrift, the car finally came to a stop at the head of a hospital column and the convoy of French aviators with their airplanes mounted on wagons. These ugly contraptions which looked as if they were going to take off at any moment stood there mocking the fugitives. Vukašin stepped out into the snowdrift and stared fearfully at a line of carts held up by the water. There was no chance of getting past; they would be snowed in on this flooded plain, which would freeze when night fell.

"Duško! Duško, my boy!" The woman who had been calling to her son ever since they left Ušće ran past.

Leaning against a wagon with its airplane, Bora Jackpot watched a gentleman in a fur-collared gray coat standing next to a car. Why did some people suffer so much more than others? This elegantly dressed man must be a minister or a member of the State Council, or else some swine of a merchant who would make Serbia pay through the nose for his discomfort. Seeing just one such Serb was enough to make one hide in an attic and wait for the Germans. And he had seen hundreds between Belgrade and here. The winds shook the airplane wings and whistled through its framework. If the bridge was not repaired—and who would repair it tonight?—thousands of women and children and wounded men would freeze in this blizzard. If only he could find Dušanka.

"Monsieur Jackpot, your platoon of engineers must repair the bridge," said Major Vitra, the commander of the French air squadron which had helped to defend Belgrade. "If we spend the night here, in this blizzard, we'll perish."

"Only Marshal Joffre could grant that request, sir. Or perhaps Monsieur Poincaré."

"I don't understand you, Sergeant."

"We're on our way to meet the French army, sir."

"Bloody swine of a Serb!" shouted the major, and walked away.

"The French are bloody swine too, sir," answered Bora Jackpot and continued marching to warm his feet.

"Sergeant, why don't you do something to get us out of this freezing hellhole?" asked Major Tallbridge, the commander of the English naval battery which had taken part in the defense of Belgrade.

"Only Lord Kitchener and his cruisers could save us. I'm only a Serbian student-sergeant, sir."

"That joke has fallen flat, Sergeant."

"Yes, sir, I know. My brain has frozen while I've been waiting for help from the English."

Bora knew that he shouldn't talk to the Allied officers in this way, but he was sick of representing the High Command to the French airmen and the English sailors after the reorganization of his regiment following the retreat from Belgrade. He was irritated by these Allied gentlemen who demanded order and organization, yet he felt sorry for them, too. Why should they suffer and perish for Serbia? It was the absurdity of their fate that prevented Bora from changing into peasant rags and running off to Belgrade, to spend his days in attics and cellars and his nights with ladies who were afraid to sleep alone. What had happened to Šunto Zlatiborac? Did he know that he had been awarded the Karageorge Star? Perhaps he was still riding through Belgrade on a white horse, sounding the reveille and the charge.

The wind carried women's cries and children's screams from the banks of the Sitnica. A few shots echoed, followed by the sound of men cursing and the wail of the *gusle*. It was that crazy Perun again who had ridden alongside the Ibar singing and playing his *gusle,* raising the spirits of the French airmen. A mockery of the epic style! The snowdrift darkened in the failing light.

He crawled under the wagon to shelter himself from the wind and smoke. Had Dušanka crossed the river? He hadn't seen her, his one military victory, since morning. He would have swum across the Sitnica to spend the night with her in this blizzard. He would have perished with her. His friends had been killed. Maybe it was a good thing that there was no one he could turn to now with his thoughts of desertion. Like a young boy, he had fallen in love in the midst of this military collapse. It was a crazy stake in wartime roulette. Dušanka was the prize. It had all happened by chance, just as he had wished it would before the war when he wanted to meet a girl, believing for some reason that love too could come to him only through chance.

The night before the retreat from Kragujevac he had decided to get so drunk that he wouldn't wake up until Kragujevac was occupied. The war would be over and he wouldn't be a deserter. What a wretched, petty fraud! He couldn't desert like a hero. That night the German shells in Belgrade had still whistled in his ears, and the wind carried a sweetish stench of gunpowder and corpses from the cemetery. As he was walking around, looking for a solitary place to spend the night, he had come upon the first-aid station of the Kragujevac hospital and rushed in to greet two Scotswomen, volunteer nurses. Then he'd heard a woman's voice cry out in Serbian: "Thieves! Help! My God!" A chill had run through his whole body. Hearing two shots he raced toward the woman, who was screaming: "These men are badly wounded! Leave their blankets alone, you murderers!" The sentry had hurried after them. In the darkness the woman had cursed the entire human race.

"You shouldn't curse people or despise them or kill them! In fact you shouldn't have anything to do with them!" Doctor Sergeev had said. "That's not true, it isn't!" the woman had cried. It *is* true, Bora had thought. He hadn't been excited by the theft, but by the nurse who had shot at the thieves. He'd followed her into the superintendent's office and in the light of the electric bulb had been astonished to see a lovely girl. Dušanka. He'd reminded her of their meeting in the summer, and of her failure to keep a date with him. She'd smiled warmly and said, "How could I have met you when I was in love with someone else?" "Are you in love now?" "What's your name, Sergeant?" "They call me Bora Jackpot." "Are you the ace?" "That depends on the game." "Was your father the owner of a gambling saloon?" "My father was an officer. But I love all games of chance." "I don't believe in luck, but I love games." "Are you angry when you lose?" "Yes, but I go on playing." "So do I. When you lose, do you suspect your partners of cheating?" "I believe it without any evidence." "Really?" "Yes." "Wonderful! You're a real gambler."

By that time he was sober. At dawn he'd set out on the retreat, making sure that the column of foreigners under his supervision would be close to Dušanka's hospital, or at least that they would stop for the night in the same place. After that conversation about the games of chance, they'd never doubted each other's feelings. The next day, as they were making their way on foot to Kraljevo, they'd taken shelter under a single tent flap, embraced and caressed and talked as if they had known each other for years. They'd spent ten nights together. For the first time he was in love. This girl gave him strength and hope. She was the one thing he had won during the war, and made up for everything he had lost.

Had she crossed this icy river? How was *he* going to do it? Indeed, why should he? Of course he would be taken prisoner or killed, he would freeze and die, but there was nowhere to go from Kossovo. His feet were numb with cold. He extinguished his half-smoked cigarette and put the stub into the upper pocket of his jacket, then crawled out from under the wagon and ran into the sleet.

He collided with the gentleman whom he had seen standing by the car. It was Vukašin Katić.

"You're Ivan's father!" Bora cried.

"Yes, I am. Are you a friend of his?"

"I'm Bora Jackpot. You tried to console me one evening in Kragujevac after the death of my father. Do you remember?"

"How could I forget? I'm delighted to see you." Vukašin embraced him as if to protect him from the wind and warm his frozen body.

"Do you hear from Ivan?" Bora asked.

"He wrote as long as he could. Come, you must meet my wife." He took Bora by the arm and led him to the car.

Bora felt slightly disappointed that Vukašin Katić was traveling by car.

On the bank of the Sitnica, which had overflowed onto the fields and the road, halting the column of carts filled with wounded at the place where the bridge had been, Perun was singing and playing his *gusle,* pausing now and then to warm his hands. As she listened to his singing, Dušanka was thinking about Bora. She knelt down in the oxcart next to Doctor Sergeev, who had pneumonia, and tried to shield his head from the wind and snow with a tent flap.

"Leave me alone, Dušanka. I don't mind the snow. At least I won't die in mud and dirt. The earth will be white and clean. Hold my hand."

"Don't be afraid, Doctor. We'll get to Priština tonight and put you in the hospital."

"I'm not afraid, Dušanka. I've lived a long time. If I freeze to death tonight, my death will not be stupid or dirty. This is the death I've struggled for, for over a year."

"Don't talk about death. The minute we get you into a hospital, you'll feel better."

"There's no hospital for me."

"If you have to talk, talk about Russia. I like your stories about St. Petersburg."

"Russia doesn't exist any more, nor does St. Petersburg. Now only I exist. And *he* exists."

"What do you mean?"

"The person whom we have chosen as father, but who doesn't acknowledge us as sons."

Dušanka didn't understand him nor did she wish to. At the cries of the wounded she turned her head. Bora's feet must be wet; they would freeze. She had some white woolen socks which she had found under the pillow of a lieutenant who had died that morning. She must find Bora before dark. Why couldn't they be alone tonight?

Mitar Slavonac had been crying out for her. He was a hero, so if he was wailing he must be in pain.

"Doctor Sergeev, it's already night. I must attend to the wounded."

"Very good, Dušanka, but promise me you'll come back."

"I promise. And I'll stay by you all night."

She stepped down from the cart into the turbid, icy water almost up to her knees, and hurried to the next cart.

"What's the matter, Mitar?"

"Lift me up, Nurse, so that I can see the Sitnica and Kossovo Field. Ever since I can remember I've heard about Kossovo, and now I can't see it."

"There's nothing to see, Mitar. It's empty. The land around us is flooded."

"It can't be empty. The peonies must still be green. The peony is a strong plant, and dies only under the snow."

Dušanka climbed into the cart, in which two other men lay beside Mitar. Mitar was struggling to raise his head above the side of the cart. As she squeezed out her soaking skirt she said reproachfully, "Where did you ever get the idea that we're in a field of peonies?"

"My father told me that Kossovo Field was red with peonies in full bloom, as far as the eye could see. And in the middle of the peonies was the church of Gračanica."

"That's a story for children, Mitar. Kossovo is empty, and it's getting dark."

"It isn't empty! How can it be? Lift me up, Nurse—I may not last till daybreak."

Dušanka took hold of him under his arms and lifted him up none too carefully. He groaned with pain, stared at the snowdrift, and said: "Kossovo Field. You can see the peonies. How could you not see such big peonies? Only they're frozen. But there are masses of them growing from the blood of heroes."

"Your wound will bleed, Mitar. I must put you down."

"Let it bleed. Hold me a little longer—please!"

"It's getting dark, you must lie down. I've got a lot to do."

"This cap I'm wearing is my own, I brought it from home. If I die, swear that you'll hold it for my son."

"I've already promised you that three times. You must settle down. I'll cover your head up."

"The man on my left has been dead since midday. Cover me with his tent flap."

She quickly removed the tent flap from the dead man, covered Mitar, and jumped down from the cart into the icy water. Ignoring the cries for help from the other wounded men, she walked along the column looking for Bora.

As she passed a covered wagon she was stopped by the Polish doctor Maria Ruseska and by Chernov, a Russian photographer.

"Why have we been waiting here so long, Nurse?"

"The bridge is gone, Doctor!"

"Dušanka, stand next to the oxen. I want to take a photograph of you."

"It's dark, Mr. Chernov!"

"If we spend the night here you'll survive only on my photographic plate, on the negative. A Serbian girl and an ox."

"I don't care!" she said and hurried off to find Bora. She hadn't seen him all day.

The wind howled. The wounded men cursed and shouted, demanding to move on.

"Brothers, don't swear, don't scold each other tonight. Have pity on your brothers and the enemy. Now only pity can save our souls and our lives." Dušanka recognized the voice of Božidar, the priest from Valjevo, but crossed to the other side of the road so he wouldn't recognize her.

Someone shouted: "The Bulgarians are in Priština! They'll be in Prizren tomorrow! Refugees from Priština are on the other side of the Sitnica! They're fleeing to our side."

Dušanka was terrified that she might be separated from Bora. She called out his name and he quickly answered. When she came up to the car, Olga hugged her:

"Dušanka, is that you?"

"Where's Milena?"

"She stayed with her grandfather."

Dušanka gave Bora the socks, then joined Olga in the car. She kissed her hands:

"Mrs. Katić, what's going on? What does Mr. Katić think?"

"I don't know, Dušanka."

"Look at all these children! That one's just a baby!"

Olga told her about Života, but when she began to talk about the other children Dušanka interrupted her: "Mrs. Katić, I'm really and truly in love now!"

Olga remembered the conversation she had had with Dušanka about Mihajlo Radić that night in Niš and for a moment felt paralyzed. But she quickly understood that the object of Dušanka's affections was no longer Radić but Ivan's friend Bora.

Meanwhile, Bora was sitting on the car's running board changing his socks, smiling. A real sign of love, these socks, he thought.

From down by the river the order was issued that all fit men were to assemble. Vukašin set out through the puddles and Bora Jackpot followed him. But when Bora realized that there were orders to take the wounded out of the carts and carry them across the river, he quickly went back to his airmen. It was his fate to die, but not to drown in an icy river for someone else's sake.

Meanwhile, Vukašin placed himself under the colonel's command and, with the soldiers, carried the wounded across the broken, ramshackle bridge in icy water to his waist. The physical effort, the cold, the danger, and the fact that he was doing something useful, made him feel that he was carrying out his decision to go into the trenches. A calm spread through him, a harmony he had not known since Ivan's departure as a volunteer. In the darkness he heard the *gusle* player's song. The wind broke the song like a dry branch, whipped people and animals, crushed anger, swept away spit and malice, and mingled with the cries of the men.

TO THE MINISTER OF FOREIGN AFFAIRS IN RUSSIA, SAZONOV:
THE SITUATION ON OUR BATTLE FRONT IS CRITICAL. THE GOVERNMENT AND
THE ARMY HOPED THAT THE RAPID ACTION BY THE ALLIED FORCES WOULD
ENSURE OUR COMMUNICATIONS WITH SALONIKA. THIS ACTION MUST BEGIN
AT ONCE.

PAŠIĆ

Today was the first day since his arrival in Priština that King Peter hadn't made a tour of the front. From his room on the first floor he looked through the window: the marketplace was swarming with people. Two days ago the refugees had surrounded the house in which he was staying, filling the marketplace and the street, and they hadn't moved. They lit fires and waited for him to appear, and when he did they shouted, "Where are we going, King Peter?" and "Give us bread!" and "Is this the end?" He had answered, "I'll be with you until the end, my children." But last night, when some women with children in their arms cried out that they had nothing to eat, he had burst into tears and said, "I'll give you everything I have in my kitchen." He had ordered that all his food be distributed to the refugees. This made him feel better. First thing in the morning he summoned Pašić and Prince Alexander, then wrote down the previous day's expenses in his diary: *Given to the kitchen for various expenses, 200. Goose 13, a pitcher of wine 18, sugar 41.* He examined his accounts since the beginning of the retreat from Topola: he'd spent much more than he should have; it upset him. Then he wrote a letter to Jelena, his favorite daughter, in St. Petersburg, and received Božidar, the priest, and Sergei, the bishop of Šabac, with whom he discussed a prayer meeting to be held in Gračanica the next day. Then he looked out the window at the marketplace again. Some merchants were being flogged for closing their shops, or for accepting only silver and gold. The mob looked on with anger and delight; he looked on with approval. But when three barefoot soldiers—deserters from the army— were brought in to be shot, the people watched with distress, and the rifle shots sent a stab of pain to his heart.

He took his field glasses to observe the slopes of Skopska Crna Gora, from which he had heard the rumble of cannon since morning. If General Bojović did not stop the Bulgarians, in two days they would take Priština, and the entire Serbian army, along with the people in flight, would be taken prisoner on the field of Kossovo. But not he. Serbian children must be able to say: Our King perished at Kossovo.

His adjutant announced the Prime Minister and opened the door for him without waiting for the King's approval. Nikola Pašić bowed stiffly. The King, disconcerted by Pašić's severity, invited him to sit down beside him on the couch. "Prime Minister, I hear that the government and the High Command are withdrawing to Prizren?"

"Yes, Your Majesty. To the last place on Serbian territory."

"Our situation is catastrophic. Yesterday Vojvoda Stepa wept in my presence. And General Šturm is no less upset. Both believe that our collapse at Kossovo is inevitable."

"Our position is difficult, Your Majesty. And it'll get worse."

"Have the Allies washed their hands of us?"

"We won't let them wash their hands of us."

"What do you intend to do? What does Vojvoda Putnik think?"

"Our intention is to make our way through the Kačanik gorge and join forces with the French and the English. We'll go with them toward Salonika, to whatever God ordains. Then Joffre and Kitchener will realize what the Balkan front means to them and they'll be fairer to Serbia."

The King looked hard at Pašić. "I want to know what your final decision is, Prime Minister. What if we can't break out of Kossovo?"

"That depends, Your Majesty."

"I want a straight answer, Mr. Pašić. Are you thinking of surrender?"

Pašić responded in a bitter, icy voice, "What's your opinion, Your Majesty?"

"It's my firm resolve not to survive the collapse of Serbia. In the morning I'll join General Bojović at the front."

"That's the one thing you mustn't do."

"I don't want to be a king in exile, Mr. Pašić. I'm a king in freedom."

"*Live* for Serbia, Your Majesty, don't die for her."

"I don't want to survive our collapse."

"Vojvoda Putnik and I are hopeful that General Bojović will force his way through Kačanik. But if we don't break through by way of Kačanik, we have another road to safety."

"May God preserve you and give you strength. I'd like to say one more thing before we part. Though I've often opposed you, I'd like to thank you most warmly, Mr. Pašić, for your loyal cooperation. And I lay this charge upon you: don't allow my successor to carry out a single important decision rashly. See that he postpones it, as you do.

And one other request, Mr. Pašić: help him to surround himself with collaborators who are honorable men and not subservient."

Pašić rose. "I'll carry out all your wishes, Your Majesty. But it would be better for both your son and the country if the two of us shared our anxieties for a few more years."

King Peter held out his hand; for the first time ever, he didn't accompany Pašić to the door. For the first time he, a constitutional monarch, had refused to accept the opinion of his Prime Minister. He felt strong. How many times had he, the King, been unjustly defeated under democracy! How many times had a man weaker than himself emerged as the stronger, had an unscrupulous man gone over his head, or one of feeble intellect acted as his equal! Well, let it all come to an end here on Kossovo!

Zdravko made a fire in the stove and lit the lamp. The King postponed dinner until Prince Alexander returned from the front lines. He couldn't remember when they had last dined together. On the eve of his departure for battle, this would be his last pleasure. He stretched out on the couch to wait for his son, and woke up just before dawn. He scolded Zdravko for not waking him when Alexander had come in, and crossed the passage into Alexander's room. He stood above his sleeping son, who had covered his head with an eiderdown. He remembered his children when they were small, in Cetinje and in Geneva, when he, instead of their mother, had put them to bed and awakened them. He thought of his wife with deep sadness and guilt, for which he could not atone by any religious penance, or even by his death.

"What's happened, Father?"

He was startled by Alexander's words. "I thought you were asleep. I was waiting for you last night so that we could have dinner together. But I didn't wait long enough."

"They didn't tell me you were waiting."

"When servants forget a king's orders, you know things are pretty bad. Get up now, we must talk. I'm in a hurry to get to Kačanik."

"Why? The Bulgarian advance is dangerous."

"I'll be waiting for you in my room," he said sharply and left.

A few minutes later Alexander appeared in full-dress uniform.

"I've summoned you, my son, to say good-by. Sit beside me."

Alexander sat down reluctantly. "Why must we say good-by? Where are you going?"

"To the battle at Kačanik. If we don't break out of Kossovo, I'll meet the same fate as Prince Lazar. I can't survive the collapse of my country. I informed Mr. Pašić of this yesterday."

"What will happen to the Serbian army if her king dies today for the kingdom of heaven, like Prince Lazar in our epic poetry?"

"My accounts with the nation are different in all respects from yours, Alexander. I can never forget that my throne rests on the dead bodies of the Obrenovići. The only way I can be absolved is to rule justly."

Alexander got up and moved away from his father. "So you're going to deal one more blow to an army that's already on its last legs?"

"I want to show the army that my head is no dearer than that of any soldier. This isn't the last Serbian battle for freedom. If we're defeated at Kačanik—God grant that we won't be—we must be defeated in such a way that our descendants consider us the victors."

"That's crazy, Father! Absolutely crazy!"

"Ah, my son, nothing great and honorable has ever been done that wasn't crazy. I must go now—General Bojović is waiting for me at Gračanica." He got up and walked over to his son. "I feel sorry indeed that we're parting like this."

"I don't suppose you want me to come with you to Gračanica, so we can take communion together and then go to Kačanik to die?"

"I'm not asking that of you. You're young, and there'll be other battles where you can prove you're a king. I wanted to give you some advice, but I have no time."

"But I need your advice! What are you saying?"

Alexander leaned against the wall, his eyes fixed on the floor. King Peter, depressed by the conversation with his son, summoned Zdravko to help him with his overcoat, took his cane, called his adjutant, went down into the street, and got into his car, which was surrounded with people. He saluted them and ordered the chauffeur to drive to the monastery of Gračanica.

He found the priest Božidar at the entrance to the monastery, performing funeral rites for refugees—some old men and women in a ditch. King Peter waited for Božidar to finish, then asked impatiently, "Where is Bishop Sergei? He promised he'd attend the morning service at Gračanica."

"The bishop may be ill."

"Disgraceful—he can't possibly be ill! The metropolitan should be here, too. With such priests, it's a miracle that people still believe in God."

"The priests are not God's hirelings on earth, sir. If you aren't responsible for your district chiefs, why should God be responsible for Bishop Sergei and Metropolitan Mihajlo?"

"But I *am* responsible for the district chiefs! I'm responsible for all the evil in my kingdom, Božidar."

"You've never said that before, Peter Mrkonjić. You've never acted like that, unfortunately for us."

General Bojović arrived with his staff and announced that overnight the Bulgarians had scattered the Vardar Division. Whole villages of Albanians with their children and livestock were going over to the Bulgarians.

"What's your estimate of our strength, General?"

"Three to one in favor of our enemies."

"What are we going to do today, General?"

"Charge with all our strength, Your Majesty! If we don't force our way through, we'll at least hold them back until the main body of our army retreats to Montenegro."

"Very good, General." He went up to the priest and whispered, "Make the prayers as short as possible!"

TO THE MINISTER OF FOREIGN AFFAIRS IN RUSSIA, SAZONOV:
ALL OUR HOPES ARE PLACED ON SKOPLJE'S BEING RETAKEN WITH THE HELP OF ALLIED FORCES. THE LAND IS THREATENED WITH FAMINE. ALL OF SERBIA IS ON THE MOVE. WE MUST BE PREPARED FOR ANOTHER EPIDEMIC. ONLY IMMEDIATE HELP CAN SAVE SERBIA FROM RUIN.

                        TRUBETSKOY

INSTRUCTIONS FROM MARSHAL FALKENHEIN, CHIEF OF THE GERMAN GENERAL STAFF:
OUR MAIN TASK NOW IS THE TOTAL DESTRUCTION OF SERBIA. OUR ARMY, TOGETHER WITH THE NORTHERN FRONT OF THE SECOND BULGARIAN ARMY, MUST PRESS ON TOWARD PRIŠTINA.

9

═══════════

TO THE MINISTER OF FOREIGN AFFAIRS IN RUSSIA, SAZONOV:
THE SERBIAN ARMY IS RETREATING SOUTHWARD. CONVINCED THAT STRONG
ALLIED FORCES WILL COME TO ITS AID, IT WILL MAKE ONE FINAL ATTEMPT
TO BREAK THROUGH TO SKOPLJE. IF THE ANGLO-FRENCH TROOPS DO NOT
ATTACK IMMEDIATELY IN FULL STRENGTH, OUR EFFORT WILL COST MUCH
BLOODSHED AND GREAT SACRIFICE. WE WILL DO OUR DUTY, BUT IF WE DO
NOT SUCCEED IN BREAKING THROUGH ALONE, THE ENTIRE RESPONSIBILITY
WILL FALL ON OUR ALLIES. WE ARE NOT YET DISCOURAGED BECAUSE WE
BELIEVE THAT THE ALLIES WILL COME TO OUR AID WITH A STRONG ARMY,
NOT ONLY TO SAVE SERBIA BUT FOR THEIR OWN SAKE, AND TO KEEP THEIR
WORD OF HONOR.

PAŠIĆ

Traveling from Mitrovica to Prizren made Vojvoda Putnik's illness worse. He lay in bed and received only Nikola Pašić and his assistant, Živko Pavlović. He gave orders that he was to receive reports only about the battle of Kačanik, which was being fought to force a way out of Kossovo. He was familiar with the rest: the disintegration of the defeated army, for which even honorable men in the command posts were blaming the High Command. Blaming him. This guilt was part of his fate. Once more he had done all he could: he had collected all the troops he could and given them to General Bojović, the commander who would fight the most resolute battle for a breakthrough toward the Allies. The fleeing population, pouring into Prizren hungry and exhausted, preoccupied him more than the front. From his bed he listened to the continuous tumult in the street, and the desperate cries: "What has happened? Where are we going?" That they saw safety in this breakthrough was no guarantee that they would find safety. Soon they would be left without hope. The despair of the people in flight would spill over into the already demoralized army and destroy what little remained of their will to fight. And he wouldn't be able to prevent the strong and the courageous from regarding Kossovo as decisive; they would capitulate.

His illness protected him from people and their endless questions, for which he had no answers. Yet not even his illness brought him the solitude he craved. A stream of people, carts, and horses flowed past his bedroom window. He felt closed in, he couldn't breathe. The walls would collapse and his bed would roll out onto the cobblestones. He would never escape those eyes—the eyes of soldiers, peasants, women, and children. He lost consciousness. With a painful effort, he came to and tried to take the hands of his two daughters, who were hovering over him. He wanted to express the tenderness he felt for them, but somehow this tenderness seemed out of place, so he conveyed instead his gratitude and concern. In this small land crushed by human folly, he cherished his good children and the infinity of heaven.

When the medications had eased the pain in his chest, he gazed at the landscape: glowering clouds enveloped the mountains, cutting off the peaks; fog settled in the valleys, obscuring rivers, hamlets, and cemeteries; whirling snowstorms leveled the trenches and tore apart the columns retreating toward the Albanian wasteland. Light and darkness succeeded each other with no clear distinction, no daybreak, no dusk.

He wouldn't die as the defeated vojvoda of a defeated army. The enemy had taken his territory, but not his country. The Serbian state was destroyed, but not Serbia's core. There was uncertainty, but in that uncertainty there was hope. And as long as there was hope, victory was possible.

Since noon he'd been listening to the ever-louder rumble of artillery: the Bulgarians had surely thrown Bojović back.

Nikola Pašić came in and sat down at the table next to the window. Putnik looked closely at this man, the only one who had given no sign that he had lost faith in victory. This Pašić, who doubted everybody and everything, didn't doubt the Allies and their promises, which they consistently failed to fulfill. Was that strength, or despair? Was he a great leader who saw what no one else could see, or a shallow, heartless, ambitious politician who would use any means to attain his end, and destroy their nation in the process?

"Have you had any news from Kačanik?" asked Pašić.

"The last was this morning. It was unfavorable."

"There's panic in the town."

"We should tell the people to turn back and go home, or give them directions for the retreat to the coast."

"How many soldiers can we take across Albania and Montenegro to the sea, Vojvoda?"

"I don't know, Prime Minister. A large number will drop out. Now even the most courageous among them will desert." He met Pašić's inquiring glance, then asked him: "Do you still believe that Allied ships will be waiting for us at the coast with food, clothing, and equipment?"

"Yes, I do."

"Have you any guarantees of this from the Allied governments?"

"Fewer than when we were preparing to receive their troops. But I'm surer now they'll help us."

"Do we dare set out across Albania with nothing but our faith?"

"We must force the Allies to help us. Given the unfavorable situation on their fronts, our surrender would be the easiest way out for them. Their failure to fulfill their promises would be justified. We mustn't let them dump us so easily."

"That's risky, Prime Minister. But I'll take the risk—for another reason."

"It's not risky. Every day, every hour of our continued existence places a greater obligation on the Allies to help. And the more of us that reach the coast, the greater and more certain their help will be."

"Yes. The more of us that die, the more certain it is that our friends will help."

Pašić interrupted him: "You no longer believe that Bojović will force his way through Kačanik?"

"No, I don't. If he doesn't strike by noon tomorrow . . ." Putnik paused, weighing his words carefully. "Then the Allied deception of our government and your deception of the High Command will become quite tragic."

"The Allies have compelled me to deceive you. I feel no guilt about that, Vojvoda. As long as they continue to deceive us, there's hope we can be saved."

"I didn't wish to accuse you of deception, Prime Minister. In war, lies are legitimate weapons. I wanted to draw another conclusion."

"I'll come see you at noon tomorrow."

Putnik, left alone, listened to the evening prayers of a muezzin from a nearby mosque. What was the military defeat of a small nation, this Serbian catastrophe at Kossovo, he asked himself, compared with those mighty catastrophes in the history of the earth, in which entire worlds ceased to exist? How trifling was their collapse, and the entire European war, compared with the collision of planets, the extinction of stars, and the destruction of solar systems!

But he didn't really believe it.

Ever since he had sent his wife and daughters off to Greece with the families of other prominent people, Nikola Pašić had been in low spirits. Although he had secured a military escort and Albanian guides for his family, and done all he could to make their journey safe, the advance of the Bulgarians toward Tetovo was so rapid that it might cut them off; they might be captured, or abandoned and killed in the Albanian mountains. He no longer had any means of finding out how they were faring. He had never shared his worries with others, and had no right to do so now.

The refugees surrounded the district office in which the government was located; his own office was besieged day and night by Allied ambassadors, foreign journalists, Serbian deputies and senior government officials, friends, and leaders of the Opposition. They all demanded help in securing accommodations and food, and asked about the Kačanik front. They all asked the same question: What will happen if General Bojović doesn't force his way through to the Allies and Salonika? He dared not give any sign that it was harder for him than for them, and in the end he asked more questions than he answered. He pressed the military commanders into accepting responsibility for the large-scale desertion of their soldiers. He listened quietly to expressions of the Opposition's dissatisfaction with the government. He didn't defend himself against angry accusations that he had used his personal influence to save his own family before all others, nor did he justify the corrupt ways in which the government and the High Command had sought safety in their flight from Prizren: it was every man for himself. He publicly took responsibility for the military defeat and the hardships of the flight.

When attacked by the High Command for deceiving the army about the Allies' promises, he replied calmly: "If the Allies hadn't deceived me, after the withdrawal from Kraljevo I'd have proposed capitulation. If I hadn't deceived you, gentlemen, you'd have capitulated after the fall of Belgrade and Smederovo. I'm still of the same opinion: deceptions make it possible to endure hardship and evil." He knew he was regarded as a devious politician, the man who was digging Serbia's grave. So be it. As long as the mob blamed him for the collapse of Serbia, he was still their leader; as long as he deceived them, they would believe in him. While they attacked and hated and cursed him, they would trudge along behind him through Albania, toward the sea.

Whenever he could, he would leave his office, wearing an officer's uniform without badges of rank. Then, accompanied by a policeman, he would walk across the square and down the main street of Prizren to face the curses of the refugees and soldiers. It alleviated their suffering for them to cry out: "Down with Pašić! He's a criminal!"

He would acknowledge them by slowly raising his clenched fist to his cap, then walk on at an unhurried pace. Soothed by his calm expression and his long, saintly beard, the mob would press behind him to hear him speak—above the ever-closer boom of the artillery.

Mihajlo Radić was approaching Prizren with Pavel Vojteh and a few hundred boys huddled into groups to protect themselves from the wind and snow. Now and then boys suffering from diarrhea slid into the ditch and pulled down their trousers. Some, not having the strength to fasten them again, trudged along bent double, holding on to their trousers with both hands. Others simply squatted on the road, then fell into their own excrement. The sight of half-naked corpses, skeletons of oxen, and dismembered horses paralyzed them with fear. Radić knew that some of the boys stopped not out of a physiological need, but out of terror. He knew also that if they headed back to Priština, they would freeze to death, be killed by Albanian brigands, or be captured by the Bulgarians. So he would call to them, go back for the ones who faltered, hold them up, beg them to be brave a little longer, threaten them, and promise them that in Prizren they'd be safe. Some obeyed him, pulled up their breeches, and continued on their way, but many remained as black shapes squatting on the frozen mud and snow.

Vojteh followed Radić with his last ounce of strength. Since leaving the Sitnica he hadn't mentioned his women, or expressed his customary contempt for the human race. When he saw Prizren in the foothills of the snowy heights, with its mosques and poplar groves, Vojteh stopped and said: "The East—I can't stand it!"

"This," said Radić, "was the famous capital city of Serbia in the Middle Ages."

"Doctor Radić, this is the end of the world."

For the boys, Prizren was the largest and most beautiful town imaginable, promising a dry resting place and a hot supper—their first hot supper since Niš. As they entered Prizren, Radić settled the boys in the camp of the prisoners of war, who were cutting down trees to keep the fires going. He left Vojteh with them and set off into the town to look for the headquarters of the Niš reserve troops. Overwhelmed by the enormous numbers of refugees, he could hardly force his way along the street. He asked for the headquarters, but no one could direct him to it. Nowhere was there a single commanding officer he knew. All the shops were closed. The cafés had been turned into hospitals or were crammed with refugees. The street was a tumultuous marketplace where people sold everything they owned and bought only the essentials. Fine ladies exchanged fur coats, dresses, and jewelry for donkeys. Portions of cornbread and small bags of potatoes and roasted chestnuts were bought with silver and ducats. Mud-spattered gentlemen negotiated with Albanians to accompany them to Debar with their mules. Cries of "How much?" and "What will you pay?" echoed all around.

It was getting dark. Radić hurried back to his boys, determined to lead them to any dry place in Prizren. To a church perhaps—or a mosque, if need be. What a crushing blow it would be when he said to them: "Well, boys, I haven't found the headquarters of the Niš reserve troops, I don't know where we'll spend the night, and I've nothing for you to eat." He lit one of his last cigarettes and pushed on through the refugees. He could no longer make out faces. Here and there lights shone through the closed shutters. A joyful cry cut through his thoughts:

"Doctor! Captain!" Bora Jackpot saluted him.

"Bora! Is it really you?"

"Who else?" Bora seized his outstretched hand and wouldn't let go.

"Do you know where the headquarters of the Niš reserve troops is?"

"The staff itself doesn't know, so don't bother looking. I'll take you to the inn where we're staying—it's a hospital now. Dušanka is there, your nurse from Valjevo. Sergeev is there, too. Prizren may be his last stop."

"Why?"

"Pneumonia. Vukašin Katić and his wife brought him here in their car."

"Where are the Katići?"

"They left for Peć at noon today in a peasant cart. They have a sick child with them, a baby. I'm happy to see you, Doctor. Dušanka will be, too."

Radić felt deceived and betrayed, as if Olga had made an arrangement to meet him in Prizren, as if he had come for her on foot from Niš and she hadn't waited for him. Throughout the retreat he had hoped to run into her, though he couldn't admit it to himself. Suddenly overcome by fatigue, he could hardly keep pace with Bora, who was leading him up a steep, narrow street. He would have turned back or simply sat down, but for the thought that he had to find a place for his boys.

"It's a small world, and Serbia is the smallest country in it now," said Bora. "Serbia is not even a country anymore, but there's still Prizren." He fell silent. Since Kragujevac, the only meeting that had given him greater pleasure was with Tričko, who had been sitting on the bridge, eating roasted chestnuts from his cap.

"Bora, do you know where I can find a place for a few hundred sick boys?"

"A few hundred? Nowhere!"

Radić stopped. "What am I to do? If I leave them in the cold tonight, they'll die."

"The only places in Prizren not already occupied are the mosques. The Orthodox churches are full of wounded."

"Where's the biggest mosque?"

"I suppose that one's the biggest," said Bora, pointing to a minaret in front of them.

They hurried up the street to the inn. Bora took him into a large room reeking with the familiar smell of wounds and the filth of military hospitals. A lamp on the wall cast a feeble light over the wounded packed closely together on the floor—they could barely make their way to a small room in the back. There they found Dušanka, who was changing vinegar compresses for Doctor Sergeev.

"God be praised!" Sergeev whispered.

Dušanka said nothing. She didn't even shake hands with Doctor Radić. Sergeev wept and kissed Radić's hand. "Stay with me tonight. I'm near the end, Mihajlo."

"I'll come back as soon as I find a place for my patients," said Radić, deeply moved. Sergeev brought back vivid memories of Valjevo. There had been hope in that suffering, even though more people had died there than in this hopeless flight. Then one had been able to do something; now one could only endure and believe in deceptions. He shuddered as he walked out with Bora.

"This is the end of your country and mine. Where do we go from here, Doctor Radić?"

Radić didn't reply.

The streets had emptied a little, but the fierce wind whipped the snow into their faces and made walking as difficult as before. On the sidewalks, under eaves and open shop counters, and around fires in courtyards sat refugees wrapped in coarse rugs. Bora and Radić soon reached the camping ground where the prisoners of war and young boys were sitting around big fires. Vojteh was in despair. Half the sick boys they had brought from Priština had gotten lost in the mob. Radić took the rest to the mosque. Inside, several dozen soldiers and refugees were crowded around braziers. He gathered the boys around him and said, "Go inside and find a place for yourselves. Doctor Vojteh and I will try to get some food for you."

Some of the boys complained, a few cursed, but they all hurried into the mosque toward the bright flames of the braziers.

Dušanka welcomed Radić and Doctor Vojteh with a smile and hot brandy, some hardboiled eggs and English canned food. They sat down to eat at a table by Sergeev's bed. Bora recounted some humorous incidents he'd had with the French airmen and their mistresses, who had accompanied them from Belgrade. Several times Dušanka laughed aloud, making Vojteh frown in disapproval. Radić didn't listen to Bora and scarcely touched his supper. He was thinking of how he could find some food for his boys tonight. Sergeev's avid, damp-eyed look unnerved him.

"Oh, feel free to smoke, Doctor Radić," said Sergeev, as Radić put his cigarette case back in his pocket. "Just think—Mrs. Katić brought me here in her car. What a coincidence!"

Nothing happens by chance in times like these, Radić thought.

"Dušanka, give me some hot brandy," said Sergeev.

Reluctantly, she passed him a cup and he drained it.

"What'll happen to this country after the war, Doctor Radić?" he asked.

"I don't know. The future doesn't interest me."

Dušanka looked at Radić: how could she have been so in love with this ugly, gloomy man?

"Something disagreeable and tedious," said Bora, lighting a cigarette. "Whether General Bojović leads us through the Kačanik gorge or we collapse and die in Montenegro or Albania, it makes no difference."

With a great effort Sergeev raised himself slightly to give more weight to his words:

"If you survive the present, you'll see a world in which people will annihilate their past—the one real thing they have. Goodness and courage won't earn respect and fame any more." He shook his finger threateningly, then sank back on his bed.

"No, gentlemen," agreed Vojteh with conviction. "After we're gone the world will be ruled by the strong and the cruel!"

"Good!" said Bora. "There'll be less hypocrisy, and people won't have to die for their country."

Radić got up and put on his overcoat.

"Where are you going?" asked Sergeev, seizing him by his coat.

"I'll be back in an hour."

Bora offered to accompany him, but Radić refused. He decided to go to the High Command. Through shameless persistence and lying, he got through to Colonel Živko Pavlović.

"The Niš reserve troops," said Pavlović, "and all the conscripts set out this morning for Albania."

"What'll I do with my sick boys, sir?"

"Take with you those who can still walk and attach yourself to an army unit. A regiment is setting out in that direction this morning."

"What about those who are seriously ill?"

Pavlović looked at him thoughtfully, twirled his pencil, and said nothing.

"I'm a doctor, Colonel. How can I leave my patients?"

"Save those who can be saved."

"I should stay with those who need me the most, sir."

"It's your duty now to be at the side of those who can stay alive and become soldiers. We must win the war, Captain."

Radić was silent for a moment, then said firmly: "I cannot sacrifice two or three hundred sick boys for any victory in this world."

"An antiquated principle, Doctor."

"How can you talk like that?"

"You're a Serbian officer, Captain. You must do your duty. Forgive me, I have an urgent task to attend to."

Radić didn't salute him when he left. On the steps of the metropolitan's residence he stopped and watched the fires burning in the darkness. An antiquated principle, was it? But why hadn't he asked for some food? He tried to go back, but the officer on duty wouldn't let him through. He lit his last cigarette and set off toward the mosque. From the minaret the Moslem's prayer to Allah was carried by the wind into the darkness. The sound sent a shudder through him.

"Doctor Radić! This place is a veritable Noah's Ark!"

He recognized the voice of Paun Aleksić and recoiled.

"What are you doing here? When last we met you were about to leave for Salonika."

"I was ready to leave for Greece—I had a railway compartment. It's that fatal sister-in-law of mine—I'm pathologically in love, I'm afraid. She didn't want to go to Greece—too much the officer's wife. Her husband's a prisoner of war so she wants to share the fate of the army—of the higher ranks, that is. And I, idiot that I am, couldn't let her go alone on this journey of no return. She came from Niš with the division staff, and I followed as her groom and orderly, loading her suitcases. Naturally someone more powerful unloaded them and found her a lodging for the night—a colonel! That's my fate."

"You've been through a lot!" said Radić. He was about to move on, when Aleksić grabbed hold of his sleeve.

"I'll make mincemeat of all the filthy whores in Serbia! Let's have a drink—I have some excellent brandy."

"No, thank you. Good night."

"I'll walk with you. Guess where she is now?"

"I'm not interested."

"She's spending the night with a French doctor in the house of the Catholic bishop. The whore! Only whores will survive the war, Radić, mark my word. But this is a mosque!"

"My patients are here."

"I'll wait for you. I want to talk some more. There are two hundred thousand Serbs in this filthy hole tonight, but not one man fit for decent conversation!"

Radić went into the mosque to visit his sick boys; he had no intention of returning to pursue the conversation.

TO THE MINISTER OF FOREIGN AFFAIRS IN RUSSIA, SAZANOV: COMMUNICATIONS WITH OUR WESTERN ALLIES HAVE BEEN BROKEN OFF. COMMUNICATION WITH RUSSIA HAS BEEN SEVERED. FROM THE START OF THE COMBINED AUSTRO-HUNGARIAN, GERMAN, AND BULGARIAN ATTACK— FOR MORE THAN SIX WEEKS NOW—SERBIA HAS BEEN FIGHTING ON THREE FRONTS. SHE NOW STANDS ON THE BRINK OF TOTAL COLLAPSE.

PAŠIĆ

In the course of the retreat from Lipljano, on the last stretch of high ground before Prizren, the special battalion of the Danube Division was halted by an order to dig in there for the defense of Prizren. Bogdan Dragović was disappointed: in Prizren he had hoped to meet with friends and acquaintances and get some reliable information about the High Command decisions before reaching the Albanian frontier. He might perhaps have found the Katići there and shared his anxiety about Milena with them. Instead he would be defending Prizren and perhaps die with this battalion. He lined up his platoon in a small wood along the road and ordered them to take turns digging the trenches—they had only ten small shovels. He sat down in the bushes and lit a cigarette. What had begun badly would end badly.

Falsely representing himself as an orderly from the division staff, Bogdan had made his way along General Bojović's front, but before he reached the regiment of his first commanding officer, Lieutenant Colonel Glišić, he learned that Glišić was dead, having refused to retreat before the advancing Bulgarians, who had wiped out his battalion. With his last grenade he had blown up both himself and the Bulgarians who were trying to take him prisoner. Bogdan decided not to save himself even from a court-martial, but he set a high price on himself: he went straight before his division commander, Colonel Kajafa, and gave him a true account of what had happened. In conclusion he said: "Please believe me, sir: I haven't been running away from death, but from injustice. And I'll accept any decision you make."

Kajafa sized him up, squinted in silence for some time, then said: "Very good, Sergeant. I'll make you the commanding officer of a platoon in a special battalion. Wait for me outside and I'll present you to your soldiers."

Bogdan was afraid this might be one of those jokes by which colonels achieved fame and confirmed their power. He didn't wait long: accompanied by a captain—a giant of a man with a moustache—Kajafa took him into a neighboring courtyard filled with convicts. The captain quickly lined them up in double ranks. When the clanking of their chains and fetters died down, Kajafa addressed them:

"Now, men, you yourselves and the court that sentenced you know why you are guilty. But I know that you are Serbs and I believe that you love freedom more than all of us who have never experienced servitude. I am giving orders that your fetters be removed, and I promote you to soldiers in the service of this small country. You will receive rifles and ammunition. Captain Popović is the commanding officer of your special battalion"—he pointed to the large, bewhiskered captain—"and Sergeant Dragović here will command your first platoon. You will get one more commanding officer. The corporals and section leaders will be taken from among your ranks. Only remember this: if any Albanian houses are looted, I authorize Captain Popović to shoot those responsible on the spot! Do you agree to all this?"

"We do! Long live the Serbian army!"

Kajafa saluted them, and many returned his salute by throwing their torn, gray forage caps into the air.

Bogdan felt happy among these soldiers, as if a great burden had been lifted from him. He made sure they carried out important orders, but to win their affection he occasionally turned a blind eye to discipline. Never had he wanted people's affection so much! Suddenly his war service had meaning. The men responded in their own fashion: they fed him roast meat and fresh bread obtained in mysterious ways and offered him tobacco and brandy. He watched them with curiosity, wondering which of them were murderers, and why they had committed their crimes, but he never ventured to ask directly. He tried to persuade them that servitude was a state of mind, not just a matter of being behind prison walls. He considered it almost a bit of good luck that he would end his war service with them, whatever its outcome.

Bogdan was startled out of his reflections by the sound of quarreling on the road. Although blows and quarrels were frequent among his soldiers, this noise did not sound like an everyday affair, so he ran out to the road. There, an ox with tall, slim horns had collapsed from fatigue in front of a baggage cart. Bogdan's soldiers had surrounded the animal with their knives and bayonets, and the baggage-train attendant was pointing his rifle at them:

"I'll kill anyone who stabs that creature while he's still alive, you hear me? I'll kill him!"

"We have to give our lives for Prizren and you won't give us even a dead ox!" said one of the soldiers, unhitching the ox. Four other men seized the ox by its feet and dragged it into the ditch.

"Don't stab him while he's alive, or I'll kill you!"

"Leave the ox alone! Get off the road! Back to your duties!" cried Bogdan, saddened by the look of the baggage-train man and angered by his soldiers. It was the first time he had shouted at them.

"I'd slaughter him if he was my father!" cried the soldier who had unhitched the ox and was now holding it by the horns. He plunged his bayonet into the animal's back.

The baggage-train man fired his rifle, and the soldier toppled next to the animal. Bogdan drew his saber and hit the soldiers who were cutting chunks of meat from the ox. One of them turned around and hissed: "Damn you, you fucking sergeant! You'll hit the dust before dark!" and went on cutting up the ox.

Bogdan stepped back to the side of the ditch and put away his saber. He stood there dumbfounded while the remaining members of the platoon stripped the ox to the bone. Only its bloody skeleton, the head, the tail, and the feet remained.

The soldiers withdrew into the wood with the meat. All but one, who helped the baggage-train man to bandage the wounded soldier with a piece of his shirt. The baggage-train man then loaded the murderer of his ox onto the cart, picked up the yoke, and, alongside the surviving ox, pulled the cart toward Prizren.

Bogdan stood motionless above the stripped carcass, staring at the ox's wide-open, bleary eyes. He looked on death but was not afraid. All he felt was revulsion. People had made him like that. Later, when snickers greeted his firm refusal of a piece of roasted ox meat, he felt ashamed. Ashamed because he understood so little.

In the dining room of the metropolitan's residence in Prizren, the government and the High Command were assembled at a long table for their last conference on Serbian territory. As they waited for Colonel Pavlović to come back from Vojvoda Putnik, the ministers stared at the military maps and calculated the distances which would have to be traversed. Prince Alexander read for the third time a report from Vojvoda Mišić about the critical state of the First Army, while Nikola Pašić stood by the window and looked at the town, which was seething with refugees and soldiers. He gazed at the mosque of Sinan Pasha, constructed from the ruins of the Church of the Holy Archangel, which Czar Dušan had built. On this patch of earth, he thought, the loss of freedom meant the loss of everything. In order to survive under the conqueror, people accepted his religion and his God, and through this change they lost their identity and their past. They had become something different. Was a transfer of faith about to begin again? His eyes fixed on the high minaret; he felt wonder and admiration for this feat of engineering.

Colonel Pavlović came in and stood at attention before the Commander in Chief: "Your highness, General Bojović has not succeeded in forcing a way through Kačanik; he has to retreat. Our effort to join up with the Allied troops in Macedonia has failed. The Austrians have entered Priština. The Bulgarians are advancing on Prizren."

Alexander asked Pavlović to sit at the head of the table. Pašić returned to the table and sat on the right of the Regent, who said despondently: "We have one course of action left."

Pašić: "There are three possibilities, Your Highness. I suggest we examine them all. First, capitulation. Yes, gentlemen, surrender. The second possibility is to continue fighting on Kossovo to the last man. The third is to retreat to the coast by way of Albania and Montenegro to join the Allies there, provided the Montenegrins cover our withdrawal."

Alexander: "Neither capitulation nor fighting to the last man can be considered. We must fight until we win. I have no faith in the Montenegrin chiefs, but I have faith in the Montenegrin army."

Pašić: "Let's weigh our options carefully—we must find the best way leading from this crossroads."

Pavlović: "Vojvoda Putnik has authorized me to inform you that the struggle on Kossovo cannot be carried on any longer. We have neither food nor ammunition. Our men have lost hope that the country can be saved. Our officers are wavering. They're all disappointed in the Allies. We have lost this war not only on the battlefield."

Pašić: "Let those who come after us decide who's to blame for the position we're in now, Colonel."

First minister: "I don't agree, Prime Minister. Right here and now it must be clearly stated that Serbia has collapsed because of our allies' failure to fulfill their promises."

Alexander: "I demand that our report of this meeting to the army and the people begin with that statement. And let the world know it, too!"

First minister: "You're right, Your Highness. I propose that a memorandum be sent to all the Allied governments, stating all the facts we've concealed from the army and the people."

Pavlović: "Allow me to remind you, gentlemen, that all our telegraph and telephone lines have been cut. Since last night the world can hear only what's being said in Vienna and Berlin."

Pašić: "Gentlemen, I warn you once again not to saw off the branch on which we are standing. It's near the breaking point."

Alexander: "How can we avoid breaking it?"

Pašić: "I'm in favor of a memorandum to the Allies. But we should tell them that we've done our duty as an ally, so at this critical time we expect help from them, help which is also in their interest. Before we do this, permit me, Your Highness, to examine some further options open to us. In a situation such as this, any nation ought to capitulate.

We have a moral right to do so in the eyes of our people and our allies."

Third minister: "Capitulation wouldn't be dishonorable. It's the logical outcome of this kind of war. But, Prime Minister—"

Pašić: "There is no 'but'! Heroes, too, surrender to the victor. The weaker have always capitulated to the stronger."

Fourth minister: "Surrender doesn't mean the end of the struggle. It can be the postponement of the struggle, and preparation for a new struggle."

Fifth minister: "Unfortunately, our capitulation wouldn't only mean losing this war. We'd also have lost all the wars we've fought since 1804 for the liberation and unification of the Serbian people."

Alexander: "Surrender, gentlemen, is surrender! As Commander in Chief of the Serbian army, I refuse to discuss it!"

Pavlović: "Your Highness, Vojvoda Putnik has authorized me to inform you that he won't sign any capitulation of the Serbian army."

Pašić: "Your Highness, permit me to finish. Although, as I've said, there are strong and morally justifiable reasons for capitulation, I maintain we should not capitulate, and for one reason only: although we have been driven out of our territory, I'm firmly convinced that we can win this war. We stand before the greatest victory in our history. It's far away, but I see it clearly." He banged the floor with his cane.

A prolonged silence followed.

Aleksa Dačić was riding with Gojko Kninjanin in an empty munitions cart and dozing. He was startled by a volley of rifle fire: in a Turkish cemetery by the road a squad of soldiers was firing at a dozen men who were tied up, while Austrian prisoners looked on from a barracks across the road.

"What's going on here, Gojko?"

"They're shooting deserters, Aleksa."

"They're still doing that, for God's sake?"

Another volley: the rest of the deserters fell among the tombstones.

"But why are those fucking officers doing that in a Turkish cemetery?"

"Never mind the Turkish cemetery. Why do it in front of the Fritzies?"

"What's this place, mister?" Aleksa asked a civilian with an umbrella and a suitcase, who looked at him in surprise. Two more rifles fired. "Where are we, mister?"

"This is Prizren."

Peering through the wet snow, Aleksa Dačić caught sight of rows of houses, minarets, church domes, and bell towers: "Was this Czar Dušan's capital?" he cried.

"Yes."

The squad which had shot the deserters was lining up in a ditch by the cemetery.

"And how far is it from here to the Albanian frontier?"

"About fifteen kilometers."

"Just two hours' walk, but into hell! Did you hear that, Gojko? We've made it right to the edge!" He jumped down into the mud and snow and went up to the battery commander: "May I have a word with you, sir?"

"What do you want, Dačić?"

"If it's not a military secret, I'd like to know where we're going."

"First to Prizren. Where after that is a military secret."

"I understand, sir." He saluted, though his curiosity wasn't satisfied. He wanted to know where they would flee when they reached the Albanian frontier. Yesterday the Bulgarians had pulverized them on Stari Kačanik, destroying two guns from their battery. God only knew how his own gun had survived. It had been chewed up by shrapnel, but he and Gojko hadn't withdrawn until its last shell had been fired. Afterward, feeling sad, he had seen that terrible General Bojović box the ears of a major in front of soldiers herded in a hollow, scolding him for retreating without orders. When a general boxes a major's ears as if he was a groom, thought Aleksa, everything is finished! But then he concluded: When a general dares to thrash a major like an ox in a cabbage patch, the Serbian army can still fight and it's not all over yet. At the next stopping place he looked through Ivan Katić's notebook, as he had many times since leaving Niš: "Who can be a coward and flee from Suvobor while Aleksa Dačić and Sava Marić are fighting?" Ivan had written. And on another page: "I'd have run away from the trenches last night if I weren't in the platoon with my grandfather's servant, Aleksa Dačić. A real man and a hero. Not another like him in the regiment!" Damn him! Why did he have to write that in his fucking notebook? His grandfather's servant, indeed— what had that got to do with it?

Shouts and cries reverberated from Prizren, sounding like a fair being attacked by thieves.

"Gojko, let's clean and oil our gun. I don't want him to go through Prizren filthy. Cvetko, take a rag and clean the axle and the spokes of the wheels."

After they had cleaned and polished the gun, Aleksa jumped down into a nearby courtyard and gathered an armful of branches and frozen chrysanthemums to decorate the gun and the horses that were pulling it. He even stuck a few flowers in his own cap, Gojko's and Cvetko's. They looked fit for a wedding. When the command was given to move off, they climbed onto the gun carriage, and, as Lieutenant Smiljanić smiled in approval, set off through Prizren. In the crammed streets every living creature moved aside to let the festive horses, gun, and soldiers pass. The men watched in awe, the women sobbed. The clattering of the gun carriage and the tramping of the horses on the cobbles were drowned by a cry: "Long live the Serbian army!"

Aleksa and Gojko rode proudly, looking straight ahead.

"Look at those mosques! Where do they come from?"

"I don't know," said Aleksa, basking in the townspeople's reception. "Prizren was the capital of our great Czar Dušan."

"Aleksa! Aleksa!" It was Adam, to Aleksa's delight.

Pašić: "For a nation, death with honor doesn't exist, gentlemen. Let's leave such chivalry to nobles and poets."

First minister: "Can Mr. Pavlović tell us whether Vojvoda Putnik believes that our run-down army can traverse the gorges of Albania and reach the coast? What will we do if the Montenegrins attack us from the rear?"

Colonel Pavlović: "Foreseeing the outcome of the battle of Kačanik, the High Command two days ago issued instructions to our armies about their retreat toward the Adriatic Sea. We've informed the Montenegrin High Command of this. That's all we can do."

Alexander: "I'm in complete agreement with Vojvoda Putnik's analysis. We must do our utmost. But we have no reason to expect that the Montenegrins will do their duty."

Second minister: "We must realize all the consequences of this decision, Your Highness. It will be the first time in modern history that a nation's government, Assembly, High Command, king, armed forces, children, and the best of its citizens have all gone into exile together."

Third minister: "And with the sacred bones of Stephen the First, our first book, and other sacred objects."

Second minister: "Who can be sure that the Lord will give us a Moses to bring us back to our country? Dare we believe in miracles?"

Pašić: "If we put our faith in miracles alone, Serbia will lose the war."

Second minister: "What will happen, Prime Minister, if the Allies don't receive us on the coast?"

Pašić: "The Allies must receive us. There'll be boats waiting for us with food, clothing, and equipment. Their ambassadors have guaranteed this."

Second minister: "Let's believe, if we must! There's no alternative. But will only a third of our army reach the sea? How many will freeze to death in the snow, die of hunger, or be killed by the Albanians?"

Pašić: "Yesterday Esad Pasha sent me a second message saying we'd be received as friends on his territory. I'm sure he'll keep his word."

Second minister: "I'll follow you, Prime Minister, but with a heavy heart. Our army will face great suffering. As for the people, can you hear them? They're waiting for our decision."

Pašić: "If one regiment reaches the Allies, if only one platoon gets there, Serbia will be saved. She'll continue to exist and will achieve her goal. And the Hapsburg Empire will be destroyed. I'll summon the Allied ambassadors immediately and inform them of our final decision."

On the way out of Prizren the battery halted. Aleksa jumped off the gun carriage and gave Adam a hug. Adam's face brightened and he told Aleksa of his brief visit to Prerovo. Aleksa interrupted him: Did you see Jelka?"

"Yes, I did. Her stomach's right up to her teeth. Your mother says the child will be born about Christmas."

"Well, it doesn't matter when, so long as she has a child. How many from our village have deserted?"

While Adam was counting, Aleksa cut him short: "The cowards!"

"You're right," said Adam. "They say we're going to retreat to Albania."

"In this cold weather and with nothing to eat?" Aleksa asked, bewildered. "But," he added quickly, "I wouldn't like to be taken prisoner!"

"Neither would I. But if we die of hunger or freeze in the Albanian wilderness, we haven't accomplished anything."

"True enough, Adam. But if we must, we must." He took a flask of brandy from his knapsack and handed it to Adam. "Too bad the sea's all water."

"Salt water, too. Not even a mad dog would drink it."

They drank their brandy in silence.

"If we must, damn it, then . . ." Their eyes met; Aleksa smiled faintly. "Then, Adam, we *must.*"

"That's what I think, Aleksa."

Their conversation was interrupted by shots nearby: Gojko and Cvetko, the shell loader, were shooting at a chicken. They missed and it scurried through an apple orchard.

"Don't shoot it! It's an Albanian chicken!" shouted the lieutenant.

But the chicken was already killed, and Aleksa smiled.

"This is a terible defeat! I don't know what to do. I don't dare be brave and honorable any more, Bora."

"Tričko, you know I could never stand high-sounding phrases about honor and heroism."

"But I'm not talking in high-sounding phrases. You'll lose your freedom, but you'll still be a Serb. Everything I've been fighting for is collapsing. Macedonia will become part of Bulgaria and I'll be a Bulgarian."

"Who knows what I'll be? We're at the limit, Tričko, and not only of our country. The limit of our own personal resources. Who knows what tomorrow will bring."

"Nothing but death."

"I feel there's something beyond death. Something I don't know and can't imagine."

"You're talking nonsense, Jackpot! What's happening now is no longer war."

"No, it certainly isn't. It's a kind of collapse that makes you disgusted—with your fellow men most of all. Let's get away from here. My teeth are chattering."

They walked into a church. "Listen, Tričko, I've had it with national ideals. I won't go to Albania and freeze to death, not for any Greater Serbia or Yugoslavia. My military oath is no longer binding. I could dress up tonight as a Moslem woman and wait for the occupying forces."

"Why don't you?"

"Because I'd be disgusted with myself. There's a certain boundary one should never cross."

"That's what I think, too. You know, Bora, the minute the Bulgarians enter Bitolj, they'll kill my father and brother. And who knows what'll happen to my mother and sisters. Our local Bulgarophiles will point out our house to the first soldier they see in Ferdinand's army."

"If you think you can save them, surrender."

"After a year of fighting for Serbia, after Suvobor and Belgrade, how can I surrender?"

Bora saw the tears in Tričko's eyes and felt sorry for him. "When I have to give sensible advice, I'm a fool, Tričko."

"What would you do if you were in my shoes?" Tričko pleaded, taking hold of Bora's overcoat. They could feel each other's breath. Bora's lips and chin were trembling.

"I don't know, Tričko. I really don't know."

"But you must tell me, one way or the other!"

"It's getting dark. I must be off. Dušanka is waiting for me. If you don't leave for Peć this evening—if you stay in Prizren, that is—come see us. We'll be waiting for you."

Bora found Dušanka under the eaves of the inn, leaning against the wall. For the first time she didn't greet him with a smile. "What happened? Where were you?"

"I've been with Tričko. He's in an agony of doubt and I don't know how to advise him."

Dušanka burst into tears.

"What's the matter?" He took her hands. Her whole body was trembling. He had never seen her like this. "What happened? Tell me!"

"I can't go with you."

"Why not?"

"I must stay with the wounded. Those are my orders. Doctor Sergeev isn't being taken to Peć—he knows it now. He didn't say anything, but his eyes were full of tears. I feel ashamed just looking at him. The first time the Austrians took Valjevo, he wouldn't leave our wounded. Milena and I stayed with him. And now we're leaving him."

"Calm down, you're not to blame. There's nothing you can do to help him. Circumstances were different then."

"We mustn't let him die alone, or be killed by the Bulgarians."

"The Bulgarians won't kill a Russian."

"Then the Germans will."

"But how could you carry a man that sick through the Albanian gorges?"

"He came to Serbia out of sheer goodness, Bora. It wouldn't be right —it would be inhuman—for us to leave him. I can't do it."

Bora let go of her hands and leaned dejectedly against the wall beside her: if she stayed behind, how could he go? Where now was that boundary he wouldn't cross? It was snowing heavily.

Dušanka looked at him and tried to understand what he was feeling. They still had this last night. She turned to go in to attend to the wounded, but looked back to assure herself that Bora was still standing there. She wasn't smiling. He could see nothing, make no decision until she spoke: "Come on, Bora, let's go."

"Where to? It's getting dark."

"Never mind that. I told Sergeev I won't be back till dawn."

Her eyes made him tremble. He couldn't go to Albania without her. There was the boundary.

She took his hand and whispered, "I know where we can go."

She led him down the street toward the square: soldiers were throwing packing cases, bits of oxcarts, and military equipment onto huge fires. The two of them crossed the bridge over the Bistrica. Huge fires were everywhere. Government property and private possessions, anything that couldn't be carried by man or beast, was burning. Bora didn't ask Dušanka where they were going. She knew and hurried on.

Just before midnight, with Nikola Pašić and Colonel Živko Pavlović in attendance, Vojvoda Putnik wrote his last instructions to the army commanders:

Complex circumstances force us to retreat across Montenegro and Albania. Our morale and discipline are poor, the men have lost faith in their country. We must explain the purpose of our withdrawal to the soldiers, and convince them of the need for it.

Capitulation would be the worst possible solution. It would mean the loss of the State. Our allies would abandon us. Our one hope is withdrawal to the Adriatic coast. There our army will be reorganized. Our allies will supply us with food, clothing, and weapons. The State will continue to exist, albeit on foreign soil, as long as there is there a Ruler, a Government, and an Army. The readiness of the Allies to support us to the end, and their inexhaustible strength, will break our common enemy, and our country will once more be free.

You must convince our soldiers that this withdrawal is designed to save the State, and that our salvation lies in the steadfastness and patience of us all, in our willingness to sacrifice, in our faith in the ultimate success of our allies.

He stopped writing and turned to the wall. What should his last sentence be? He wanted to turn out the lights, send Pašić and Pavlović away, and think it out alone. It needn't be about victory. There was far too much about the State and victory and faith in others. These were Pašić's ideas, a politician's conceptions of war and history. He should say something about the fate of man and nations on this frozen earth. Or should he simply write: Protect your health! A sick man has no need of freedom or fatherland. No, Živojin Mišić would laugh at him. In a similar situation the ancient Greeks had said, "It isn't ramparts that make a town, but people," and then had retreated to the high seas. He ought to have said: "The country isn't the state's territory, the country is freedom."

"Should I call the doctor, sir?"

Putnik looked sternly at his assistant and added the last sentence: *We must persevere to the end.*

"You add the date and the hour, Colonel," he said, handing the paper to his assistant.

"Vojvoda," said Pašić, "allow Colonel Pavlović to add the following: 'We will destroy the Austro-Hungarian Empire, for centuries the deadly foe of the Slavs, just as we destroyed the Ottoman Empire.' Just like that. Write it down."

Putnik didn't object; it no longer mattered to him. When Pavlović left the room, he turned to Pašić and said: "You're now a prime minister without a state, and I'll soon be a commander without an army. We've worked together so many years, Mr. Pašić; everybody in Serbia knows you except me."

"Does that surprise you, Vojvoda?"

"I guess not. Still, I'd like to know which evil Nikola Pašić hates the most."

"It depends. But I shrink most from braggarts and ambitious men. They're dangerous in their weakness."

"You're right!" said Putnik, suddenly livening up. "I've laughed at such men mercilessly—they find laughter hard to take. What have you been most afraid of, Mr. Pašić?"

"Of men who kill for an idea. No good can come of killing a fellow man just because he thinks differently."

Putnik wondered if Pašić had given him a sincere answer, this man whose sincerity had been doubted by the whole nation, but who now commanded belief more than anyone. He was startled by a question from Pašić:

'What evil do you hate most, Vojvoda?"

"There's no greater evil than cruelty. And perhaps what I've most feared are people who don't think of their own death."

"Good night, Vojvoda," said Pašić thoughtfully. "I'll wait for you tomorrow evening at Ljum-Kula."

Putnik was alone. He drank up the elderflower tea brought by his orderly. He told the orderly to go to bed immediately and rest up for the long journey, but then called him back and asked for a jug of hot water, a bowl, and some soap. He tried to wash his hands himself, but he was so weary that the orderly had to do it for him. He then asked him to turn up the wicks in the lamps—he wanted as much light as possible. These last few nights in his country were his very last; he wouldn't return as a victor. He wanted to enjoy the first comfortable bed he had had since Kragajevac. He looked with satisfaction around the warm, clean room, furnished with cushions, and tapestries, and permeated with a light, feminine fragrance. This agreeable atmosphere fortified him and gave him a sense of his own personal dignity.

He wanted to reflect on some of his happy times—his promotion to the rank of captain, his betrothal, the births of his children, their school celebrations, his military victories, his women, and those early morning rides through the fields and meadows around Kragajevac. In spite of everything, it would have been good and soldierly for him to mount a horse in the morning, ride slowly through Prizren and then along the Bistrica, speed up to a trot toward the Albanian frontier, and, just before the border, fall off his horse. Ever since the military academy he had believed that falling from a horse at full gallop was the right death for a soldier. But his illness would deprive him of a fine death. Of course it had also freed him from the fear of defeat and, in the eyes of the army and the people, given him an excuse which even those who bore him the greatest ill will had to accept. Twenty years ago, even ten years ago, he wouldn't have dared or wished to issue an order such as the one he had issued tonight. Now he really had no right to be afraid of death; he had outlived that privilege. The time that was left him—the most painful of all—should be as simple as possible. He must become an ordinary man. He didn't want to be carried across Albania on a stretcher. The day before, he had ordered a small sentry box built that would hold one comfortable chair. He would sit on this chair and, unseen, depart from his country, travel across the mountains of Albania to the coast—to the unknown, to the place where he had promised his army they would find hope and safety.

A defeated man is attended by contempt, a victor by envy; both contempt and envy are repulsive, though perhaps envy more so because it's concealed. In a sense, then, he was fortunate: he would die between defeat and victory. He would be glorified without envy or hatred, free of lies and exaggeration. The best death leaves behind confusion and illusions; and the worst leaves behind the truth. There's no creature on this earth who doesn't lose something when the truth about him emerges.

O Lord, forgive me for seeking such consolation.

Behind the rostrum of an empty classroom in the Prizren seminary, King Peter was writing in his diary by candlelight:

A great pile of paper is burning in the courtyard. They say it's old accounts too heavy to be transported. They're really accounts that would confirm theft and misappropriation by the ministers or their relatives, for whom there is no law. Blessed are the thieves. The High Command has received a report that the French are returning to Salonika, fearing an attack from the Greeks. The Russians are still concentrating their forces; there's no hope that they'll attack soon. Perhaps they never will. Serbia should rely on its own resources.

He blew out the candles and sat down in the glow from the embers of two braziers. He was thinking of how, without hurting him, he would tell his son what was on his mind. That unfortunate man was too suspicious of advice. He had laid the burden of the throne on him too early, much too early.

Prince Alexander came in and peered around the empty room. "Are you alone, Father?" he asked gently.

"I've been waiting for you. I want you next to me while the crown is being buried."

Alexander came up to him. "I'm not sure that what you're doing is wise. It'll be a terrible blow to the nation if our enemies discover it."

"You're forcing me into exile, the hardest thing I've ever done in my life. I agreed to it only so I could share the suffering of my people and the army. But I refuse to carry the crown in my backpack. Let it stay in Prizren; let the town that saw our greatest glory now witness our darkest misery."

"Father, I don't like making a theatrical performance out of matters of state, and treating our military defeat like a requiem for Serbia. What's the point of burying the crown on the Albanian frontier?"

"Let it stay on the frontier and keep guard over our enslaved land."

"Where will you bury it?"

"On the ground floor. I've chosen the spot. You can hear the pick-axes. They're breaking up the floor."

"I don't like it!" Alexander paced up and down the empty classroom, striking his left hand with the clenched fist of his right. He frowned at the creaking of the floorboards and stopped in front of his father. "I'm leaving for Ljum-Kula at four in the morning."

"I know. You must rest. It's a long, hard journey. How many soldiers are you taking with you?"

"Twelve cavalrymen from the Guard. And some of Esad Pasha's men will accompany me to Skadar."

"That Albanian is now worth more to us than all our great allies put together. That's what we've been reduced to: seeking friends among enemies. If God grants that you return to our liberated country, you must never forget the kindness and friendship of Esad Pasha. There's one other thing I'd like to say to you. That crown they're digging a hiding place for was made from cannon used in the uprising. It was forged by freedom and should be worn in the service of freedom. You must listen to me. This may be the last time I can advise you. From now on you'll have the advice of only toadies and yes men."

"Whom do you have in mind?"

"Courts have always been full of corrupt men. And you're becoming increasingly fond of them."

"Putnik and that old fox Pašić have been putting crazy ideas into your head again."

"Unfortunately, I have no friends with whom I can share my anxiety about my son. That's a curse inherent in kingship and political authority. People lie to the king and to the government. That's the law of mankind."

"I know people very well. They won't deceive me, Father."

"Unfortunately, Sandra, the best people are farthest from power. You'll neither see nor hear them. He went over to his son and seized his coat sleeve. "With all my heart, I beg you: guard against being vengeful to your opponents. When you dig up the crown that we're burying tonight, defend it not with prison walls and sabers, but with freedom and justice. Please, my son, protect the throne not with the help of valets and policemen, but with the help of men who love truth and justice. Respect your supporters, and respect your opponents even more."

"Who are the opponents that deserve my respect?"

"You'll be the king. Anyone who has any reason to oppose you or is bold enough to do so will deserve your respect. That's the only way you can respect yourself."

"Not likely, Father, not likely! Among us Serbs, when you show respect for someone, he thinks either you're cheating him or you're afraid of him. If I ruled according to your advice, Apis and his band would have my head rolling down the main square in Belgrade."

"That's not so. Our people have been contaminated by power and politics. They're more dangerous to the government as supporters than as opponents. We've been enslaved for a long time, and we find it easiest and feel most secure when we obey and endure."

Alexander strode over to the window. From the dark hills, the Albanians were shooting at the town. Tomorrow, without artillery or equipment, the Serbian army would look like a band of destitute rebels. He turned to his father and said:

"I'm unhappy, Father, because you respect me no more than my enemies do."

"My son, I know you're not bad at heart. But you don't realize that power and the throne make the best people evil and the strongest weak. On a throne a man bends like a blade of grass. Power bends him, and the force he possesses eludes him. Man is weak, he doesn't know where the cracks are, where the rot has set in. He's easily broken. Never have more faith in yourself than in another man."

There was a sound of floorboards breaking, then dull, muffled thuds. Alexander moved away and said bitterly, "People are evil and dangerous!"

"Yes, they are. And heartless and mean and slippery. They're ready to commit any crime or wickedness for personal gain. But a king must not defend himself by fear. You should use force only to defend yourself against praise and lies. There's no grandeur that can't be toppled by lies and glory."

"What you're saying, Father, would be suitable for a speech from the throne on a great national holiday in peacetime. Apis and the Black Hand are spreading the rumor at headquarters that the High Command is to blame for our collapse. And I most of all, as Commander in Chief."

"Maybe they are, my son. People bring their quarrels even to a funeral. Let them!"

"What do you mean—let them? My head is at stake!"

"There's a Brutus behind every throne. He should be neither bribed nor driven away. You must behave in such a way that Brutus will find no sympathizers among those close to you. Brutus never kills alone. He never kills a king, only a tyrant—especially one who rules by humiliating people. The humiliated take the hardest vengeance."

"All right, Father. Since we aren't parting tonight forever, I hope, there'll be opportunities for you to advise me. I must go to bed now."

"Good night. I'll see you off in the morning."

King Peter went downstairs to examine the hiding place for his crown.

Bora and Dušanka lay on a pile of cornstalks in a field outside Prizren. They couldn't tear themselves apart, though it was nearly morning. In reaction to Bora's silence Dušanka kept repeating that he must go with the army, that he mustn't be a deserter.

They heard footsteps and a rustling sound, then the crackling of fire. Leaping to their feet, they rushed forth into the murky dawn. In the fields around Prizren piles of cornstalks had been set alight and were now burning, filling the fog-laden dawn with smoke and flames. Dušanka clung to Bora in terror. A bullet whistled over their heads. They ran between the fires and the piles of embers until they reached the entrance to the town, where Serbian troops were being lined up for the march. The Albanians had set fire to the cornstalks to prevent the Serbian soldiers from using them to feed their oxen and horses.

Bora and Dušanka hurried into the town. In the main square of Prizren, now thronged with soldiers and refugees, they embraced warmly and then separated.

At the entrance to her hospital Dušanka saw two Albanians carrying out wounded men. She threatened them and cried for help, but the wounded said the Albanians had promised to hide them and save them from the Bulgarians and the Germans. She went in to look for Sergeev, but didn't find him in his room. She returned to the empty inn and saw Mitar Slavonac with a large wound in his head, dumped in a corner, dead. She ran after the Albanians who were carrying the wounded men into their courtyard. They told her that about midnight Sergeev had gone outside and hadn't returned. Just before dawn all those able to move had left, and Mitar Slavonac had killed himself. She went back into the inn, and took from Mitar's hand the cap he wanted to have passed on to his son. She stood still on the threshold of the inn for a few moments, unable to weep, then hurried off to look for Bora, feeling both intense pain and joy.

Meanwhile, on the outskirts of Prizren, in the Albanian courtyard where they had spent the night, a battalion of conscripts and young boys from Valjevo was lining up. The battalion commander was crossing off his list the names of those who had deserted in the night, while at the same time carrying out an inspection of clothing and footwear. Under the eaves of the house the priest Božidar was talking to the woman in whose courtyard they were camping. Having completed his inspection, the commanding officer reported to Božidar that nineteen conscripts had fled. Božidar went up to the boys, raised his arms, and said: "Come closer to me, children." Slowly they gathered around him. "We're setting out now for our homes and families, from which we've been separated by the enemy. We're going to our freedom along a steep, narrow road filled with drifting snow—the only road by which we can reach our birthplace and our homes. To arrive there alive and well, we must love each other, we must believe in the Lord God who alone can save us. And remember this, children, we can reach home with all of us together. No one can do it alone. Take hold of one another's hands so the weak can support the strong, and the strong can pull along the weak. When you feel afraid, draw close together and look into one another's eyes. You're all my grandsons now. Call me 'Grandfather.' If you need something, ask me for it. If you're sick or in pain, complain to me. If you're hungry, ask me for bread. If you can't go any farther, take hold of my cloak. Would you like me to walk in front of you or behind you?"

"In the middle, Grandfather! In the middle!"

"Very well, children. Now, Captain, you do your duty."

The battalion commander lined the boys up in double ranks. Their Albanian host stood at the gate with a basket of corn, and his son, the same age as the boys from Valjevo, brought two baskets of red apples. As they filed out the gate each boy took an apple, but only a few took an ear of corn.

Before he set out, King Peter examined his case in which Zdravko had packed two changes of underwear, two pairs of socks, and a few small items he couldn't do without. In front of the seminary his adjutant reported that the horses reserved for his baggage train had been sent by mistake to Peć that morning. The King was angry and went into the church to pray. Afterward he set off on foot with his adjutant and Zdravko through the empty town. The shops and houses were locked and bolted. Standing behind their counters, the Albanians watched him with curiosity, while the local Serbs peered through the shutters and wept. The King was followed at a suitable distance by a crowd of beggars and a dozen wounded men on crutches. At the other end of the town the King gave the beggars some money, then climbed into an oxcart and proceeded slowly toward the Albanian frontier.

At infrequent intervals the sound of muffled shots echoed through

Prizren—the last shots fired by the Serbs—as the wounded committed suicide.

In Prizren their driver ran away, so Vukašin and Olga Katić set off for Peć in a hired oxcart with a priest from Srem and his four children. They decided to go to Peć in an oxcart because Vukašin was still unwilling to use his government connections to obtain horses and a military escort through Albania, as many of his Opposition colleagues had done. Also, Olga was afraid to cross over into Albania with Života, who was sick. For her, going to Peć was a life-saving solution, albeit temporary.

Just beyond Djakovica, however, they were ambushed by Albanians. The priest traveling with them was killed before the eyes of his children. The Albanians took their oxen, seized their possessions, and removed Vukašin's coat and boots. Vukašin would have hurled himself at the brigands rather than have his boots removed at gunpoint, had it not been for Olga's protests. He felt the responsibility for Olga and this child who wasn't his own to be a heavy burden. He couldn't contain himself: "Do you realize what you've done by leaving Prerovo?"

Olga's lips trembled, but her eyes, though astonished, were dry. The priest's children fell on their father's body, crying uncontrollably. Then an artillery battery came along and opened fire on the robbers, who fled. The soldiers removed the dead priest from the road and loaded the children onto their gun carriage. Olga was deafened by their screams. She and Vukašin followed the gun on foot. Vukašin carried Života, striding through the mud and snow, feeling much more humiliated than frightened. Olga, rigid and speechless, walked behind him carrying the basket and some milk for the baby.

At Metohija, night fell and the frost clamped down. Just beyond Dečani the gunners settled them in a deserted inn which soon filled up with refugees. Olga and Vukašin forced their way into a corner and stayed there, hemmed in by strangers whose faces they couldn't see in the darkness. All night long refugees kept arriving at the inn, the one dry place by the road; they fought each other for a spot under the eaves or on the threshold. Olga and Vukašin were not so much troubled by physical discomfort as by the presence of the strange people around them. Vukašin was angry at himself for his inability to accept as brothers those who shared his hardships. What would he gain from this ordeal—he who had never loved these people as a Christian, but who had always been ready to struggle and sacrifice for them? Olga held Života in her lap, her whole body wrapped around him. She felt that he was now hers, the child of her womb. Until they reached Prizren this child had been a burden, and a reproach for having left Milena; but now, among these strange and dangerous people, the child was the only warm thing in the night, the one good thing in the world, incapable of threatening anyone, of doing any harm. His helplessness gave her a feeling of protection, a sense of security which she had lost on seeing Vukašin at the mercy of the robbers. Because Života was asleep, she felt no need to close her eyes; because of the warmth of his tiny body, she didn't feel cold.

In front of the inn the imploring cries of men and women never ceased: "Have pity on us! Have mercy, brothers! You've been in a warm, dry place since last night. Give us a chance!" No one moved.

"Do you hear that, Olga?" Vukašin whispered. "No one can do any good any more without endangering his own life. You and I will be forced to do wrong."

"Yes, I know. Let's not go to Albania. I'm afraid of that country."

"So am I. But I can't surrender."

She said nothing. He rubbed her hands and feet to warm them.

At dawn they left the inn; it was a frosty morning. An Albanian boy sold Vukašin a pair of artilleryman's boots for one ducat; Vukašin refused to think of how the boy had come by them. Carrying Života, he hurried toward Peć, where he hoped to find Mišić, who might help him get horses for his journey to Albania. He would have to ask him; he had no alternative.

A blue cloud of smoke hung over Peć as if the town, their last hope of deliverance, had been burned to the ground. They forced their way through ragged throngs of refugees and soldiers, through the market where they bought some apples, a slice of pumpkin, and some chestnuts. Then the search began for a room, a bed, any place where they could light a fire, but everything was taken. The local people directed them to the monastery, but the guesthouses and courtyards of the monastery were crammed with refugees. The church too was full of people who had come for a prayer service over the relics of Stephen the First. Drawn toward the narthex by the hundreds of candles and intoxicated by the warm, thick smell of wax and incense, they pressed themselves against the portal. The sound of muted incantation echoed from the church:

> Better in noble deeds to meet our death
> Than live a life besmirched by shame;

Better to die in battle from the sword than
Yield to our enemies.
Thou drivest us out;
Thou killest us and feelest no pity.
Thou hast made us outcasts in the midst of these people.
Fear and the pit have come upon us,
Wastelands and ruin lie before us,
Already our eyes are worn,
Looking in vain for help that does not come;
We have waited for a people that cannot deliver us,
Our last days draw near,
Soon they will be over,
Our end is at hand.

Vukašin pulled Olga away from the portal, then asked a monk if there was a place for them to rest; he directed them to the stables. From the veranda of the guesthouse Auguste Boppe, the French ambassador, called out to Vukašin and led him into a warm room he was sharing with his secretary and a doctor from the French medical mission. Olga burst into tears of gratitude.

"I must tell you, Monsieur Katić," said Boppe, "that after what I've witnessed in Dečani and here in this monastery, I've come at last to understand you Serbs. You won't lost this war, because you're waging it with your spirit. There's something of eternity in your spirit. You'll outlive defeat!"

Vukašin found Boppe's words both soothing and unsettling.

"The exodus in our time," the French ambassador continued, "this fantastic decision to leave your country in the cause of freedom, was made by Pašić, the most practical politician in Europe, and by Putnik, a classic example of a cautious and sensible military leader!"

Vojvoda Mišić received the order for the retreat to the coast by way of Albania and Montenegro as a crazy product of Pašić's politics and Putnik's strategy. He couldn't agree to the final annihilation of the Serbian army—he couldn't. out of a strong sense of personal responsibility. But driven back into Peć, with his army reduced by a third and his soldiers hungry, naked, and barefoot, how could he pursue his own vision and avoid this suicidal move in which there was no heroism or honor?

He shut himself up in the guest room of the house in which the army staff was accommodated. His entire family was there, too, which made him feel so guilty that he refused to eat or sleep with them. Dragutin lit a fire in the stove and brought him some tea and hard-tack. The night before, he had brought him a basket of the best Metohija apples. Mišić told Colonel Hadžić to report only on the Montenegrin front and on changes in the present situation. But the enemy was advancing rapidly, the artillery had been booming since dawn; time was rushing by, making it more and more difficult to change Putnik's decision. He stood by the window and watched the blue columns of smoke rising to the snow-covered slopes of the Prokletije Mountains.

Nevertheless, he had summoned the army commanders who were withdrawing through Peć, to try to persuade them not to carry out the High Command's last order. While he waited for them, his adjutant announced Vukašin Katić. Mišić was reluctant to see this friend who very likely approved of the army's exile. He resented Vukašin's ability to defend the most dangerous ideas by powerful arguments. He decided not to see him until the following morning, by which time he'd have made all his decisions. Vojvoda Stepa Stepanović, General Pavle-Jurišić-Šturm, and General Mihajlo Živković came in. They greeted each other solemnly and took their seats.

Mišić began immediately: "I've called you here so we can share our thoughts regarding our next move. The government and the High Command have fled to Albania. The four of us, along with our absent colleagues Bojović and Gojković, are responsible for what remains of our army and people."

"We're responsible," said Stepanović, "only to the extent we're authorized by law and the High Command."

"Stepa, the State has collapsed along with its laws, and the High Command is outside the country. Now all responsibility is ours. We've been retreating toward our allies who promised to help us, but there's no sign of them. It's obvious to every Serbian shepherd that the Allies have been playing games with us, that they've betrayed us! And yet our High Command is sending us off across Albania to the Adriatic, in hopes the Allies will be waiting for us! Only feeble-minded and unscrupulous persons could issue such an order, and only despairing men and cowards could carry it out!"

"If you go on like this, Mišić," said Stepanović, "I'll be forced to walk out. This is the army headquarters, not a tavern!"

"The situation is desperate," said Šturm. "We've lost contact with the High Command, and our communications are poor even with our own troops. It's extremely important, gentlemen, that communications among the four of us not be disrupted. As regards our salvation, there's no counsel on which we can rely."

"Tell us why you've summoned us, Mišić," said Stepanović.

"In the first place, so we can agree about our situation. I'll list the facts; repudiate them if you can. The morale of our army is collapsing. We've had large-scale desertions—regiments have been reduced to battalions. We have food for men and animals, if we stretch it out, for four to five days, but our march to the coast will take eight or ten. In the mountains of Albania we can't obtain food even by force from the poverty-stricken inhabitants, who hate us and will rob us and murder us."

"That's true," said Živković and Šturm.

"We'll get no food in Montenegro, we'll starve. Our soldiers are in rags. Exhausted by hard fighting and long marches, they'll die of cold in the mountains of Albania and Montenegro. And the Albanians will be lying in wait."

"That worries me, too," said Živković.

"Before we set out into this trackless wasteland, we must destroy all our artillery, baggage trains, and draft animals, all our equipment except rifles and cartridge belts. We'll be reduced to beggars! Are these facts, or are they not?"

Šturm and Živković nodded. Stepanović frowned.

"Vojvoda Putnik," continued Mišić, "has ordered us to persuade our troops to have faith in the Allies."

"And to persevere to the end!" said Stepanović. "As befits the leaders of the Serbian army!"

"For what reason, Stepa, should we persevere in this deception? How can we believe now that the Allies will be waiting for us at the coast when all autumn they've been telling us, 'Hold on for a few more days, help is on the way, victory is yours'? That, gentlemen, meant one thing only: Serbs, fight to the last man!"

Mišić's voice cracked; he was trembling.

Stepanović broke the silence: "All that is true, but it isn't the whole truth. If the Allies hadn't given us weapons and a war loan, we'd have given up last autumn. If we hadn't had allies, Austria-Hungary would have crushed us long ago. Perhaps they can't help us because they've suffered heavy defeats on every front. Our suffering hasn't been caused by the deception of the Allies, but by their weakness, gentlemen. But it's by no means certain who'll win this war."

"Then," said Mišić, "it's imperative that we not destroy what's left of the army in vain. As for the powerlessness of the Allies to help, that, Stepa, is your pitiful naiveté. The collapse of Serbia and the loss of the Balkans reveal not the Allies' military weakness, but their strategic stupidity. They've underrated us and sacrificed us!"

Stepanović interrupted him: "What do you propose we do now?"

"Gather our troops, give them a few days' rest, then attack in the direction of Mitrovica or Skoplje." All three of them looked at him in amazement. "Yes, gentlemen, we have only two options: carry out the suicidal order of the High Command, or launch an offensive! If we attempt to save ourselves, we might succeed."

Again Stepanović interrupted him: "What if we don't?"

"If we don't succeed, at least we'll have done all that we could."

"Do you really believe our army capable of an offensive?" asked Živković.

"I know our prospects are meager, but they do exist. If we make this move, that is. Didn't we work a miracle last year? There's still the strength to fight in our army!"

"There can be no thought of an offensive with the army in its present condition," said Šturm. "That would be a vain and heartless sacrifice."

"Very well, but do you really believe the Allies will be waiting for us on the Albanian coast? What will happen to us if they're not there?"

"I too doubt we'll get help from the Allies," said Živković. "Yet that's less of a risk than the offensive you propose."

Stepanović was agitated: "I'd like to end this unnecessary discussion. There is not a single valid condition for the offensive proposed by Mišić. It would be a desperate adventure in which we'd sacrifice the army and destroy all chances of continuing the war and liberating our country. An army can survive every defeat, Mišić, but it can't survive failure to carry out the orders of the High Command. Especially this order, which you can oppose only by violating your oath!"

There was a long silence. Mišić was alone, all was lost.

Stepanović rose and said: "Let's eat, then get back to work. The orders of the High Command must be carried out."

Distressed and humiliated, Mišić did not say good-by to them. He remained sitting at the table. Colonel Hadžić came in, but Mišić waved him away. He walked across the room filled with packing cases belonging to the staff. He stopped by the window and looked at the Peć cathedral: from here, two centuries ago, Patriarch Arsenije Čarnojević had led the Serbs into exile in flight from the Turks—led them northward, across the Sava and the Danube, on a journey from which they never returned. Weren't the Serbs now departing into exile, this time southward toward the sea, never again to return? Why not admit defeat and seek peace? Remain in bondage, but in one's own land, then again raise a rebellion and make a bid for freedom? What were state laws, military oaths, and national honor in face of survival? What was it that still prevented him from following his own instincts?

Colonel Hadžić put two telegrams from Cetinje on the table. Mišić didn't look at them. He walked up and down the room, smoking and listening to the bells of the cathedral, still suffering from his defeat at the hands of the army commanders. Tomorrow morning he would leave Peć for Skadar by way of Podgorica, where his career as vojvoda would come to an end. Hadžić came in again:

"Have you read the telegrams, sir?"

Mišić picked them up: the Serbian representative at the Montenegrin High Command had sent the text of an official German communiqué, stating that Germany had achieved her objectives in the war with Serbia and would suspend further operations against her. The second telegram, from Lyons, announced the withdrawal of the German forces from Serbia to the middle Danube.

"Now for an offensive!" cried Mišić excitedly, slapping Hadžić on the back.

With a smile Hadžić handed him two reports from the divisions, conveying intelligence to the effect that Austria-Hungary would withdraw its troops from Serbia and transfer them to the Russian front, where a major Russian offensive was imminent.

"Surely this is as good a time as any for an offensive, Hadžić!" cried Mišić again, and took a bite of an apple. He immediately summoned the army commanders. They arrived looking gloomy and suspicious, and he, calm and confident, handed them the telegrams and reports.

Stepanović spoke first: "This certainly indicates a change in the military situation. But we have to know for sure."

"Let's send out cavalry patrols deep into the enemy's rear to investigate their movements," suggested Šturm.

"I agree," said Stepanović quietly.

"We should immediately cease carrying out the High Command's order to abandon our territory," Mišić said firmly, "and instead order the division staffs to prepare their troops for an offensive." He was surprised at the ease with which the commanders accepted his proposal. The fact that even Stepanović agreed was the strongest proof he was on the right track.

In the anteroom Dragutin crouched beside the packing cases, put his ear to the keyhole, and listened to the army commanders talking in low voices. There was a lot he couldn't catch, but he understood clearly that they wouldn't go to Albania, and that the Serbian army would launch an offensive. He ran down the stairs into the courtyard to announce the offensive to the soldiers and drank a flask of brandy with them to celebrate; then he ran off through Peć to spread the unexpected, life-saving news: "Brothers and sisters, no need to be afraid any more! We're not going to Albania! Vojvoda Mišić is launching an offensive!"

"Long live Vojvoda Mišić, the man who smashed Potiorek on Suvobor! Anybody got some brandy? I'll give ten dinars for a bottle! Oil your guns, gunners! We're starting an offensive! I'm from the First Army headquarters. May I never see my children if I'm lying!"

"You hear that, Aleksa?"

"So I do! Our gun is oiled already. Folks, haven't I told you that even God Almighty can't do anything with the Serbs? Shoot at the sky, not at Prokletije! Where's your flute, Živorad? If we have to die, at least we'll do it in style!"

"Folks, you needn't buy horses and donkeys. No need to sell all your property. We're not going to Albania! The generals have ordered an offensive! You women and children get ready to go home!"

"Who's that idiot? Vojvoda Mišić's adjutant, sir. The Russians have reached Budapest and they've captured Varna! The French and English have retaken Skoplje! The Bulgarians are fleeing! Have you really had mercy on us, O God?"

"Go on, folks, hug and kiss each other! We'll be home by Christmas!"

"What's that man saying? He's a major from Mišić's staff! He knows for sure that the prisoners of war have arrived! Where are they? In the headquarters courtyard. Several hundred of them, and more to come!"

Soldiers and civilians set off toward the courtyard of the First Army headquarters. Only ten prisoners were there. Arguments erupted between those who believed the news about the offensive and those who didn't. All over Peć people burst into song. Soldiers fired in the air from sheer exuberance. Aleksa Dačić led a reel around his gun, to the accompaniment of a flute. People embraced each other; many wept for joy. The renewed faith in salvation was celebrated in Peć until midnight like a military victory.

Late that night Dragutin returned to headquarters and stuck his chest out in front of Mišić: "I've been rejoicing with the people, sir!"

"You're drunk!"

"It's the offensive, sir!"

"Go sleep it off!" said Mišić, smiling. It was the first time he had smiled since Valjevo. He went back to the window and opened it to hear the flutes playing among the fires in Peć. That was how it had been last year, too, before the Suvobor offensive. But suddenly he was afraid and closed the window. He lit the stove, and the fire leaped into flames; he sat beside it and cut a large, red apple in two. He gazed at the dark, shining pits: it was a mighty tree when flowering in the wind and the sun, but then was bent low under its load of fruit. He didn't eat the apple.

Stepanović, Žiković, and Šturm entered his room unannounced. Mišić immediately sensed that something was wrong. Before they had even sat down, Stepanović handed him reports from three divisions: the Bulgarians, together with bands of Albanians, had taken Djakovica and slaughtered the Serbian inhabitants and those soldiers who hadn't withdrawn; the enemy was thirty kilometers from Peć and the Serbian regiments were fleeing in disorder; the plundering of Albanian houses and desertions from the army had assumed massive proportions. Mišić said nothing. He read the last report: "The troops are no longer capable of fighting, least of all in the proposed offensive. They are few in numbers, hungry, and barefoot; the animals are exhausted and incapable of work." He said angrily:

"They're running away. Why should they want to die while retreating to Albania? But if they were ordered to go forward—home—they'd move against the enemy like wildcats!"

"Empty words, Mišić," said Stepanović. "Our situation is deteriorating so rapidly that we dare not delay carrying out the High Command's orders. We've lost two days to no purpose, which means two days' less food for the soldiers and horses. We should immediately destroy the artillery and all the equipment we can't carry. The first thing tomorow morning we'll leave Peć." Šturm and Živković agreed.

Mišić put his head in his hands. Once again he was alone. What could he do alone? He raised his head and said firmly: "I cannot agree to the destruction of my army in Albania."

"How would you agree to see it destroyed?"

"I won't agree, Stepa, to a flight which will end in destruction! I won't finish it off with cold and hunger! I can't tell them the Allies are waiting by the sea! I won't lead them to their deaths with lies!"

"Enough!" said Stepanović. "We know what you don't want to do! Now tell us what you *do* want to do!"

"I want to gather all the troops, join with the Montenegrins, and try to force our way through Sandžak! Or in another direction, toward Skoplje and Salonika, if you're convinced the Allies will be there. I'm in favor of a decisive battle, one way or the other!"

"And if we lose?"

"If we lose, Šturm, we'll ask the enemy for peace!"

"Peace?"

"That would be an honorable peace, Živković, peace for the survival of our people."

"Who authorized you to propose capitulation?" they all shouted.

"*You* favor a shameful capitulation! You're fleeing like cowards from your land! Why don't you throw away your braid?"

Dragutin was crouching by the door, his head pressed against the keyhole. He trembled as he listened to the commanders quarreling and threatening one another. Mišić's wife and sons came running from their room. Officers, orderlies, and sentries filled the passage and staircase of the headquarters. They listened to Stepanović dictating his orders:

"Artillery, gun carriages, and ammunition are to be buried or demolished, but the breeches and sights are to be taken along. All carts and harnesses and all military and medical equipment are to be burned. Healthy draft animals will carry food; tired animals are to be slaughtered."

"That isn't property you've inherited from your father! That's the toil and sweat of the peasants! Who's given you the right to destroy it? Why don't you fire the shells at the enemy, you cowards!"

" 'Cowards'? Take that back!"

"I won't! And you won't get out of here alive, unless you sign a record of this capitulation for your descendants, you bastards!"

Mišić's wife Louisa screamed, his sons took him away to their room, the officers retreated into their offices, and the orderlies hurried down the stairs, but Dragutin remained by the door. Someone had turned off the light in the hallway, so he stumbled downstairs into the courtyard, where a group of prisoners had gathered around the fire. Several soldiers stood next to a shed.

"All is lost!" cried Dragutin.

Mišić spent the night alone, staring at fires burning all over Peć; the flames were high and bright, the smoke rushed up into the sky. The old houses shook, beams and ceilings creaked from explosions. Mišić put out the lamp. Dragutin didn't come to start the stove; the reflected light of the fires lit up the room and chased the shadows on the walls and ceiling. Mišić felt warm from the embers glowing under Prokletije. Where would they go after such a conflagration and so many ashes? What was burning tonight under the cathedral of Peć? Not just war material and what the refugees couldn't carry into the mountains. It was the life-giving force and will of the Serbian people that was burning, something of much greater value than the State of Putnik and Pašić. Was this happening according to the dictates of fate and divine law, or was it the result of their sin and guilt? He pondered all that he had done since the beginning of the war and couldn't see that his actions were wrong. But suddenly he was seized by fear at his lack of guilt and his self-confidence. He paced back and forth: what could he still do when the day dawned? The bells of the cathedral began to toll. The fires were pale now, and the smoke had condensed into a dark cloud. Day dawned, yet it was dark. The apple tree in the garden was a black shape; so was the man hanging from one of its branches. The cathedral bells tolled on. He opened the window and called out: "Sentry!" The officer on duty ran up to his window. "Who hanged himself?"

The officer ran to the apple tree, swung the dead man around, stared at him, then slowly walked back and said: "It's your orderly Dragutin, sir."

"Yes, it's Dragutin!" Mišić took off his cap. *I'm to blame,* he said to himself; *I bear great guilt before men, I'm a sinner in the eyes of God and my children.* When he had told his mother he'd become a major, she paused for a moment, then said: "I'm glad, my boy, that through your intelligence you've reached a position where people obey you. But I'm frightened when a man has a lot of power, and one of my own flesh and blood, too. No good will come of it." The war was indeed lost on Kossovo, and he had lost it. He shut the window.

He gave orders to Colonel Hadžić that Dragutin be buried immediately. He burned all the staff archives, fired all the artillery shells, followed the orders of the High Command, and executed the decisions of the army commanders. Without waiting for his family to prepare for departure, he mounted his horse and issued his last order in Peć: the military band was to play marches until all the soldiers had left.

My dear son,

I'm taking advantage of the kindness of Monsieur Auguste Boppe, the French ambassador, who will deliver this letter to you.

We're now retreating before the enemy; your mother and I are in Peć, Milena has stayed in Prerovo. At dawn we'll leave for Skadar and the Albanian coast across the mountains of Montenegro and Albania, together with the army and numerous refugees. I don't know whether we'll reach our destination or if safety awaits us there. I want to explain what's happening here, though I know that a hundred years must pass before Serbia's position in this war can be assessed.

We're a small nation with great aims, in conflict with the world and its laws. In our struggle for survival we've defined some of these goals as necessities. Some evolved from our illusions, and of course the hardest have been imposed on us by our enemies and by history.

We had to destroy the Ottoman Empire, which had been destroying us for centuries. We had to oppose Austria-Hungary, who by her annexation of Bosnia and Hercegovina at bayonet point proclaimed that she wouldn't permit the liberation and unification of the Serbian people. If we had to fight a war with Turkey and wanted to, the war with Bulgaria was one we lacked the wisdom to avoid; the war with the Hapsburg Empire was one we couldn't escape.

For understandable reasons events here have been chosen as the pretext for a European war, and judging from what's happening, we're condemned to be its victim. In the trenches we've been defeated by a powerful enemy, and behind the trenches we've been betrayed by our allies. Now we don't know what's worse: military defeat or betrayal by the Allies. I think the latter, though I've come to realize that small nations often suffer equally from powerful conquerors and from their own great protectors; the former trample them underfoot, the latter smother them in their arms. A small nation can sometimes defend itself against a stronger enemy through heroism and cunning, but there's no salvation from saviors.

Serbia's military collapse was inevitable, but the betrayal by the Allies was not. If in August we'd handed over eastern Macedonia to the Bulgarians—a policy I championed in the Assembly, and so was spat upon as a traitor—our front would now be around Skoplje and we'd be retreating toward Salonika and Greece, not into Albania. But

Pašić and his generals followed the illusions of the nation, and were subsequently forced to withdraw the people and the army by the most dangerous route. Of course we've rarely used the means usually employed by the small and the weak. Yet even tonight I don't believe that was done simply to prove our greatness.

We aren't accepting history's law that says the vanquished must surrender to the victor, and the betrayed flee from those who've betrayed them. We're doing just the opposite: we're not admitting defeat, we're abandoning our country and remaining faithful to our faithless allies. Serbia is going into exile, Ivan. We're going into an uncertain future, of our own free will, fully aware of what we're doing. By refusing to capitulate and by leaving our land we're transforming our military defeat into a victory over history, something only a great nation can do. And the price of that greatness is very high. Freedom alone wouldn't deserve that price; and this difficult feat will probably not bring us happiness. But our goals are higher than freedom, greater than happiness. We want to unite all the Serbs and all the South Slavs; we want to destroy the Hapsburg Empire. We're determined to become different and more important than we were before 1914. We must do all we can to ensure that our defeat in war becomes more than an affair between us and our enemies; we must do our utmost to make the Allies bear the guilt of our tragedy, to make the defeat of Serbia the defeat of Europe and her democracy, and of Russia and her Panslavism. We're building our fate into the fate of the world.

If our descendants and other small nations learn from our experience, we'll have suffered and died for the future. If our action doesn't help our children and your children to see some meaning in existence, we'll have sacrificed ourselves for nothing. And I am partially responsible. You must be my judge, my son.

Vukašin dropped his pen and went out onto the porch. Broad tongues of flames leaped into the night sky above Peć. He smoked two cigarettes, then returned to the cell. Was he telling Ivan the truth? Truth was what he wished to leave behind him. He continued:

All human barriers have been destroyed. Our nation is capable of enduring unimaginable suffering and horror, but also, at times, of great weakness. If in freedom our nation doesn't protect itself from it own faults, the future peace won't justify our present suffering.

He reflected again, then wrote:

Perhaps our sacrifices will send a shudder of horror through our descendants in peacetime. Perhaps we're nothing but a tragicomic mistake of history, painful misfits in space and time, an historical absurdity. I question everything tonight.

He stopped, crossed out every word of doubt, and continued:

This morning we'll set out for a foreign land, carrying beggars' baskets and sticks. Who knows how long we'll have to suffer. When something unknown begins, it doesn't begin with words. "In the beginning was the Word"—that's not true. The Word comes after everything, including the end.

Vukašin felt such pain that he couldn't go on. He couldn't even sign the letter. He gave it to Olga when she returned from the church. She wrote:

My dear son,
This evening in the Peć cathedral I prayed to the Mother of God for you and Milena. It was the one thing I could do for you before we leave our country. In this great misfortune God has blessed me with a three-month-old child to look after. This will give me strength to endure human wickedness. Don't blame me, Ivan, for giving you the following advice: find a kind person and try to be kind in return. It will save your life.

> *With love,*
> *Mother*

On the high ground above the Peć cathedral, at the entrance to the Rugov gorge, the remaining artillery was arranged in rows as if for inspection. Next to the guns, the gunners stood at attention. In front of them were Vojvoda Stepanović, General Šturm, and General Živković. Ten priests sang the burial rites for the Serbian artillery. The bells of the Peć cathedral tolled. Aleksa Dačić wept.

The priests sang the final words; the generals turned toward the guns, stood at attention, and saluted. Then Stepanović gave the command:

"Soldiers, perform your last duty!"

Stepanović departed with the generals and his suite. The battery commanders ordered the barrels to be removed, taken into the forest above the monastery, and buried; the breeches and aiming devices were to be taken on the journey. The soldiers didn't stir. The battery commanders repeated the order threateningly. Slowly the gunners began to dismantle their guns, all but Aleksa, Gojko, and Cvetko. The gun carriages rolled down with a clatter toward the rooftops and the domes of the cathedral, then into Bistrica. The battery commander shouted: "What are you waiting for, Dačić? Destroy your gun!"

Aleksa stepped forward: "The three of us have decided, sir, to drag it with us as long as we can."

The commander looked bewildered, then ran off to catch up with Stepanović and tell him of their decision. Stepanović immediately gave his approval, and asked to be informed in Skadar about the fate of the one gun not destroyed.

Mišić's command was being carried out: in the fields outside Peć the First Army gunners were firing the remaining shells at the enemy. The rumbling of the guns drowned out the bells of the cathedral, and the soldiers and refugees about to leave for Albania stopped in their tracks. Scattered among the large fires lay piles of wheels and axles, cases of archives, barrels of gasoline, telephone and telegraph installations, stretchers, and books. People of all occupations and ages—women and children, volunteers from Austria-Hungary, doctors, nurses, and journalists—listened to the guns while in the square the military band played marches. Soot from the fires that had burned all night had turned the snow to gray slime and blackened the trees, the houses, and the faces of the people; the whole town was covered with soot, as were its inhabitants, except for the president of the Peć town council and two local officials, who stood in front of the band in festive Montenegrin costumes. Large snowflakes began to fall.

On the bank of the Bistrica, Vukašin Katić was loading his meager belongings onto the horse. With Života in her arms, Olga was looking at the snow-capped peaks of Prokletije, transfixed with fear. She didn't want to go on this journey. She beseeched Vukašin with her eyes; he didn't notice her.

The noise of the guns ceased, and a brief, heavy silence descended from Prokletije. Then the cathedral bells tolled, the band played, women wailed. The army and the people began the march up Prokletije toward the Rugov gorge, trampling the sooty snow. The town officials called out to the soldiers: "Good luck to you, heroes!"

"Let's go, Olga," said Vukašin.

Olga placed Života in a basket on the packsaddle and covered him with a blanket. The wife of the man with whom they were sharing the horse put her little girl in the other basket. Vukašin took the halter and led the horse behind the column of officers and a group of Austrian prisoners. Olga and her companion could hardly keep up. They passed through a double row of wailing women offering red apples and tiny yellow roasted pumpkins. At the outskirts of Peć the procession stopped to let through the monks carrying the reliquary of Stephen the First. They were holding lighted candles and murmuring prayers. But a group of officers on horseback urged the refugees to get going again. Those who couldn't move were to get off the road.

Epilogue

NOVEMBER 29, 1915

INFORMATION FROM THE GERMAN HIGH COMMAND:
OUR IMMEDIATE GOAL HAS BEEN REALIZED: A LINK WITH BULGARIA AND
TURKEY HAS BEEN ESTABLISHED. THE SERBIAN ARMY NO LONGER EXISTS.
SOME REMNANTS ARE SCATTERED IN FLIGHT OVER THE WILD MOUNTAINS
OF ALBANIA AND MONTENEGRO WHERE, WITHOUT FOOD AND IN THE FREEZ-
ING WEATHER, THEY WILL MEET THEIR DEATH.

EMPEROR FRANZ JOSEF EXPRESSES HIS THANKS TO MARSHAL VON MACKEN-
SEN FOR THE DESTRUCTION OF THE SERBIAN ARMY.

ANNOUNCEMENT FROM LORD KITCHENER, BRITISH MINISTER OF WAR:
YES, UNFORTUNATELY IT IS ALL OVER WITH SERBIA. WE MUST WITHDRAW
FROM SALONIKA. I MUST THINK NOW OF THE DEFENSE OF EGYPT.

ANNOUNCEMENT FROM SAZONOV, RUSSIAN MINISTER FOR FOREIGN AFFAIRS:
SERBIA HAS BEEN DESTROYED. ENGLAND IS TO BLAME. THE FRENCH GOVERN-
MENT TOO BEARS A SHARE OF THE RESPONSIBILITY. IT DID NOT REALIZE
THE IMPORTANCE OF THE BALKAN THEATER OF WAR.

ANNOUNCEMENT FROM KING CONSTANTINE OF GREECE:
SERBIA HAS FINALLY BEEN DESTROYED!

At a conference of representatives of the French and British general
staffs held in Calais on December 4, 1915, a decision was made to
abandon the Balkans. The collapse of Serbia was considered a *fait*

accompli. However, due to pressure from public opinion in the Allied countries, especially France, and Russia's strong dissatisfaction, a change took place. At the determined initiative of Aristide Briand, supported by Lloyd George of Britain, a new conference of Allied representatives was held at Chantilly on December 5–7, 1915. France and Russia agreed not to abandon the Balkans and Salonika, and to save the Serbian army retreating to Albania. Italy came out in favor of not abandoning the Balkan peninsula, but wished to defend it within the framework of her own territorial interests. Serbia once more set her hopes in vain on a powerful Allied army in the Balkans, convinced, as was the Russian general staff, that Austria-Hungary and Germany could be smashed on the Balkan battlefield.

After these decisions Lloyd George, the British Minister of Munitions, announced in the House of Commons: "We set out from here too late, we arrived there too late; we made this decision too late, made those preparations too late! At this time the mocking specter 'Too late!' haunts the footsteps of the Allied troops; if we do not hasten our step, a curse will fall on the holy cause for which so much heroic blood has been shed."

In the rear guard of the retreating Serbian army the last battle on Serbian territory, waged against Bulgarians and Albanians, was fought by the platoon of former convicts commanded by Bogdan Dragović. They fought bravely and many died. As he climbed up the slopes of Prokletije through a snowstorm, Bogdan had some doubt as to whether 'freedom' and 'country' were the same thing; but the brotherhood of man had more meaning for him than ever before.

Sitting beside a fire in Fletija, King Peter was writing in his diary:

It's freezing cold. The path is bad—I cover most of it on foot, some on horseback. Uphill and downhill over goat tracks, taking one's life in one's hands. I've seen Vojvoda Putnik. Tonight's lodging was without windows, but had braziers. I couldn't sleep—my rheumatism made me stiff, a stabbing pain on my left side. At about eight o'clock I had to leave this niche à chien *to let in some wounded men and some women with children. So I'm spending the night outside by a fire, the coldest night so far. In the morning I'll set out on foot, up and down steep slopes. The king mustn't turn his gun on himself; he can only be killed. I want to be killed. I didn't succeed at Kossovo, but I will in Albania.*

The soldiers no longer stood at attention before him. Back home he had been Uncle Peter to them, but in Albania he was simply a companion in endless suffering.

The Serbian government and High Command reached Skadar before the troops, but neither there nor in the harbor of Medova did they find the aid promised by the Allies. Instead they were met with the news that the Allies had abandoned the Balkans. Nikola Pašić was deeply concerned, but even now he didn't lose hope in victory.

DECEMBER 6, 1915

TO THE AMBASSADORS OF THE KINGDOM OF SERBIA IN ST. PETERSBURG, PARIS, LONDON, AND ROME:

AT THE MOST CRITICAL MOMENT FOR OUR COUNTRY, WHEN OUR SUFFERING AND DEPRIVATION ARE AT A PEAK, WE ARE HUMBLY ASKING OUR ALLIES TO REPLY TO THE FOLLOWING QUESTIONS:

DO YOU INTEND TO ABANDON THE BALKAN THEATER OF WAR AND LEAVE THE SERBIAN PEOPLE TO WANDER THROUGH THE MOUNTAINS AND GORGES OF ALBANIA, LOOKING FOR SALVATION?

HAVE YOU REPUDIATED THEIR PROMISE TO SEND TROOPS TO SERBIA'S ASSISTANCE, OR DO YOU INTEND TO HELP REORGANIZE THE SERBIAN ARMY IN MONTENEGRO AND ALBANIA?

PAŠIĆ

It's impossible to relate how we trudged along and how we arrived. Worn out and starving, the people looked like ghosts; they picked flesh from the bones of the dead horses, extracted grains of wheat and corn from their excrement. The soldiers cried, "Give us bread!" and Vojvoda Mišić repeated this cry to the High Command. For ten days we trudged along goat tracks, over treacherous mountains, and through drifting snow, with the enemy on all sides. Whenever someone collapsed from exhaustion, he was left behind. No one looked back. Everyone's eyes were fixed on the steep rocks past which they were climbing, and to which they clung with their nails. People staggered up steep slopes and slipped down chasms through ice and snow, climbed into the clouds and plunged into abysses. There was no resting place; Albanians were everywhere, lying in wait. The moment one sat down beside a fire to rest, rifles cracked. Cavern floors were strewn with the carcasses of animals. Everybody was hostile, angry, bitter; old friends looked at each other with suspicion and hatred; all were obsessed by the thought of bread and a night's lodging. Waiting for bread made the hours long, and each day stretched out into eternity.

—From the notebook of Milorad Pavlović

One morning after an overnight stop in a shepherd's hut, Vukašin and his traveling company found, instead of their horse, a skeleton with their packsaddle: hungry men had slaughtered the horse and stripped off the flesh. Vukašin and Olga continued on foot through waist-deep snow. The column of soldiers and refugees grew thinner; many who stopped from exhaustion did not get up again. It was growing dark. Someone suggested that the men go on ahead, find a place to spend the night, and have fires waiting for the women and children. Olga urged Vukašin to join the men and secure a place for her and Života beside the fire. Olga, carrying Života, stopped only occasionally—to listen to his breathing. But the procession of women thinned out. A group of soldiers passed them; soon thereafter she and two women, no longer able to see the soldiers' tracks, lost their way in the gathering darkness. They tried to make a new path in the snow; Olga now went first. She felt dizzy, and her heart ached from the effort. In the distance she caught sight of a fire and hurried to reach the safety it promised. But she couldn't get close to it; the snow grew deeper; the fire grew smaller, it vanished, then it gleamed forth once more. Summoning all her strength, she called out to her companions, but no one answered. She turned back, caught sight of another fire below and set out toward it; then the wind extinguished the fire and she could go no farther. Feeling drowsy, she sank into the soft snow. She pressed Života tightly to hear his breathing. In the thick of the night she saw the spark of Radić's cigarette on the train to Valjevo.

Vukašin waited for her by the fire in a hollow; two women arrived who couldn't account for the others. Vukašin and several men rushed into the stormy darkness to look for their women. They searched until daybreak. The wind died down. Day dawned, quiet and clear, with the vast blue expanse of the heavens stretched over garlands of snow-covered hills shot through with coniferous forests. Vukašin set out again to search. Suddenly it occurred to him that Olga might have gone past the fire the previous night in the snowstorm so he hurried on ahead.

By the time they reached Žljeb, neither the monks nor the soldiers could carry the bones of Stephen the First in their ark any longer; from the ice-covered goat track people and horses were plunging headlong into the abyss. The soldiers wanted to transfer the sacred relics to a sack and take turns carrying it, but the monks wouldn't agree to this sacrilege. They cursed the blasphemous soldiers and threatened them with divine wrath and eternal punishment. Bora Jackpot shouted:

"Throw those old bones into the abyss, so we'll be punished! There's no hope for us anyway, but at least we can find out if God exists. I don't believe he does, but that would remove all doubt!"

Dušanka begged him to calm down. He pushed her aside: "I want that belief exposed as a lie! Throw the bones away, soldiers, so we can see what more God can do to us. If he doesn't do anything, all we have to deal with are our fellow men."

After a scuffle with the monks, the soldiers dumped the sacred bones into a sack that they then carried to the accompaniment of the monks' wailing and Bora's laughter.

For eight days the soldiers carried Vojvoda Putnik in the little white sentry box across the trackless waste of Albania—over ice and snow, under clear skies, and through an ambush—and brought him to Skadar. Prince Alexander and his entourage greeted him by asserting that he was unfit for duty and responsible for the army's catastrophe. Someone had to be blamed; Putnik understood and submitted without protest. He asked Alexander to remove him as chief of the High Command for reasons of health. The Commander in Chief acceded to his request that same day. Putnik complained to no one about this last and greatest pain inflicted on a worthless clod of earth in the infinity of the heavens.

On a patch of rocky ground dotted with juniper bushes, a squadron of Bulgarian cavalry overtook two hundred conscripts and boys who were retreating with a column of Austrian prisoners led by Mihajlo Radić and Pavel Vojteh. The boys scattered to one side like frozen, starving partridges and hid in the bushes. The Bulgarians surrounded them, dismounted, and killed them one by one with sabers and bayonets. Several conscripts who had rifles resisted, others rushed headlong toward the river. Some of the prisoners tried to defend the boys with the rifles of those who had been killed. Vojteh was wounded and captured by the Bulgarians, while Radić hid in a clump of thistles. Radić didn't fire one bullet in defense of the boys. Paralyzed by fear—fear of the bayonets, not of death—he listened to the last cries of the slaughtered. When darkness fell, he climbed out of his hiding place and looked at the battleground. With a shudder he sank back, sank into the very depths of his betrayal. Time stood still; space was obliterated. Cold, damp, endless nothingness. He lit a cigarette, took two or three puffs, and felt nauseous. He threw away his cigarette, threw away his backpack of medicines, and walked down the hill, stumbling over the dead bodies. No one ever saw him again.

The Albanians plunder the dead. Naked bodies are covered with a thick layer of ice, smooth and transparent as glass. Some have been stabbed by bayonets, others hit by bullets. Terrible wounds: gashes on the nape of the neck through which one can see teeth. A naked man, lying on an icy hillside with his arms outstretched and his head thrust back, crucified.

—From the notebook of Henri Barbi

The soldiers reached Skadar in small groups, cavalry mixed with infantry. Here and there a detachment had retained its military bearing, but vast numbers were without weapons. They moved with painful effort, emaciated, hollowed-eyed, gloomy, their faces ashen. The sad procession continued for days on end. As if driven on by evil fate, they walked in silence, only now and again muttering "bread."

—From the notebook of Auguste Boppe

Aleksa, Gojko, and Cvetko arrived at the outskirts of Skadar with their gun. They stopped to clean it properly, groom the horses, and wash up. Then Aleksa and Gojko climbed onto the gun carriage. They got down, lifted up the animal, stroked it, and gently urged it to move off. Aleksa began to sing "Oh, Morava," but quickly realized that people were in no mood for a song. He admonished Gojko and Cvetko to march in a soldierly manner and did so himself. A damp wind blew off his cap; if Gojko hadn't run after it, Aleksa would have arrived at Skadar bareheaded—as if for a funeral.

In Skadar, in the lobby of the Europa Hotel, whose owner had refused to serve the Serbian government, Prince Alexander opened the meeting of the government:

"The Allies have deceived us, and we have deceived the army. We hoped that Allied ships would be waiting for us with food, equipment, and weapons. Instead we learn that we've been crossed off. The Italians have persuaded the other Allies that what remains of the Serbian army is only brigands and small groups infected with cholera. This morning I received information that the Italian military authorities now controlling central and southern Albania have forbidden us to cross the river Vojuša and reach Valona and its harbor. At least forty thousand soldiers and boys have died of hunger in central Albania. Italy wants to destroy us today, so that we won't take Dalmatia and Istria from her tomorrow. All in all, gentlemen, Serbia is dead to the world. What do we do now?"

They were all silent. The murmur of thousands of soldiers and refugees gathered in front of the hotel reached them in waves.

"What do you have to say, Prime Minister?"

Pašić gripped his stick tightly between his knees, bent his head over it, and said nothing.

"No comment from any of you?"

They were still silent, their heads lowered. Alexander looked at his watch: he had given them twenty-five minutes.

"The meeting is over!"

Alexander left; the ministers filed out behind him. Pašić remained alone in the hotel lobby. Bombs dropped by Austrian airplanes exploded all around.

Italy would not allow the retreating Serbs to set foot in her "sphere of interest." An Italian expeditionary force held the Serbian army on the banks of the Skumba, Semena, and Vojuša rivers, where they died of hunger, disease, and exhaustion in large numbers. Italy put pressure on England, France, and Russia to refuse Serbia's demands for unification with Croatia and Slovenia, and to make Serbia renounce Dalmatia and the Adriatic coast.

England announced that her fleet could not help save the remnants of the Serbian army, nor could she accept General Alekseev's plan to maintain the Balkan theater of war.

Italy stated that her navy did not have sufficient vessels to supply the Serbs with food and transport them from Albania. Moreover, since there were cases of cholera among the Serbs, maximum hygienic measures would have to be undertaken to save the fleet and the mainland from disastrous epidemics.

Esad Pasha, the ruler of Albania, continued to be loyal to Serbia, even though his own authority was being undermined by the revolt of the Miridith tribe, and his people were starving. He offered the Serbian soldiers food and resting places, and kept fires going for them through the night. One man who could still do good.

General Bertoti, commander of the Italian forces in Albania, came to the Albania Hotel, where King Peter was installed with his doctor, his adjutant, and his orderly.

"I regret to inform Your Majesty that you must leave Valona immediately."

"Why? Am I a criminal?"

"These are my government's orders."

"I'll need time to pack and pay my bill."

"You have four hours. The boat that will take you to Brindisi hasn't arrived yet."

"How am I to interpret this, General?"

"As an act of generosity, Your Majesty. My orders were that you should leave Valona as soon as you arrived. When I saw you looking so tired, I felt sorry for you. My kindness has not been received well in Rome. I am now acting on my new orders, which are distasteful to me."

"Thank you, General, for all the kindness you have shown me and will show to my soldiers. Please tell your government that I see clearly Italy's intention to kill off the Serbian army by starvation, and to conquer Dalmatia without firing a single bullet. But I'm firmly convinced that the Yugoslav land cannot be won by your clever tricks. Good-by, General."

Still hoping that Olga had joined the refugees heading for Skadar, Vukašin arrived there on the verge of exhaustion. He made a frantic search for her in the streets, courtyards, cafés, churches, and mosques. Unsuccessful, he set out for Medova to look for her there among the refugees who were waiting for boats. On the outskirts of Skadar he ran into Auguste Boppe, who embraced him and immediately asked about Olga. Vukašin told him what had happened, and asked if he would add to the letter to Ivan an account of the journey between Peć and Skadar.

"A letter's too little, Monsieur Katić! I'll write a book, a whole book! You Serbs are no longer suffering for freedom and national goals. You are suffering for something beyond human comprehension. You are being wiped out by history! The metaphysics of evil is coming to pass! Good-by, Monsieur Katić. Rest assured I will hand the letter to your son and tell him all!"

Vukašin put up his collar so the rain wouldn't trickle down his neck, and hurried to Medova.

TO THE AMBASSADORS OF THE KINGDOM OF SERBIA IN ST. PETERSBURG, PARIS, AND LONDON:

PLEASE INFORM THE ALLIED GOVERNMENTS THAT I HAVE SENT THE FOLLOWING TELEGRAM TO ROME TODAY: OUR ARMY IS STARVING. IF WE DO NOT RECEIVE FOOD IMMEDIATELY, OUR CAPITULATION DUE TO HUNGER IS IMMINENT. THREE DAYS AGO WE WERE PROMISED THAT BOATS WOULD ARRIVE IN MEDOVA AND BAR. DO THE ALLIES INTEND TO SEND US FOOD, OR TO BRING ABOUT OUR DEATH BY STARVATION?

PAŠIĆ

While the Serbian army was retreating to the Adriatic coast, some forty thousand Montenegrins, upset by the Serbian defeat and the Allies' betrayal, held a five-hundred-kilometer front against the Austrians. Their army covered the withdrawal of the First, Second, and Third Serbian armies, while the half-starved population of Montenegro shared their last morsels of bread with the soldiers of Mišić and Stepanović.

At Sveti Jovan Medocski the Serbs are sprawled on the ground. They are cramming damp earth into their mouths and eating grass. A hundred meters away Italian ships lie at anchor ready to transport the troops—ships equipped with life-saving provisions, but which haven't taken a single refugee or given a grain of flour.
—From the notebook of Hermann Vendel

The Serbs were scattered all along the coast, watching the open sea, waiting for boats. The fires they lit were extinguished by the rain. Women poked about the horse manure looking for undigested grains, which they cooked in water from the puddles; man stripped the dead horses, hunted for shells, saw imaginary boats.

Meanwhile along the muddy shore, Colonel Kajafa made a daily inspection of what was left of his division. He checked the officers' watches, reprimanding those whose watches didn't work. "Gentlemen, in spite of everything, time does not stand still." It didn't matter to him whether their watches were accurate, but only that the officers continued to have a sense of time. They simply had to keep them going.

He checked his soldiers for lice: "Have no patience with those pests! Kill them, heroes! Every Serb can kill a battalion of lice in a day!"

The soldiers would then take off their rags and kill the lice. Some would eat them as they stared out to sea, their teeth chattering in the moist, salty wind.

Božidar the priest, in a torn mantle and crumpled cap, was leading his surviving boys, their feet bleeding, on the road to Elbasan. Half the battalion which had set out from Prizren had died on the way, and ten had been killed with their commanding officer in an Albanian ambush. Suddenly Božidar caught sight of an empty stone building by the road, and gave a prayer of thanks to God for His mercy. He asked the boys to collect dry twigs in a nearby forest and made a fire in the middle of the large stone chamber. He told the children to take off their wet clothes and shoes and spread them out to dry, and gave them each three of the large walnuts he'd bought from an Albanian. When they reached the sea it would be warm, he assured them, and big ships would take them to a land where the trees bore the sweetest and most fragrant fruits in the world—oranges and lemons. He felt tranquil sitting by the fire, the children's eyes on him. Suddenly a grenade, which was banked up in the ashes, exploded, killing the priest, one of his own grandchildren, and some of his adopted ones. The survivors scattered into the darkness and rain. The wounded were left whimpering in the ruins.

Hunger, cold, disease, and death reconciled the Austrian prisoners and the Serbs. The Serbian soldiers no longer guarded the prisoners. There was no longer any difference in the way they were dressed. Columns were confused. Both Serbs and Austrians carried the remaining rifles: together they defended themselves against Albanian brigands and ambushes. Austrian prisoners helped the women, carried Serbian children and wounded; they shared food, and warmed themselves around the same fires. Above the abysses they gripped each other's hands, supporting one another in the snowdrifts. The stronger Serbs helped the weaker Austrians; many Austrians accepted the fate of the defeated and exiled Serbs as their own. Suffering makes brothers of enemies in war.

TO NICHOLAS II, CZAR OF RUSSIA:
IN HOPE THAT ON THE ADRIATIC COAST MY ARMY WOULD RECEIVE SUPPLIES AND REORGANIZE ITSELF WITH THE ASSISTANCE PROMISED BY THE ALLIES, I HAVE LED IT OVER THE MOUNTAINS OF ALBANIA AND MONTENEGRO. HAVING FOUND HERE NOTHING OF WHAT WAS PROMISED, MY ARMY NOW STANDS ON THE VERGE OF DISASTER. AT THIS DIFFICULT MOMENT I AM TURNING TO

YOUR IMPERIAL MAJESTY, IN WHOM I HAVE ALWAYS PLACED MY LAST HOPES, WITH A REQUEST FOR YOUR INTERVENTION IN THE HIGHEST QUARTERS, SO I MIGHT SAVE MY ARMY AND PREPARE FOR NEW EFFORTS. TO ACCOMPLISH THIS, IT IS ESSENTIAL FOR THE ALLIED FLEETS TO TRANSFER MY NORTHERN ARMY AS SOON AS POSSIBLE FROM SVETI JOVAN MEDOVSKI TO A SECURE PLACE NOT FAR FROM THE SERBIAN FRONTIER, PREFERABLY NEAR SALONIKA. THE HUNGRY AND EXHAUSTED ARMY CANNOT COME OVERLAND FROM SKADAR TO VALONA, AS PROPOSED BY THE ALLIED HIGH COMMANDS.

PRINCE ALEXANDER

TO PRINCE ALEXANDER:

WITH PAIN I HAVE FOLLOWED THE WITHDRAWAL OF THE COURAGEOUS SERBIAN ARMY THROUGH ALBANIA AND MONTENEGRO. I WOULD LIKE TO EXPRESS TO YOUR ROYAL HIGHNESS MY SINCERE ADMIRATION AT THE SKILL WITH WHICH THE ARMY UNDER YOUR LEADERSHIP HAS OVERCOME ALL THE DIFFICULTIES OF THE RETREAT, REPELLING THE ATTACKS OF AN ENEMY FAR SUPERIOR IN NUMBERS.

IN ACCORDANCE WITH MY INSTRUCTIONS, THE MINISTER OF FOREIGN AFFAIRS HAS SEVERAL TIMES CALLED UPON THE ALLIES TO ENSURE THE SAFETY OF THE SEA ROUTE ALONG THE ADRIATIC COAST. THESE REQUESTS HAVE BEEN RENEWED AND I HOPE THAT THE GLORIOUS SERBIAN ARMY WILL NOW BE GIVEN THE OPPORTUNITY TO LEAVE ALBANIA. I BELIEVE THAT YOUR ARMY WILL SOON RECOVER AND ONCE MORE PLAY ITS PART IN THE STRUGGLE AGAINST OUR COMMON ENEMY.

VICTORY OVER THIS ENEMY AND THE RESURRECTION OF THE GREAT SERBIAN NATION WILL CONSOLE YOU AND OUR BROTHER SERBS FOR ALL THAT YOU HAVE LIVED THROUGH.

NICHOLAS II

The Allies, not knowing what to do with the Serbs in Albania, made agreement after agreement and exchanged many diplomatic telegrams. Finally, when Russia threatened to secede from the military alliance, and on the resolute initiative of France, Italy evacuated the Serbian army from the northern coast of Albania to Valona in the south. However, for security reasons Italy, supported by England, refused to pick up the Serbs from Medova, insisting that they cross on foot to Drač and Valona. The Serbian government and High Command refused: their people were in no condition to walk another three hundred kilometers over swampy ground. Prince Alexander asked Poincaré, the French president, to transport the Serbian army from Medova to Drač and Valona, but the French too refused for reasons of security.

TO THE AMBASSADORS OF THE KINGDOM OF SERBIA IN ST. PETERSBURG, PARIS, AND LONDON:

OUR ARMY IS BEING DECIMATED BY HUNGER. WE HAVE BEEN ON THE COAST WAITING FOR SHIPS FOR TWENTY-TWO DAYS. TWENTY OF THOSE DAYS IT HAS RAINED. WE HAVE NO TENTS. THE ARMY IS BARELY SURVIVING.

PAŠIĆ

When Vojvoda Mišić arrived in Skadar from Podgorica, Prince Alexander reprimanded him angrily for attempting to go against orders of the High Command; officers and politicians accused Mišić of advocating capitulation and suspected him of treason. Exhausted by his own futile efforts and exasperated with the Allies and his country's leaders, he resigned the command of the First Army and left for Italy, a sick and despairing man.

The Serbian army turned to France, their last hope. Pašić sent a message to General de Mondésir, chief of the French mission in Albania:

WE ARE IN YOUR HANDS. DO WHAT YOU WILL.

At last the French responded.

Faced with a threat from Austria-Hungary in the north and with the starvation of their army and the refugees, the Serbian government and High Command agreed to lead the army and the people down the coast toward Drač and Valona. The terrible retreat—through the swamps, in the December rains—lasted several days. Without bread and without hope.

Although he was recovering from an operation in Skadar, Prince Alexander firmly refused the invitation of the Italians to leave for Bizerta: "I shall embark with the last of my soldiers!" he declared.

Making the rounds of his soldiers, now scattered in the swamps of the river Maća, Colonel Kajafa climbed a willow tree and shouted:

"Wash your faces, men! And remember, death doesn't get everybody! I swear it. Since the beginning of time, someone has survived every disaster, fire, or epidemic! Not even death is all-powerful. Someone always survives!"

JANUARY 7, 1916

AT THE INSISTANCE OF GENERAL JOFFRE AND THE MINISTER OF THE NAVY, THE FRENCH GOVERNMENT HAS FINALLY DECIDED TO TRANSPORT THE SERBIAN ARMY TO THE ISLAND OF CORFU.

The Austrian army launched a decisive attack on Montenegro, though the Hercegovina detachment offered fierce resistance. For several days the Sandžak army fought a battle at Berane and Mojkovac with bayonets and hand grenades. These were battles for honor, glory, and epic poetry. King Nicholas and the Montenegrin government sought an armistice, and in a few days capitulated.

The capitulation of Montenegro and the rapid advance of the Austrian troops toward Skadar forced the Serbian government and Allied diplomats to flee from Skadar to Medova, where an Italian ship was to meet them to take them to Corfu via Brindisi.

In icy wind and rain Pašić, his ministers, and the diplomats arrived at Medova. The docks were crowded with thousands of refugees, sick and wounded men, and soldiers who gazed at the undulating, foam-flecked sea, waiting for the ship. The Prime Minister, wet to the skin, could hardly make his way through the crowds to the harbor office. Pašić and the ministers entered the shack of Admiral Tallbridge, the Allied harbor commander. Later that evening Captain Leniani informed them that the *Cità di Bari* had arrived; but according to orders from Brindisi, it would take only the Kings of Serbia and Montenegro, the governments of both states, and the Allied diplomats—fifteen persons in all. Pašić was astounded by this decision, which at once spread all over the harbor. Thousands of despairing people flung themselves against Tallbridge's shack, crying for help, threatening, and cursing:

"Where are you, Pašić, you criminal? You're running away, leaving the people and the army to die of hunger and be slaughtered! Why have you deceived us, you murderer?"

A shudder ran through Pašić: for the first time in his life he was frightened of his fellow men, offended, humiliated, powerless. The ministers and Allied diplomats fled outside into the wind and rain. The cries and threats of thousands of men, women, and children mingled in the darkness with the weeping of the wind and the sea.

Captain Leniani asked Pašić, the ministers, and the diplomats to board a launch which would take them to the brightly lit boat rolling gently in the waves offshore. He counted fifteen, then pushed the sixteenth away; the launch moved off toward the *Cità di Bari*, accompanied by the frenzied wailing of the refugees gathered on the dock. Several people, including Paun Aleksić, jumped into the sea to grab hold of the launch, but missed.

After ten minutes the launch reached its destination. Soldiers pulled the ministers and diplomats up a rope ladder. The ship's doctor was waiting for them with a light and a spoon in his hand:

"Open wide!" he commanded.

He examined their throats, then let them disperse to their cabins. The last person hauled up the ladder was Pašić; the doctor shone his light on his large white beard. He was so awed by it—no one had such a beard except God as portrayed in pictures—that he dropped his spoon. Carrying his cane and his small black case, Pašić stepped onto Italian territory without a medical examination.

We retreated through mud and mire, through melancholy water lilies and reeds, through a monotonous expanse of peat. No clear horizon, not a single distinct feature of landscape. This dark, blurred region of mud and puddles, filled with the swollen carcasses of horses, with abandoned ammunition cases and cartridge belts, with debris and rags, this terrible land pulsed beneath us and inside us, possessing our every thought. It was as if we'd been treading through oozing slime since birth.

—From the recollections of the poet Stanislav Vinaver

A living graveyard. Dead bodies scattered in the mud. Living skeletons walk over their dead companions, who have been stripped naked by the enemy. At every step you meet a desperate creature sunk in the mud, waiting for death with a crazed expression in his eyes. A man dying of hunger; we have nothing to offer him. Weary and half-conscious we trudge onward, up to our knees in the mud, and ford rivers, climb fences, and give our last dinar for a piece of cornbread. This desperate journey through swamps where death hovered in the air lasted six days.

When the poet Milutin Bojić reached Drač at dusk he ran down to the sea to wash his face. He came upon his friend Stanislav Vinaver and they embraced warmly.

Vinaver asked: "What kind of poetry will we be writing after this war, Bojić?"

"A great epic about our generation, a great poem about Serbia which I shall call 'Red Baptism.' I'll write about the new messiah of the South Slavs, about the unconquerable life force, about human strength and greatness. About the grandeur of our pain and pride."

"No, Bojić. After what we've gone through, poetry will be muted—muted and mystical. Then suddenly we'll burst into laughter and piss at the stars!"

"You're wrong. The Serbian people must be praised in verse."

"You can't put the people into a poem, Bojić. The future of poetry lies in the invisible and inaudible quiverings of the soul. Its fear and trembling before the flickering light of the unknown."

"Nonsense, Vinaver! A great thing must be expressed in great and holy words."

"Grandiloquent words about death soon become banal. The atom holds together by different charges, Bojić. So do the world and the universe. Causality is the law of Newton's mechanics."

"What about Aeschylus and Shakespeare? Racine and Victor Hugo?"

"May they rest in peace! Only a person who understands the old and can throw it away is modern. But for our work one needs genius a hundred times greater than Homer's!"

A man wrapped in a coarse rug and accompanied by a woman interrupted them:

"Surely you two don't believe that the survivors of this debacle will need art? Those who invented the arts and believed in them are dead. Shut up and listen to the sea!"

"Is that you, Jackpot? So God has spared you! Go wash yourself! The three of us we can have a game of poker in Drač tonight!"

"It's a deal. Let me introduce you to my wife."

Dušanka held out her hand and smiled.

Over one hundred and forty thousand Serbian soldiers and refugees died of hunger, cold, and disease in Albania or were killed by Albanian ambushes. Of the forty thousand conscripts and boys mobilized and pushed along before the advancing enemy, about seven thousand reached Drač and Valona.

From mid-January to April, 1916, the French transported one hundred and fifty thousand Serbian soldiers from the Albanian coast to Corfu. Also, they and the Italians transferred to Italy, Bizerta, and France about twenty-five thousand Austrian prisoners of war and over eighty thousand Serbian refugees.

On the shores of Albania were left the human corpses, some twenty-five thousand horses of the Serbian army, about thirty dogs belonging to the refugees, one cat, and a cavalry squadron of the Morava Division.

The famished horses, with no riders or loads, filled the swampy valley behind Drač and ate up all vegetation. They began kicking their hind legs, banging their heads together, and biting one another to get at the remaining clumps of grass and weeds. Enticed by the green reeds in the swamp, some pressed toward them and drowned without a sound in the black mud of the bog. Those even hungrier trampled over them, submerged their heads in the mud, bit frenziedly at their necks, and then sank. The more they resisted the faster they sank. Meanwhile the hungriest of all fed with blood-flecked muzzles on the manes and tails of the dead and on the dying, who stood on their front legs, feebly defending themselves with their eyes closed. At night, with rain falling heavily and a strong wind blowing from the sea, the horses huddled together in groups for protection and warmth. Their heads were turned away from the sea, toward the mountains and the north where they had come from. From time to time one gave a prolonged neigh, perhaps for oats and a meadow, or simply for a rider. The neighing of the horses would start the dogs in the abandoned camps yelping and barking.

The French captains of the last two transport vessels announced that they could take only thirty-five hundred horses. The officers in charge ordered the cavalry squadron to select the youngest and healthiest, then kill the rest so they wouldn't be left for the enemy. Under the supervision of the squad commanders the troopers plunged among the horses, looking into their glassy, troubled eyes, not recognizing a single one, yet knowing them all. Which should they save?

Adam Katić saved all the horses except those too weak to stand. The squadron commander berated him and beat the horses he had picked with his saber. Adam became more discriminating, but still spared the handsome ones, even if they had deep wounds and were at death's door. He tried hard to sneak them past the commanders, who, dissatisfied, made a new selection and killed the rest. A strong wind blowing from the sea muffled the revolver shots; dead horses were piled high on the shore. The surviving animals were slowly driven onto the docks, where they were bound with steel ropes and lowered into the boats by cranes. The soldiers worked with painful effort, dawdling, talking, moving along the edge of the never-ending herd. They felt deep sorrow for the finest and swiftest animals, which were the only proof that these men had ever had homes, that they had been something and could go where they pleased. For the officers, though, the land and the native countryside were something different. Dissatisfied with the soldiers and their selection, they threatened to leave the men to the Germans and Albanians along with the dying horses. Using their sabers, they made the soldiers wade into the swamp and pull out the horses that looked healthy and still fit for riding and fighting.

At dusk the French captains threatened to sail off without them unless the number of horses was reduced by half. The officers and men began to slaughter the horses that pity had reprieved. When at last all was quiet on the docks at Drač, the local people stripped the skin off the dead but still warm horses by the light of their lanterns. By morning the rain had ended. The squadron commander lined up the troopers and ordered them to kill the rest of the horses that couldn't be saved. The soldiers moved reluctantly toward the horses, and on command shot them one after another between the eyes. Some soldiers wept as they remembered how the animals had carried them to weddings or on swift rides through crooked lanes. Adam Katić killed several and sobbed aloud; he tried to save one black horse, but the squad commander hit him and forced him to go on with the slaughter. This was the hardest thing he'd done since the beginning of the war.

After several thousand horses had been killed, the surviving ones suddenly became restless. They herded in groups, pawed the ground, and moved against the killers. The soldiers fired their rifles in terror, but through pools of blood the horses continued to advance. The soldiers fixed bayonets and retreated into the sea, and the officers fired their revolvers, but the horses wouldn't stop. They came right up to the men who were now waist-high in the sea, drenched by the waves. The men talked softly to them, begging their forgiveness for all the times they had let them go hungry and thirsty, for all the rides, the spurs, and the blows, for the slaughter in the name of the fatherland. A few paces from the men the horses halted. The wind howled and the sea bathed them in foam.

From the north, three Austrian airplanes flew in over Drač and dropped their bombs. Wind and sea muffled the explosions; men and horses were reconciled in a single death, their blood and bones mingling, their bodies floating helplessly on the waves. The living lowered their rifles and gazed at the sky. Some remembered that they could flee down the sandy shore but, hungry and exhausted as they were, they knew they would never make it. Among those who dared to save themselves were Adam Katić and Uroš Babović. But the horses didn't stir; following the example of the men, they lifted their heads to the sky until death came to them.

The surviving soldiers snatched up the one cat and crawled into the boats among the chosen horses; a few dogs sneaked into a boat behind them. Vukašin Katić came on board and sat down beside his nephew Adam, but they didn't notice each other. The engines roared and the boats moved off, carrying them toward the end of the glowering sky.